MEXICO 21

Mark Joseph

GRAFTON BOOKS
A Division of the Collins Publishing Group

LONDON GLASGOW
TORONTO SYDNEY AUCKLAND

Grafton Books
A Division of the Collins Publishing Group
8 Grafton Street, London W1X 3LA

Published by Grafton Books 1990

Copyright © Mark Joseph 1990

A CIP catalogue record for this book is
available from the British Library

ISBN 0-246-13344-9

Printed in Great Britain by
William Collins Sons & Co. Ltd, Glasgow

Contents

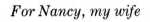

For Nancy, my wife

Poor México! So far from God and
so close to the United States.

Porfirio Díaz

PROLOGUE
SEPTEMBER 1990

With five minutes to relax before soccer practice, Lucio Serdán lifted his bad leg onto the heavy oak desk, crossed his shattered knee with the good one, tilted back his chair and blew smoke at the chalkboard. The forty-two year old schoolteacher held his Delicado with three fingers and thumb, letting the pungent smoke filter through his nostrils. The grey cloud briefly obscured the green slate scrawled with algebraic formulae, residue of the morning's lesson. The ceiling fan twirling over-head pushed the smoke into the dead still air of Colonia Las Palmas, the poorest district in Chilpancingo.

A panoramic view of green mountains filled the open window. The rugged Sierra Madre del Sur surrounded Chilpancingo de los Bravos, cradled in a valley 4500 feet above sea level. Chilpancingo, the 'place of wasps' in ancient Nahuatl, embraced a university, a pretty colonial square surrounded by outdoor cafés, the government of the state of Guerrero, an infamous mercenary bar called 'The Death of Maximilian', and a long tradition of nurturing bandits and revolutionaries, often the same people.

Like his ancestors and neighbours, Lucio Serdán harboured a deep mistrust for the government. A respected *maestro* who taught mathematics and coached the soccer team, Lucio limped through life on a right knee shattered by a government bullet. For twenty-two years his halting gait had been a symbol of indomitable will to the people of his district. To feel the suffering of his people, Lucio read the scars on his heart. To know their hatred for tyrants, he had only to take off his pants.

He snubbed out his cigarette and listened to his soccer players shouting and laughing outside. Fifteen boys kicked a ball in the dust and waited for him to lead them through the Colonia Las Palmas to the empty lot where they practised.

A pile of ungraded maths tests lay on his desk. He picked up the top sheet, glanced at the name, Tomás Rodríguez, and rows of neat figures. He reached for a red pencil, let it hover over the paper a moment, then returned the exam to the pile. To this kind, stern master, teaching was an act of love. Later, in his modest apartment, he would check each calculation, applying each red correction as delicately as a kiss.

His eyes drifted back to the mountains. Each summer he drove his pick-up deep into the Sierra and lived in the villages among the fiercely proud mountain people. Lucio moved like a priest among the peasants and farmers, sharing their tortillas and pulque, distributing books and teaching their children numbers.

He knew their secret. For twenty years the people of the Sierra had lived by growing opium poppies. Twice each year the farmers sliced open the green opium fruit, collected the milky fluid, dried it in the sun and pressed the sticky residue into dark brown bricks. Soldiers from the 27th Infantry came in trucks, took away the bricks and left the farmers enough money to feed their families for another six months.

The soldiers trucked the raw opium to factories in Acapulco and Zihuatanejo, where chemists processed the opium paste into a brown powder the colour of cinnamon and sugar. Packed into plastic bags, this powerful narcotic sold on the streets of America as Mexican Brown.

For twenty years a river of Mexican Brown heroin flowed out of the Sierra without hindrance from the authorities. Lucio Serdán understood how the farmers, chemists, soldiers and legions of smugglers operated with impunity. The heroin traffic in Guerrero was a pyramid with the farmers at the base and one man at the apex.

In the mountains men spoke his name with whispered curses. Women crossed themselves and made signs to ward off the evil eye. In México City his name provoked shudders of fear and frustrated bursts of outrage. Millions knew the terrible truth which no one uttered in public.

Alfredo Mendoza, the heroin king of Guerrero, held the rank of Federal Minister of Government, a post which placed him in control of the entire Méxican police apparatus. Second in power only to the President, Mendoza made no secret of his desire to occupy the National Palace himself.

14

Lucio knew the people of the Sierra had no choice. If they failed to produce an opium crop, they would starve. He never scolded or called them *narcotraficantes*. Born among them, the son of a mason and a tortilla maker, Lucio Serdán encouraged the people to educate their children, to send them to the universities and fill their heads with ideas. Only then would they free themselves from Alfredo Mendoza and the monstrous system he represented.

In his youth Lucio had won a scholarship to the National University in México City. For three years he had pursued his study of mathematics and had earned a degree. In the late summer of 1968, as he prepared to return to Chilpancingo to begin teaching in the *secundaria*, a wave of revolutionary fervour had swept across México City, a wave which in that watershed year had rolled through Paris, Prague, Tokyo, Beijing, Chicago, Saigon, New York and Berkeley.

The august Olympic Games were scheduled to start in México City on 12 October. Inspired by firebrands around the world, hundreds of thousands of students took to the streets of the Méxican capital to protest against the games, claiming the money spent on the Olympics was an insult to the impoverished millions of México. As the summer progressed, demonstrators widened their protests to criticize the authoritarian policies of the government, and by October they threatened the government's very existence.

From late July to late September violent clashes took place every day between demonstrators and the police. In August riot police and soldiers occupied the university.

Studying for exams, Lucio neither attended rallies nor marched in demonstrations, but he understood what was happening. The government was treating urban middle-class students like peasants in the Sierra. The result was open rebellion.

In the faculty of science Lucio had become friends with a brilliant young mathematician from México City named Máximo Levín. Scion of a family of wealthy silver merchants, Máximo had the advantages of wealth and education, but he also had the rudiments of a charismatic vision of a new México, a modern México free of tyranny and corruption. Máximo spoke passionately of a future dominated by computers, lasers, optical fibres,

15

a dizzying world of high technology that Lucio barely understood. The obstacle to this wonderful future was a political system run by dinosaurs.

The two students from opposite worlds spent long nights arguing and discussing the state of mathematics, the state of the world and of the republic. Young Máximo raved with frustrated bitterness at the government. True, Lucio Serdán agreed, the government is oppressive and corrupt. True, one must protest, but demonstrations or long, carefully worded tracts accomplished nothing in the dirt streets of Colonia Las Palmas or the ravaged villages of the Sierra Madre. Yet, in spite of his doubts, the sight of helmeted riot police running amok in México City pushed Lucio Serdán closer to the brink of revolution. Finally, like millions around the world in that terrible year, Lucio Serdán took to the streets.

On 2 October 1968, in the Plaza of Three Cultures in Tlatelolco, the oldest and most historic district of México City, Lucio Serdán and Máximo Levín joined a demonstration organized to protest against the police occupation of the university.

As the games approached, the student movement had lost steam. The rally at Tlatelolco drew only five thousand, many of whom were families who came from the public housing project which overlooked the square. Ten days before the opening of the games, with foreign reporters arriving in México City, the government decided to crush the student movement for good.

When Lucio Serdán and Máximo Levín arrived at Tlatelolco, they saw the troops and riot police surrounding the square. A police helicopter hovered overhead. Máximo parked his car three blocks away, and as they approached the plaza they saw the helicopter drop a green flare on the crowd below.

Troops hiding in the excavated Aztec ruins adjacent to the square suddenly rushed up the stairs from the ancient temples and burst onto the pavement with heavy .50 calibre machine-guns.

Before the two young men reached the square, they heard an officer shout an order. Lucio Serdán never forgot the sight of the officer's contorted face.

Alfredo Mendoza screamed, 'Fire!'

The troops unleashed the machine-guns. Hundreds fell. What

came to be known as the massacre of Tlatelolco seared the minds of a generation. *No one ever would forget* . . .

Lucio took a bullet in his right knee. Miraculously unhurt, Máximo half-carried, half-dragged his friend to his car and drove him to a private hospital.

A month later, his leg in a cast, Lucio had returned to Las Palmas and had settled into the quiet life of a teacher of mathematics. He taught children algebra, coached the soccer team, and prayed that Tlatelolco would never be repeated.

In the classroom Lucio shook the memories from his mind. A black and white soccer ball flew through the open window and knocked over a desk. He laughed, picked up the ball and tossed it outside, following the trajectory until it reached his boys dressed in white jerseys and red shorts, standing together with arms draped over one another's shoulders.

Tomás Rodríguez, the team captain, shouted at him, 'Come on, *Maestro*. Let's go.'

'All right. Just a minute.'

Lucio changed into red sweats and white Nikes and went outside. The team straggled across the schoolyard and up the dusty unpaved street through Las Palmas, kicking the ball back and forth among the dogs, chickens and naked toddlers.

As he passed a row of adobe houses with corrugated aluminium roofs, a woman, the mother of two of his players, ran out of one of the houses.

'Maestro Serdán,' she shouted breathlessly. 'Maestro Serdán. The police came today, and men with trucks. They closed the field.'

Lucio stopped in the middle of the road and looked quizzically at the woman, 'Pardon me, Señora?'

'They closed the field where the boys play, and put up a fence.'

Lucio said, 'The field is public land. It belongs to the City of Chilpancingo.'

'Go see for yourself.'

The team had turned the corner out of sight. In a moment Lucio caught up and found the boys standing before a chainlink fence eight feet high which completely surrounded the practice

17

field. Some leaned against the fence, clinging to the steel wire links. Others stood back, talking quietly.

A sign riveted to the fence proclaimed, 'No trespassing! By order of Alfredo Mendoza, Minister of Government.'

Lucio gathered his team around him and said, 'I'll go to the Municipal Palace and file an *amparo*, a redress of grievances. A judge will hear my petition within three days. It's the law.'

'But where can we play, *Maestro*? We need to practise.'

'Play in the street. Stay out of the field or you'll get in trouble.'

Lucio limped back to school, changed into a coat and tie, and drove to the Municipal Palace. Twenty years of anger boiled behind his eyes as he pushed through the revolving doors and limped with dignity across the marble lobby.

He presented himself in the office of the court clerk and announced, 'I wish to file an *amparo*.'

The clerk, an obsequious civil servant, replied, 'On behalf of whom?'

'On behalf of the students of the Secundaria Emiliano Zapata.'

Pretending not to know Lucio, the clerk asked, 'And who might you be?'

'You know who I am. I taught your sons! My name is Lucio Serdán and I am their teacher.'

'And whom do you wish to charge, *Maestro*?'

'Alfredo Mendoza, Minister of Government.'

The clerk began to giggle, trying unsuccessfully to hide his laughter behind a fluttering wrist. Finally he said, 'You can't be serious.'

Lucio leaned over the barrier which separated the clerk from the public and shouted, 'Give me a form! I have the right!'

Reluctantly, the clerk found a blank *amparo* form and handed it to Lucio with the advice, 'You're asking for trouble.'

Lucio snarled, 'It's shitheads like you who let people like Mendoza get away with anything. He fenced in public land.'

'Oh, that. Yes, of course. I'm familiar with that. The city sold that lot to the Minister.'

Lucio exploded. 'What's Mendoza going to do? Plant a field of opium poppies in the middle of Chilpancingo?'

Shocked, the clerk shouted back, 'Now see here. You're talking about the Minister of Government . . .'

'Go to hell,' hissed Lucio Serdán. 'How much does he stick in your pocket, you snivelling *cabrón?*'

The clerk's voice turned viciously patronizing as he said, 'I understand the Minister is going to build apartments on that lot. Very nice ones, I should think, and it won't be long before he pulls down that nasty slum, Las Palmas. Very bad for the tourist trade, you know.'

Lucio snatched the form and asked, 'How much did he pay for the lot?'

The clerk shrugged his shoulders and answered, 'That's privileged information.'

'Nonsense. It's public land, it's on public record. If you don't tell me, I'll come back behind the counter and look it up myself.'

The clerk stammered, 'One hundred pesos.'

Lucio shook his head, dizzy with rage. One hundred pesos was less than the price of a beer in a cantina. He stammered, 'God help us all.'

Quickly, he filled out the form and insisted that the clerk give him a court date.

'The day after tomorrow,' said the clerk, 'but you're wasting your time.'

'We'll see about that,' said Lucio Serdán, turning on his heel and stomping out of the clerk's office.

The case was scheduled for five in the afternoon. At a quarter to the hour Lucio assembled his team in the public square which faced the Municipal Palace. The boys wore their soccer uniforms. A light rain began to fall, chasing away late shoppers. Around the square shops and restaurants began to open after the afternoon siesta, but few customers occupied the tables. A tiny green hummingbird darted from café to café, investigating the dying flowers in vases on the tables.

Lucio said to the boys, 'Be silent in the courtroom. Show respect for the judge, and remember, the law is on our side.'

Led by their teacher, the brigade of soccer players in red shorts and white jerseys marched up the stairs to the doors of the Municipal Palace. A policeman stood on either side of the entrance.

The doors were locked. One of the policemen spoke tersely to Lucio.

'The Palace is closed. The judge is not here. Go home.'

Lucio grabbed the door and pushed against the lock. He said to the policemen, 'This is outrageous. I have a court date. It is my right!'

The policeman grabbed Lucio's arm and snarled, 'You have no rights, asshole. Go home.'

Lucio jerked his arm away and said, 'We will wait.'

For an hour the teacher and his team stood on the steps of the Municipal Palace in the rain. At six o'clock Lucio told Tomás Rodríguez to go to the offices of the newspaper and bring back a reporter. Ten minutes later Tomás returned and told his teacher that the newspaper was closed.

At eight o'clock the people of Las Palmas began to filter into the square looking for their children. When Lucio explained what had happened, the mothers and fathers decided to wait with their boys. Tacos and Pepsi Colas appeared. More people came into the square and by ten o'clock two hundred people milled around in front of the Municipal Palace. As the shops and restaurants closed, workers joined the crowd. Word spread to the furniture factory, and from there to the union halls.

At eleven o'clock, with five hundred people in the Zócalo, the police arrived *en masse*. The chief of police ordered the crowd to disperse and was answered with jeers and catcalls. Lucio stood on a chair and tried to calm the people. He said he would wait all night with his boys until the judge arrived in the morning.

The chief responded by ordering his men to arrest Lucio. As the police moved toward the stubborn teacher, the crowd surrounded Lucio and his soccer players and threatened the police with fists and stones.

Frustrated and angry, the chief called the army garrison from the headquarters of the 27th Military District. At one in the morning two green army trucks rolled into the square. Angry officers quickmarched forty soldiers armed with assault rifles from the trucks onto the steps of the Municipal Palace.

The crowd turned silent and glared their hatred at the soldiers, forty frightened, nervous farm boys barely older than Lucio's soccer players.

An officer raised a bullhorn and bellowed to the crowd, 'I am

Colonel Arturo Durazo. I command you to leave. You have sixty seconds to clear this square.'

He then turned to the soldiers and shouted, 'Load and lock.'

The nervous riflemen jammed clips into their M-15s and the ominous sound of steel bolts ramming home galvanized the crowd. People began to run, trampling one another as they fled.

Only Lucio Serdán and his soccer players remained in the middle of the square. The air seemed to thicken like curdled milk. Brave and defiant, the boys stood shoulder to shoulder and began to sing the national anthem.

A sharp crack split the night.

Someone on the edge of the crowd, no one ever learned who, fired a pistol and shattered a window in the façade of the Municipal Palace. Screaming, the crowd recoiled toward the side streets leading away from the square.

With no experience of crowd control, the badly trained soldiers began to sweat, confused by the noise of the crowd. Officers shouted unclear and contradictory orders. First one panicked, then two more terrified privates lost their control and fired full thirty-round clips into the square.

Time stopped for Lucio Serdán. In slow motion, like a nightmare that wouldn't end, he saw his boys falling to the granite paving stones of the square, spurting blood from shattered chests and broken faces. Decades swept away as he relived the horror of Tlatelolco.

Seven boys died instantly. Lucio felt a hot sting in his shoulder and knew he, too, had been shot. He saw Colonel Durazo screaming into his bullhorn but could not understand his words. Lucio crawled on hands and knees behind the shelter of one of the army trucks, then crawled out again and began pulling boys to safety. The screams erupted in his ears. People swirled around him. He felt himself being pulled up and into a truck. Tomás Rodríguez was at the wheel, driving through the crowd. Seven boys, including two wounded, scrambled into the rear of the truck.

A wild bullet had flattened a front tyre on the other truck. By the time the soldiers recovered from the shock of what they had done, Lucio and his charges had disappeared.

Tomás drove for hours, deep into the Sierra. In the village of Atoyac, Lucio knew a doctor who tended his shoulder and the injured boys. One had a bullet in the leg and would survive, but the other had suffered a massive chest wound. The next morning they buried him in the mountains.

In the truck the boys found a cache of M-15 assault rifles and ammunition.

'Teach us to shoot, *Maestro.*'

Lucio said, 'You must return to your families.'

'No, *Maestro.* We're dead.'

They would never go back. This time, Lucio Serdán would fight.

1993

26 AUGUST

1

Redemption

You name Beno? You are the *espía*, no? We kill the *espía*, squash him in his black blood. We kill you maybe slow. Make you talk a little first. You are twelve years in México, long time, time to learn much, write reports, CIA espider, espider, spider, spy . . . 'This is my final report, Fred. Two hundred pages on your buddy, Alfredo Mendoza. Two hundred pages of the truth if you can stand it. Two hundred pages pages pages . . .'

Beno Alvarado woke up in a sweat. Bad dream. Part movie, part novel, part memory, one hundred per cent nasty hangover. The report was real. His resignation was real, too, but Beno knew no one ever made a clean break with the agency. Once a spider, always a spider. You cain't run an' you cain't hide. Who said that? Oh, *por Jesús*, a litre and a half of tequila.

You got shitfaced drunk, Beno. Ain't every day a career officer dresses down his station chief and quits the CIA, but that's what you did. In spades. Adiós, motherfucker.

Beno sat up in bed and watched his hands shake. His eyes felt like jelly rolls stuffed into his head. His dick felt like a pickled mescal worm. His life felt like a burning fuse racing toward his brain. Ka-boom!

He made his legs carry him into the bathroom. The mirror. What a face! No mother could love that. Red eyes and the sheen of dishonest sweat. Women often thought him handsome. They liked his black Latin eyes, bushy eyebrows and strong chin. Beno saw only a lip quivering with bitter cynicism under his moustache. In place of glib wit he found burning rage.

Don't kill yourself with booze, Beno. No honour in that.

Honour? Do I have any left?

How much honour sticks to a man who has spent twelve years lying, cheating, deceiving and dissembling? Tradecraft, the spy's art, wonderful stuff in the cinema but bad news on planet earth. In the name of Old Glory, Beno had deceived and stolen more times than he could count. He had murdered three men,

27

shot two, a Cuban and a Russian, and carved one Méxican with a knife. To save his ass, yes, in the line of duty, yes, all in a day's work, yes yes yes, but dead men haunted his dreams and made him want to puke. Guilt? Yes. Fear of retribution? Definitely. Remorse? None, but each duplicity had chipped away a little piece of his soul. Each crime had reduced his self-respect until, finally, Beno realized, his essence had been whittled down to almost nothing. What once had been a man had become a ruin. The core of his life had been the CIA, but his disillusionment was complete. Now, before his self-respect was thoroughly demolished, he intended to redeem himself.

The report on Mendoza had been the first step toward redemption. Fred Lowry, the station chief in México City, had ordered Beno to file a report on Lucio Serdán. Instead, Beno had filed a report on Mendoza.

Furious, Lowry had shouted, 'Stability is the name of the game, Beno. Stability at any price. We can't afford chaos on our border. Is Serdán a communist? Is he a threat to the stability of México?'

Preposterous questions. Beno had shouted back, 'Every kid in the slums of Acapulco knows Lucio Serdán is a hero, but a genuine threat? Don't be ridiculous.'

Lowry had replied, 'Beno, you're a royal pain in the butt. That's why I stationed you in Zihuatanejo in the first place. You're on the CIA slow track to nowhere. If you don't like agency policy, tough shit. We want Mendoza to become the next president of México. To preserve stability. To maintain the status quo. To keep the growing power of the leftists in check. To avoid a Nicaragua on a gigantic scale.'

In a century of miscalculations and political blunders, this was the last ideological straw. Beno had said, 'You're full of shit. I quit.'

Beno had drunk all night and slept all day. When he emerged from the bathroom showered and shaved, he climbed up a ladder that led from his first-floor bedroom through a trap door to the flat, decked roof.

The bay of Zihuatanejo curved away to his right. The centre of the old town lay at the foot of the bay, two miles down the beach. Directly across the bay a ridge of hills separated Zihua-tanejo from Ixtapa, the glittering zircon emerald of the Méxican riviera.

To his left the sun was sinking into the Pacific Ocean. A para-glider floated over the bay, suspended like a bait fish between a speedboat and a parachute. A quarter of a mile down the beach the boat driver reduced his speed, and the parachutist landed neatly in front of the Villa del Mar Hotel.

Beno's house stood exactly one hundred metres from the sea at high tide. The back yard was filled with palms and a lime orchard enclosed by a whitewashed brick wall. Beyond the wall the white sands of Old Clothes Beach sloped down to the sea. Private beaches are not allowed in México, and from his roof Beno could watch an endless parade of fishermen, peddlars, tourists, hustlers, hicks, secret policemen and smugglers.

His time in Zihuatanejo was growing short, and he was going to miss the sea and bay and even the tourists. Zihuatanejo had been a nice gig, drinking at the bar of the Villa del Mar and taking home rich women on vacation. Some cover for a CIA officer, playboy on the beach.

Beno tried to juggle the attitudes he carried around in his hip pocket like an English character actor, but his well of charm was empty. He couldn't disguise his disillusionment. He had thrown his resignation in Lowry's face, and sooner or later the station chief would send someone down from México City to debrief him. A CIA officer cannot simply wipe the slate clean, and Beno's was very dirty. His concern was with México and his own personal redemption. Lowry had pushed him over the edge of acceptable behaviour. He was going to turn rogue and help Lucio Serdán kill Alfredo Mendoza, Minister of Govern-ment, heroin king of Guerrero.

Beno watched a hovering red hummingbird suck nectar from an azalea, then dart into the jungle.

To protect his empire Mendoza had suborned the officers of the 27th Military District, the infantry battalion stationed in Chil-pancingo. To maintain his influence throughout the republic of México, Mendoza had the powerful resources of the infamous Directorate of Internal Security, the DIS. This secret police force had at its disposal an arsenal of high-tech weapons and surveillance equipment supplied under a secret protocol by the CIA.

Lucio Serdán had a band of teenage guerrillas and a few assault rifles. Beno intended to even the odds.

Lucio Serdán was waiting in Chilpancingo. Beno climbed down from his roof, walked out of his house, started his old VW bus and drove down the coast highway toward Acapulco, one hundred and twenty miles south.

In Acapulco he stopped for fuel, then turned east on the broad, modern highway that crossed the Sierra to México City. Eighty miles inland he pulled off the highway and drove slowly through the centre of Chilpancingo.

The night was quiet. A pack of dogs howled from the direction of Colonia Las Palmas. In front of the Municipal Palace a lone policeman slept at his post. Around the public square the cafés were deserted, their umbrellas folded up for the night. Beno slowly drove around the plaza, parked on a side street in the old part of the town, and walked half a block to a dark alley.

At the foot of the alley a dark, dimly lit tavern, The Death of Maximilian, hunkered down in the shadows. Run by a French ex-Legionnaire named Laluce, The Death of Maximilian catered to mercenaries, gun runners, dope dealers and defective units of all types. A small plaque on the door read, 'No women, no firearms.' Inside, Laluce had an ample supply of both.

The decrepit four-storey Hotel Juarez stood on the corner. Pale yellow light showed at the windows on the alley side. Beno knew Lucio's men were in the hotel and on the roof.

Lucio had rejected all other locations for their meetings. Lucio felt safe in Chilpancingo in the bosom of his people. He trusted Laluce, and the Frenchman knew a betrayal of Lucio Serdán was a death warrant.

Beno strolled down the alley and entered the smoky tavern. The narrow room was jammed. Half the mercenaries in Latin America crowded around a large, round table near the door where two men in suits were holding court. Bald, fat, moustachioed Laluce worked the bar, pouring good whisky and decent tequila. Whores buzzed like mosquitoes among the men.

Beno pushed his way to the bar and signalled Laluce.

The Frenchman greeted him with a smile.

'Ça va, Monsieur Alvarado?'

'Hello, Laluce. How about a shot of gold Sauza and a Negrita.'

Laluce poured Beno a jigger of tequila, set a cold bottle of Negra Modelo beer on the bar.

Beno stared at the large painting behind the bar, *The Execution of Maximilian.* A Méxican firing squad aimed muskets at the unfortunate Austrian archduke who had presumed himself emperor of México.

'Busy tonight,' Beno said to the bartender.

Laluce rolled his shoulders toward the front table and said, 'These guys from Panama hiring eighteen merc for a job down south.'

Beno gulped his tequila and asked, 'What're you getting?'

'Fifty dollar a head.'

'Not bad. Pour me another shot.'

Laluce poured and said, 'They tell me they can use four more specialist. You have interest?'

'Listen, Laluce, have I ever hired out?'

'*Non.*'

'Then stop asking.'

Laluce sauntered toward the rear, disappeared behind a curtained doorway for a moment, then returned and switched on the radio. A slick upbeat salsa added to the din.

Beno set his beer on the bar and looked at himself in the back bar mirror between the rows of bottles and *The Execution of Maximilian.* His eyes had narrowed into combat alertness and his shoulders flexed and stretched.

Laluce leaned over the bar and said quietly, 'Your man is here. Pay up.'

Beno slid two hundred dollars cash across the bar. Laluce pocketed the money and said, 'Go in back. Last door on the right.'

Beno pushed through the curtain. A small figure suddenly blocked his passage and silently frisked him. When the guard stepped back, Beno recognized him as one of Lucio's teenage guerrillas.

Beno followed the boy along a narrow corridor and waited while his guide passed through a door. After a moment he returned and signalled Beno to enter. Beno passed into a grubby little room with a table, a filthy bed, candlelight and two low chairs.

Lucio Serdán sat in one of the chairs, an AK-47 assault rifle placed casually across his knees, his bad leg stretched out in front of him, a cigarette burning between his fingers. A cheap Radio Shack two-way radio rested on the table.

Dressed in a schoolteacher's coat and tie, Lucio wore a wispy beard around his dark, Indian face. In the flickering light his eyes burned like a fallen angel's. He extended a hand, and they shook.

The guerrilla said, 'We meet again, Mr Alvarado.'

'I'm honoured, Mr Serdán. Thank you for coming.'

'Please sit and share a drink with me.'

Beno squeezed into the vacant chair. Lucio produced a bottle of tequila and two glasses, poured, raised his glass and said, 'To the children.'

Beno repeated the toast and they drank. For thirty seconds the two men stared at one another. Beno felt flutters in his stomach.

The guerrilla leader picked up the radio and said, 'Paulo?'

He listened to the response, replaced the radio on the table and said to Beno, 'It appears you came alone. That's a good sign.'

'You didn't. Your men are outside and in the hotel.'

Lucio puffed his cigarette and said, 'There are twenty men out there drinking with Laluce who would kill me if they knew I was here.' He smiled and asked, 'Do you think I'm worth the price on my head?'

'How much is it now?' Beno asked.

Lucio furrowed his brow in mock concern and answered, 'I'm not sure. It fluctuates up and down like the peso. In truth, I'm probably worthless.'

The schoolteacher laughed, a soft, gentle laugh that rolled over Beno like a warm Sierra breeze.

Beno smiled at the joke, then frowned and said, 'I don't like this place. I've never liked it.'

Lucio waved his hand in a gesture of dismissal and said, 'We're safe. Laluce makes a good living here and wants to continue. Besides, the army believes I'm going to attack one of their outposts tonight.'

'How do you know that?'

'Just believe that I do.'

Beno asked, 'Have you searched this room?'

'Of course.'

'May I?'

'Certainly.'

Beno made a quick check of the primitive, exposed wiring and nodded with satisfaction.

Lucio smoked his cigarette and said, 'You speak well for a *chicano*. You sound Méxican.'

'My grandfather was born in México City.'

'But you are *puro gringo*.'

'Yes.'

Lucio paused again, thinking, watching, twirling the glass in his hand, then said with a smile, 'I trust you anyway.'

Beno asked, 'Are you happy with the AK-47s?'

Lucio held up his machine-gun and stared at it with an expression of surprise, as if he were seeing it for the first time. Then he made a sad clown's face, and said, 'I'm not a soldier. I'm a schoolteacher. I'm going to lead my boys to their death.'

'Are you going to give up the fight?'

'No.'

'Good,' said Beno. 'I need the business.'

Lucio twirled his glass in his hand as he said, 'You summoned me here, Mr Alvarado. Please tell me why.'

'I have more weapons, if you're interested.'

'Perhaps.'

'I have hand-held rockets, very small, very deadly.'

Lucio laughed and said, 'It sounds as if you want to turn us into real soldiers.'

Beno said, 'Ask one of your men to come with me to my vehicle.'

Lucio called out, 'Tomás.'

Tomás Rodríguez came into the room and Lucio said, 'Go with Mr Alvarado.'

Beno led the boy out of the back door of the tavern, circled the block to his VW and retrieved the armour-piercing rockets.

Returning to the room, he zipped open the bag and took out a bullet-shaped, foot-long missile and a disposable launch tube.

He said to Lucio, 'This is a Soviet-made anti-tank missile, an RPG-16. As you see, it's small, but deadly.'

Beno loaded the launcher onto the grip and explained the simple sighting and firing mechanisms.

He said, 'This is a fire and forget weapon. Once you pull the trigger, the missile does the rest. It has infrared radar which guides the warhead to the target where it explodes. You can't miss.'

Lucio looked at the rocket but didn't touch it. He asked, 'How did Russian weapons find their way to México?'

Beno answered, 'War surplus from Afghanistan. Soviet weapons are quite readily available if you know where to look. They're simple, reliable, and durable.'

Lucio said, 'They look expensive.'

'One thousand dollars apiece.'

'I don't have that much.'

Beno suggested, 'Rob a bank.'

'I don't rob banks. I'm not a bandit.'

'Would you like to have them, Mr Serdán?'

'I'm not sure.'

Beno said, 'With this, you can ambush Alfredo Mendoza. You can avenge the massacre of three years ago.'

Lucio asked, 'Why are you offering these to me? Any of Laluce's patrons can easily double your price.'

'I want you to have them. You pay me when you can.'

Incredulous, Lucio asked, 'You want to give me these weapons? Mr Alvarado, you're a businessman. Don't tell me you believe in my cause.'

Beno answered carefully, 'I have no love for Alfredo Mendoza. He's bad for business. He's killing my customers.'

'Then why don't you take your rockets and kill him yourself?'

Beno said tersely, 'I prefer to stay in business, but even a businessman can believe in justice.'

His friendly smile turning wary, Lucio said, 'You have a house in Zihuatanejo. Perhaps you are more than a businessman. Perhaps you're from the DIS.'

'If I were DIS, you'd be long dead.'

Lucio shrugged.

Beno said, 'You're a good man, Lucio Serdán. In an honest world you'd never come near a place like this. Do you think me a fool if I respect that? I'm rich. I can afford to give you a few rockets which cost me little. If you don't want them, I'll sell them at a profit. I'm offering them to you because you can use them. You need them. How that benefits me is my business.'

Lucio said, 'It is disrespectful to decline a gift.'

Beno said, 'Pay me when you have the money.'

Lucio stood up and said, 'One of my men will be in the bar. His name is Paulo. He will stay with you for one hour. I'm sure you understand. Good night, Mr Alvarado.'

'Good night.'

Lucio returned the missile to the duffel bag, picked it up and disappeared through the rear door.

Beno re-entered the bar, ordered a drink and stared at himself in the mirror. An unsmiling young man sat down at the next stool.

Beno said to Laluce, 'Give him a drink.'

It felt good to be on the side of the angels, buying back a piece of his soul with rockets.

After an hour, Beno left the bar and walked to his bus. When he was gone, Laluce went into a little room behind the bar, picked up a telephone and dialled México City.

A gravelly voice answered, 'Yes?'

'Mr Lowry?'

'Yes.'

'Alvarado was here again.'

31 AUGUST

2

The Finding

Fifty-five year old Fred Lowry sat down to breakfast in the kitchen of his house in Polanco, a wealthy neighbourhood near the embassy in México City. He felt robust and hungry.

'Good morning, Mr Lowry,' said his cheerful, pregnant maid.

'Hello, Teresa,' said Lowry with a big smile. He pointed at her swollen belly and smirked, 'I wish that were mine.'

She grinned and asked, 'What can I get you today?'

'The usual. Ham and scrambled, coffee and orange juice. Where's Mrs Lowry?'

'Tennis.'

'And the children?'

'School.'

'Already?'

'It's half past eight.'

Lowry ate breakfast and scanned the morning papers, the *New York Times*, *Washington Post*, *Wall Street Journal* and three México City dailies, but his mind drifted. He had less than a month of service remaining in México City before returning to CIA headquarters in Virginia.

In his own considered opinion, Lowry was leaving México City station in far better shape than he had found it in 1988, five years before. For the first time in fifty years, the CIA had thoroughly penetrated the huge KGB station in México City. Cuban influence in México was declining. Lowry believed these positive changes arose from his astonishingly workable relationship with Máximo Levín, the enigmatic, reclusive director of the Méxican Directorate of Internal Security. The DIS co-operated with the CIA to an extraordinary degree. Quid pro quo, the CIA provided hardware, and the DIS provided hard intelligence on subversives, communists and activity at the Soviet embassy.

As usual, the Méxican economy verged on collapse. Strikes ravaged the republic. Besieged by inflation, the middle class countenanced rebellion. And down in Guerrero Beno Alvarado threatened treachery, a minor inconvenience in the grand scheme of things. Lowry intended to let the new station chief take up the issue of Beno Alvarado and Lucio Serdán with the DIS. The directorate would have no qualms if asked to terminate a renegade CIA officer.

Breakfast over, Lowry went to the garage and drove his Buick out under a hot yellow sky. A thick blanket of smog lay over the Federal District, etching away the majesty of the great city.

He waved at the policeman assigned to guard his block and plunged into traffic for the short drive to the embassy. He had a pleasantly giddy sense of anticipation. With luck, today he would learn México's most carefully guarded secret. This morning the leaders of México's ruling party, the Institutional Revolutionary Party, known by its Spanish acronym as the PRI, were meeting in executive session to choose the party's candidate for the 1994 election. The party expected the candidate to assume the presidency for six years, the *sexenio*, six years of untempered power. For sixty-five years the party had not lost a major election. Since 1928 its candidates had followed one another like dynastic kings into the National Palace to sit upon the presidential chair.

The selection procedure was simple. The President listened to the party leaders, then he alone chose. One man would receive the *dedazo*, the big finger. President Salinas had narrowed the possibilities to two men, Ricardo Solida, the Foreign Minister, and Alfredo Mendoza, Minister of Government. Lowry had backed Mendoza. He was so sure of himself that he had bet the ambassador one hundred dollars that Mendoza would get the big finger.

Across the city in the ancient district of Tlatelolco, the high-rise headquarters of the Directorate of Internal Security rose twenty storeys to a sharp peak, a modern pyramid of glass and steel aimed precariously at the future. On a clear day the upper floors afforded a spectacular view of the Federal District.

Underground, in a multi-storeyed basement crammed with electronic gear, DIS technicians surveilled the entire republic.

Tall, thin, ascetic Máximo Levín, creator and director of the

DIS, lived in a small apartment on the upper two floors of the pyramid and rarely left the building. Always formal and correct, he dressed in a DIS regulation plain suit, white shirt and narrow tie. A mass of curly black hair spilled down his scalp like a thundercloud. Thick glasses magnified his large brown eyes, creating the aura of an all-seeing wizard.

His staff called him 'el genio', the genius. Charismatic, equally adept at manipulating people and electronic machinery, Máximo dwelt in the visionary upper echelons of the human intellect. Where others saw chaos, Máximo perceived order. While others served themselves, the director served only a vision of his country's future. Aloof, remote, terrifyingly brilliant, his enemies compared him to Feliks Dzerzhinsky, founder of the Soviet secret police.

This morning Máximo sat alone in his library on the nineteenth floor and faced a bank of television monitors. On the main screen he watched the proceedings at party headquarters. The party leaders were about to cast their votes.

On a second screen he monitored the activity in the communications room in the first sub-basement. Half a dozen operators were recording and decrypting every telephone call to and from the American and Soviet embassies. Other screens monitored vital functions of the Bank of México, Pemex, the state oil monopoly, a multitude of police agencies and various military communication channels.

On the main screen President Salinas began to poll the leaders. To Máximo, the result was a foregone conclusion.

Light California oak panelling and an array of antique maps adorned Lowry's windowless embassy office. For five years he had ruled his CIA fiefdom from this room, but he had tired of México. The Russians and their huge KGB operation in México City no longer interested him. His mind had gone south. With all his heart he believed the era of the American Imperium was dawning in the western hemisphere, and Lowry was moving up to man the Latin America desk in Virginia.

He spent an hour fiddling with papers, pretending to work while waiting for the phone to ring. Finally, at ten o'clock his secretary told him that Máximo Levín was on the scrambled line.

Lowry picked up the phone and said, 'Yes, Director.'

Máximo's rich voice and perfect English were undiminished by the scrambler mechanism. He said simply, 'It's Mendoza. I'll have details for you tomorrow, perhaps the day after.'

Lowry jumped to his feet and in a gesture of triumph thrust his fist in the air.

'Thank you, Director. Thank you very much.'

Lowry replaced the phone in its cradle, rang his secretary and shouted gleefully, 'Get me Langley. I want to talk to the DDO right away.'

When Al Mears travelled, the world adjusted to his time zone. No matter where he was, the DDO, Deputy Director of Operations, ran on Langley time, stretching his electronic umbilical cord to CIA headquarters in Virginia, the centre of his universe. The DDO believed in C cubed I, command, control, communications, and intelligence, with emphasis on control. Sixty-five years old, veteran of wars never mentioned in school history classes, the DDO relished his role as a secret potentate of a secret world. In his mind he was eminently qualified to sit like Zeus on lofty Olympus and fire thunderbolts at unruly mortals below.

Today, his lightning was aimed at México, America's alien neighbour.

Mears hated México City, loathed the smog and despised the traffic. The sprawling city filled the vast Valley of México to the brim with thirty million people. To Mears the Méxican capital seemed to exist on the brink of anarchy, and that prospect frightened him. From his distant perch in Langley, México City filtered into his consciousness as a nasty bed of pests which he occasionally had to swat. Up close, driving through the crowded streets on his way from the airport to the embassy, the city confirmed his smug belief that his sworn duty was to keep it under control.

From the rear window of his Lincoln Continental sedan Mears watched the sprawling metropolis roll past, block after block of weird surreal juxtapositions, high-rise blocks next to shacks, faded pastel stucco houses jammed against the stone façades of colonial buildings with wrought-iron balconies. He stared at the brown faces, knowing their destiny was in his hands, knowing they would resent it if they knew, and feeling indignation at their imagined resentment.

He arrived at the embassy in a rotten mood, but a glimpse of the splendid chancellery uplifted his spirits. Surrounded by a fence of sharpened steel spikes, the gleaming white stone embassy reminded him of a fortress, defiant and proud, that bespoke an America of goodness and light. Al Mears' mission in life was to impose that image on the rest of the world, whether the world wanted it or not.

The driver wheeled the car around to the garage. A waiting Fred Lowry, hand extended in greeting, opened the door. Mears emerged looking at his watch.

'I want to be out of here in six hours,' said the DDO.

'No problem, Al,' said Lowry. 'The safe room is ready for our briefing, then lunch with the ambassador and back to the airport.'

The safe room behind Lowry's office consisted of a twelve by twelve foot hermetically sealed steel box encased in lead. No electrical leads went in. A sealed battery pack provided power for lights, air-conditioner, small refrigerator, paper shredder and decoder, which looked like a fax machine attached to a computer. The furniture consisted of two uncomfortable folding steel chairs and a table.

Mears laid his briefcase on the table, sat down and watched his station chief take a bottle of vodka from the refrigerator and pour a tumbler half full.

Mears said, 'Your message caused quite a stir. I know you've been saying all along that Mendoza would be the anointed one, but no one believed you, including me. To tell you the truth, I could spend a lifetime trying to sort out the Méxicans and never understand them. They're worse than the Russians.'

Lowry beamed and said, 'Since I sent that message, I've learned how Mendoza was chosen. It's a classic, Al, a real piece of work.'

The station chief swallowed a mouthful of vodka and said, 'To start with, Mendoza has the army behind him. He has generals begging him to move his heroin production to their districts so they can get a piece of the action. They let it be known that if Mendoza wasn't chosen, they were prepared for a *coup*.'

Surprised, Mears blurted, 'He threatened the party with a *coup d'état*? Incredible!'

Lowry nodded joyfully, saying, 'He reminded the party leaders in very emphatic terms of what they already knew. The party has won every election since 1928, but in the last election, Salinas got only 51 per cent of the vote. If the next election is honest and democratic, the party candidate is going to lose. Guaranteed. The party will be dethroned unless they cut loose all their muscle. That means using the army to control the polls. Mendoza is the only guy with balls enough to do it, and Salinas and the rest know it. If the party loses, the army loses, and in that event they will attempt a *coup d'état*.'

Mears nodded and allowed, 'We could live with that. Yes, indeed. It would be a hell of a lot better than having the damn socialists win the election.'

Lowry said, 'Yes, but the threat of a *coup* didn't scare them. Mendoza has been a top cop for twenty years. He created the DIS specifically to collect dirt on everyone. The DIS has dossiers on every politician, corporate executive, union leader and army officer in the republic. He blackmailed every one. When it came to a vote, the hands went up unanimously for Mendoza.'

Mears said, 'Your friend, the Director of the DIS, told you this?'

'Yes. Máximo Levín.'

'The Jew. Strange, a Méxican Jew.'

Lowry said, 'I'm certain Mendoza ordered Máximo to tell me. I think it's hot shit, Al. Mendoza is the most pro-American, anti-communist Méxican politician to come along in years. He ordered the DIS to co-operate with us, and even Salinas doesn't know that. They feed us everything they have on the Russians. It's been fantastic. Mendoza will make a great president. He loves us.'

Mears snapped, 'Because we protect him. Because we give him everything he asks for. Because he beats up the socialists.'

Startled by the DDO's tone, Lowry asked, 'What are you getting at?'

'We've protected Mendoza for years, and he has a dossier on us, too,' said the DDO. 'What do they call him? They have a nice name for him.'

44

'The heroin king of Guerrero.'

'Yeah. The bloody king, the heroin king. Jesus. A few years ago Mendoza's drug production was small-time, low-key, easy to overlook, considering what he did for us. Now he's built a fucking empire. You know exactly what he's doing. You filed the report yourself, flying dope into the US in his own god-damned government plane under diplomatic cover. The son of a bitch. Every month, into Las Vegas of all places, thumbing his nose at the DEA, and we have to tell the Drug Enforcement Agency to keep their hands off him.

'This is going to blow sky high, Fred. Mendoza has gone too far, way too far. He has no sense of balance. His heroin factory is the worst kept secret of all time. He's far more dangerous to us than that little prick Noriega in Panama ever was. If he becomes president, he'll have us by the short hairs. DEA will leak the story and we'll get a black eye. Are you beginning to get the picture, Fred? State is prepared to back up DEA, so there is only one way to save our ass, make State and DEA happy, and do a service to all mankind to boot.'

Lowry said slowly, 'Pull the plug on Mendoza.'

'As you so quaintly put it, yes,' said Al Mears. 'Your powers of deduction have not been diminished by your intake of vodka.'

Lowry stood up and paced across the small room. 'Jesus Christ,' he said. 'Mendoza is the best source we've had in years. Having the DIS is like having three thousand agents watching the Russians, the Cubans, the Nicaraguans. México station is coming up with more product than any other station in the world. Cut out Mendoza and we lose all of it.'

Mears said, 'Lose the battle, win the war. Mendoza is out.'

The DDO turned on the decoder. The monitor displayed a blinking cursor and he typed in, 'Fire'. An option menu appeared and he selected, 'Insert key'. He typed in five digits and then punched, 'Insert Document'. He removed a sheet of paper from his briefcase and inserted it into the machine. The fax scanner read the neat columns of five digit code groups and sent the coded message to the computer. A moment later a sheet began to roll off the silent laser printer.

Lowry knew without looking that the document was a finding of the National Security Council. Rated much higher than top secret, a finding spelled out American policy with no regard to public statements or public opinion.

Mears set the coded version aside to be filed in the Secure Documents Room and ripped the sheet of clear English off the printer. He handed the document to Lowry, who read it quickly, then re-read it slowly, memorizing the peculiar language.

Finally, he read part of it aloud, 'Alfredo Mendoza's becoming President of the United Méxican States threatens the security of the United States. The Central Intelligence Agency is hereby ordered to sever all relationships with Alfredo Mendoza, and to establish relationships with any and all groups or individuals who are opposed to Alfredo Mendoza's candidacy for President of the United Méxican States.'

Lowry handed the document back to Mears who ran it through the shredder.

Petulant, Lowry said, 'This undoes everything I've done here in five years.'

Mears nodded his head slowly and said, 'I know, Fred, but it makes sense. México has changed; the world has changed. If Mendoza forces his way into the National Palace, he'll have a real revolution on his hands, and we'll be forced into helping him. My God, we might even have to send in troops. The liberals will scream, "Vietnam." The conservatives will go apeshit over the dope. Mendoza has to go. That's all there is to it.'

Deflated, Lowry sat down and declared, 'How can we get people to trust us when we fuck them over like this?'

Mears replied, 'If you don't want to handle this operation, I can bring in a new station chief tomorrow.'

Lowry shook his head and said, 'I'll do it. You know me, Al. When the crunch comes, I toe the line and salute. I'm a good trooper.' He tilted his head toward the shredder and asked, 'Does the NSC know they're asking for a *coup d'état?*'

Mears said, 'They're not idiots. They recognize the possibility, but they're subject to pressures, like this drug thing. If the army ends up in control of México, no one in Washington will object.'

Lowry scoffed, 'The drug issue is bullshit.'

Mears said, 'I know that, but neither you nor I want to pick up *Time* and read about the heroin king and his contacts in the

CIA. That's what's going to happen unless . . . Look, you know what to do under the standard guidelines. No clear agency involvement. No loose ends.'

'I follow. What's my time frame?'

'You mentioned in your report that Salinas would announce Mendoza as his party's candidate on 16 September during the Méxican Independence Day celebrations. Mendoza should be out of the picture before then.'

'That's not much time. A little over two weeks.'

'Quick and dirty, Fred.' Mears paused, then said, 'Just get the job done. We're counting on you. Now, let's get on with the bloody lunch. I need to be back in Virginia.'

1 SEPTEMBER

3

Sam

As the polluted brown cloud over México City receded into the distance, flight attendants on the Méxicana 737 speedily distributed a quick round of drinks. After ten minutes of level flight, the plane began its descent to Zihuatanejo.

Samantha Louise Black sipped a Cuba libre and gazed over the green mountains of Guerrero marching like soldiers to the sea. Pert, bright, a little giddy, Sam tingled with excitement as she approached her first field assignment. Trained as a computer systems analyst, she had been trying for months to escape the silicon gloom of México City station's secure documents room.

She checked her reflection in her compact mirror, red hair, milky white skin, blue eyes, an all-American svelte body. She looked like a tourist, acted like a tourist, but she felt as if the letters 'CIA' were tattooed across her forehead.

Fred Lowry had shown her several photos of Beno Alvarado, service record mug shots, passport portraits, and a candid shot set against the pyramids of Teotihuacán. In each picture Beno's black, brooding eyes reflected a lethal intelligence. She found him very attractive.

Sam had said, 'He looks Méxican.'

'*Chicano*, third generation Californian,' Lowry had replied with a thin smile. 'He won't like you. He'll give you a hard time.'

Sam Black had encountered few men in her life who didn't like her. The idea intrigued her.

Fred Lowry had told her, 'He's expecting to be debriefed. Check into the Villa del Mar and wait. He'll show.'

Suddenly the plane banked and the window filled with the wide blue of the Pacific. Palms, mangoes, and a pristine white beach bordered the sea. After two stiff bounces the plane taxied to a stop.

Eighty light-hearted tourists shuffled toward the illusory

México of travel brochures. Waiting for the aisle to clear, Sam stared across the tarmac at a Gulfstream jet carrying Méxican national colours, which she recognized as the private conveyance of Alfredo Mendoza who owned a mansion in Zihuatanejo, the notorious El Partenón.

As she crossed the soft asphalt, the heat of September struck her like a sunspot come to rest on earth. In the terminal, the air-conditioning had failed. Sweat dripped off her like a tropical storm. Indolent policemen with machine-pistols patrolled the airport, smoking cigarettes and scrutinizing passengers. They stared at Sam as she waited for her small valise. In the heat her simple cotton shift clung to her body as if transparent, revealing her identity along with her form. For an old hand in the spy game, delivering a simple message to a field officer would be routine, even boring, but Sam felt an almost erotic excitement. She felt vibrant, alive, primed for the unexpected.

She collected her bag and took a taxi to the huge, glitzy Camino Real Hotel in Ixtapa. For half an hour she dawdled in the lobby bar, watching the entrance, then summoned another cab and presently stood in the cool, air-conditioned foyer of the elegantly understated Villa del Mar on Old Clothes Beach. The low-rise inn surrounded a central courtyard which contained a thatched tropical bar, restaurant and pool open to the sea.

She checked in. From the balcony of her room she heard laughter and music floating up from the bar. Methodically, she examined her room as she had been taught, opening drawers and looking into the light fixtures, telling herself she wasn't playing at being a secret agent – this time she was one.

So far, the CIA had been a disappointment. Sam craved excitement, adventure, even passion. Instead, she had found the dull routine of petty bureaucracy, men and women whose emotions ranged from smug arrogance to grim cynicism. Modern espionage had degenerated into a vastly complex electronic game. Human intelligence, humint in spytalk, had little value compared to the data generated by satellites, computers and dehumanized technicians. The agency seemed more like a mediocre corporation living off a fat government contract than a secret service dedicated to the preservation of democratic institutions.

Now, alone in the field, to keep her head from buzzing with

anticipation, she reviewed her instructions: stick to procedure, do everything according to the book, remember your cover. A cover was a licence to cheat. In pursuit of truth she was supposed to lie. Did that make her an actor, a puppet, an extension of national sovereignty? Or was she merely a frustrated computer systems analyst pulled out of a pool of live bodies to function as courier for a low priority assignment?

She suspected the latter, but the tension in her neck and shoulders made her feel as if hers was the most important mission on earth. What the hell, that's why people came to the Villa del Mar: a few drinks, a lot of sun, and the tension melts away.

Fat chance. The tension would rise like a rolling Pacific wave until it crashed into the surf when she met Beno Alvarado.

She showered, changed into a one-piece Spandex swimsuit, winked at herself in the mirror, and went downstairs.

As she passed the bar, the bartender flashed a radiant smile and asked politely, 'May I get you something, señora?'

She returned his smile, shook her head, and said, 'Pool first, then the beach, then a piña colada.'

'Very good, señora.'

The half dozen guests lining the bar turned to stare as she plunged into the pool. Waves of pleasure rippled through her body as she breast-stroked back and forth, observing the guests out of the corner of her eye. After a moment they resumed their conversations.

She pulled herself from the pool and walked onto the beach. In the stifling heat of August the long strip of white sand was sparsely occupied. Fishermen fished, beachcombers collected shells, body surfers plunged through the mild waves which rolled in like quiet, distant thunder. Sam waded shoulder deep into the surf and turned to look at the hills rising above the line of hotels.

A mile away, high above the town, perched on a black granite plateau, Alfredo Mendoza's El Partenón loomed majestically, its gleaming white pillars a statement of supreme arrogance, a full-scale replica of the Parthenon in Athens.

Rumours describing Mendoza's grotesque habits frequently enlivened dinner conversations in México City. Sam had heard that Mendoza detailed agents of the Directorate of Internal

Security to comb the beaches of Zihuatanejo for beautiful women. The DIS offered the women drugs, then arrested and hauled them to El Partenón to service the Minister.

Disgusted, Sam turned her eyes away, whirled and dove into the sea, cleansing her mind with salt water. Ten minutes later, eyes downcast, she returned to the row of beach chairs and thatched palapas in front of the hotel. She felt lulled, seduced, wonderful.

At that moment reality confronted her in the form of a ragged, dark-skinned Méxican girl of six or seven, ankle-length dress in tatters, face smeared with grime, palm held up holding a pathetic, broken sea shell.

'Please buy, señora?'

Confused, even a bit frightened, Sam could only shake her head. Without a word the girl moved through the beach chairs, collecting nothing, and trailed down the beach to the next hotel.

'Don't worry, you'll get used to it,' said a cheerful male voice.

Sam turned as the bartender passed with a tray of drinks.

On his way back to the bar he asked, 'Can I get your piña colada now?'

'Yes, please.'

He snapped his fingers. 'One happy pineapple en route.'

She stretched out on a chaise-longue, slathered herself with sunscreen, and settled down to wait. Her moment as a novelty had passed, and she became another rich tourist soaking up sun and icy drinks.

An endless parade of souvenir vendors marched up and down the beach offering carved swordfish, ceramic birds and glittering beads. After an hour of staring across the bay she fell into a dreamless sleep.

When she awoke the sun had set and guests were gathering in the restaurant for dinner. She dined alone on delicious grilled shrimps and then settled in the bar, enduring the flirtation of every male on the premises.

At one in the morning she was alone in the bar. The bartender politely polished sparkling clean glasses, waiting for her to say good-night.

Sam shifted on her stool for a moment to watch the surf, and when she turned around, Beno Alvarado was sitting two stools away as if he had materialized out of the warm breeze.

Strong, powerful arms rested on the bar, cradling a beer. He wore a plain white Mexican short-sleeved shirt, tan linen pants and Cordovan boots. His unshaven face had the ravaged, knowing look of a weather-beaten sailor. Sam saw more Spanish adventurer than Aztec in his Mexican features. Having read a portion of his file, she knew he carried a Ruger .38 in his left boot.

No computer pusher or satellite jockey, Beno Alvarado was a flesh and blood spy. Within a heartbeat, she knew she desired him.

The bartender retreated to the kitchen.

Without looking at her, Beno said, 'Lowry sent you.'

Startled, Sam asked, 'Is it so obvious?'

Beno turned toward her, his eyes penetrating like lasers into hers. His face softened as he asked, 'Do you want to play agency games, pass code words back and forth and all that crap?'

Sam conceded, 'There isn't much point, is there?'

Beno asked, 'What's your name?'

'Samantha Black.'

'Do your friends call you Sam?'

'Yes.'

'Are you here to debrief me, Miss Black?' Beno asked, pointedly avoiding her intimate nickname.

'No,' she answered, 'I'm here to deliver a message. Can we talk somewhere else?'

'In your room?'

'Yes.'

'I was just in there,' he said. 'Look what I found.'

Beno reached into his pants pocket and brought out a miniature microphone.

Sam muttered, 'Oh, shit.'

Beno laughed quietly and said, 'Don't get excited. I put it there.'

'But I didn't find it,' Sam said. 'I feel pretty foolish.'

Beno recited, 'Samantha Louise Black, passport number F109887. Born Key West, Florida, 4 November 1968. No weapons, no agency trademarks, appropriate clothes for a few days on the beach. Not too much make-up.' He smiled and added, 'I like that. You're too beautiful to be vain.'

Sam felt naked, exposed, revealed. She asked, 'How long have you been watching me?'

'All day.'

'You're a cautious man, Mr Alvarado.'

'The bold die young in this business,' he replied. 'The bartender wants to close up. Let's go to your room.'

As he followed her up the short flight of stairs, Beno could smell her desire, and it caught him off balance. He had no room for agency women in his life – little room for the agency at all, but he liked her, liked the way she looked in her swimsuit, liked her enough to listen to her message instead of sending her back to México City.

After she closed the door, he asked, 'Is this your first assignment outside the embassy?'

'Yes.'

'Nervous?'

'Something like that.'

'Sit down.'

Sam sat on a sofa and watched Beno pace, filling the room with a taut, predatory presence. When he glanced at her, she felt as if he were probing directly into her brain. She knew she would never trifle with this man.

2 SEPTEMBER

4

Beno

All day Beno had been trying to fathom Lowry's reasons for sending this young woman to Zihuatanejo. He had concluded that Lowry had written him off. A resolute cold warrior, Lowry saw the agency not as an apparatus for gathering accurate intelligence, but as a weapon of war. Beno's announced reluctance to serve in that war had made him disposable.

Beno asked abruptly, 'What's your security clearance?'

'A two.'

'Okay. Let's have your message.'

'It's in two parts. Hummingbirds prefer red flowers.'

Lowry wanted him in México City immediately. Beno already knew that.

'What's the second part?'

'RPG-16,' Sam said, blithely adding, 'That's the NATO designation for a Soviet anti-tank missile, I believe.'

Now he knew why Lowry hadn't come himself. Lowry knew of Beno's supplying rockets to Lucio Serdán. Where was the leak? Serdán himself? Laluce?

Beno had expected to be discovered, but it seemed as if Lowry was doing him a favour, telling him to get out before he got dead.

Beno recovered enough to answer, 'Yes, that's right. Lowry mention why he wanted you to say that to me?'

'No.'

He scrutinized her but couldn't tell if she was lying. While his mind cleared, he began to fire questions.

'Do you know what your message means?'

She answered, 'I have no idea.'

Coaxing, he said, 'You must have tried to decipher the code.'

'You're right,' she said. 'I guessed. Hummingbirds prefer red flowers. It's a simple book code known only to the sender and receiver. I think "hummingbirds" is you. That's as far as I can go.'

'Are you married?'

'No.'

'Regular boyfriend?'

'No.'

'Good. I don't want to worry about pillow talk. What I did on my vacation by the sea.'

Slightly miffed, Sam asked, 'Are you concerned with my sex life or my security?'

'Not your security,' Beno replied. 'Mine.'

He lit a cigarette and asked, 'How long have you been in México?'

'Seven months.'

'Speak Spanish?'

She lisped, '*Sí. Cómo no.*'

In clipped México City Spanish Beno commented, 'You have a Castilian accent.'

'I spent a year in Spain.'

Sarcasm tinged Beno's voice as he asked in English, 'Junior year abroad?'

He was pleased to see a spark of anger in her eyes as she answered, 'My father was a naval officer, assigned to Rota.'

'A Navy brat. Was Daddy an admiral?'

'Captain.'

'Naval intelligence?'

'No. He's a nuclear engineer.'

He asked, 'What's your job in the embassy?'

'I'm a computer systems analyst.'

'Do you sleep with Fred Lowry?'

'What is this?'

'*Answer my question!*'

'No.'

'Do you like him?'

'He's a pompous ass.'

'Do you *like* him?'

'No.'

'Do you hate him?'

She hesitated, then replied, 'No. I hardly know him. I only met him twice before he sent me on this assignment.'

He thrust his face close to hers, narrowed his eyes, and hissed, 'I hate his fucking guts.'

Her face registered shock and a trickle of sweat dribbled down her temple.

Beno pulled back, took a drag off his cigarette and said, 'Don't worry. Lowry knows that. He doesn't like me much, either.'

He could see she was uncomfortable, but she was standing up to him and earning his respect. He sat down on the opposite side of the coffee table and asked, 'Did Lowry tell you that this is a dangerous mission?'

'No.'

'That figures. You're expendable, the same as me.'

'Are you trying to frighten me?'

'Yes.'

'You're doing a good job.'

Beno took a long drag on his Marlboro and said, 'Thank you. I don't think you should have illusions about the kind of work the agency does, sometimes to its own people. You're fresh, untried, and therefore expendable cannon fodder.'

Chagrined, Sam asked, 'Are you saying I might be killed? By whom?'

Beno ignored her question and asked, 'How much did Lowry tell you about me?'

'Very little. Your file said you carry a revolver in your boot.'

'The file's out of date. Once something like that gets into a computer data bank, shit, it'll get you killed.'

'I see.'

Beno said, 'I bet you want to be a field officer and carry a gun in your boot, right?'

'I'll admit it,' Sam said.

'You won't have much of a chance as long as Lowry is in charge of México station. He thinks women are cunts. He's also not fond of niggers, spics or gooks.'

'So what?'

He smiled, seemed to relax slightly, and asked, 'Mind if I help myself to a beer?'

'Be my guest.'

He took a bottle of Dos Equis from the servi-bar, opened it, and asked, 'Did Lowry send you here to seduce me?'

'That's a bit much.'

'Are you objecting to my question as a woman, a human being or an employee of the Central Intelligence Agency?'

'All of the above.'

He knew she was right. Impudent and outspoken, Sam's resentment mirrored his own. He hated the agency for turning two people who liked each other into enemies.

Sam snapped, 'I resent being tested and probed.'

Surprised, Beno asked, 'You do?'

'Yes, damn it.'

'But you were trained to expect it.'

'Yes, of course, but that doesn't make me resent it less.'

'You want me to treat you with dignity? Not ask you embarrassing questions?'

'Yes.'

Beno scratched his chin and said, 'Well, I'll be damned. Suppose I said, well, okay, acted like a perfect gentleman, and then you shot me in the head.'

He raised his eyebrows, wrinkling his forehead, and stared right into her face.

Sam protested, 'Do you think . . .'

Beno held his stare until she stared back, then he dropped his eyes and said, 'No, not you. I don't think so, but I'm not the most popular guy in México station. I have unsavoury opinions. If you're cleared for security level A two, as you say, you should know what happens to people like me.'

'What exactly are people like you, Mr Alvarado?'

'Pissed off people who quit.' Beno paused, then asked, 'Didn't Lowry tell you I resigned?'

'No.'

'Figures.' Beno shook his head and said, annoyed, 'Well, Miss Black, you have delivered your message to ex-CIA officer Alvarado, Alpha Seven, México station. I told Lowry to stick it up his ass. You can go back and tell him you did your job, and I refused to co-operate.'

Sam scratched her head, went to the servi-bar, found a miniature of Bacardi 151 rum and a can of Coca-Cola. She mixed a drink and asked, 'Can you tell me why you resigned?'

'Sure,' Beno said, then asked, 'Have you noticed El Partenón?'

Sam nodded, 'The Greek palace on the hill? Sure. You can't miss it.'

'You know who owns it?'

'Alfredo Mendoza.'

'Ever meet him?'

'Thank God, no.'

Beno smiled coldly and said, 'If you stay in México long enough, you will. Mendoza gets a thrill from hanging out with agency types.'

Sam said, 'From what I've heard, I don't think I'd like that much.'

Beno said, 'You were shocked when I asked if Lowry had sent you to seduce me. Lady, he sends women to make love to Minister Mendoza. Sometimes Mendoza likes a gringo sandwich. Lowry parks his agency whores here at the glorious Villa del Mar.'

Sam said, 'Sounds like business as usual. You're not quitting because the station chief does favours for a politician with perverse tastes.'

Beno chuckled and said, 'You're sharp. That's right, I'm not.' He asked, 'What do you know about Lucio Serdán?'

She paused and sipped her drink. Beno raised his eyebrows and pressed, 'You've heard of him?'

'Yeah, sure. People in the embassy grouse about him once in a while.'

'Tell me what you know.'

Vague, almost flippant, Sam said, 'He's a revolutionary with a guerrilla band in the mountains near here. The Méxican army has been after him for years. He's a communist.'

Beno fired back a question, 'How do you know he's a communist?'

Sam answered defensively, 'That's the word. Lowry says so. The DIS says so.'

Beno nodded and said, 'Fred's a kill-the-commies-at-all-costs kind of guy. To him, anyone who goes into the mountains to fight a friendly government has to be a red.'

He asked, 'Ever been up in the Sierra Madre?'

She shook her head.

'It's beautiful,' he said. 'Clean and rugged. The people are simple and ignorant, like mountain folk everywhere.'

63

He tilted the beer and drank.

Sam said, 'That sounds idyllic.'

His eyes flashed around the bottle and he said wistfully, 'I wish it were, but there's nothing romantic about being stone poor in paradise. The people have nothing, and so they take what they can get. They grow opium poppies for Alfredo Mendoza.'

Beno resumed pacing, and began to speak softly, measuring his tone.

'The people call Mendoza the heroin king of Guerrero. Last year his net profits were sixty million dollars. That's a secret known by every reporter in México City. In all of México only Lucio Serdán has the courage to challenge Mendoza.'

As Beno told her the story of the children's massacre in Chilpancingo, his cheeks flushed with passion and his voice quivered with emotion. He finished by saying, 'Lucio is fighting a losing battle. Mendoza will get him. Is Serdán a threat to Mendoza? No. His band is too small, too ill-equipped. He's a symbol for the opposition, but he's no Fidel Castro. Is Serdán a communist? Likewise, no.'

Sam asked, 'Do you have proof?'

'Proof? Jesus Christ, isn't the blood of children proof enough? Aren't a million junked out Americans enough? You hear endless shit about the Colombians and their cocaine. The Méxicans love that. It takes the heat off them. This is right on our border. Assholes like Mendoza send a million Méxicans a year across the river to the other side, and you want proof that one righteous man is not a member of some grand communist conspiracy.

'Listen,' Beno snarled, his face contorted with rage. 'I wouldn't give a shit if he was Leon Trotsky.'

He puffed furiously on his cigarette, the reflection of the ember glowing in his eyes. After a moment he said, 'The fact is that Serdán has no ideology of any kind. He's a simple man, a hero to his people. I don't know if a bright young sophisticate like you can understand that.'

Sam thought he was going to strike her. Her voice wavering with fear, she said, 'I'm sorry. I deserved that.'

His fury spent, Beno said, 'Hell, it's not your fault. All you know is what you learned at Langley and the kind of crap that passes for intelligence at the embassy. I'm sorry if the real world doesn't conform to those views.'

He opened the servi-bar, grabbed another bottle of beer, popped the top, and took a long swig. With a thoughtful look, he stared at the wall as if he could see through to the deep valleys of the Sierra.

Sam had met few men with such volatile emotions. In her heart she knew Beno Alvarado was telling the truth, but she was troubled.

She said, 'There's something I don't understand. If Alfredo Mendoza is trafficking in narcotics, why isn't the DEA on his case?'

Beno laughed, a rumbling mirthless chuckle. He said, 'The DEA gives millions of dollars in equipment to the god-damned Ministry of Government, to *Alfredo Mendoza*, which is a bad joke.'

'Don't they know what he does?'

'Sure they know, but they can't touch him. Their job is to look good in front of congressional committees and appease an hysterical population. People in *gringolandia* want to believe these brave drug warriors are combating a scourge. Some of them are. There's a DEA guy in Acapulco named Antoine Bonmarche who would bust Mendoza in a minute if he had a chance, but what can he do? He can't arrest the Méxican Minister of Government. He can't bust every soldier in the Twenty-seventh Military District. That's absurd. Maybe Nancy Reagan should come down and tell Mendoza to just say no. See what I mean? It's public relations, sensational headlines and bullshit.

'Mendoza sends soldiers into the mountains and Serdán kills them every chance he gets, which isn't often. The soldiers are fighting quote communist guerrillas unquote. The cold war angle is a veil, a myth that paints Serdán as a dirty commie rat. To smooth things over, Mendoza shows off corpses of farmers and dealers who won't co-operate. He presents a few kilos of smack to the DEA so they can report back to Washington what a good job the Ministry is doing.'

Sam asked, 'Are you saying the DEA is involved in Mendoza's operation?'

Beno paused for a moment, considering his reply, then said,

'No, Sam, the DEA is not involved. We are. The agency. The CIA supports Mendoza, just like it supports every asshole the pricks in Washington think is anti-communist.'

'That's a serious accusation.'

Beno laughed and blurted, 'No foolin'. The DEA has orders from Fred Lowry to keep their hands off Mendoza. He's going to be the next president of México, a friendly, pro-American president. It's the same old cold war policy that doesn't work any more, if it ever did. This goes higher than Mendoza. Millions of dollars are involved, and that kind of money reaches deep into the National Palace in México City and all the way to Washington. That's not my department.'

Sam smiled and said, 'You're an angry man. You sound as if you'd like to start a war.'

Beno rolled his head around, stretching his neck muscles, and then said, 'I'd just as soon prevent one. If Mendoza becomes president of this godforsaken country, it'll be a bloody mess.'

Beno cracked open the balcony doors and peered outside. With his back to her, he said, 'There's one more thing, a personal message from me to Fred. Tell him to keep his hands off Lucio Serdán.'

Sam said, 'That sounds like a threat.'

'It is.'

She asked, 'You care about Lucio Serdán, don't you?'

'Yes.'

'And you aren't supposed to, right?'

'Right again.'

'You're saying there's a war on and we're on the wrong side.'

'It's a very small war in some mountains far away. It doesn't matter.'

'It matters to you, doesn't it, Beno?'

'I opted out. The analysts in fancy suits don't know what to do with real information. I'm not going to write any more reports that nobody reads.'

'The agency needs you, Beno.'

'I don't need them.'

He turned around and discovered she was standing quite close.

Sam could sense that he was going to leave, but she wanted him to stay. She wanted to feel his rage, know his heat. If he

66

left, he would be gone forever, like a dream. She felt a tinge of panic, a flood of unfamiliar emotion. In Sam's life relationships had been cold, distant, calculated. What she felt for Beno was unexpected, immediate, irrational, the kind of feeling she had been taught all her life to avoid. Being near him, she felt alive. She knew he was a killer, a dangerous man, but standing next to him she felt safer than ever before. She wanted him.

Her odours almost overpowered him. Sex, perfume, sunscreen, rum and Coca-Cola. She moved closer.

She reached up to kiss him but he gently pushed her away.

He smiled and said, 'You don't want to get involved with me. Lowry will quiz you, and you don't want to lie to him.'

Unaccustomed to sexual rejection, Sam's face turned down in a pout.

Beno said, 'Go back to México City and keep out of this.'

He slipped out of the door and disappeared into the sultry night.

Sam pulled the blankets tightly around her. That night she couldn't sleep. Bugs outside sounded like dive bombers; music in the bar thundered like a rock concert. Her mind filled with horrific images of children lying dead in pools of blood, of poppy fields ripening in the sun, of teenage guerrillas prowling the mountains. Behind these pictures crowding past her mind's eye, she saw the towering shadow of Beno Alvarado, the most provocative and disturbing man she had ever met.

3 SEPTEMBER

5

México City

The next day Beno drove his VW bus to México City, timing his arrival for midnight when traffic was bearable and the smog invisible.

Dark and menacing on the best of nights, the Federal District was suffering a brown-out caused by striking electrical workers. In the northern precincts cars moved through the streets like luminous fishes in the deep ocean. Beno guided his bus like a great white whale, glad to have an Uzi tucked under the front seat.

He inhaled the peculiar mix of lime dust, exhaust fumes, ozone and rotted citrus fruit that distinguished the world's largest metropolis from other cities.

México City reminded Beno of a nightmarish future, a crowded, menacing *Blade Runner* world of smoke and danger. He always felt there as if the earth beneath him would melt and erupt. If the lava didn't explode, thirty million choking, thirsting pressure-packed people would.

In the light of flickering charcoal braziers, entire villages of *damnificados*, México City's countless homeless, clustered on pavements of despair. Beno played Dire Straits' 'Brothers in Arms', and the hauntingly sinister music bounced off rotted walls plastered with political posters.

The Left. The Right. The Centre Party crushed between them. Hundreds of posters, giant, billboard sized faces with inflated dignity and patriotic slogans. Violent graffiti indiscriminately defaced the entire political spectrum.

'Fuck Marx.'

'Fuck the government.'

'Fuck the church.'

'Fuck you, Fascist.'

México was being polarized, fragmented, politically shattered, a bomb waiting to explode, and Alfredo Mendoza was a primed fuse. Should he become president, socialist México City

71

would revolt, and the result would be a bloodbath. His death would prevent a thousand, perhaps a million, deaths.

A fire engine screamed past, blue lights flashing, sirens whining. Beno cruised through the darkened streets, fantasizing that his Uzi was a nuclear device destined to blow México City off the planet.

Full power had been restored to the centre of the city, providing illumination to government buildings, embassies and tourist hotels. Using a standard American passport issued in the name of Pedro Alvarado, Beno checked into the plush, old-fashioned Hotel Majestic on the Zócalo.

He sat for an hour in the hotel's elegant hardwood panelled bar, drinking good cognac and thinking of Sam. She had been so hungry, so eager, so fresh. He wanted to root around in her mind, plunder her body, be with her.

An expensive, heavily made-up whore tried to make small talk, but he ignored her, paid his tab and went upstairs.

In his room he turned on CNN news, and counted four wars, three revolutions, seven government lies, twelve commercials and two acts of terrorism while he waited.

At two-thirty in the morning the young duty officer in the embassy's CIA station was fighting off sleep with coffee, cigarettes, George Thorogood's hammerhead guitar and his own improvised lyrics.

'Bam bam bam bam bam oh yeah! Let there be light oh yeah! And the truth shall make ye free oh yeah! Let all the shit come down on somebody else's shift oh yeah oh yeah oh yeah!'

The phone rang six times before he noticed the blinking light, picked it up and said, 'Four three nine one.'

The voice at the other end said, 'This is Alpha Seven. Put me through to Flame.'

'Just a moment, please.'

The duty officer turned down the music and shook the echoes out of his head. He said, 'Please say again.'

Annoyed, Beno repeated his code and added, 'I don't have all night.'

The duty officer noticed that his hand was shaking enough to

72

turn his Winston into a smoke signal. He asked, 'Are you calling from a secure phone?'

'Fuck no, you idiot, or I'd call him myself.'

'Please hold.'

Alpha Seven, Alpha Seven, Jesus. Okay. He pushed the hold button, unlocked the agent code book and flipped it open to the roster sheet on the first page. Calls from agents coded alpha were extremely rare and always tense. Next to Alpha Seven was the code word Hummingbird. He punched the button again.

'Okay, give me the next sequence.'

'Hummingbird.'

'Hang on.'

Fred Lowry was asleep in his house in Polanco when the phone rang. His wife slept soundly in her bed on the other side of the night stand.

Groggy, hungover from an embassy reception, he answered, 'Flame here. What is it?'

'Duty officer, sir. Sorry to bother you. I have Alpha Seven on the line.'

'You sure it's him?'

'He gave the correct code sequence.'

'Secure line?'

'No.'

That meant the DIS was eavesdropping on the call.

'Put him through.'

Pause, click.

'This is Flame.'

'Howdy, Fred. I like your messenger service.'

Lowry reminded him, 'You're not on a secure line.'

'I lied,' Beno said. 'This is a secure line.'

Irritated, Lowry demanded, 'What do you have to say?'

'Message received, but I was wondering why you didn't deliver it yourself. Makes me think I'm not very important.'

Lowry intended to use Beno, dupe and betray him, perhaps kill him, yet in spite of himself, the station chief admired his operative's survival skills.

Lowry asked, 'Are you going to come in, or do I have to send more of my people after you?'

'Fred, I want to talk about the messenger. You filled that

girl's head with ideas. We're supposed to be intelligence agents, not party hacks. I told her a few tales, but I saved the best to tell you in person.'

Fully awake now, the effects of embassy vodka pushed away, Lowry propped himself up in bed and turned on the light. His wife, accustomed to calls at odd hours, continued to sleep soundly.

Lowry asked, 'You didn't trust her?'

Beno retorted, 'Would you trust me if I had?'

Lowry said, 'Okay. Drop three, tomorrow.'

Beno said, 'I have a better idea. How about right now?'

'Are you close?'

'I'm right down the hall. In your study.'

'You . . .'

The line went dead.

Lowry smiled to himself. The only way to bring Beno in was to make him angry, and it had worked. Lowry slipped out of bed, retrieved a pistol from the night stand drawer, wrapped a bathrobe around his middle and stepped out of the bedroom.

At the far end of the corridor a slash of pale bluish light spilled out of his study.

Cautiously, Lowry crept down the hall and pushed the study door open.

Beno sat in Lowry's leather chair, boots propped on the desk, smoking a cigarette.

Grinning, Beno chirped cheerfully, 'Hi, Fred.'

'How the hell did you get in here?'

'Your alarm system isn't worth a shit. You should have it replaced.'

'Christ almighty.'

Beno lowered his feet to the floor and said, 'Put away the gun.'

Lowry asked, 'I take it you're armed?'

'Never leave home without it. Agency rules.'

Lowry commanded, 'Put it on the desk.'

Beno shook his head and said, 'Go to hell.'

Lowry ordered, 'Stand up.'

Beno shook his head again and said, 'Relax, Fred. I'm pissed at you, but nobody's going to get hurt. Let's not wake up your kids. I brought you a present from Alfredo Mendoza.'

Beno reached under the chair and dropped a large plastic bag full of powder on the desk.

He said, 'One kilo of Mexican Brown.'

'Cute,' said the station chief. 'Very dramatic.'

'Care for a snort?' Beno asked. He flicked his wrist and a long, thin knife slid into his hand. He plunged the point into the bag spilling powder across the top of the desk.

Beno said coldly, 'How about your kids? Maybe they'd like a hit.'

'What's the point, Beno?'

'It's all politics to you, Fred. Policy, professional hypocrisy, expedience, whatever you call it. I thought you might like to see the real thing.'

'What do you want me to do with it?'

'What do you think?' Beno said. 'You can sell it, stick it in your arm, flush it down the toilet. I just wanted you to be around it for a little while. Now put your gun away.'

Lowry hesitated, then opened a cabinet, put his pistol inside and took out a bottle of vodka and a pair of glasses.

Pouring, he said, 'I'm not surprised you defeated my alarm. You've always been a pretty good burglar.'

Beno said, 'That's another way of saying you're getting old and sloppy.'

'Maybe,' Lowry replied, setting a glass of vodka on the desk for Beno. 'I wanted to see you. Glad you could make it. Cheers.'

Lowry drank. Beno left his glass on the desk. Lowry stepped toward the window and gazed at the streetlights glowing yellow in the gloom of Niagra Street. A policeman walked slowly up the street. Lowry wondered idly how Beno had evaded him.

Beno said, 'Tell me there was a good reason for you to send an amateur to Zihuatanejo, Fred. Make me feel loved and secure.'

Without turning around, Lowry said, 'If I had come down and said "RPG-16", I think you would have tried to kill me. You still might, but it's a chance I have to take.'

'That's great, Fred. Real brave.'

'You've gone over the edge, Beno, selling rockets to the guerrillas. People have died for less.'

Beno asked, 'Where are you getting your information about

Serdán? Serdán doesn't mean shit to you, Fred. I want to know how you learned about the rockets.'

Lowry answered with a smile, 'From Máximo Levín. He has a man inside Serdán's guerrilla group. He doesn't know about you, just the rockets. I put two and two together and they added up to Beno Alvarado.'

Beno said, 'If that's true, why doesn't the DIS wipe out Serdán?'

'The Méxican government needs an identifiable enemy. As long as they can point a finger at the "dangerous, communist guerrillas", they distract attention from themselves and get support from us. Serdán justifies the very existence of the DIS. Answer this question: is Serdán a genuine threat to the government of México?'

Beno answered, 'Are you kidding? He's starving to death. He has a dozen fuzzy-headed kids pretending to be soldiers of the revolution.'

'Right. Then why can't the Méxican army get him?'

'Good question, Fred. Partly because the people protect him, and partly – this is guesswork – because he has a friend inside the government.'

'Who?'

'I don't know. If I did, I sure as hell wouldn't tell you. You'd run straight to the DIS and tell Máximo Levín. Then a lot of people would die.'

'Very clever, Beno. Máximo Levín is his protector, but without Serdán being aware of that fact. The government needs Serdán as a scapegoat. I suppose you're going to tell me Serdán is not a communist.'

'That's right.'

'And also that the agency has its head up its ass for supporting Mendoza.'

'You must be prescient, Fred.'

'You like the guy? Serdán?'

'Yeah, but he's not much of a soldier. He's a schoolteacher.'

'Does he trust you?'

'I doubt it. He believes I'm a merchant of death with no scruples.'

Lowry turned away from the window to face Beno and said, 'For once the National Security Council agrees with you. If

Mendoza becomes president of México, his entire operation, and our generous support, will become public knowledge. He's become an embarrassment. We think Serdán is just what we need.'

'Need for what?'

'Mendoza has become a problem, and Serdán is the solution.'

'What are you saying, Fred? Jesus.'

'We want Serdán to kill Mendoza.'

Astounded, Beno croaked, 'You're full of shit.'

Lowry said, 'There was a finding.'

Beno worked his mind to make himself believe what he was hearing. He said softly, 'I'll be damned.'

Leering, Lowry said, 'You will be. We all will be.'

Beno's eyes narrowed as he said, 'You're fucking with my head. I don't know what you're after, but you're giving me a stroke job.'

Lowry said, 'Pick up the phone. Call the DDO in Langley. Al Mears will tell you the same thing. Look, this wasn't my idea. I don't like it.'

Beno could see Lowry was not bluffing. The sly old bear was telling the truth.

Beno said, 'You want to waste Mendoza to protect yourselves.'

Lowry tilted his head to an arrogant angle and asked, 'What difference does it make to you?'

'You want Serdán to do it?'

'Yes.'

'What happens to him?'

'That hasn't been decided.'

'I don't like the sound of that, Fred.'

'First things first, Beno. You're the contact. You set it up, and we'll give Serdán some real firepower. We can give him a Stinger.'

Beno cocked his eyebrows and said, 'A Stinger? You want to give him a surface to air missile? Jesus!'

Lowry nodded his head, sipped his vodka and said, 'Why not? He can't miss. I'll have the armourer cook up a Stinger with serial numbers from a stolen lot. *No problema, señor.* It'll be ready tomorrow.

'Mendoza's selection as the party candidate is to be made

public on 16 September, during the Independence Day ceremonies. That's less than two weeks from tonight. His plane should go boom before then. On the second Friday of every month, Mendoza flies jet to Las Vegas to gamble. He's well known in the casinos, a real high roller. He flies in his private jet, the Gulfstream. Security around the plane is lax. All Serdán has to do is get within a mile of the runway. Bye-bye Mendoza. Think Serdán will go for it?'

'You're a treacherous son of a bitch, Fred.'

'Yeah, I know. Treachery is my strong point. Now, get the hell out of here and let me go to sleep. And take that . . . that . . . dope with you.'

Beno laughed and said, 'Sorry, that's yours. It's a fantastic analgesic. Cure your hangover right away.'

4 SEPTEMBER

6

Stinger

At nine the next morning Sam Black sat in Lowry's office waiting for her chief's attention. Lowry pushed papers around his desk, unlocked, opened, closed and locked three cabinet drawers, pulling a file from one drawer and placing it in another.

Sam glanced around the expensively furnished room. Over Lowry's right shoulder a nineteenth-century map of the British Empire blazed in faded crimson glory. Over his left shoulder, the empire of sixteenth-century Spain circled the globe. Around the walls the lost powers of Rome, China, Japan, Persia and Imperial Russia completed Lowry's vision of history. Her thoughts drifted to Beno's black eyes and how much he hated the station chief.

After a long silence Lowry asked, 'How did Alpha Seven react when you gave him the message? Did he seem, say, unbalanced, a little out of control?'

'Quite the opposite,' Sam replied. 'I don't think I've ever met anyone quite so sure of himself.' After a moment she added, 'You didn't tell me he had resigned.'

Lowry said, 'I don't take his resignation seriously.'

'He does. He's quite angry at the agency for supporting Mendoza.'

Irked, Lowry said, 'Idealism is for children. In the real world one compromises. Alpha Seven knows that.'

'He didn't seem like the compromising sort to me, Mr Lowry. I wouldn't want him as an enemy.'

He studied her for a moment, wondering what effect Beno Alvarado had really had on her.

Finally, he stood up and said, 'You've done an excellent job, Ms Black. Congratulations. Naturally, your report is top secret, and you'll keep it to yourself. Thank you.'

He walked around his desk, opened the door, and resisted the temptation to pat her on the butt. It wasn't like the old days. She'd probably hit him, or bring him up on a charge.

* * *

Across town Beno was eating breakfast on the balcony of his hotel room overlooking the Zócalo. Below, ten thousand demonstrators from the United Opposition Parties protested against the economic policies of President Carlos Salinas de Gotari. Under a grey sky, banners fluttered in the breeze, including several which bore the image of Lucio Serdán.

While hundreds of police looked on, workers and students shouted slogans against the government. For two hours the Zócalo reverberated with impassioned rhetoric, but at eleven o'clock the rally ended peacefully. The square cleared of everyone save the *damnificados* who maintained a permanent delegation in front of the National Cathedral.

Beno went to the movies and watched a revival of Alejandro Jodorovski's *El Topo* and *The Magic Mountain*. After the show he refreshed himself with beer and tacos *al carbón*, the great México City speciality.

At ten in the evening Beno stepped out of a taxi at the foot of Niagra Street in Polanco, twelve blocks from the embassy.

Hands in his pockets, Uzi micro-pistol concealed under a corduroy sports coat in a Galco holster, Beno approached the solitary uniformed policeman assigned to patrol Niagra Street.

Sitting on a low wall half hidden by shrubbery, the young cop eyed Beno with indifference, more interested in a soccer game he was following on a Sony Watchman.

Beno asked, 'What's the score?'

'Zero zero. Guadalajara sucks.'

'Quiet night tonight.'

'Hmmmm.'

Beno flashed a forged DIS identity plate and the cop's neutrality vanished. He jumped to his feet, saluted, and stammered, 'Yes, sir!'

Beno asked, 'What time did you come on duty?'

'Six o'clock.'

'How long have you been assigned to this beat?'

'Two months.'

'Do you read the logs of the other men who cover this beat?'

'Yes, sir. I want to do well, get promotion to a squad car.'

Beno pointed at a large stucco house surrounded by a brick

wall across the street and asked, 'Do you know who lives in that house?'

'Yes, sir. A North American, an embassy official.'

'How many servants?'

'Three, more when they have parties.'

'Anything unusual happen in that house in the last few days?'

'Yes, sir. The day before yesterday the woman and her children and much baggage left in a limousine and didn't return.'

'Is the man in there now?'

'Yes, sir.'

'Who else?'

'The maid.'

'What's your name?'

'Noriega.'

'Okay, Noriega. In ten minutes the man will drive out of the gate in his car. I want you to stop him. Be polite. I'll get in the car with him. Next month you'll be in a squad car. I'll put in a good word with your captain. Understand?'

'Yes, sir. Of course, sir.'

'Okay.'

Beno walked to the pay phone on the corner and called Lowry's home number.

Fred Lowry enjoyed being alone in the big house. Dressed in evening clothes, he sipped a vodka and lime and waited for the phone to ring. He was expecting a call from General Guillermo 'Billy' Vargas, who was going to introduce the station chief to an exclusive club in San Angel. With his wife and children in Virginia, Lowry intended to sample the more decadent pleasures of the Méxican capital.

A Stinger IV missile, an astonishingly compact aircraft killer, was locked in his wall safe. The serial numbers had been removed by the embassy armourer who knew how to keep his mouth shut.

The phone rang, the open line.

'Lowry.'

Beno said, 'Hello, Colonel Fred. Drop six, ten minutes.'

Lowry replied instantly, 'Check,' hung up and dialled General Vargas at the Officers' Club at Military Camp Number One.

'General, I'll be an hour late.'

'No problem, Mr Lowry. They never close.'

Lowry retrieved the missile in its aluminium case, put it in the boot of his Buick Electra, and drove down the driveway and out through the electrically powered gate.

The young cop stood in the middle of the street, his hand raised in the universal gesture that means stop.

Annoyed, Lowry lowered his window and asked, 'What is it, Officer?'

Beno stepped out of the shadows and said, 'Surprise.'

Lowry unlocked the passenger door. Beno waved at the cop and got into the car.

As they drove down the street, Lowry said, 'You don't take chances, do you, Beno?'

'You're getting old, Fred. When you saw the cop, you should've backed into your driveway.'

'Fuck off. The cop's on my side.'

'He did a hell of a job, didn't he?'

Lowry asked, 'Where do you want to go?'

Beno scanned the Buick's dashboard and asked, 'You wired for sound in this boat?'

'No.'

Beno opened the glovebox, took out maps and a flashlight, felt around, and closed it. He lifted the car phone, jerked the cord free and threw the handset out of the window.

Lowry muttered, 'You prick.'

Beno turned on the radio, slowly wound through the FM band and picked up no interference from a transmitter.

He smiled and said, 'Well, maybe you're not wired. Let's just drive around and talk. Are you going to give me a missile?'

On Niagra Street agent Noriega used the pay phone on the corner to call Máximo Levín at DIS headquarters.

Máximo took the call in his library on the nineteenth floor of the glass pyramid.

'Yes?'

'Noriega here, Director. The gentleman returned and left with Mr Lowry in the official's car.'

'Excellent work, Noriega. Make a full report when your shift ends.'

The big Buick wallowed through the quiet streets of Polanco.

Lowry said quietly, 'There's a hitch with the Stinger.'

Beno turned to face the station chief and replied hollowly, 'There always is.'

Lowry said, 'For argument's sake, let's say Lucio Serdán blows Mendoza away. What happens next?'

'C'mon, Fred. The Méxicans pick some other asshole to be president.'

'Right,' Lowry agreed. 'Anybody they pick will be the same or worse, and somebody else will take over Mendoza's operation. Nothing will change. It never does.'

Lowry turned onto Avenue de los Insurgentes Sur and followed the broad boulevard south. The wildcat strike had ended and streetlights blazed a shimmering yellow. The stoplights were working. Huge posters announced the latest films, *Lethal Weapon VI, The Voyage of the Bijou, Cathedral.*

Beno asked, 'Are you playing games with me, Fred?'

He pulled the machine-pistol from his belt, pressed it against Lowry's temple and said, 'Turn here, right now.'

Lowry swung the wheel to the right and the car turned into a side street. At the end of the first block, Beno said, 'Turn left.'

Another block. 'Pull over to the kerb and stop.'

Lowry stared through the windscreen and said nothing.

Beno asked, 'What's the hitch?'

In a steady voice Lowry replied, 'I'll give you the Stinger. Serdán blows up Mendoza's plane, and you kill Serdán.'

'Why?'

'He'd be a loose end, a connection to the agency.'

'If I agree, you'll give me the missile?'

'Yes.'

'When?'

'Now. It's in the trunk.'

Beno pulled the gun back and patted Lowry on the cheek. 'I knew you'd come through, Freddy.'

Lowry asked, 'Is it a deal?'

'I'll think about it.'

'You know what'll happen if you don't do it.'

'Sure,' Beno said, smiling. 'I'll lose my pension and credit cards. Open the trunk.'

Lowry pushed a button on the centre console and the lid popped open.

Beno growled, 'Get out. Put your hands on your head.'

Lowry opened the door and stepped into the street. Beno slid across the seat and followed him out of the driver's door.

On the street Beno reached inside Lowry's coat, pulled the station chief's Smith and Wesson .38 Police Special from his shoulder holster, emptied the cartridges onto the pavement, and stuck the gun into his belt. He glanced into the boot, saw the buff metal case and asked, 'What have we here?'

'One Stinger IV surface to air missile with all serial numbers removed.'

Beno said, 'You'd better tell me now if anything's been tampered with, Fred.'

'It's a straight up aeroplane killer. No tricks.'

'Let's hope so.'

'You set up the meet in Chilpancingo?'

'Why? You want to come along?'

'I want you to have a back-up.'

'I don't think our friend would like that.'

'It's procedure, Beno.'

'Fred, if I even smell one of your people in Chilpancingo, I'll kill him then come after you.'

'Be careful.'

'Sure, you bet. Now, walk to the corner.'

'What about my car?'

'Take a cab. You'll find your car in the morning.'

Beno closed the boot and drove away without another word.

Lowry smiled as he watched Beno disappear in his car. The station chief didn't believe that Lucio Serdán could shoot down an aeroplane with an entire battery of Stingers. Serdán was a decoy, a red herring. What Lowry needed was a genuine killing machine, someone who loved his work, not a peasant schoolteacher.

On the corner he found a pay phone and made a credit card call to Acapulco.

'Andrés?'

'Who's calling me in the middle of the fucking night?'

'Flame.'

'Oh. Yes, sir.'

'How soon can you be at the usual place?'
'Day after tomorrow.'
'No sooner?'
'Very busy tomorrow.'
'Okay. Day after tomorrow.'

5 SEPTEMBER

7

Andrés Obregón

Andrés Obregón, DEA, Cuban refugee, cocaine addict and master of the dope deal sting, adorned his skinny body with a wide bandito moustache, wrap-around sunglasses and a ruby stud in his left earlobe. For two weeks he had combed the beaches of Acapulco looking for gringos stupid and greedy enough to have come into town cold, without a contact, but with a lot of money to buy drugs. Having almost given up, Obregón took a seat at the poolside bar of the Holiday Inn, intending to get drunk. Tomorrow he would cure his hangover by driving to Zihuatanejo and trying his luck there.

Obregón was working on his third tequila lime when two guys walked in with New York accents as wide as Long Island Sound, pretty faces full of perfect teeth and lean good looks draped in flashy clothes.

Obregón carried his drink to the bar, sat down next to the Americans, and eavesdropped.

The blond one said to the bartender, 'Two margueritas, Ricardo.' He leaned over the bar and asked, 'You gonna get us some coke or what?'

Grinding his teeth, the one with black curly hair said, 'Yesterday you said today, man. What's the hangup?'

The bartender smiled, showing off his gold teeth, and said, 'Come back at five o'clock, okay? That's when I get off.'

'Okay.'

They picked up their drinks. The blond one signed for them, adjusted his sunglasses and led his friend toward the beach, saying, 'What do you think, Barry?'

Wiping sweat off his forehead, Barry answered, 'Joel, my man, I think it's too hot to think.'

Obregón laid ten thousand pesos on the bar and whispered to the bartender, 'Let me see the tab that guy signed.'

The bartender hesitated, then looked at Obregón's hands

resting on the bar, hard, calloused hands. Without looking up, he produced the tab.

Room 364.

Obregón hated walking on the beach in shoes, but he crunched through the sand until he found Barry and Joel sitting under an umbrella with fresh drinks.

Obregón crouched in the shade and said, 'That bartender's a DEA informer.'

Startled, Barry glanced furtively around toward the bar and hissed, 'How do you know that?'

Obregón shrugged casually and replied, 'I live here, and I hate to see anybody get burned. Hell, everybody's a cop. That's okay. The cops sell dope, too. You just have to pick the right one.'

Joel asked, 'Are you a cop?'

Obregón answered with a sly smile, 'No. I'm CIA.'

They all had a big laugh at this joke.

Obregón said, 'You can get hurt trying to buy drugs from the wrong people.'

With an arrogant lilt Barry said, 'I suppose you're Mr Right, hey?'

Obregón answered, 'I know the right people, but you don't, my friend.'

He stood up, faced the sea, said, 'Don't forget the sunscreen,' and started to walk away.

He was halfway to the bar when Joel caught up with him and said in a stage whisper, 'Hey, man, can we talk to you for a minute?'

'What about?'

'You said you know the right people.'

Obregón asked, 'Why should I trust you?'

'We're cool, really. I mean, come back and talk.'

Obregón reluctantly followed Joel back to the umbrella.

Barry asked, 'Can you get us a little coke?'

'How much?'

'A couple of grams.'

Obregón looked from one to the other and laughed. He said, 'You're a couple of punks. You think I mess around with lightweights?'

Barry said, 'If you can get us a little coke, then maybe we'll talk about what we really want.'

Obregón said, 'Two grams, sixty bucks, twenty minutes.'

Barry and Joel looked at each other, then Barry said to Obregón, 'We'll be right here.'

In the hotel lobby Obregón approached the bell captain and discreetly flashed an embossed brass, red and green enamelled identity plate from the Directorate of Internal Security, the secret police.

The bell captain stiffened slightly and said, 'Yes, sir. What can I do for you?'

'Open up room 364.'

'Follow me.'

In the cupboard Obregón found a Mac-11 machine-pistol and a suitcase stuffed with hundred-dollar bills. He shook his head. Some people were just asking for it.

From the lobby he telephoned the headquarters company of the 27th Military District and asked for Colonel Durazo.

A few minutes later, Obregón returned to the beach and handed Barry a small package of cocaine. An hour later, when the coke was gone, Andrés Obregón had become Barry and Joel's best friend. He spent the day with them, bought them drinks, found them girls, and listened to their life stories.

At midnight, loaded and laid, they told him that they wanted to buy two kilos of heroin.

Obregón said, 'Two kilos of Mexican Brown, fifty thousand dollars. Can you handle that?'

Joel asked Barry, 'What do you think?'

Barry answered, 'This is what we came here for, isn't it?'

'I can even help you get it out of the country,' Obregón told them. There's these guys, see, at Oakland Air Freight Company, who will fly the shit to California and get it through customs. They *own* customs at the San Francisco Airport. Guaranteed.'

'What's it cost?'

'Five grand per kilo.'

'Expensive.'

'Yeah, but worth it.'

93

'We'll think about it.'

'Tomorrow,' Obregón said. 'I'll pick you up here at two.'

The next day Obregón piloted a rented Chevrolet Lumina north from Acapulco on Highway 200, windows open, stereo blasting out Warren Zevon's 'Roland the Headless Thompson Gunner'.

The windscreen framed a postcard perfect view of the Méxican coast. The towering mountains of the Sierra Madre del Sur loomed over the jungle on the right. The Pacific Ocean rolled blue and benign on the left. Palms swayed over pure white beaches. From time to time they passed a donkey laden with coconuts or firewood, a *campesino* in white clothes and huaraches trailing behind.

Barry sat in the back seat, coked to the gills, poking the muzzle of his Mac-11 out the window at passing cars and shouting, 'Zap! Zap! Hahahahaha.' Good-looking in a silly Hollywood way, he wore two gold chains, a shirt open to the waist, and expensive, pleated cotton pants.

Joel lounged in the front, sandalled feet propped on the dashboard, a joint dangling from his mouth, babbling incessantly about the Ferrari he wanted to buy with money from the dope deal. As far as Obregón could tell, Joel's goal in life was to drive from New York to Los Angeles collecting speeding tickets.

Obregón said, 'You guys watch too much TV.'

'Wha . . .?'

'Forget it.'

He had always wondered why the Aztecs' victims climbed willingly to the top of a pyramid to have their hearts ripped out. He had heard that they were force-fed drugs. Barry and Joel definitely were not forced, but they were on their way up.

They flashed past the burnt-out hulk of a late model Cadillac rusting on the shoulder of the road.

Obregón said, 'Did you see that?'

Joel looked around and asked, 'See what?'

'That wreck.'

'No.'

Obregón gestured toward the surf and said, 'The sharks aren't out there, man.' He pointed toward the sea, and said, 'They're over there.' His finger swung toward the jungle.

Barry stuck his head over the back of the front seat and asked, 'What do you mean?'

Obregón answered, 'This is Guerrero, the most violent state in México. This is where they grow all that nice smack you're gonna buy. Up in those mountains they still practise human sacrifice. If they don't like you, they cut out your heart.'

'No kidding,' said Joel. 'Wow.'

Barry scoffed, 'You're full of shit.'

'Think so?' said Obregón.

'Yeah, I think so.'

Barry leaned back in his seat, popped the clip out of his machine-gun, jammed it back in and popped it out again, muttering to himself.

Obregón cruised down the highway, admiring the pristine jungle and deserted beaches, making small talk. Ninety miles north of Acapulco he turned onto a badly paved road that led into the mountains and the village of Atoyac. Within a few miles, the coastal jungle gave way to dense forest. Clouds of butterflies swarmed over the Chevy as Obregón ground the gears through the switchbacks, rapidly gaining altitude. A mile short of Atoyac Obregón smelled the delicious odour of cooking fires and noticed the sides of the road were deserted. A bright green hummingbird hovered in front of the windscreen, peering through the buggy glass at the occupants of the car. Coming around a sharp bend over a ridge, Obregón sensed the roadblock before he saw it.

In a quiet voice of command he said to Barry, 'Put that gun away and no matter what happens, don't touch it.'

The young smuggler didn't argue. The Mac-11 disappeared under the front seat. Obregón slowed, the bend straightened, and they saw a military Chevy Blazer parked sideways across the road. Two soldiers stood behind the truck, M-15 assault rifles trained on the car.

Obregón stopped and said, 'Stay here. There'll be others hidden in the brush.'

Nervous, Barry squawked, 'What is this? Jesus. What if they search the car?'

Obregón replied, 'Shut up. This is your connection.'

'Cops?'

'No. Soldiers. Welcome to Guerrero.'

Slowly, Obregón got out of the car and approached the soldiers.

'Good afternoon, gentlemen,' he said, smiling. 'I believe your colonel is expecting me.'

'Who are you?' said the sergeant.

Obregón produced his DEA badge and ID card.

The sergeant inspected the ID and asked, 'You have the money?'

Obregón jerked his head and said, 'In the car.'

'Bring it.'

Obregón shook his head and said, 'I mean no disrespect, but, I deal with the colonel.'

An officer in fatigues stepped out of the brush into the road and said, 'Good afternoon, Andrés.'

Obregón smiled and said, 'Good afternoon, Colonel. A profitable afternoon, I'm sure.'

'Where did you find them?' Durazo asked.

'In Acapulco. They're from New York.'

'The money's right?'

Obregón nodded and stroked his thumb with his forefinger.

Durazo flicked his head toward the soldiers standing twenty feet away, waiting respectfully for the colonel, and whispered, 'Them, too.'

Obregón let his eyes roll toward the sergeant and the private, both young, both armed. He raised his eyebrows to Durazo and said, 'You sure?'

Durazo nodded, an almost imperceptible bob of his head, and barked an order at the sergeant.

The soldier pulled a wooden packing crate from the rear of the Blazer and used a crowbar to prize off the top. Obregón looked inside and saw two plastic bags crammed full of powder the colour of cinnamon and sugar, two kilos of Mexican Brown heroin.

He said, 'My friends wish to perform a test.'

'Naturally,' said the colonel. 'After I see the money.'

Obregón returned to the car and said to Barry, 'All right. Bring the money and don't say a fucking word.'

To Joel he said, 'Bring your chemistry set. If it gets funny, hit the deck.'

Barry asked, 'What are you getting us into, dude?'

96

'You never know until you go, kid.'

Obregón stayed back and watched Barry heave the heavy suitcase onto the front seat of the Blazer. The colonel unzipped one corner and smiled.

Joel opened a small bag of test tubes and chemicals. The soldiers and smugglers glared at each other like hostile chess players. Barry swatted at bugs. Colonel Durazo stood well off to the side with his hands on his hips, feet wide apart, humming a tune.

Obregón opened the rear door of the car, reached under the seat for his nine-millimetre automatic loaded with Glasser bullets. With the cocked pistol at his side and a smile on his face, he walked toward the soldiers whose attention was on the smugglers. In one swift motion Obregón raised the pistol and shot the sergeant in the face, whirled and shot the private twice in the chest. As he toppled forward in slow motion, the private pulled the trigger of his assault rifle, firing wildly and pouring half a clip into the young smugglers.

The two soldiers and Barry were dead, but Joel was breathing erratically. Blood pumped out of a hole in his chest.

Obregón stood over him, said, 'Sorry, kid. No Ferrari this week,' and administered a *coup de grâce*.

A hummingbird hovered above the bright red patch growing on his chest.

Durazo clapped slowly as he would applaud a bullfight.

'Bravo,' he said. 'Well done. Now, help me get these poor unfortunates into the truck.'

Durazo took care not to smear blood on his uniform. When the four corpses were covered with a tarpaulin in the colonel's truck, Obregón split the fifty thousand dollars. He knew better than to ask Durazo why he wanted his soldiers dead.

Obregón gave Durazo the suitcase, stuffed his share in his pockets, and drove back down the mountainside, playing his stereo full blast, wondering what Fred Lowry had in store for him tomorrow.

8

Antoine Bonmarche

On the way back to Acapulco, Obregón smoked a joint, snorted half a gram of cocaine and drank two beers. He stopped for a few more beers in a roadside cantina, and when he arrived in Acapulco at one in the morning, he was ready for action, DEA style.

Dark and deserted, the Acapulco airport was closed for the night. Obregón drove a mile past the passenger terminal and crunched to a stop on the gravel in front of a small corrugated aluminium warehouse adjacent to the freight terminal, Oakland International Air Freight. He wanted to go inside and add the twenty-five thousand to his private piggy bank.

Obregón loved to visit his money. Over the years he had stashed close to half a million dollars inside a secret container, bounty from drug dealers, smugglers and corrupt Méxican officials. His goal was to amass a million and return to Florida with his fortune. On nights when he was a little high, he liked to go inside the warehouse, swim in his money like Scrooge McDuck and dream of a big score.

He took one step inside and froze. The muzzle of an automatic shotgun was an inch from his nose.

'Easy,' he whispered. 'It's me, Andrés.'

The thin face of a long-haired Anglo hippie grinned behind the gun. He wore a black t-shirt imprinted with silver letters that read 'Oakland Raiders'.

Two more black-shirted Raiders emerged from the shadows.

Obregón asked, 'The boss in?'

'In back.'

Loud rock music rolled over pallets laden with shipping crates. Obregón recognized the funky sound of Dr John, The Night Tripper.

Obregón took several steps toward the office and called out, 'Antoine?'

A booming voice shouted, 'Who's there?'

'Obregón.'

'What the fuck do you want?'

'Can I come into the office?'

'You alone?'

'Yes.'

'Come on back.'

Bearded, robust Antoine Bonmarche sat in his messy office, sipping whisky and smoking his forty-seventh Marlboro of the day. A quarter full bottle of Wild Turkey rested on his desk.

Absent-mindedly wiping ashes off his Oakland Raiders t-shirt, he yelled at Obregón, 'I been waitin' for you, asshole.'

Obregón yelled back, 'Turn down the music!'

Bonmarche reduced the volume on the tape-recorder and said in a voice dripping with courtesy, 'I been waitin' for you, asshole. Thought you might bring that scumbag Durazo with you. DIS called. Said your deal went bad. What happened, Andrés? CIA tell you to waste a few folks, just for practice?'

Obregón's face turned ugly as he said, 'What the hell is that supposed to mean?'

'It means you work for them, asshole.'

'That's crazy, Antoine. You're drunk.'

'Yeah, I'm drunk. So fucking what? So drunk I don't mind telling you I'm sick of you and your CIA buddies.'

'I don't know what you're talking about, man. I just came by to write a report.'

Bonmarche stubbed out his cigarette, set his glass on the desk, pulled himself up to his full six foot four height and said, 'What for? These little dinky busts don't mean shit. I don't think I give a fuck any more.'

The big man poured more whisky into his glass and asked, suddenly congenial, 'Want a drink?'

'Sure. Why not?'

Bonmarche handed him the bottle and pointed at the paper cups stacked on a water cooler. Obregón poured a small shot of bourbon and smiled at his boss.

Antoine Bonmarche, a veteran narc from New Orleans, had served as DEA Regional Director in Guerrero for a year. Obregón knew him as a good-natured, easy-going drug cop who never rocked the boat. He had never seen him drunk.

Bonmarche said, 'You think I'm a real asshole, don't you?

99

You think I don't know what goes on around here? You think I don't know you work for CIA? Well, little Andrés, I do know, so fuck you. You got a joint on you? C'mon, I can smell it.'

Obregón produced a roach. Bonmarche lit it and took a deep drag.

Bonmarche continued, 'The thing is, I don't give a shit. You're in my unit and I keep tabs on my people. I figure you been here, what? five, six years? Long enough to be wired solid into Mendoza and he's plugged into CIA way up, way up.' Bonmarche gestured vaguely toward the ceiling and finished by slurring his words.

Obregón said, 'You're burned, Antoine, fried to a crisp.'

'Me? Burned out? Are you shitting me? I'm a hard-nosed DEA guy. Tough. I was here a week before I figured out that my job was to protect Alfredo Mendoza. God-damn! It took me a whole week. So I coasted, set up Oakland Air, busted every nickel and dime dealer came through here . . . I seen you operate, Andrés. You're slick. I seen you hang with them dudes from El Partenón, Colonel Durazo.'

'You want me to write up my report now?'

Bonmarche took another drag off the roach and smashed it into the ashtray.

'I don't give a shit if you ever write your report. You ain't never gonna write a report on Mendoza, are you? Fuck it, neither am I. Do that and poof! Disappear.'

'Why don't you take a vacation, Antoine?'

Bonmarche sat down heavily. On paper he was a tremendous success with a long list of drug busts to his credit. Oakland Air, his creation, was being copied by the DEA all over the world.

Oakland Air's entrapment operation was simple and effective. DEA agents in Acapulco posed as drug sellers and talked their buyers into shipping their wares on Oakland Air. When the smugglers picked up the dope in California, the DEA arrested them on the spot. The dope went back to Acapulco and was sold again.

Bonmarche emptied the dregs of Wild Turkey into his glass, tossed the bottle at a wastebasket, missed, and said, 'You know what I think, Andrés? I think you have a private scam going with Mendoza. I think when a really big buyer comes along, you steer him to Mendoza's people. I think that's what happened with these two kids from New York. You and Colonel Durazo blew them away. You know anything about that? Like what happened to the dope and the money?'

'There was no money, Antoine. That's what freaked out the soldiers. They started shooting, then the punks started shooting.'

'Bullshit. It was your kind of set-up.'

Obregón looked pained. 'For Christ sake. All I wanted to do was bust the guys. I didn't know they didn't have any money. I wouldn't double-cross a guy like Durazo. He's one mean son of a bitch. He has too many friends.'

'Like Mendoza?'

Obregón nodded emphatically, raised his voice and said, 'Yeah, like Mendoza. Nobody fucks with Mendoza or his friends. Jesus.'

Bonmarche raised his glass in a toast. 'Here's to the heroin king of Guerrero. *Viva! Viva!* God, it's like a bad movie, or one of them weird foreign jobs where the bad guys win. Fuck. C'mon, Andrés, you killed the soldiers and the smugglers. How much did you walk away with?'

'Listen, Antoine. It was just a buy that went wrong. Shit happens.'

Bonmarche scoffed, 'Oh yeah, sure. You'd like me to believe that, wouldn't you? I think it was you. What was it, a five-kilo deal for a hundred grand? You got a spare hundred grand, Andrés?'

'You're drunk. You can't think straight.'

'This is Guerrero. Hell, nobody thinks straight here. If you think straight, you go over the edge of the cliff. You gotta be bent, real bent.'

Obregón drained his cup, dropped it in the wastebasket and said, 'Fuck this, Antoine. I'm going home. I came in here to go to work. Instead, I get a ration of shit about the CIA, about Durazo, about I don't know what.'

'Right. Go home. Go home to Miami, to Havana, wherever the fuck you came from.'

'Relax, Antoine. Get some sleep. Take a vacation.'

Obregón walked out of the warehouse, got in his car and drove away.

Bonmarche opened another bottle of Wild Turkey, poured

himself a drink, and told himself for the millionth time that trying to stop the flow of drugs into the United States from México was like trying to stop an armoured division with BB guns. The *narcotraficantes* had billions of dollars, the co-operation of both governments, no scruples and a huge, insatiable demand to feed. To oppose them, the DEA had righteous indignation, pious, puritanical morality, lots of expensive, useless high technology, bad laws, and little luck.

He lit another Marlboro and entered the warehouse to inspect half a dozen crates labelled 'Genuine Ford parts'. Each crate contained a half-kilo of Brown Mexican heroin inside an oil filter casing.

'How is it?' he asked one of the Raiders, a freak with three earrings in his left ear.

'Fair to middlin',' came the answer. 'Grade B.'

'What the hell,' said Bonmarche. 'Junkies take what they can get. Ship it.'

'Okay, boss. You know what they say. If there ain't no solution, become part of the problem.'

6 SEPTEMBER

9

Al Robo

Late the next afternoon Lowry stood in a drizzle on the vast plain of the Zócalo, México City's great square, watching the changing of the presidential guard in front of the National Palace. Six soldiers in flashy black uniforms commanded by a tough-looking officer quickmarched across the First Courtyard and out of the main gate. The officer posted two guards on the pavement outside the fortified gate, seated the others on a bench inside, then marched alone in a heavy, aggressive military manner alongside the low, wide Palace, scanning the Zócalo.

Devoid of greenery, with nary a bench, the Zócalo could be cleared by troops or swept by gunfire. For the moment it was populated by pigeons and government clerks scurrying for the subway and home.

The pink façade of the Palace shimmered in a ray of light. In the centre of the square the banner of México hung limp, soaked by the passing storm.

Above the gate, under the Bell of Liberty, construction workers were building a new balcony where the President of the Republic would stand and deliver the traditional Independence Day Speech. Giant DiamondVision television screens were being installed around the square.

September 16 was ten days away. Fred Lowry intended to enjoy the President's speech, the long military parade that would precede it, and the fireworks afterwards as well. On the following day he was scheduled to hand México City station over to the new station chief and fly away from México forever.

Lowry wore a grey Brooks Brothers two-button suit and a shirt which had been white that morning but now was the fuzzy brown colour of México City's thin air. Inconspicuous and unremarkable, even beggars and shoeshine boys ignored him. The subway rumbled beneath his feet. In front of the Palace the people went about their chaotic, colourful business. Traffic swirled around the square, faster and faster like a whirlpool that sucked everything into the vortex of the National Palace, the black hole in the centre of the Méxican universe.

As Lowry took a few steps closer to the Palace, he realized the officer in charge of the changing of the guard was General Juan Jalapa, Minister of Defence and a member of Máximo Levín's informal DIS national security committee. Lowry believed Jalapa was the man who had planned to lead the *coup d'état* if Mendoza had not been selected as candidate.

The General returned to the guard post, scowled at the Zócalo once more, then disappeared into the depths of the First Courtyard.

By 16 September, Mendoza would be dead and Salinas would have to pull a new name out of his hat. Fred Lowry felt an intense pleasure from the feeling of power this knowledge gave him.

Scuffing his soles on stones which formed the very soul of México, Lowry pondered briefly upon the President's ultimate predecessor, Hernan Cortés, the great conqueror. When Cortés discovered that the Aztec empire was founded on human sacrifice and cannibalism, the fierce Spaniard reacted with violent revulsion. He swore to shatter the spirit of the Aztecs. After the conquest, Cortés destroyed the sacrificial pyramids and broke the idols of the fearsome Aztec god of war, Huitzilo-pochtli. No fool, the greatest of Spanish brigands retained entire the Aztec system of patronage and tribute. Gold and silver continued to flow into the palace Cortés built upon the ruins of the Aztec Wall of the Dead.

Like the conqueror's palace, that system remained intact. For almost five centuries viceroys, regents, emperors, presidents, generals, dictators and revolutionaries had dispensed patronage and collected the tribute which flowed incessantly into the house of Cortés.

Following the ancient pattern, Alfredo Mendoza, heir apparent to the Palace, was taking in millions, only the money no longer was called tribute, but rather *la mordida*, the little bite, even when the appetite was voracious.

Lowry knew the details of Mendoza's heroin operation, the schedule of payoffs, the secret bank accounts, the false accounting methods, the whole dirty laundry list, including satellite photos of the poppy fields in Guerrero. He knew far more than he filed in his reports to Al Mears. On Mendoza's monthly flights to Las Vegas the minister did not always carry heroin, as Lowry had told the DDO. Mendoza frequently carried cash, millions of dollars which he deposited in a Las Vegas bank as part of a money laundering scheme.

For the five years Lowry had been in México he had thought to himself, 'So what?' The most powerful American in México had believed that Mendoza's heroin business posed no genuine threat to the security of the United States. The dope was of no consequence. In fact, it provided employment for thousands of American cops. In any case, he rationalized, Mendoza's death would not stop the drug traffic, only divert it to other hands.

What mattered was the money and who got it. Lowry was as greedy as the next man but for years had held his greed in check. Like Beno Alvarado he had lied, cheated, deceived, even killed for a pat on the back and a handshake. Unlike Beno, he felt no outrage at the corrosive wealth that flowed into Mendoza's bank accounts. He felt envy. He wanted a few of those millions for himself.

In México he had acquired a taste for luxury, and he did not intend to leave empty handed. If Mendoza was going to die, Lowry saw no reason why he shouldn't profit from that event.

Lowry shuffled toward the subway entrance and descended into the maze of the Zócalo station. After changing trains three times, he emerged an hour and a half later in the southern district of Coyoacán, hailed a taxi, rode ten blocks, then walked another six blocks to an obscure, working-class cafeteria.

He pushed through the door, stopped at the counter, bought a bottle of beer, and walked through the restaurant. Sitting in the rear of the smoky, dank room, he found the small, lithe, Andrés Obregón dressed in beach clothes, a flowery Hawaiian shirt and pleated white cotton pants.

The Cuban had polished nails and slicked back hair. His delicate gestures appeared Méxican, but his inflection, as he said, 'Seat yourself,' had the clipped tones of a native of Havana.

For a moment the other patrons of the cafeteria observed the be-suited gringo, but their idle curiosity quickly waned.

'Speak English,' said Obregón, 'and keep it short.'

Lowry watched the DEA man scoop up beans with a tortilla

and shove the food into his face. Obregón served as number two man in the Acapulco DEA office but had worked in secret for five years as a CIA plant within the DEA. Obregón's primary responsibility was to ensure that Mendoza's operation ran smoothly while freelancers and outlaws were busted.

Lowry asked, 'How are things in Acapulco?'

Obregón answered, 'A little touchy. I set up a sting yesterday that went bad. Two gringos and two Méxicans got wasted.'

Lowry sucked his cheek and nodded. He said, 'Too bad. Consul take care of it?'

Obregón shook his head and said, 'I don't think the consul will be informed. It's not an affair of state.'

Lowry asked, 'How are things between you and Bonmarche?'

'Antoine? He's a fat fuck. He thinks this is a war.'

'Does he suspect you work for me?'

'He doesn't suspect, he knows. Not much he can do about it, is there?'

Lowry asked abruptly, 'How much are you taking down from Mendoza?'

Obregón stopped chewing and slowly lowered his tortilla onto his plate. A dangerous, murderous look passed over his face.

Lowry knew the Cuban was capable of knifing him then and there. When Obregón said nothing, Lowry said, 'I have a gun aimed at your balls.'

Obregón snarled, 'What the fuck are you talking about?'

Lowry's lips curled into a smile and he said, 'You've got a sweet thing going, Andrés. You're working both sides against the middle. You set up buys, the smugglers cop the dope and ship it to Frisco on Oakland Air Freight. The DEA busts the bad guys in California, but you set up the sellers with Mendoza. The army goes in, rips off the money and you get a nice kickback.' Lowry smiled and added, 'Now it sounds like you and Durazo added a new twist. I know it, and I'm sure Bonmarche knows it. I'm trying to save your ass, Andrés, not put you away.'

Obregón asked, 'Did you hear this from Bonmarche? You been going behind my back?'

Lowry said, 'I have my own people, Andrés. We're the spooks. We're everywhere.'

Obregón relaxed and grinned. He said, 'Suppose you're right.

I'm still working for you, Fred. Bonmarche would bust Mendoza in a hot minute if CIA didn't want his highness the minister left alone. Suppose I shake hands with Mendoza once in a while. Suppose Bonmarche knows it. What's he going to do? Call DIS and play tattle-tale? No? Call CBS and put it on *60 Minutes*? Come on, this is México. Everybody gets a little piece of the action.'

Lowry said, 'Bonmarche will bust your ass if he finds out what you're doing. He might even kill you. Bang bang. You're dead.'

'I can take care of myself.'

Lowry shook his head and said, 'Not forever.'

Obregón ate more beans and said, 'What do you want? You wanna bust me for my own protection, what?'

He snapped his fingers. 'No, I got it. You wanna shake me down. You! Righteous Fred Lowry, pride of the CIA. Mr Up-and-up himself. My my. You wanna get dirty, Fred? I'm shocked. Go ahead. Shoot me in the balls. Fuck you.'

Obregón ducked his head under the table and saw Lowry's nine-millimetre automatic. He popped up and said, 'Oowee, it's a nice one. Make a big noise in here.'

Lowry said, 'I don't give a shit about your deal with Mendoza, but it can't go on forever. I'm leaving México. I'm going back to Virginia in ten days.'

Startled, Obregón blurted, 'Jesus, Fred, if you're leaving, that means my time is short, too.'

'That's right. We have barely enough time for one big score.'

'What do you mean, one big score?'

'Who's the biggest?'

Obregón's eyes popped wide open. His voice went high and squeaky as he asked, 'Mendoza? You wanna rip off Mendoza? You're a big shot, Fred, but I don't know if you're that big.'

Lowry said, 'Didn't you just say, "This is México. Everybody gets a piece of the action." Let's say I want my piece. I want the plane.'

'The Vegas plane? You're out of your fucking mind.'

'There's a lot of money on that plane every month.'

'I know that, Freddy boy. What do we do? Walk on and say, "This is a stick-up"?'

Lowry answered emphatically, 'Yeah! That's exactly what you do.'

'Me?'

'Yeah, you.'

'You're shitting me.'

Lowry continued, 'You get on. The plane makes an unscheduled stop. You and the money get off, the plane goes on its way but never arrives.'

'Mendoza dies?'

'Killed by terrorists. You're officially dead, too, because you were on the plane.'

'I'm not sure I like that part. How do I get on the plane?'

'I'll leave that up to you.'

'You really do want to rip off Mendoza, don't you, Fred?' Obregón grinned and said, 'I like it. Yeah, I do.'

Lowry said, 'We want to make sure DIS believes Lucio Serdán brings down Mendoza. I want you to go to Chilpancingo. Do you know how to hardwire a bug?'

'Sure.'

'You know The Death of Maximilian?'

'The mercenary bar. Sure.'

'There's going to be a meet there. We need a tape of that meeting.'

'One of your people, is it?'

'That's the way it goes. I'll pay you ten thousand dollars for the tape.'

'Tell me about your guy.'

'Don't go near him, and don't get caught. He'll rip your eyes out.'

'All you want is a tape?'

'Yeah. Ten grand.'

'I never thought you had it in you, Fred. You're a real *pinche cabrón. Simon, Maestro. Toma tu cerveza. Al robo.*'

Lowry lifted his glass and concurred, '*Al robo.*' To the robbery. Suddenly he laughed, for the Cuban's Spanish toast reminded him of the movie, *Butch Cassidy and the Sundance Kid.* Sundance, Butch and Sundance's girl went in to rob their first Bolivian bank, but neither of the men knew how to pronounce the traditional, 'Hands up! This is a robbery.'

The girl muttered, '*Este es un robo,*' and Butch stammered a repetition. It was a hilarious image of a botched heist. Then Lowry remembered that Butch and Sundance had died in Bolivia.

At least they died like outlaws, which Lowry thought was better than joining the living dead in the suburbs of Virginia.

8 SEPTEMBER

10

Betrayal

With a sense of foreboding, Beno returned to Chilpancingo. Lowry had been too glib, too slick, too eager to push the Stinger into Serdán's hands. Clearly, the CIA wanted Mendoza dead, but Lowry's twisted logic was so murky Beno couldn't see through the smoke.

He pulled off the highway, parked his VW bus near the rear entrance to the bar, and carried the Stinger in its case around the block and down the alley.

The Death of Maximilian was almost empty. Reeking boredom, half a dozen whores occupied a corner booth. In the rear, three Venezuelan mercs sat around a table.

'*Ça va, Monsieur Beno?*'

'Give us a beer.'

Laluce popped the top off a Negrita and said, 'The girls are giving it away tonight, Monsieur Beno. Half price.'

Beno looked at the women in the back bar mirror. Three were fat, two were skinny, one was old, and all wore too much make-up. He shook his head and stared at *The Execution of Maximilian*.

'Slow tonight,' he said to the bartender.

'All my best clients are in Panama.'

'My man here?'

'*Bien sûr.*'

Beno set his beer on the bar and looked at himself in the mirror under *The Execution of Maximilian*. He felt like the dying Austrian prince in the painting.

He paid Laluce his two hundred dollars and passed through the curtain.

Lucio Serdán waited in the same filthy room. He shook Beno's hand and they shared a drink.

Beno asked, 'Did you try one of the rockets?'

'Not yet. Have you come to collect payment?'

'No. I have something else for you, something much more potent.'

'You are the Father Christmas of the arms industry, Mr Alvarado.'

Beno asked, 'Have you searched this room?'

'I did when I arrived,' answered Serdán. 'I've been here eight hours. Do you feel the need?'

At that moment, in the hotel on the corner, Andrés Obregón felt a surge of alarm. He had managed to bug each of the four rooms in the shoddy whorehouse to the rear of the bar. The bugs were first class, hard-wired into the electrical system, each on a different frequency, but if Alvarado made a thorough search, he would find the microphone in the skirting-board.

Obregón wasn't going to wait in the hotel until Alvarado came after him. Quickly, he packed his receivers, left the hotel, and headed for México City on his motorbike.

Beno said, 'I do.'

He started at the stark electric bulb and worked his way down the exposed wiring to the skirting-board. Serdán watched with amused interest. Three minutes after he started looking, Beno found Obregón's bug, a sub-miniature microphone.

Beno thought to himself, 'Lowry.'

He held his finger to his lips and gestured Serdán to follow him into the corridor.

Hurriedly, Beno whispered, 'Take the case. It contains an anti-aircraft missile . . .'

Serdán interrupted, 'Whose microphone?'

Beno shook his head, 'I don't know. DIS, perhaps. I'll take care of it. Take the case and get out of here.'

Rapidly he added, 'Mendoza flies out of Zihuatanejo at least once a week. Security around the plane is lax. Mendoza believes no one in his right mind would tamper with his plane. You have only to be within a mile of the airport. Once the pilot starts the engines, you can destroy the plane on the ground.'

Serdán grinned and said, 'Not very sporting, is it, Señor Alvarado?'

'The sporting part comes next,' Beno said. 'Once you shoot, they know where you are. The airport is right on the beach. I

116

would go in by boat, perhaps shoot from the boat, but there are other possibilities. You might make it out.'

Serdán said, 'It's suicide.'

'Perhaps. Shoot him wherever you like. In México City, anywhere. Go. Quickly. Go with God.'

Serdán leaned his face close to Beno's and said, 'I know you are CIA.'

Beno didn't flinch. He said, 'It's true, I was, but not any more. Not after tonight. They'll kill me for this.'

'The microphone came from them?'

'Yes.'

'I should kill you now,' said Lucio Serdán.

'I won't stop you,' Beno replied. 'But you serve your people better if you kill Alfredo Mendoza. Avenge Chilpancingo and the memory of Tlatelolco.'

'I may be a fool, but I believe you,' said Serdán.

He grabbed the case and vanished through the rear door.

Beno returned to the room, jerked the bug from the skirting-board and walked into the bar.

Laluce saw the grim look on Beno's face and began moving stealthily down the bar toward his shotgun. Beno vaulted the bar and shoved the tiny microphone into the face of the shocked Frenchman.

'I didn't know, Monsieur Beno. I swear to God.'

Beno reached under the bar, pulled out the bartender's sawn-off twelve gauge, cracked it, checked the shells, and snapped it into firing position.

The whores panicked. The Venezuelans reached for their pistols. Beno swung the L. C. Smith toward the men and yelled, 'Stop! This doesn't concern you. Hands on your heads. Now!'

The Venezuelans froze. Beno said, 'Good. Keep your hands where they are. Walk out the door and don't come back. Don't move, Laluce.'

The Venezuelans scurried out the door and Beno said to the women, 'After them. Adiós. Good night.'

The whores disappeared. Beno came around the bar, keeping the shotgun trained on the Frenchman, and locked the door.

'Come out from behind the bar, Laluce. Hands on your head. That's right. Don't go for the knife behind your collar. You'll never make it. Sit down on the floor. Good. Now, who did this?'

Laluce said, 'I'm trying to think. Maybe it was Lucio. He was in there all day.'

'Horseshit. He couldn't wire a battery to a toy car. Think harder.'

'There was a Cuban. Yes, I'm sure it was him.'

'What Cuban?'

'A little man, very horny, fucked all the girls. He stayed a day and a half, spent a lot of money, slept in the rooms.'

'What was his name?'

'He say he was call José, but nobody use a name. What's a name? José.'

'Why didn't you tell me?'

'What was to tell? He was a customer. He spend money.'

'When did he leave?'

'Two days ago. He signed for Panama. He left with them.'

'A lot of those guys must have been in the back rooms with the girls. What's so special about the Cuban?'

'The Panamanian call me asking for some money return. The Cuban crap out, disappear in México City. I'm sorry. It's not my fault. Are you going to kill me?'

'Why? You want to say your prayers?'

'I am *légionnaire*. I don't want to die on the floor blubbering in my own piss.'

'*Vive la mort, vive la guerre, vive le joli légionnaire* and all that shit, hey, Laluce? Fuck you. No. Your time in México is over. Go back to Algeria. I guarantee your Cuban will come back. Shall we wait for him?'

'No.'

'How about we walk over to the hotel and see if he's waiting?'

'I don't know where he is.'

'You're finished, Laluce. Whatever he paid you wasn't worth it. By tomorrow, every merc in México will know you can't be trusted.'

Andrés Obregón waited for Lowry in a two-bedroom suite in the Holiday Inn on the Paseo de la Reforma. To pass the time he had rented two Japanese girls from an expensive escort service.

When Lowry banged on the door, Obregón felt like a piece of ripe sushi. He peeled off the girls who stuck to him like grains

118

of vinegared pearl rice, put on a terrycloth bathrobe and opened the door.

Lowry stood in the corridor and twitched his nose.

'You alone?' he asked.

'No.'

'You fool. Get rid of her.'

'I got two, Fred. Want one?'

Lowry looked at his watch.

Five minutes later the women rushed past Lowry and scurried toward the elevators.

Lowry walked into the suite.

Obregón said, 'You bring my money?'

'Did you bring the tape?'

Obregón said, 'I have Lucio Serdán and his guerrillas, Serdán and one of Laluce's whores, and your man and Serdán having a drink. Two minutes after he walked in he found the bug.'

'Oh, shit. What happened then?'

'I split. You got my money?'

Lowry dropped two thick stacks of hundred-dollar bills on the coffee table and said, 'Go back to Acapulco, stay cool and think about Mendoza's plane.'

Obregón surveyed the line of cabs in front of the hotel.

'Taxi?' said the first driver in line.

Obregón handed the driver a fifty-dollar bill and said, 'Make sure we're not being followed.'

'Si, señor.'

The driver jammed the accelerator to the floor, jerked the wheel, stood on the brakes, brought the rear end of the car around and charged two blocks through traffic the wrong way on a one-way street.

Obregón screamed, 'Yes yes yes, do it do it!'

Scattering pedestrians, the driver jumped a red light and pulled onto Avenue Cuauhtémoc at normal speed.

'Okay, boss?'

'Beautiful. Now, Coyoacán.'

The taxi dropped Obregón on the Avenue de los Insurgentes South.

'Wait fifteen,' he said to the driver.

He walked a block to a cheap roominghouse, pushed open the

119

heavy plate glass door, waved at the sleepy desk clerk and went up to his first-floor room.

He keyed the triple locks, opened the door, quickly crossed the room to the bed, lifted the mattress and switched off a simple timing device.

With the motion sensors deactivated, he relaxed for a moment and admired his handiwork. Anyone who broke into this room would never walk out again. Four ounces of C4 high explosive would take out an intruder and half the first floor. A man had to protect his money.

He opened a large wooden armoir and added the ten thousand dollars to forty thousand in the cabinet, reset the sensors and returned to the waiting taxi.

'Calle Fresnos.'

'Anything you say, boss. Fast or slow?'

'Take your time.'

Lowry stopped his Buick at the red light at the foot of Niagra Street. The driver's side window was down. Suddenly the twin barrels of an L. C. Smith shotgun appeared an inch from his face. He thought he was a dead man.

'Keep your hands where I can see them and move over,' said Beno.

Bursting into sweat, Lowry slid across the front seat. Beno opened the door, sat down behind the wheel, reached inside Lowry's coat and took his gun. Putting the shotgun down on his left side and keeping the pistol pointed at Lowry, he drove the car slowly away from the light.

'Tell me, Fred, old buddy, what should I do with you?'

Lowry said nothing.

Beno asked, 'Why did you bug my meeting with Serdán?'

'I don't know what you're talking about.'

'Going to stonewall me, Fred?'

Lowry said, 'We spend a lot of time in this car with you waving guns at me.'

Beno said, 'Let's be logical. Who might have put a bug in the room at Laluce's bar besides you? Two possibilities, Serdán himself, or the DIS. Serdán? No chance. DIS? Tell me it was them, Fred. Convince me. Save your life and the interior of your nice car.'

Lowry said, 'Meeting in a hole like that mercenary bar was a mistake in the first place. If you say it was wired, I believe you, but Laluce could have done it himself. Anyone could have done it. It could have been an old bug, been there for years. Who knows?'

'You do.'

'Jesus, Beno, whatever thin cover you had, it's time to rotate you out of México.'

Beno snapped, 'It's time to rotate you to heaven. Do you think you can talk your way out of this? You knew I gave Serdán the RPG-16s. How did you know that? I didn't find the bug that time, but this time I did.'

Thinking Beno was going to kill him, Lowry said, 'I'm not going to pretend I like you, Beno, but you're one of my people. You were in Chilpancingo setting up an operation to kill Alfredo Mendoza. It sounds to me like the DIS would take an interest in that.'

'Then why didn't they come in and blow me and Serdán away?'

'I can't read their minds.'

Beno exploded, 'Because it wasn't them. It was you. It was a Cuban named José. You know a José?'

'Half the people in México are named José.'

'Fred, I'm sick of your bullshit. I know I'll regret it, but I'm going to let you live, not that you don't deserve to have your brains splattered all over the dashboard. But I'm out. Consider this a punctuation point to my resignation. Don't send any forms. Don't send some asshole down to Zee to debrief me. Just keep away from me. And keep away from Serdán, or I'll change my mind.'

Beno hit the brakes hard causing Lowry to bang his head on the windscreen. Taking the shotgun and pistol, Beno got out of the car, walked around a corner out of sight and dropped the car keys through a sewer grating followed by the pistol and shotgun shells. He left the L. C. Smith in the gutter, jammed his hands in his pockets, and went off in search of a cab.

11

Máximo Levín

Autonomous, aggressive, ubiquitous, the Directorate of Internal Security could tap any phone, invade any data bank or compile a dossier on any person in México. With high speed Cray computers and advanced electronic surveillance technology provided by the CIA, the DIS existed as an agency of political information, prediction and control.

The President, party and Federal Judicial Police had created the DIS as a modern version of thought police, but when political control is invested in technical means, the technicians become all powerful. The day the Cray computers were switched on in the basement of the glass pyramid, real power, the power of information, shifted from the National Palace to Tlatelolco. Only one man in the republic recognized that a subtle revolution had taken place. When the switch was thrown, Máximo Levín, director of the DIS, became *de facto* head of state.

Born and raised in México City, the son of a wealthy silver merchant, by training a computer engineer and by default a policeman, Máximo had been entrusted with the power inherent in DIS because of his brilliance and because, as a Jew, no Méxican expected him to seek overt political power in his own right.

Máximo passionately embraced the ideals of the great Méxican revolution. In 1911 Zapata, Villa, Madero and a host of others overthrew the forty-year dictatorship of Porfirio Díaz. In 1994 Alfredo Mendoza intended to restore Porfirio's chair to the National Palace, the ultimate betrayal of the revolution.

A zealous patriot, Máximo was dedicated to a single goal, the creation of an advanced, rational society prepared to plunge into the twenty-first century as the leader of a new, powerful Latin America. To achieve this goal he had followed Lucio Serdán's advice, given on the sad night of the massacre of

Tlatelolco. Máximo had made a pact with the devil and found a patron.

He had surrendered his soul to Alfredo Mendoza, but in the DIS he had created the means to overthrow the regime. Using his mandated power to gather information from any source, Máximo had networked every significant computer system in México into the Crays in the basement of DIS headquarters. At any moment he could seize control of the operating systems of critical mainframes in the Bank of México, the police, the armed services, the various ministries, the media, and the national communication system.

The programs were written, the instructions prepared, the machines waited as Máximo himself had waited for a quarter of a century. For twenty-five years Máximo had lived a life of rigid self-denial, devoting every minute and all his energy to his service. He rarely displayed emotion, even when alone. His was a life of sacrifice and solitude, monklike in its abstinence.

To the thousands of DIS employees beneath him in the pyramid and the millions whose lives they surveilled and controlled, Máximo Levín was a man of wire and silicon, an automaton, a ruthless, efficient extension of his computers, but behind his icy mask the tense director seethed with anger.

As keeper of the republic's secrets, no secret was more precious to the director than his private agenda. Revolted by Mendoza's excesses, Máximo had come to despise the Minister of Government. When Mendoza had ordered the DIS to begin collecting dossiers on the party leaders, Máximo correctly predicted that Mendoza would secure the *dedazo*. The director had concluded that Mendoza was the worst possible choice as the next president of México. With Mendoza ensconced in the National Palace, all the savage violence hidden just below the surface of the republic would erupt like a thousand volcanos. Violent revolution would roll over México like a river of lava, burning everything in its path.

For decades Máximo had planned a silent, electronic revolution. One day eighty million Méxicans would wake up and discover that control of the nation lay in the DIS computers. Mendoza's candidacy caused the director to alter his plan and push that day forward, precisely to 16 September, the day Salinas was to announce Mendoza as his successor.

At first, Máximo had considered assassination. Despite all precautions Mendoza was as vulnerable as any public figure. Yet killing Mendoza would only remove a symptom, not cure the political disease of one-party dictatorship. Máximo was determined to destroy not only Mendoza, but the corrupt one-party, anti-democratic system which had produced him.

An essential component of that system was the support of the United States. A political realist, the director ignored the machinations of the Department of State and watched the CIA in order to discern genuine American policy. The CIA had supported Mendoza for years, and a side effect of that support was the official co-operation between the DIS and the CIA.

Unofficially, Máximo treated the CIA as the meddling secret service of a latently hostile power. Like all Méxicans, Máximo was acutely aware that the only possible enemy who could threaten his nation was the colossus to the north. In 1848 the United States had taken half of México by conquest. Since then the interests of the United States had been served by stability in México, but Mendoza represented the greatest threat to stability since the revolution.

Máximo believed the CIA understood the danger Mendoza represented, but he also knew the CIA was a loose cannon inside the American government, serving its own interests rather than the good of the American people on either side of the border.

At the precise moment when Beno Alvarado entered the tavern in Chilpancingo, Máximo sat in his library atop the glass pyramid, eyes locked on his bank of monitors. He had intended to dine alone in his apartment, but his meal remained untouched. He had scarcely eaten for days.

The central screen displayed a log of all the calls going in and out of the CIA station in the American embassy. An audio speaker quietly relayed calls taken by the CIA duty officer.

The director had ordered all DIS field agents to observe the movements of CIA operatives throughout the republic. As Máximo had expected, the American spies had reacted to Mendoza's selection as candidate with a flurry of activity. Immediately after learning that Mendoza had received the big finger, Lowry had telephoned Al Mears in Langley. The American National Security Council had held an urgent meeting on México, and the DDO had promptly visited México City.

Most disturbing to Máximo Levín was the fact that Lowry had sent a courier to Zihuatanejo to summon Beno Alvarado to México City. Lowry had met Alvarado on two successive days.

The DIS dossier on Beno Alvarado was inadequate. From time to time, both with and without the CIA's approval, Alvarado had sold small arms to revolutionary groups, including Lucio Serdán's guerrillas. Máximo understood the CIA's motive. No single group of armed guerrillas posed a real threat. Their existence could be touted as part of a grand communist conspiracy. If necessary, the DIS could eliminate the guerrillas at any moment, but Máximo had other plans for Lucio Serdán.

By eavesdropping on communications from the American embassy, Máximo had intercepted a memo in which Lowry had complained bitterly about Alvarado to his superiors in Langley. The station chief did not believe that his agent would eliminate the guerrillas if ordered to do so. Given the order to kill Lucio Serdán, Lowry believed that Alvarado would rebel, and perhaps join the guerrillas.

Máximo thought it possible that Lowry had ordered Alvarado to terminate his selling of arms. That scenario suited the director who absolutely wanted Mendoza alive on 16 September.

A moment later one of Máximo's most private lines rang.

Máximo answered, 'Direction.'

'This is the schoolteacher. I must see you now.'

Máximo hung up and called for his helicopter.

12

Lucio

Forty miles north of México City at Teotihuacán the ancient pyramids of the sun and moon loomed over the Valley of México. Máximo's helicopter landed at the base of the pyramid of the moon, and the director walked unarmed and alone along the Street of the Dead.

On the first level of the pyramid of the sun he found Lucio Serdán and two of his guerrillas.

Máximo greeted his old friend with a warmth he rarely displayed. 'I was hoping to hear from you tonight. Did you meet Alvarado?'

Serdán replied, 'Yes, but nothing went as expected. He gave me this.'

Serdán showed Máximo the Stinger. 'The CIA wants me to kill Mendoza.'

Máximo became furious. His mind flashed white as he saw his carefully laid plans go up like the high-explosive warhead in the missile.

Serdán said, 'The room where we met was bugged. Someone was listening.'

'The CIA.'

'Yes.'

'I must protect Mendoza. We must have him alive on the sixteenth. Do you have tapes for me?'

'Yes.'

Serdán handed Máximo a box of 8mm videotapes.

Máximo said, 'It's time for you to come out of the Sierra, Lucio. I want you in México City on the sixteenth. If the CIA wants you to kill Mendoza, they'll be after you soon enough.'

Serdán said, 'I don't trust this man Alvarado. I know where he lives. I want to kill him.'

'No. That would alert the Americans. The enemy of your enemy is your friend.'

'I'm not convinced.'

'Be patient, my friend,' said Máximo. 'Bring your people out of the mountains as soon as possible. Go with God.'

Again they embraced. Máximo walked to the waiting helicopter and flew back to DIS headquarters.

Assassination does not require death. Neither a bullet nor a surface to air missile can destroy with the finality of a television camera.

In his library Máximo picked up the secure, voice encrypted, scrambled telephone and dialled General Juan Jalapa, Minister of Defence.

The two men had known each other since childhood. Jalapa had been party to Máximo's schemes since they were twelve. Many years before, when Máximo said, 'I need a soldier. We need an army,' Juan Jalapa had volunteered.

After twenty-five years Máximo's army was finally positioned for a *coup d'état.*

'Juan?'

'Yes, Director?'

Even the security apparatus could not remove the authority in Máximo's rich, cultivated voice. He said, 'I want you to come to DIS at once.'

'Half an hour.'

Máximo's next call tracked down Ricardo Solida, the Foreign Minister, at a party at the home of the First Secretary of the French Embassy.

'Come to Tlatelolco.'

'And forgo this gorgeous wench who is about to reveal all her secrets, Professor?'

'At once.'

Máximo telephoned four more old friends. Javier Vatiz, the chairman of Pemex, the state oil monopoly, was en route by corporate jet from the oil fields to México City and would land in twenty minutes.

Guillermo Guzman, executive director of Televisa, México's privately owned television network, was in the control room of Televisa Studios checking the tapes in the hopper against the log for the early morning broadcast when Máximo called. Guzman handed his clipboard to an assistant and called for his limousine.

Guzman's counterpart at Imevision, the government network, Manuel de la Roca, was sound asleep but waking up quickly.

Tomás Molina, Chief Executive Officer of the Bank of México, was visiting his mistress in Polanco when Máximo's call reached his car phone. His driver sighed and called Molina on his beeper.

Máximo Levín, Juan Jalapa, Ricardo Solida, Javier Vatiz, Guillermo Guzman, Manuel de la Roca, Tomás Molina. Old friends. México 21.

13

México 21

That night a general alarm fire raged through the México City suburb of Netzahualcóyotl. The fire had started with an explosion in a propane distribution centre and quickly spread into the surrounding slums, the *colonias perdidas*, the lost settlements, where uncounted millions lived without running water, sewers, electric power or police protection. The fire was the seventh such conflagration in ten days. México City was slowly consuming itself.

At one in the morning the first fire brigade to arrive at the burning propane centre had been stoned by vandals. The firemen had remained in their trucks until a group of local residents persuaded the chief *bombero* to sell them water from the pumps to save their homes. The Netzahualcóyotl police had negotiated the settlement in return for a commission for their services. Nevertheless, by four a.m. ten thousand citizens of the Valley of México had been added to the unwritten list of *damnificados*, the homeless without hope.

Ten miles west the huge blaze was visible from DIS headquarters in Tlatelolco. Throughout the night an easterly breeze carried a fine white ash from Netzahualcóyotl across the Federal District.

The residue of the fire fell like acid rain, marring the finish of the limousines discharging passengers at the glass pyramid. As the cars entered the underground garage, their occupants cast furtive glances at the fire as if calculating how quickly the flames were burning toward them.

The guards had been briefed on the arrival of the director's 'Committee for State Security', six powerful individuals who were frequent visitors to DIS headquarters.

One by one they rode in the director's private elevator up to his apartment and assembled in the library. Máximo warmly greeted each man with an embrace and a polite inquiry after his family, the children and the elderly. Despite the crisis, Máximo performed this ritual without fail, for, in classic Méxican fashion, he was their *patrón*.

As *patrón*, Máximo had used his influence to manage the career of every member of México 21. Each man owed his present high rank to the director of DIS. In return for Máximo's protection and influence, they gave him absolute loyalty, but their bond went deeper. The members shared his vision of a new México, a great México for the twenty-first century. Like Máximo, they despised Alfredo Mendoza and the regime he represented.

Within the government, Máximo and his group of powerful friends functioned as an informal committee on national security. On the nineteenth floor of the glass pyramid no pretence was necessary. México 21, the 'Committee for State Security', was in fact a revolutionary cabal, a secret society of determined radicals.

In the ancient, feudal pyramid of power Máximo himself had a patron, no less an individual than Alfredo Mendoza, whom Máximo had served for twenty years, first in the México City Police, then in the Federal Judicial Police, and finally in the Ministry of Government. Mendoza considered Máximo his grey eminence, his Hebrew mandarin.

Mendoza had first noticed Máximo in 1973, when the bright young computer engineer was hired to computerize the México City Police Department. The power of high technology, and the wizardry of the man who made it work, so impressed Mendoza that he made Máximo his personal assistant.

Máximo quickly developed an aptitude for police work and a willingness to exploit the police powers of the state. Within a year he became the *de facto* chief operating officer of the México City Police Department, actually running the department on a day-to-day basis. He served as Mendoza's shield, freeing the Chief to pursue the business of getting rich.

As Mendoza's corruption reached unprecedented levels of depraved excess, Máximo began to prepare his cabal to strike a fatal blow against the regime which had nurtured them all. When Mendoza was selected as the candidate, México 21 chose the date.

On 16 September, México's Independence Day, a long military parade would meander through México City from Military

Camp Number One to the Zócalo. Both television networks would televise the ceremonies from the National Palace, which would culminate with the President's speech from the balcony.

At that moment México 21 would usher in the new millenium.

At four in the morning Javier Vatiz of Pemex arrived at DIS headquarters from the airport. Máximo led the members of México 21 into the library.

Standing at the head of the table behind the recorder, Máximo addressed his cabal in a sombre voice. 'Gentlemen, the CIA is going to attempt to assassinate Alfredo Mendoza.'

The polite decorum evaporated. Angry shouts erupted around the table.

'Why?'

'When?'

'How?'

General Juan Jalapa shook his head in dismay and muttered, 'The gringos will never leave us alone.'

Máximo waited until the table was silent, then said, 'Tonight in Chilpancingo a CIA officer named Beno Alvarado provided a surface to air missile and a great deal of money to Lucio Serdán. Even the CIA would not depend on one man with one rocket. There may be others.'

Javier Vatiz, president of Pemex, rumbled in his deep bass voice, 'How did you learn this, Máximo?'

Maximo responded, 'Directly from Serdán.'

Vatiz asked, 'Does he intend to use this weapon?'

'Of course not, Javier. He's one of us.'

'Are you sure?'

'Yes,' Máximo said. 'But that does not remove the danger to Mendoza.'

'Has the President been informed?'

'No,' Máximo said. 'Not yet.'

Guillermo Guzman, the tall, obese director of Televisa, asked, 'And Mendoza?'

Máximo said, 'I'm going to Zihuatanejo tomorrow.'

Ricardo Solida, the Foreign Minister, still in the elegantly tailored dinner jacket he had worn to the diplomatic party, said angrily, 'We must control our own destiny. I've said before and

I say again, we cannot let the CIA interfere with our history to suit their purposes. Arrest Alvarado.'

Máximo asked, 'On what grounds? We cannot use the word of a supposed enemy of the state.'

De la Roca said, 'Then disappear him, Máximo.'

Máximo said, 'I'm not convinced that he's responsible. He answers to his station chief, Fred Lowry. If we eliminate Alvarado, Lowry will replace him.'

Solida said, 'I can call Lowry in and throw this in his face.'

Máximo said, 'I believe there may be a proper moment for that, but not yet. Gentlemen, let us not be distracted by the CIA. We must focus on Mendoza. The time has come to assemble the final round of evidence from Guerrero. Serdán provided me with more videotape, and there may be yet more to come. We can deal with the CIA after the sixteenth of September. Let's remember our goals and prepare ourselves.'

9 SEPTEMBER

14

El Partenón

Every Thursday afternoon Alfredo Mendoza entertained a different young woman in his private apartment in El Partenón. No matter what she called herself, he called her Maria.

On this drizzling, hot Thursday in September Mendoza's Maria was an eighteen-year-old aspiring actress the Minister had noticed in a commercial for Pan Bimbo, México's Wonder Bread. As it happened, her real name was Maria, and she smiled nervously as Mendoza's huge bodyguard, Ramón Santiago, escorted her through the back corridors of the mansion. She paused to gaze in awe at the rich furnishings, then skipped and hurried to keep up with the bodyguard's great strides.

Only the façade of El Partenón resembled its Greek namesake. The pillars which looked down on Zihuatanejo and Old Clothes Beach ringed the terrace of the mansion's primary swimming pool. Hidden from view, the main body of the house contained 47 rooms, a twelve-car garage, stables, tennis courts, three courtyards, two more pools, a television studio, a casino, a Roman bath and a dog track.

Ramón and Maria arrived at the door to Mendoza's apartment. Ramón extracted a printed form and pen from the breast pocket of his expensive, Italian suit and said in a gruff voice, 'Sign this.'

Dazzled, Maria maintained the presence to ask, 'What is it?'

'Release. Says you were never here. Says you heard nothing, saw nothing, said nothing. Says no one is responsible for any consequences.'

Maria's eyes bounced. She hesitated, then asked, 'What consequences?'

Ramón peered down at her and a tiny smile pinched the corners of his eyes. He said, 'He didn't ask you here to shoot craps, you know? Don't come back and lay no babies on the Chief's doorstep, understand?'

She nodded, picked at her clipped, dyed blonde hair, and signed.

Ramón added, 'One more thing. Call him "Chief". He likes that. Before he was Minister, he was Chief of Police for all México City, and before that, Chief of Motorcycles. Call him "Chief".'

'Okay.'

'Don't worry. He won't hurt you.' Ramón knocked on the door and tenderly stroked her neck. 'If he doesn't like you, I will.'

The door opened. Alfredo Mendoza, 57 years old, dressed in the uniform of the Chief of Motorcycles replete with dark glasses, peaked cap, holstered pistol, handcuffs, ticket book, flashlight and portable two-way radio, ushered in his Maria with a courtly gesture. He watched Ramón shuffle down the corridor to his post in an alcove in front of a television set.

Mendoza closed the door and said, 'Sit down, my dear. Let me look at you.'

Maria was wearing the same blue chiffon party dress she had worn in the Pan Bimbo commercial. Mendoza led her to a blue velvet chair and she sat. The Minister looked to her just like he did on television, a fleshy, high-cheekboned, jut-jawed, almond-eyed mestizo. Maria knew that for twenty years, longer than her life, Alfredo Mendoza had been the most hated and feared man in the republic.

Mendoza grinned and asked if she wanted a drink. Meekly, she asked for a Pepsi. He opened a small refrigerator, filled a glass with ice and cola, and poured himself a large cognac.

He asked, 'Do you recognize that chair? The one you're sitting in?'

Puzzled, she looked at the heavy oaken arms under her elbows and shook her head.

Mendoza sipped his cognac and grinned. 'You've seen the President on television, I suppose?'

'Oh, yes, Mr Chief. Many times.'

'Then you have seen the Presidential Chair, the red one, embossed with gold leaf?'

'Yes, it is very beautiful.'

'I'm going to tell you a private joke. The red chair is a fake, part of a television set. The real chair is the one you're sitting on. Notice the elegant blue velvet, the brass studs, the heavy oak frame. That chair is the genuine article. That chair supported the ass of Porfirio Díaz.'

Mendoza laughed again. Confused, Maria stared at her glass of Pepsi.

With a confident smile the Minister asked, 'You don't know who he was, do you?'

'He was President once, I think.'

Mendoza removed his dark glasses and asked, 'Did you ever hear of Emiliano Zapata?'

'Zapata? Oh, sure. He was the leader of the revolution.'

Mendoza bent close to Maria and said, 'One day in 1915 Zapata walked into the National Palace in México City, gazed upon Porfirio's blue chair, and sneered, "This chair is bewitched. Whoever sits in this chair will become wicked." Did you ever hear that story?'

'No. No, sir, Chief, I didn't know that.'

Mendoza emptied his glass, set it down, and loosened his belt. His voice dropped an octave and he groaned, 'It's true. Whoever sits in this chair becomes terribly wicked. You are sitting in the bewitched chair, Maria. Do you feel wicked?'

With his belt unhooked and fly unzipped, the Minister reached behind him for his handcuffs and whispered, 'I feel wicked.'

Mendoza's father had been a México City policeman. For thirty years he had supplemented his meagre income with a thousand *mordidas*, 'little bites', small, regular bribes from shopkeepers on his beat. More bribes came from the crooks who stole from the shopkeepers, and still more *mordidas* from the fences who sold the goods back to the shopkeepers. Part of the money always filtered up the pyramid of tribute as party and union dues, benefits for associations and widows, pension plans or straightforward 'donations'. For decades this workable system of tribute and patronage had provided a kind of stability and order to the republic.

When Mendoza turned eighteen, he followed his father into the police. His ambition was to join the motorcycle patrol. In those days a man who wanted to be a motorcycle cop in México City had to buy his ride from a certain Harley-Davidson dealer. A few thousand pesos were tacked onto the price, the *mordida* for the Chief of Motorcycles. Mendoza paid, and swore on his shiny new Harley that one day he would become Chief of Motorcycles. Ten years later he succeeded, and owned the dealership as well. After only five more years he became Chief of the México City Police and laid the foundation of his fortune.

Now, as Minister of Government, Mendoza was one step away from the pinnacle of the pyramid. In a year and five months he was going to take his place as the ultimate benefactor of the Aztec system of tribute which Cortés had discovered in the Valley of México.

The phone rang for a long time before Mendoza rolled his heavily larded body off Maria and picked it up.

'Yes, what is it?' snarled the Minister.

A polite but firm sergeant of the guard replied, 'The Director of the Directorate of Internal Security is here to see you, Chief.'

Astounded, Mendoza said, 'Máximo Levín, here?'

'Yes, sir.'

'Put him on.'

A moment later Mendoza recognized Máximo's voice.

'I'm sorry to disturb you, Alfredo, but I'm afraid we must discuss an affair of the greatest importance.'

'Concerning what?'

'Lucio Serdán and your security.'

'All right. Meet me in the casino in ten minutes.'

'I prefer outside if you don't mind, Mr Minister.'

Mendoza pulled up his pants, buttoned his ruffled white shirt and stared out of the window at the second courtyard, a serene enclave of elm trees and stone benches. While he changed into a polyester leisure suit, he watched Máximo cross the little park, escorted by the sergeant of the guard.

Reaching for the door, he noticed Maria, naked, one hand cuffed to the bedstead, the other holding a can of Pepsi. He picked up a remote control, turned on the Televisa evening news and said, 'Watch the news. Maybe you won the lottery.'

He shut the bedroom door and stepped into the corridor.

Ramón Santiago sat in an overstuffed chair also watching the news. When he saw the Minister, he waved, wiggling his fingers, a ludicrous gesture from a man who stood six feet seven inches tall and weighed twenty stone.

Mendoza ordered, 'Come with me.'

Ramón raised his eyebrows and gestured with his head toward the door to Mendoza's suite.

Mendoza said, 'She's not going anywhere.'

The casino had all the amenities of a miniature Las Vegas. A mirrored ceiling reflected the glitter of a bank of slot machines and the sparkle of pearls adorning the neck of a topless cocktail waitress. Army officers in civilian clothes clustered around a spinning roulette wheel. The flash of dice at a craps table entertained a quartet of high rolling smugglers from Acapulco. The croupiers stopped the action momentarily to greet their chief.

As Mendoza passed the roulette wheel, General Guillermo 'Billy' Vargas stopped him and said, 'Congratulations, Alfredo! The big finger!'

As commander of the 27th Infantry, Vargas held the highest military rank in the state of Guerrero. He had sworn the allegiance of his battalion to Mendoza.

Mendoza playfully put a finger to his lips and said, 'Shh! That's a secret.'

He leaned on the wheel and whispered to Vargas, 'Bet on the double zero.'

The General smiled. The croupier spun the wheel and let the ball fly.

At the craps table the smugglers were losing. Mendoza watched the action for a moment, then quietly asked the croupier, 'How much?'

'We're into the guy in the blue suit for twenty thousand. The others, about five or six thousand each.'

'Good. Let them have half of it back.'

To the blue suit he said, 'Need anything? A girl? A little candy for the nose?'

Shaking the dice, the man said, 'All I need is to make my point.'

To Ramón Mendoza said, 'I'll be outside by the pool. See that I'm not disturbed.'

15

Security

Máximo Levín stood on the terrace of El Partenón behind a thick sheet of bullet-proof glass and surveyed the bay of Zihuatanejo below. A cruise ship was discharging passengers into motor launches. Para-gliders pulled by speedboats floated over the blue-green water. Sailing boats dotted the bay like candles on an aquamarine cake.

Máximo turned his back on this playground for the oblivious and looked up at Mendoza's forty-six Doric columns, thinking the Minister would have fitted in perfectly with the bloodthirsty ancient Greeks and their violent gods.

Emerging from the house, Mendoza smiled expansively and said, 'Well, you skinny Jew, I've been trying to get you down here for years. Maybe you finally got horny, hey? You want a girl, maybe two? What can I do for you?'

Máximo focused on his patron and said, 'Spare me your jokes, Alfredo.'

Máximo placed his hands on his hips and said, 'We learned from the CIA that a shipment of Stinger surface to air missiles has arrived in México. Some of those missiles have fallen into the hands of Lucio Serdán.'

Mendoza scratched his belly, looked at the sky and said, 'That's your problem, no?'

'Are you crazy, Alfredo? This is serious. Serdán knows details about your operation, and that worries me.'

'What details?'

'The flights to Las Vegas, for example.'

Mendoza swore softly, 'Damn. How do you know?'

'We have identified the man who sells Serdán arms. We're looking for him now. Until we find him, you need to make drastic changes in your security here and elsewhere.'

A loud burst of laughter boiled out of Mendoza's throat. He waved his arms at the heavily armed soldiers patrolling the grounds and shouted through his laughter, 'What do you want

140

to do? Count the bullets in their guns? That's ridiculous, Máximo. No one can get in here, Jesus bloody Christ.'

Máximo insisted, 'That's not the point, Alfredo. I'm telling you Serdán knows *details*. This place is not secure. You have faith in your soldiers and all their guns. Okay.'

Máximo pointed at the nearest soldier and said, 'Tell me how much you pay that man.'

Mendoza shrugged and said, 'Shit, I dunno. Regular army pay plus a bonus. Five, six hundred a month, I suppose, and all the booze and dope and girls he can do.'

'Right. Suppose Serdán offered him twenty thousand.'

Mendoza snarled, 'I'd kill him. I'd strangle him with my bare hands and he knows that. Every one of my men knows that.'

Patiently, Máximo said, 'You can't kill them all, *patrón*. Guns and fear are not enough, not in this world. You have to modernize El Partenón, and you'd better start now. Otherwise, some bright boy with a camera and a laser microphone will bring you down.'

'A what?'

'A laser microphone.'

'What the hell is that?'

Máximo gestured at the soldier and said, 'Call him over here.'

Mendoza waved, and the soldier, a boy of nineteen, trotted over, snapped to attention and saluted.

Máximo asked him, 'Do you know what a laser microphone is?'

The soldier looked confused, then frightened at his own ignorance. Kindly, Máximo said, 'Don't be afraid. Just answer the question.'

'No, sir. I haven't no idea.'

Máximo said, 'That's all. You're dismissed.'

The trooper glanced at Mendoza, who nodded curtly, and the soldier ran back to his station.

Máximo opened his jacket, removed a small radio and said into it, 'Velásquez, come here.'

To Mendoza he said, 'Look over there on the next hill. See that truck? That's one of my agents, and he's two hundred metres away. He's been recording our conversation.'

Five minutes later Inspector Velásquez arrived carrying a laser microphone, a device which looked to Mendoza like an electric eye, which it resembled. The DIS agent handed Máximo a tape recorder and drove away in his truck. Máximo and the Minister listened to the recording.

Máximo said, 'It picked up the vibrations in your plate glass shield around the pool.'

Shaken, Mendoza said, 'Come inside, Máximo. We must talk about this.'

In Mendoza's apartment the Minister poured himself a brandy while Máximo quenched his thirst with soda water and lime.

Mendoza said, 'What do you have in mind?'

Máximo replied, 'First of all, you have far too many people here, and everyone is a security risk. Everyone. Instead of all these people, you need systems like those we use at DIS. One man operating remote cameras is far more secure than twenty men walking around with rifles. Men get drunk, they go to sleep, they talk, they take bribes. Cameras don't.

'In the second place, you need to use bank transfers to move the money. These flights to Las Vegas must cease. You're too vulnerable.

'Thirdly, you need to distance yourself from the heroin operation. You're going to be President, Alfredo. You'll be in the public spotlight every day. You need to find someone you can trust and put him in charge.'

Mendoza worked his heavy jaw and stared at his secret policeman before he said, 'If anyone else spoke to me like this, I'd shoot him.'

Máximo replied calmly, 'I know, but someone has to tell you.'

The Minister sipped more brandy and said with a chuckle, 'I don't understand you, Máximo Levín. You don't smoke, don't drink, don't swear, don't fuck. I think you don't even eat. You don't do anything a man is supposed to do, but you have more guts than anyone I ever met.'

Máximo tasted his soda water and said, 'We've worked together for twenty years, Alfredo. You should know me by now. My only pleasure is to serve your interests. Without modesty, I'd say I've done my job well. You're a rich man, and now you're going to be President. As you would say, don't fuck it up. Serdán got close, too close, and there will be others. You must take the steps I outlined.'

142

'You say I must put someone in charge. Any suggestions?'

'Yes. Juan Jalapa.'

Frowning, Mendoza asked, 'The Minister of Defence? Why?'

'He's wealthy so he won't steal. He obviously understands security. He knows how to handle the press and the public. He has a grasp of high technology and modern accounting, but most importantly, he's loyal to you. He's demonstrated that many times.'

Mendoza's scowl deepened as he said, 'I'd have to tell him everything. We're not children, Máximo. Very few people can handle this information.'

'Someone must. You can't run this operation from the National Palace. It simply isn't possible.'

'I agree with you in principle, but I reject Jalapa. He's a good man, but no.'

'All right. How about Tomás Molina?'

'The banker? No. Another good man, but I don't know him well enough. Look, forget your list. There's only one man I would trust with my secrets, one man who knows most of them already. You.'

Humbly, Máximo said, 'I anticipated this, *Patrón*, and prepared my answer. When you become President, I hope to become Minister of Petroleum. Heroin is a lucrative business, to be sure, but I thought you might take a greater interest in Pemex. Oil, Alfredo, is far more precious than drugs to many more people.'

Mendoza broke into a fit of laughter, deep giggles that rattled in his throat. Shaking his head with mirth he said, 'You're a mad genius, Máximo. You really are. I don't know what I would do without you. God help me if you should ever turn against me. It has to be you. You can run El Partenón and be Minister of Petroleum. You can't say no.'

'Of course I can say no.'

Mendoza stopped laughing and said, 'Yes, you can, but you won't.'

'Why not?'

'It's a challenge, like any other. You want to install computers. Fine. Do it right. Use your imagination. You can do anything you like. In fact, if you run El Partenón, you'll save me money. You won't spend it on foolish toys.'

'This was not my idea, Alfredo.'

Mendoza laughed again, 'What's the matter? Are you turning squeamish? You work for me. You do what I want you to do. You're the only man I trust with this. You're different from the others, and you'll make no mistakes.'

Máximo made a great show of sighs, looking out of the window and scratching his head. Finally, he said, 'All right, you're correct. I know most of the details of the operation already, but there are a few things I don't know.'

Mendoza poured another brandy and said with genuine happiness, 'You'll do it? You'll take over El Partenón for me?'

'I will. With reluctance. It's the only way I can keep my eye on your best interests.'

Mendoza clapped his hands and slapped his thighs. 'You must have a drink. Just one.'

Rigidly, Máximo declared, 'That I will not do.'

Mendoza grinned and lit a cigar. He smiled broadly and said, 'All right then. You must understand that most of the heroin goes to the United States, and to ship the quantities we handle we must have the co-operation of the gringo authorities. There's a DEA agent named Andrés Obregón with ties to the CIA . . .'

For three hours Mendoza explained to Máximo the details of his heroin operations while the director recorded their conversation. The drug was manufactured high in the mountains in restricted zones protected by the army, and transactions with smugglers took place in the coastal resort towns of Zihuatanejo and Acapulco. Ramón Santiago and his lieutenants supervised the deals and turned freelance smugglers over to the DEA. Only the money moved through El Partenón which was used as a pleasure palace.

By the time Mendoza finished he had drunk enough brandy to intoxicate three men yet remained on his feet. He escorted Máximo through the casino and showed him loaded dice, the crooked roulette wheel and rigged slot machines, saying, 'We bring a smuggler up here, cheat him, cause him to incur debts, and then he works for us for very little. Sometimes, if one does a good job, we let him win. No matter. Everyone has a good time. I let army officers win just enough to keep them in line.

144

The girls are free, and we have boys, too, for the women and men whose tastes run that way.'

Mendoza laughed, 'That's why I go to Las Vegas, to learn humility. I let them cheat me. But you're right, no more, no more. One more shipment of cash, but I'll let Ramón take it.'

'That would be wise, Alfredo.'

Mendoza returned to his Maria, still handcuffed to his bed.

He asked her, 'Did they announce the winning lottery numbers?'

Maria pouted. She said, 'My wrist hurts and my arm's asleep.'

'I asked if they announced the winners?'

'Not yet.'

Mendoza smiled. 'Good,' he said. 'I want to see your eyes when you win.'

Maria's pout changed into a look of amazement. She gasped, 'Can you do that?'

Mendoza puffed himself up to full ministerial stature and announced, 'Shit, girlie, I'm the Chief of Motorcycles. I can do anything.'

Máximo had a team of technicians waiting at the airport. Within the hour electricians and computer specialists began turning El Partenón into an electronic fortress. They installed infrared sensors on the grounds and mounted cameras and microphones in every room.

At midnight Mendoza left for México City by car, reluctantly accepting Máximo's admonition to stay out of his aeroplane.

When he was gone, Máximo walked through El Partenón turning off the lights.

11 SEPTEMBER

16

Airport

A tropical storm washed over Zihuatanejo, ushering in the annual rainy season. In the accounting room of El Partenón Ramón Santiago watched Máximo Levín count out fifty thousand dollars.

Máximo said, 'This is the last flight to Las Vegas, Ramón. The Minister isn't going. I believe Mr Mendoza gives you this amount to squander on each trip. Take it. It's yours. I want you to call as usual when you arrive in Las Vegas.'

'Fifty thousand? That's all? We take millions. This is nothing.'

Ramón hated Máximo for his cultured accent, his wealth and power, and for being a Jew. Things had changed quickly in El Partenón, virtually overnight, and Ramón was upset. Cameras recorded everything, especially activities in the accounting room. The casino was closed, the girls gone, the soldiers replaced by DIS guards in cheap suits.

Máximo said, 'From now on the money will be transferred to Switzerland by wire. If you don't want the fifty thousand, I'll send someone else.'

'I'll take it.'

Ramón stuffed the money into a Louis Vuitton suitcase and descended to a subterranean lounge. In México the bodyguard of a man of consequence has a bodyguard. Ramón had Jesús Platón, who sat at the bar, cleaning and polishing an Uzi.

Ramón barked, 'You ready?'

Jesús grinned, shoved a pair of clips into the pockets of his raincoat, and asked, 'Where's the Chief?'

'He's not coming.'

The two men bent themselves against the rain and crossed the open courtyard to the garage to Ramón's big Mercedes. Ramón tossed the suitcase in the back seat and drove to the airport.

* * *

Mendoza's Gulfstream was parked in the section of the airport reserved for government planes. Painted white with sleek red and green pinstriping, the jet looked like a toy compared to the sinister attack helicopters squatting on the tarmac. Soldiers ringed the runway facing away from the plane, watching for the glint of metal or the flare of a rocket.

Dressed in a mechanic's overall, Inspector Velásquez of the DIS and a camera crew clustered under the belly of one of the helicopters, posing as a repair crew. The Gulfstream's image appeared on a large video monitor in one of the mechanic's diagnostic circuit testers. The pilot and co-pilot were visible in the cockpit.

Máximo had ordered Velásquez to record Ramón getting on Mendoza's plane. Tight as security was around the airport, it was lax around the plane.

As Velásquez watched, a Méxicana service truck appeared from behind a hangar and slowly approached the plane. Wearing a Méxicana jumpsuit, the driver nonchalantly stopped in front of the plane's nose and held up a bottle of Scotch for the pilot to see. He parked the truck and carried a box of supplies up the stairs and into the plane.

Velásquez scratched his chin and shook his head. One of the technicians asked, 'What's going on, Inspector?'

Velásquez said, 'It's nothing. Booze for the boys.'

Andrés Obregón stuck his head into the cockpit, smiled at the pilot and co-pilot and said, 'I've got Scotch, tequila, rum, bourbon, Coca-Cola and limes. Where's the flight attendant?'

'There isn't one on this flight.'

'Okay, I'll just put this stuff away.'

'Hurry up.'

Even the jaded Andrés Obregón was stunned by the opulence of the cabin. Rather than seats, the Minister of Government and his passengers rode on luxurious leather couches. Persian carpets covered the floor and side panels, and a sixty-inch television screen turned the cabin into a theatre for in-flight movies.

Obregón exclaimed loudly, 'So this is Mendoza's plane. Pretty fancy, very nice. Hey! This cabinet door is stuck. Can one of you guys help me?'

Captain Saltillo said to his co-pilot, 'Go see what he wants.'

A moment later the co-pilot emerged from the cockpit, crossed the cabin to the galley, and asked, 'What's the trouble?'

When he saw no one he frowned and asked, 'Where are you?'

The barrel of a silenced .22 calibre automatic pistol peeked out from behind the lavatory door, and Obregón shot the co-pilot in the back of the neck. The gun made a quiet pop, and the man collapsed on the galley floor.

Obregón shoved the corpse into the lavatory, put on the co-pilot's hat and jacket, and entered the cockpit.

The pilot kept his eyes on his instruments and asked, 'Everything all right, Eugenio . . .?'

He looked up straight into Obregón's pistol. 'Who the . . .?'

Obregón put his finger to his lips and said, 'I can fly this aircraft, and therefore do not need you. You will do exactly as I say or you will die. Do you believe me?'

The pilot looked at the silenced automatic. The elongated barrel loomed huge and lethal in his eyes. He noticed the fresh manicure on the fingernail gripping the trigger.

Without looking at Obregón's face, he said, 'I believe you.'

'Good. Have you turned on the flight recorder?'

'Yes.'

'Turn it off.'

The pilot complied.

'Are you armed?'

'No, but there are weapons on board.'

'You won't need them.'

Obregón looked at his watch, 'How soon do you expect Mendoza?'

The pilot replied, 'The Minister is not coming. Only his bodyguards.'

Obregón considered this information and asked, 'With the money?'

'As far as I know.'

'You'd better be right.'

Velásquez could see two men in the cockpit of the plane. On the far side of the tarmac the Mercedes appeared.

Ramón's voice crackled in the pilot's earphones.

'Fire that sucker up, Saltillo.'

151

The pilot started his engines and the sweet whine of jet turbines filled the air.

Jesús climbed out of the car, scanned the tarmac and peered around the corner of the hangar. Ramón got out with the suitcase, and they walked the hundred yards to the plane. Ramón could see a bottle of Scotch waiting in the luxurious interior.

Jesús carried his Uzi with safety on and muzzle pointed at the ground. As they climbed the stairs, Ramón spoke glowingly about the casinos in Las Vegas and the looks on the women's faces when you threw hundred-dollar bills onto the roulette table.

Jesús, then Ramón, stepped into the plane. Ramón winked at the pilot through the open hatchway to the cockpit, and yelled, 'Let's go!'

Jesús set his Uzi on the bar, looked around, and complained, 'How come there ain't no stewardess?'

Ramón laughed. 'On the way back you can have as many as you like. We can watch tapes, pretty good home movies. You like girls named Maria?'

Jesús said, 'I like girls named anything, even better if they don't have no name.'

Both men started to remove their raincoats, momentarily pinning their arms. Obregón stepped out of the cockpit and stood face to face with Jesús, who hesitated, then reached for his machine-pistol. Ramón blinked, confused, thinking of his body armour. With deadly precision Obregón shot Jesús in the throat, and the Uzi clattered onto the bar.

Ramón grappled for his pistol too late, his face obliterated by three rapid shots.

Captain Saltillo had never seen human beings shot at such close range. His face turned white and he started to hyperventilate. Obregón pushed him into his seat and poured a double shot of Scotch.

The highjacker said, 'Drink this and fly us out of here, just like you always. Do it!'

The pilot swallowed the whisky, coughed and nodded. He began talking to the tower and the plane moved.

Obregón saw the core of fear behind the man's eyes. The plane taxied toward the runway.

* * *

152

Velásquez stared across the tarmac at the empty service truck. 'Damn!' he exclaimed. 'The service guy never got off the plane.'

He called the tower and shouted, 'Stop the Minister's plane!'

The air traffic controller responded, 'Who the hell are you? What are you doing on this frequency?'

'DIS! Order the pilot to remain on the ground.'

Saltillo heard the command come over the radio, 'This is Zihuatanejo air traffic control. You are not cleared for take-off. Please return to service area.'

The pilot hesitated.

Obregón asked, 'What's the matter?'

'Nothing.'

'Go,' commanded the Cuban. 'Fly or die.'

Saltillo took a deep breath, pushed the throttles forward and took off. The plane quickly rose over the Pacific and headed out to sea.

Unnerved, shaking with fear, the pilot asked, 'Where are we going?'

Obregón gave him the co-ordinates of an abandoned DEA airfield one hundred miles north-west in the high desert of Michoacan.

With a halt in his voice, the pilot asked, 'And then?'

'I might as well tell you, I intended to kill you after we landed, but I have a better idea,' said the Cuban. 'How much is usually in that suitcase?'

Sweating, feeling sick to his stomach, the pilot answered, 'Four, five million dollars.'

Obregón said, 'I want Mendoza to think dear Ramón and you stole his money. You're the lucky one. I'm going to give you a hundred thousand dollars and send you on your way. You can do what you like, take the money back to Mendoza, tell him what happened and take your chances. You can disappear. In any case you will leave a trail that will lend credence to my programme of disinformation.'

'A hundred thousand?'

'What's the matter, shithead? Not enough? Shut up and fly.'

Obregón returned to the cockpit to open the suitcase.

* * *

153

Inspector Velásquez immediately called Máximo in El Partenón. Shaken by the unexpected turn of events, Velásquez said, 'Director, a man in a Méxicana service uniform got on the plane before Ramón, and he was on the plane when it took off. I called the tower and tried to halt the plane, but the pilot took off anyway.'

'Did you recognize him?'

'No, sir. None of us knew who he was.'

'Were you taping?'

'Yes, sir.'

'Bring the tape here as quickly as possible.'

Máximo called the control tower at the airport, identified himself, and asked the air traffic controller, 'Do you have the Minister's plane on radar?'

'No, sir. He wasn't following his flight plan when he took off. He must be flying at low altitude.'

'Do you have an Air Force squadron nearby?'

'Only helicopters and they'll never catch him. The closest fighter squadron is in México City.'

'How much fuel does he have?'

'He has a range of two thousand five hundred miles, enough to reach Las Vegas with a reserve. Should I notify the Air Force?'

'No. Not yet. Our conversation is confidential. Keep it to yourself.'

'Yes, sir.'

'If you hear from the pilot, notify me immediately. That's an order.'

Twenty minutes later Velásquez arrived with the videotape. Máximo put the two-inch professional quality tape into a playback machine and quickly fastforwarded to the arrival of the service truck at the plane. He reduced the speed to single frame slow motion. After a moment, the face of Andrés Obregón filled the screen.

Uncharacteristically, Máximo swore. Softly, he said, 'Damn.'

Velásquez asked, 'Do you know who it is?'

Máximo nodded and replied, 'Yes. Listen, Velásquez, get your crew in here and keep them here. No one, especially Mendoza, must know of this.'

'Yes, sir.'

Velásquez moved slowly toward the door, a quizzical expression on his face.

Máximo said, 'It's Andrés Obregón from the CIA.'

Velásquez said, 'Oh, shit.'

Máximo agreed. 'My sentiments exactly.'

17

Bad Guys, Worse Guys

A hundred miles west of México City Fred Lowry parked his Buick in an abandoned field and waited. Precisely on time, a civilian helicopter from a charter service in Guadalajara landed. Carrying a buff aluminium case, Lowry ran to the chopper, climbed in, and put on a headset.

'Mr North?' queried the pilot.

'Yes.'

'Can I see some ID?'

Lowry presented credentials which identified him as a vice-president of Ford of México.

'Okay,' said the pilot. 'Where to?'

Lowry handed him a flight plan and ten thousand dollars, and said, 'Stay off the radio.'

'It's none of my business,' said the pilot. 'But what's going on?'

'Industrial espionage.'

For fifteen minutes Mendoza's jet swept up the west coast of México at an altitude of three hundred feet, then banked inland south of Manzanillo.

Built on a plateau in the foothills of the Sierra three miles from the village of Aguililla, the abandoned DEA landing strip had not been graded for two years. As the Gulfstream approached the plateau, Obregón radioed a brief message, and two lines of bright blue lights popped up from the surrounding hills.

The jet touched down hard on the packed gravel, blew one

rear tyre, skidded part way round to the right, and came to a stop. The blue lights faded into the darkness.

Sitting in the helicopter, an elated Fred Lowry could scarcely believe his eyes when the plane appeared in the starlit western sky. He had convinced himself that Obregón was going to take the plane and money and disappear.

At first he thought the plane would crash, but it slid to a stop and the engines wound down to silence. The snap and pop of cooling metal rang out clearly in the night air.

He swore at the blown tyre.

The helicopter pilot said, 'Jesus, that's a government jet.'

'You're very observant,' said Lowry, and shot him twice in the chest. He reached across the body, opened the hatch and pushed the dead pilot onto the ground.

In the cockpit of the Gulfstream Obregón said to Captain Saltillo, 'Well done. I congratulate you. Tell me, Captain, what are you going to do with the money?'

Saltillo blinked several times, grateful to be alive, then answered, 'What concerns me is my family. The moment Mendoza realizes what has happened, he'll take them as hostages.'

'I see,' said Obregón. 'That would be a concern.'

The Cuban stood up from the co-pilot's seat, moved toward the cabin, pointed his pistol at the back of the pilot's neck, and pulled the trigger.

To Saltillo's corpse he said, 'I lied. I can't even fly a paper plane.'

He pushed the body out of his way, released the pressure locks and opened the hatch.

Walking toward the plane, Lowry heard the muffled pop of a silenced pistol. He ducked under the fuselage, pulled out his gun and waited. After a moment, the cabin door opened but no staircase descended to the ground.

Lowry called out softly, 'Andrés?'

The answer came in the form of an entire clipful of nine millimetre bullets tearing up the ground.

Lowry yelled, 'What the fuck is going on in there?'

Obregón shouted, 'Put your hands on your head and come out where I can see you.'

Lowry shouted back, 'No way. Not until you tell me what's happening in there.'

In a normal voice, Obregón asked, 'No goblins out there, are there, Fred?'

'No, I'm alone.'

'Where's the chopper pilot?'

'Dead.'

'I have a problem,' said the Cuban matter-of-factly. 'This was an interesting flight, but there was no Mendoza.'

Then Obregón screamed, 'And no money!'

Lowry, who had been holding his breath, let it all out in one long whoosh. Breathlessly, he asked, 'Are you shitting me?'

'Ramón had fifty thousand dollars on him. What the fuck is going on, Fred?'

'Jesus Christ,' Lowry said, feeling his life begin to crumble like a burnt match. 'Jesus Christ.'

Obregón said, 'I'm coming down.'

Servos lowered the staircase. In a state of shock, Lowry inched forward to see the inside of the blood-spattered cabin. Obregón popped open the pilot's wing window escape hatch, slid down to the ground and surprised Lowry from behind.

The Cuban whispered, 'Drop the pistol and put your hands on your head.'

Lowry let out an audible sigh of frustration and let his gun fall to the ground. Obregón took his finger off the trigger of the Uzi and picked up Lowry's gun.

Lowry thought Obregón was going to shoot him. For a crazed moment he considered attacking the Cuban the way ancient Romans ran on their swords. No Mendoza, no money, only shit deeper than he had thought possible.

Obregón said, 'You can put your hands down now.'

Mosquitoes began to attack the two sweating men.

Obregón said, 'This is really fucked, Fred. If I didn't need you to fly us out of here, I'd blow you away.'

Hollowly, Lowry asked, 'Why wasn't Mendoza on the plane?'

Obregón shook his head and answered, 'How the hell do I know?'

'Do you think he suspected a set-up?'

'That's a stupid fucking question if I ever heard one. The real question is who?'

157

Lowry said, 'He's going to be one very pissed off Minister of Government.'

'Yeah,' said Obregón. 'Brilliant deduction, unless he's laughing himself silly.'

Lowry asked, 'Is the pilot alive?'

'Hell no.'

Lowry sputtered, 'I told you to leave him alive. Shit. What else can go wrong? I was going to blow the plane in the air.'

'Too bad. Blow it on the ground.'

In the forest half a mile from the landing strip two woodcutters from Aguililla had watched in awed silence as the helicopter, then the plane had landed on the deserted airstrip. They heard the machine-gun and saw men walking around on the ground.

'Juan, let's get out of here. We must tell the police.'

'Wait, Pedro. Let's see what happens.'

'You heard the gunfire. You wait. No planes have been here for a year, and when they did come, it was always bad men, dangerous men. Now, they're back. Let's go.'

Lowry positioned himself a hundred yards behind the plane, aimed at the warm engine in the tail, and fired the Stinger. The plane exploded like a balloon. Pieces of burning fuselage bounded into the woods.

In terror, the woodcutters rushed into the safety of the woods. Three hours passed before they returned to their village and woke up the local policeman.

Lowry silently cursed himself for letting the Cuban get the drop on him. Beno had been right, he had turned old and sloppy. He had intended to kill Obregón who now was more of a liability than ever. Butch and Sundance, botched heist, good God.

As they flew south-east in the noisy helicopter Lowry said over the intercom, 'I want you out of the country tonight.'

'Forget it,' answered Obregón. 'I expected to walk away from this with millions. For that, I would have left everything behind, but not now. No way.'

'One phone call to Bonmarche and you're gone, Andrés.'

'Listen to me, Mr CIA hot shit, fuck with me and I'll kill you,

you motherfucker. I'll call Langley and blow the whistle on you.'

'They'll laugh at you.'

'Wanna try me?'

Below, the dark shapes of the Sierra gave way to the scattered lights of the bajio plain. Lowry concentrated on manipulating the controls as his mind struggled for coherence. Al Mears could accept an ill-conceived mission, but he had no tolerance for loose ends. Station chiefs were not authorized to go into the field. The agency was not to be directly involved. Personal gain was not supposed to be part of the picture.

Lowry said, 'Blowing the whistle on me cuts your own throat, Andrés.'

Obregón ranted, 'I'm not a station chief. I can go back to Cuba if I have to. I can disappear into the Amazon. You can't. You have a wife and kids, and if you think they're safe in the States, think again. If I can get onto Mendoza's plane, I can get to your family.'

'So what are you going to do, Andrés?'

'The world is supposed to believe Lucio Serdán did this, right? You're going to plant the story with the media, right? You aren't going to fuck up that part, right?'

'Right. Everything's in place.'

Obregón said, 'Good. You go back to México City and I go back to Acapulco. We do our jobs and act surprised when we pick up the papers tomorrow and learn that Serdán blew up Mendoza's plane with a Stinger. And I wait around until you figure out how to keep me quiet. I'm talking money, Fred, a hot million. You got that? You have a week. Some time in that week you're going to waste Mr Beno Alvarado. He's one guy who will figure this out. He'll get to Serdán and Serdán will say it wasn't him. You with me?'

'What about Mendoza?'

'I don't care about Mendoza. That's agency bullshit. I'm your problem now, asshole. You fucking CIA idiots haven't learned shit since the Bay of Pigs. You didn't learn shit from the Contras.'

They went back and forth, bitching and puling at one another until Lowry landed the helicopter on the deserted field where he had picked it up. He tossed an incendiary grenade into the engine compartment and destroyed the aircraft.

They argued all the way to México City.

As dawn illuminated the twin volcanic peaks that watched over México City, a rain shower sprinkled the capital. White garbage trucks collected bounty for the *damnificados*. The whores went home to the *colonias perdidas*, and the motorcycle patrols began their daily rounds. Downtown, beggars stirred from their doorways and took up stations in the subway.

Lowry dropped Obregón at a cabstand in Coyoacán. The Cuban took the fifty thousand, got into a cab and blended into the morning commuters.

Lowry drove home. With his wife and children already in Virginia, no one occupied the Lowry house except a maid who woke up and found Lowry sitting in the kitchen with a large vodka and lime. He told her to close the house in the morning. He would be gone.

Lowry knew Obregón had been right about Beno Alvarado. Beno would learn what had happened and come after him. If he didn't, Obregón would. Within the hour Lowry had moved out of his house and taken up residence in his embassy office. He told the duty officer that he disliked living in an empty house and that he intended to sleep in his office until his tenure was up.

Mendoza owned a house in Las Vegas. At eleven the next morning Ramón had been instructed to call Mendoza in México City and announce his safe arrival in Nevada.

At eleven-fifteen Mendoza began to pace around his official residence in Las Lomas de Chapultepec. Considerably smaller than El Partenón, the house still dwarfed its less imposing neighbours.

At eleven-thirty the Minister phoned Máximo at El Partenón and directed him to call Las Vegas.

Ten minutes later Máximo called back and declared, 'Ramón never arrived.'

Mendoza exploded, 'What do you mean? Check the Las Vegas airport and see if the plane landed.'

'I already talked to them,' said Máximo. 'The American

160

authorities say the plane never entered US air space. It disappeared.'

'Find the plane, Máximo, and find Serdán. He did this. I can feel it in my blood.'

12 SEPTEMBER

18

Glorieta

The embassy operator said, 'Mr Lowry, the Director of the DIS is on the line.'

Surrounded by his maps, Lowry picked up the phone and said, 'Yes, Dr Levín, what can I do for you?'

'Good morning, Mr Lowry. I have a matter to discuss if you could stop by the Directorate.'

'I'm on my way.'

Lowry showered, shaved, changed into a fresh suit, and popped a dexedrine. He snared one of the Marines from the embassy detachment and ordered the soldier to drive him across town. For the duration of the ride, Lowry watched the rear view window, scanning the traffic.

Máximo awaited the CIA station chief in his seventh-floor office in DIS headquarters. In the sunlight he could look down on the Plaza of Three Cultures and see the clearly defined pits in the paving stones, indentations left by .50 calibre machine-gun bullets in 1968 when the army slaughtered hundreds of demonstrating students a week before the opening of the Olympic Games. The pain and sorrow of that day never left him.

On this day his fury with the American plot to kill Mendoza had resolved into a ruthless scheme. The Americans had interfered with his plan to depose Mendoza, and that he would not allow to pass without retribution.

His telephone rang.

'Velásquez here, Director. I'm calling from Michoacan. The plane has been found, destroyed on the ground by rocket fire. Two villagers witnessed the explosion and said a helicopter took off shortly afterward.'

'Thank you, Inspector. Get a forensic team up there.'

'They're on their way.'

'Try to get a description of the helicopter.'

'Yes, sir. The men are being questioned now, but I don't think they'll be able to tell us much more.'

'Do your best. Thank you.'

So. Obregón had an accomplice, possibly Beno Alvarado.

The phone rang again.

'Mr Lowry from the American embassy is here to see you.'

'Send him up.'

Máximo cordially greeted Lowry and offered the American a comfortable chair. The Méxican said, 'I have a delicate matter to discuss, Mr Lowry. Last night the plane of the Minister of Government was attacked. We believe this episode was an attempt on Mendoza's life, but fortunately he wasn't on the plane. We have information that Lucio Serdán was in possession of anti-aircraft weapons.'

Lowry's expression showed alarm. He said, 'This sounds serious, Director. We also have a confirmed report that Serdán has acquired one or more Stingers.'

Máximo said, 'We're releasing a report to the media that Serdán attacked Mendoza's plane. I have informed the Minister and the President that Serdán is responsible, but,' Máximo paused, took a sip of iced water, and continued, 'we know the plane was highjacked and destroyed by Andrés Obregón.'

Lowry didn't have to feign surprise. An agonizing pain gripped his belly, and for a brief moment he thought he was going to vomit.

Máximo said, 'I know this must be a shock. Are you all right?'

Lowry said, 'Obregón? Holy Jesus, he's one of ours, or rather I should say, he belongs to DEA. Are you positive it was Obregón? Did you see him?'

Máximo answered, 'We have him on videotape.'

A moment later Lowry was staring at a freeze-frame image of Obregón's face. Fear settled in his stomach like an insoluble mineral. He asked, 'How did you come by this tape?'

Máximo answered smoothly, 'An Air Force maintenance crew was working on a helicopter nearby, conducting a training seminar. The tape machine was rolling. It was a lucky coincidence.'

Lowry twisted his eyes away from the screen to regard Máximo Levín. The Director didn't look like a secret policeman, but rather a university professor whose elegant manners disguised a mind sharp as a guillotine.

Máximo inquired, 'Are you quite sure you're all right?'

Shaking his head, Lowry replied, 'I'm looking at one of our people who's turned into a loose cannon. It's embarrassing, to say the least. Who do you think he's working for?'

The Director sipped more iced water and said, 'Probably himself. This man Obregón is a scorpion, a deadly nuisance. Mendoza's security is my responsibility, and I consider this attack a personal affront. I appeal to you, Mr Lowry. If your agency can help me find him, quietly of course, I will be profoundly grateful for any assistance. We're keeping this under wraps. Neither the President nor Mendoza knows of this. Should word leak out, we would have an international incident on our hands. As you say, Obregón is one of yours. If you eliminate him, and his accomplice, the matter can be closed before Obregón can make another attempt on the life of the next president of México.'

Lowry asked, 'Why do you think Obregón wanted to assassinate Mendoza?'

'I was about to ask you the same question,' Máximo replied. 'Great quantities of South American cocaine move through México, and the Ministry of Government has the responsibility of stopping this traffic in narcotics. Obregón may have been corrupted by smugglers. This is simply conjecture on my part, but clearly, since Obregón works for the DEA, drugs must play a role in this affair. As you know, vicious rumours surround the Minister and his alleged involvement in the drug trade. This may have been a misguided attempt by Obregón to exact retribution on Mr Mendoza. There are myriad possibilities. We won't know until we question Obregón. If he dies, we may never know, but I would not object to forgoing that knowledge.'

Lowry said, 'Well, I'm more than happy to co-operate. I'm pleased to have the opportunity to get my own house in order. I'll find him.'

Máximo smiled. 'I'm glad you see it that way. I knew I could count on you. Naturally, we'll keep this between ourselves.'

'Of course.'

'Would you like a copy of the videotape? It may assist you in your search.'

* * *

167

Lowry rode back to the embassy certain that he was being followed. He sensed that Máximo Levín knew more than he had said, but he had no doubt that the Director wanted Obregón dead. Mentally, he kicked himself for having lost the opportunity to kill the Cuban on the airfield in Michoacan.

Sam Black saw red lights flash in her rear view mirror and pulled her Avis Plymouth to the kerb. She cursed, first in English, then in Spanish, then looked up at the golden wings of the Angel of Independence, wishing she could fly away. As the early morning México City traffic spun around the *glorieta*, a traffic roundabout with the Angel in the centre, half the male drivers seemed to be whistling and waving at her.

The motorcycle cop took his time. Not often did he have the opportunity to stop a beautiful, red-haired tourist on the Paseo de la Reforma a block from the American embassy. The DIS wanted this car stopped right here, and his job was not to ask questions. He had the licence plate number, a description of the car and driver, and orders to hold her for ten minutes.

The cop sat on his bike watching Sam through the rear window as she fiddled in her purse. Tourists never knew how to offer a bribe. Most offered nothing, the rest too much or too little. With this one, well, all he really wanted was to look at her, delay her transit across the city, then let her go.

Sam had committed no traffic offence. For a brief moment she considered pulling her diplomatic passport from her purse and unloading on the cop, but CIA policy was never to pull rank except in an emergency. Instead, she retrieved an ordinary passport, a valid tourist card and a California driver's licence and pulled her dark glasses over her eyes.

The cop barely noticed the legless beggar who suddenly appeared sitting on his wide skateboard on the pavement next to the car. Sam never saw him. Wrapped in a filthy *sarape*, the man started bouncing a cracked rubber ball on the pavement. The ball got away and rolled under the rear wheel of the car. The beggar quickly retrieved it and resumed his demented game.

The cop advanced to the driver's side window and said, 'Good morning, Miss.'

168

To his surprise she responded in Spanish. 'It was good, but you just ruined it.'

He frowned and snapped, 'Papers.'

She handed them over and he studied them. Without looking at her he said, 'You were speeding.'

Inside the passport he found a five-thousand peso note and palmed it. For a moment they stared at each other through dark glasses, his flat black wrap-arounds, hers polarized Vuarnets. He grinned. She wrinkled her nose. He handed back her documents and without another word climbed onto his bike and roared away.

She thought, five thousand pesos, two bucks. Half goes to his chief, half of that to his chief, and so on up the pyramid until, she figured, she had just contributed one hundred pesos to the welfare of Alfredo Mendoza. What a lovely way to start the day.

She drove to the embassy and circled around to the garage.

'I was stopped by the police,' she said to the guard. 'Check the car.'

A mechanic crawled under the frame and popped back out holding a miniature transmitter.

'Fourth one today,' he said. 'We're making a lot of new friends.'

Inside the building the windowless offices of the CIA, the DEA, and the defence and legal attachés occupied a fortress within a fortress. An inner core of steel and lead protected the spies from assault, radiation, bio-chemical warfare and electronic espionage. Of late Sam had found it depressing, not because of the paranoid construction, but because the winding down of the cold war had stripped away the main purpose of the intelligence agencies.

Her office was in the secure documents room on the second floor. To get there she passed through three security checkpoints. At the last checkpoint her right thumb and the retina of her left eye were checked against official records before she was allowed to pass into the inner sanctum of México station.

Sam wore little make-up. As she walked through the maximum security area the fluorescent lighting treated her

169

less harshly than the women who sweated under layers of cosmetics.

Even in a gabardine business suit, her hair pulled back in a knot and tortoiseshell glasses perched on a button nose, Sam turned heads. As the guard twisted his neck to read her security badge, his eyes lingered on her chest.

'May I pass?' she asked.

'Of course. Excuse me, Ms Black.'

'Thank you.'

Fred Lowry was waiting in her office, appearing slightly dishevelled, as if he had passed a night without sleep.

Lowry sucked in his breath and said, 'I want you to go back to Zihuatanejo and give Beno Alvarado a critical assignment. I'm going to clear you to access some classified information. Sign this form.'

She signed. Lowry showed her the videotape given him by Máximo Levín, gave her instructions for Beno and sent her to the airport.

At the Méxicana counter she learned that the Zihuatanejo airport was closed. She had to fly to Acapulco and drive one hundred and twenty miles.

19

Elizalde

That morning Beno woke up in his house in Zihuatanejo. His bedroom window framed the green dome of the distant Sierra under a sky blue as a leaping sailfish. He smelled coffee and flowers and stretched with pleasure as the exotic olfactory onslaught of old México ravished his nose.

Suddenly he was completely awake. Coffee? When he had fallen asleep, the house had been empty. He blinked several times, grabbed a revolver from the nightstand, and crept down the stairs to the living room.

Someone stirred in the kitchen. Beno was halfway to the

kitchen door when a voice said politely, 'Put on your pants, Mr Alvarado, then join me for coffee.'

Beno recognized the mild baritone of Alonzo Elizalde, the local representative of the DIS.

'Mr Elizalde?'

'At your service.'

'I'll be with you in a moment.'

Beno returned upstairs and dressed in jeans, huaraches and a flowery Hawaiian shirt. He felt no animosity toward Mr Elizalde. The DIS was not required to respect his rights. He had none.

Beno walked into the kitchen. The morning was hot, but Elizalde wore a dark suit, white shirt, skinny tie and ultrablack sunglasses. At least the shades made sense.

The thin, frail looking DIS man said, 'I wished to be discreet, and your door was open.'

Beno poured himself a cup of coffee and let Elizalde spike it with a healthy dose of El Presidente brandy.

'How are you today, Mr Alvarado? Hungover, I hope.'

Beno swallowed a mouthful of coffee, smiled coldly and said, 'I wasn't expecting a guest, or I would have fixed breakfast.'

The DIS man sipped his brandy and said, 'You've been here in Zihuatanejo a long time, almost two years.'

Beno sat down, prepared for a siege. A polite Méxican never came directly to the point, and Elizalde would not be rushed.

Beno replied, 'I feel at home here. It suits me.'

'You like the countryside as well, no?'

'Sure.'

'You like to drive around in your old VW bus, talk to farmers and villagers?'

'I do. I get tired of sophisticated people with all the answers. Simple country people see things more clearly.'

'Ah, yes, perhaps. Perhaps they do, but rural México is passing away, don't you find? We are an urban nation now. México City is the largest city in the world.'

Beno smiled and said, 'That's why I live here. Not too many people, no pollution, clean air and water.'

Elizalde nodded his head in sympathy and said, 'Yes, it's tranquil here, except for the tourists.'

Elizalde pushed his glasses onto his forehead, looked directly at Beno and said, 'You've spent considerable time in the countryside asking farmers and villagers about Lucio Serdán.'

Beno nodded and allowed he had been doing just that.

Elizalde said, 'You understand, I must report your activities to the head of the Directorate, Dr Máximo Levín.'

'Certainly.'

'I have observed you some considerable time now, Mr Alvarado. Tell me, why are you so interested in Lucio Serdán?'

Beno leaned back in his chair and said, 'The people sing songs about him in the cantinas. His picture is on posters which are torn down as soon as they are plastered on the walls. You know what I am, Mr Elizalde. I must determine whether Lucio Serdán poses a threat to the security of the United States.'

'And your conclusion?'

'At the moment, his guerrilla army is very small. If it continues to grow, he might possibly threaten the stability of México, and a stable México is in the interest of the United States.'

Elizalde removed his sunglasses and said, 'It seems that he's trying to do precisely that.'

The DIS man unfolded the front page of *El Sol*, a major México City daily. A huge photograph showed a small jet in ruins on the ground.

A banner headline screamed, 'Notorious Communist Bandit Lucio Serdán claims attack on government plane.'

The secondary headline read, 'Minister of Government's plane destroyed in terrorist attack. Mendoza safe.'

Beno read the headlines and blinked. Serdán missed. Oh shit. Beno forced himself to grin and said, 'Mendoza's a lucky man.'

Elizalde stated, 'I think you should revise your opinion of Lucio Serdán.'

Beno grabbed the brandy bottle, filled his coffee cup and drank deeply. He asked, 'May I keep that paper?'

'Of course.'

Elizalde stood and asked, 'You were here last night, were you not?'

'I most surely was.'

'Well, I must be going. Good morning, Mr Alvarado.'

'Good morning, Mr Elizalde.'

20

Zihuatanejo

Every day Beno drove into town to the *Playa Municipal*, the city beach, to take his coffee at his favourite café and have his boots shined. Made to measure, Beno's boots were crafted of good Cordovan leather, pigskin dyed a deep burgundy, and shaped with narrow, square toes and modestly raked Andalusian heels. High on the outside of each boot the cobbler had stitched in the silhouette of a tiny green bird in full flight, a hummingbird.

Just for fun, Beno played a game with the shoeshine boys, urchins who clustered near the beach, pestering every adult male with an ubiquitous, English, 'Shine, mister?'

By Beno's count, there were forty-three ways to approach the beach, and he paid double to any kid who spotted him before he reached one of the benches in the little square that opened onto the *embarcadero*.

This afternoon he circled behind the municipal palace and approached the square from the direction of the public market. Elizalde's news had spoiled his morning, and his heart thumped sadly in his chest. His time in México was over. Mendoza lived, and México lurched toward chaos and revolution. Beno wanted to be far away. Costa Rica, France, Jamaica, somewhere he would find a new life.

He walked to the beach and scanned the square. In front of the faded pink municipal palace two policemen watched for pickpockets. Mr Elizalde's black Ford was parked in front of the palace. A fruit juice vendor waved flies away from his brightly coloured jars of sugar water. A handful of tourists were drinking at the Mother Lode, the least expensive of the cafés. Across the square, the shoeshine boys congregated in front of the Farolito, Beno's favourite café.

He strolled slowly toward the café, watching the boys. One barefoot youngster broke from the pack and raced toward him, lugging his shoeshine pack and wad of rags. His rapid movement

173

agitated a flock of birds perched in the trees, and hundreds of sparrows suddenly took flight, wheeled around the municipal palace and returned toward the plaza on a kamikaze flight path.

The breathless shoeshine boy stood grinning before Beno.

'Shine, Mister?'

Beno didn't hear him. When the boy had started to run, the other bootblacks had moved away from the Farolito, clearing the view of the café terrace, and Beno saw Sam Black sitting at a corner table. Her dark red hair spilled over her shoulders and the straps of a simple white dress.

'Shine, mister?'

Beno fished in his pockets for 2000 pesos. 'Not today, son.' He gave the boy the banknote and said, 'I'll look for you tomorrow. Okay?'

'Sure, mister. Tomorrow you find me.'

Under the cloudless sky, Beno studied the square. If Sam had company, it wasn't obvious, but the plaza, as always, sprouted numerous strangers.

'Hey, *chico*,' Beno called to the shoeshine boy. 'See the lady with red hair at the Farolito?'

'Pretty lady.'

'Did you see her arrive?'

'Sure.'

'She come alone?'

'I didn't see nobody else.'

'Okay, you go tell her to come over here.'

He gave the boy another 2000 pesos.

Beno slipped into a waiting taxi, handed a small banknote to the driver and said, 'Start the engine and wait.'

The silent driver nodded his head. Beno watched the boy approach Sam, speak to her and point across the square. As she walked through the plaza, several heads turned to stare, but no one moved to follow. Beno let her walk past the taxi while he eyed the square until convinced she was alone. He dismissed the driver, stepped out of the cab and stood behind her.

Her white cotton knee-length dress flowed like a sheet over her hips. Her feet were wrapped in romanesque sandals with straps that wound halfway up her calves.

Beno whispered, 'Bang bang, dirty imperialist swine.'

Sam whirled, and grinned, 'You bastard.'

174

His boots added two inches to his six-foot stature, his Panama another two. He wore jeans and a red checked cotton shirt.

He asked, 'You come to pass a quiet morning in the plaza? Maybe cop some dope from a retrograde hippie?'

'Very funny, Beno.'

'I don't think you came to Zihuatanejo to improve your tan.'

Hands on her hips, Sam demanded, 'Are we going to stand out here on the street and be clever, or can we go some place and talk?'

Beno took her elbow in a firm grasp and escorted her into the roofed public market, past stalls piled high with mangoes, papayas and limes, to a *liquadora*, a juice stand. The building hummed and buzzed, a quiet cacophony of flies, Waring blenders and civilized commerce. Short, almond-eyed Indian women stole sly glances at the gringo queen.

They sat on stools and Beno ordered two alfalfas.

Sam looked around and said, 'We can't talk here, Beno.'

'Yes, we can, and you'll say enough for me to decide if I want to hear the rest. Let me guess. You're here because all the Russians in México City are going home and you're out of work. Lowry gave you notice and you want to rusticate in quiet Zihuatanejo. No?'

Sam said, 'I'm scared to death. I thought you might shoot me on sight.'

'I still might,' Beno said with a chill in his voice. 'You've violated every security rule in the book. Not the agency book, my book.'

Sam acknowledged this statement with a nod and said, 'I know. This is nasty business, Beno, the worst.'

Beno sighed sadly and said, 'Whatever it is, it doesn't concern me. I'm *hors de combat*, as they used to say. I think Fred Lowry is a bigger asshole than ever, but, fuck it. I know you're just the messenger. It's not your fault.'

Sam took a deep breath and asked, 'Do you have a VCR?'

'Why?'

'I want you to see a tape.'

Beno smiled sadly and said, 'Is this an assignment from Fred?'

'I suppose it is. Yes.'

Beno said, 'Go away. You're an illusion, a fantasy. You're not

175

here. I never saw you. Drink your alfalfa juice and go back to México City.'

'Orders, Beno. I'm supposed to show it to you.'

Turning to face her, his eyes black embers, he asked, 'Why don't I trust you?'

'You don't trust anyone.'

Beno said, 'I'm selling my house and leaving town. If the airport weren't closed, I'd leave today.'

Sam said, 'Let me do my job, Beno. Let me show you the tape and report back that you saw it. Please.'

Beno guzzled his juice, winked at Sam and said, 'Okay. I guess I've been bored sitting around this town hustling tourist ladies and meditating on my sins. Let's go.'

Beno's house nestled behind a whitewashed adobe wall, invisible from the street except for a small satellite dish on the roof. The brick patio led to a stone porch whose french windows gave way to a comfortable living room. In one corner a heavy oak colonial desk was piled high with papers and books. A 27-inch Sony monitor dominated one wall faced by an array of chairs and benches. Beer cans and ashtrays made a mess of the impromptu theatre.

Beno waved at the residue and said, 'Last night was Monday Night Football, and a few of the boys were over.'

Sam asked, 'Who are the boys?'

'A mixed lot. The usual ex-patriots, midget bandits and outlaws, dopers pretending to be artistes. One guy owns a bar. One guy's a real writer, science fiction best sellers, but I'm the only one who knows because he writes under a fake name.'

'Sounds like a nice life, Beno.'

'It was.'

Sam sauntered over to the busy, crowded desk and examined the pile of books and manuscripts, and the rattletrap Adler typewriter. She glanced over the titles, most of which were in Spanish. *The History of Guerrilla Warfare in Western México. The CIA in México. The Hummingbird and the Hawk. The Massacre at Tlatelolco, México City, 2 October 1968.*

'Writing your memoirs?' she asked, adding, 'You can't do that without permission, you know.'

Testily, Beno snapped, 'I know the regulations. Now, cut the crap. I could've left you sitting in the café by the plaza. This better be good.'

She opened her bag and handed him a videotape. Beno shoved the VHS cassette into the machine, turned on the television, and sat down in a front row seat to watch the show.

21

Refusal

When the brief tape ended with white snow on the screen, Beno was certain that Obregón had been Laluce's mysterious Cuban, José.

He shut off the machine and said to Sam, 'Okay, tell me what Lowry said this tape is supposed to be.'

Sam recited, 'A highjack. Obregón thought Mendoza was going to be on the plane, but he wasn't. According to Máximo Levín, this was an assassination attempt that went wrong. Lowry wants you to find Obregón and terminate him.'

Beno smiled sardonically. 'I love that word, terminate. It's only used by people who don't kill people.'

'I'm just a messenger, Beno. Lowry's word and Lowry's orders.'

Beno scoffed, 'He's ordering me to murder Andrés Obregón. How sweet. Where did Lowry get this tape?'

Sam replied, 'From the DIS. Máximo Levín gave it to him personally.'

Beno rewound the tape, removed the cassette from the machine and replaced the previous night's football game.

He returned the cassette to Sam, saying, 'All I saw was Andrés Obregón in a Méxicana jumpsuit getting on a plane. Then two guys get on and the plane flies away.'

Sam insisted, 'This was a highjack, Beno. The plane was found this morning in Michoacan, burned on the ground.'

Beno asked, 'You see the plane?'

'Of course not.'

'Suppose you did see the plane. How would you know who

177

stole it, or if it was stolen at all? How would you know Mendoza hadn't been on the plane?'

Beno caught in her eyes a glimmer of doubt. Patiently, in a quiet voice, he asked, 'Why did Máximo Levín give this tape to Lowry? It doesn't make sense.'

'I don't know. I'm frightened.'

Instead of sympathy, Beno felt a snarling sarcasm. He said, 'Maybe Andrés Obregón works for the DIS. Maybe they staged this little show. These Méxican cops are Mendoza's private army, and this whole thing stinks of a set-up. Why did Lowry send you here? Why not come himself?'

'I can answer that,' said Sam. 'You threatened him. He thinks you'd kill him.'

'Why?'

'I don't know.'

Beno said, 'This is horseshit. Lowry wants me to cover his ass by killing Obregón. What I can't figure is Máximo Levín. That guy has the most devious, sinister mind ever developed in México. Nothing he does is obvious or direct. He's playing Lowry like a harpsichord, and you're trying to play me. I'm sorry. You're out of your league. Did the DIS follow you here?'

'If they did, I didn't notice.'

'I'm sure you didn't because they're very good. Anything unusual happen in the last couple of days?'

Sam nodded, 'I was stopped by a motorcycle cop this morning on the Reforma. The embassy mechanic found a transmitter under my car.'

Beno said, 'DIS knows you're Lowry's messenger. Máximo is Mendoza's number one guy. His job is to protect Mendoza and exact vengeance. This was not an attempt on Mendoza's life, Sam. Millions of dollars were on that plane. Obregón wasn't after Mendoza, he was after the money, Mendoza's dope profits.'

Subdued, the fire gone from her voice, Sam muttered, 'Oh, shit.'

Beno continued, 'Máximo wants Obregón silenced before Mendoza finds out and really sets fire to the shithouse. You've been conned into helping Mendoza collect his blood money. You come down here, probably with the entire DIS after you like the birds who followed Hansel and Gretel.'

Beno shook his head, went to the kitchen and started grinding coffee beans. After a moment Sam followed him. He set a kettle of water on the stove and lit the flame.

Sam asked, 'Did Lowry know there was money on the plane?'

'I'm sure he did.'

The kettle whistled. Beno dumped the ground coffee into a filter and poured water into the dark aromatic mound.

'I'm beginning to understand why you hate him,' Sam said, then asked, 'Why don't you go to Langley and talk to Al Mears?'

'Because I carry no weight, Sam. I can't prove anything. I don't know if there really was a finding, or what it said.'

'I don't know what you're talking about. What finding?'

Beno said, 'This has been a classified operation from the beginning. I can't tell you more than that, but I can tell you how I feel.' Beno curled his hand into a fist and said, 'I feel like the man who murdered Trotsky. I want to bury an icepick in Lowry's head!'

No longer under control, Beno's voice rose to a shout. He punctuated his exclamation by slamming down the coffee pot and sloshing hot coffee over his hand.

'Damn,' he swore. 'I won't because I'm out. O-u-t. I don't give a shit any more.'

He poured one cup of coffee and stared at her. She lowered her eyes and said, 'I guess I'll go back to México City.'

After a pause, she raised her eyes and asked, 'What are you going to do now?'

'Clear out of here, if I have time. Something is brewing. Something big is behind Lowry sending you on this little errand. Maybe he's behind Obregón. Ever think of that? The DIS will pursue the little bastard to the ends of the earth, and anybody else involved, and kill them all. You, me, Lowry, Obregón and anybody else. Sam, these people have more passion for a vendetta than the Mafia. They are more powerful than the Union Corse and have greater discipline than the KGB. In this country if you know too much they cut out your heart. You're dealing with Méxicans in their own country, not Russians and Bulgarians and Czechs, and I'm positive you don't know the rules. I'll make it easy for you. The only rule is: if the DIS want you, you die. Neither the CIA nor the American flag can protect you.'

Beno ended with a snort, took a long gulp of coffee, and

179

added, 'If I were you, I'd take my videotape back to the embassy and stay there until my assignment was up. Go home as soon as possible and never think about returning to México. That tape is a death sentence.'

He flexed his knuckles and said, 'This isn't one of your espionage games with the Russians. You've done enough damage to my psyche for one day. I have to pack, find a car and hit the highway. I don't think I'll get far, but I'm not going to sit here and wait for them to come after me.'

'Are you going after Obregón?'

'Gee whiz. Who do you think'll win the Superbowl this year? I'm a diehard San Francisco 49er fan myself.'

'I think I've worn out my welcome.'

Beno shrugged and muttered. 'Adiós, Sam.'

He strode to the door, passed through into the courtyard, opened the gate and stood there until she walked through into the Street of the Inquisition. She glanced back once, then disappeared around the corner.

He shut the gate and kicked it, scuffing his boot and banging his toe. He swore the most vile curses he could think of, at the gate, his toe, his boot, Sam Black, Máximo Levín, Fred Lowry, Andrés Obregón, Alfredo Mendoza, and every other god-damned son of a bitch who had screwed up his life. When he ran out of curses, he vented his anger on the pathetic little garden in the forecourt, tearing up the prickly cacti, then on slamming open the door and storming back to the kitchen. He poured his cup of coffee down the drain and opened a cold beer and poured it down the drain.

Suddenly, the scenario jelled in his mind. The Cuban in Chilpancingo, the bug, the Stinger, Obregón.

He went back outside and found Sam turning her car for the long drive to Acapulco.

'Come back inside,' he said. 'Let's talk.'

22

Guerrilleros

Sam parked the car and asked from the driver's seat, 'Are you all right?'

'If you're asking if I'm a little crazy, the answer is yes. Crazy and pissed off. Come into the house.'

Beno led Sam into the kitchen, sat her down at the table, and straddled a chair backwards, facing her. He rested his chin on his hands and asked, 'If I were to change my mind and look for Andrés Obregón, how am I supposed to find him?'

Sam shook her head. 'I don't know.'

'Did Lowry give you an address?'

'No.'

'Did the question occur to you?'

'No.'

'Do you realize what that means? The truth is that Lowry wants Obregón to kill me.'

Surprised, Sam asked, 'Kill you? Why?'

'Because I know the two of them set up Lucio Serdán and highjacked Mendoza's plane. It all makes sense to me now.'

'You mean Fred . . .?'

'Yes, Fred was in on it.'

'Why?'

'I don't know. Maybe he had orders from higher up.'

She shook her head, 'That's hard to believe.'

Beno said, 'After you've been in the agency a little longer, you'll encounter much stranger things. Everybody lies all the time. It's a way of life. If you think about it, you'll realize our entire government runs that way. You're not allowed to work for the federal government unless you're allergic to the truth. Nobody is honest. Americans pick on Méxicans because they have a tradition of corruption, but we're worse, much worse. We pretend to be honest. We hide our corruption behind snappy phrases like "ethics committees". We haven't had an honest president since Harry Truman, and I have doubts about him.

181

This really isn't the issue here. If I change my mind and decide to go after Obregón, you have to help me. You said you work as a computer analyst. Are you assigned to the secure documents room?'

'I really can't answer that question, Beno, no matter who asks.'

'This isn't a training seminar, Sam. You're involved whether you like it or not. Lowry and Obregón will kill you if they believe you're a threat to them. You said as much yourself.'

He thought she was going to break down, but she maintained a grip on herself. He said, 'In the secure documents room you can access the DEA personnel files and come up with an address for Señor Obregón. That would give me a jump start on finding him.'

'That's a federal crime, Beno.'

'Sam, everything the agency does is criminal. That's the nature of a secret intelligence service. Us, the KGB, MI6, Mossad, the DIS, all criminal by nature. So what? Here in México we break Méxican law when we wake up in the morning and brush our teeth. DIS guys in Washington do the same thing. So what?'

'That's not what I mean. You want me to break our laws.'

'So you do work in the secure documents room. I thought so.'

'I haven't said I do or don't.'

Beno said, 'I know I'm putting you on the spot. You took the oath. You signed the National Security Act. So did I. So did Richard Nixon, Oliver North, Joe McCarthy and a hundred guys worse than them who never got caught. You want to play by the rules? Fine. Go back to México City and ask Lowry why he never told you where to find Andrés Obregón. You think it over while I pack. I know one thing for sure. Lowry and Obregón have my address.'

Beno went upstairs and continued up to his roof. A lone policeman had taken a position in front of the house.

He returned to the bedroom to find Sam standing at the top of the stairs.

'Beno,' she said, close to tears. 'I want to help you but I'm afraid.'

He stopped tossing clothes into a suitcase and asked, 'Do you think you can access the personnel files?'

'I'll have to steal the codes. It's not that difficult.'

She stood close and put her arms around him.

'Beno, hold me.'

He straightened up, turned to face her, and her arms slipped up around his neck. She pulled his head down and kissed him.

'Sam, we have to get out of here.'

She kissed him again, deeply pushing her body against his. This time he kissed her back. When they came up for air, she breathed, 'I've wanted you since the minute I saw you in the hotel.'

Against his better judgement, he felt himself grow hard. He said, 'We have to get out of here.'

'Don't you want me?'

She took a step backward, pulled her dress over her head, unhooked her bra and stepped out of her panties.

He had never seen a more beautiful, desirable woman. Her breasts had the sheen of pearls, her pubic hair flared crimson.

And then he was out of his clothes and inside her, forgetting everything but the silkiness of her skin. Years of suppression exploded in passion, an erupting galaxy of sensation as they melded together. Beno had had many women, but for the first time he knew he was making love. His mind disappeared.

Sam felt as if a rocket had ignited inside her womb. Every muscle in her body contracted and extended in one great spasm, and then they lay quietly, licking and smelling and stroking one another.

At that moment, with his senses heightened to a new sharpness, Beno heard a sound he normally never would have perceived, a sound he had not heard for many years but would never forget, a sound so ugly it jolted him to his feet before he was aware of his reactions. It was the horrible crack of a man's neck breaking.

He whispered, 'Get dressed. Stay away from the windows.'

'What is it?'

'We have visitors.'

Naked, he crept up to the roof. The policeman had vanished. Beno slipped off the roof, down the stairs and retrieved his Walther. He picked up the phone and hurriedly dialled Elizalde. No one answered.

Shouting, 'Sam, come down here,' Beno clawed his Sony

monitor off the wall, ripped open the back panel and pulled out his Uzi machine-pistol.

Pulling her dress over her head, Sam rushed downstairs. Beno yelled, 'Can you shoot?'

'Give me the gun!'

He handed her the Walther and said, 'Go up on the roof. Don't kill the neighbours, but if anyone comes over the back wall, shoot him.'

Sam spun the cylinder, grabbed a box of ammunition and ran back upstairs.

Beno jammed a clip into the Uzi, tiptoed toward the front window as a rocket flared over the wall from the street. The warhead hit the façade of the house under the roofline and exploded. Adobe cascaded onto the patio.

RPG-16.

'Oh, shit.'

He heard Sam's Walther blasting from the roof, three shots. Beno kicked open the door and saw Lucio Serdán holding the Stinger's launching grip coming through the gate. Two more guerrillas with AK-47s followed him through the gate.

Beno screamed, 'Lucio, stop! You're making a mistake.'

The guerrillas answered with gunfire. Lucio struggled with the rocket launcher. Beno saw the point of the warhead aimed at his heart and the Uzi popped in his hands. Lucio toppled backwards and pushed the Stinger's fire button. The rocket roared out of the launcher on a high trajectory over the roof and out into the Pacific where it landed harmlessly half a mile away in a spray of steam.

Lucio fell to the ground, dead. The warriors behind him retreated into the street. Gunfire erupted from behind the wall.

In tears Beno ran to Lucio who lay broken and bloody on the stone patio.

'Lucio, Lucio, you dumb shit. My God!'

Beno's chest heaved. He thought his heart would burst. The frail body lay limp in his arms. His mind recoiled in horror at what he had done. He had killed Lucio Serdán!

The two guerrillas made a second suicidal charge through the gate. A short burst from Beno's Uzi dropped them on the patio. Sirens sounded in the distance.

He heard more shots from the roof, turned and ran into the

house and up the stairs. Sam lay on her belly, the pistol held in a two-handed grip.

'I got one,' she said, dead calm, 'but there's another one down there. Who are these people?'

'Lucio's guerrillas.'

'Holy Christ.'

She shifted her eyes away from her field of fire and saw Beno's face, smeared with blood.

He forced himself to say, 'I killed him. I killed Lucio Serdán.'

They heard more gunfire from the front of the house. Beno said, 'This is fucked.'

Sam glanced toward the yard and yelled, 'There he is! Behind the tree!'

Bullets sprayed adobe chips around them. Beno stood up and unloosed the machine-gun. The man dropped.

Naked, crazed, Beno sprayed bullets until the gun was empty. Beyond reason, he jerked the trigger again and again.

They heard footsteps below. Beno whirled around, aimed the Uzi at the stairwell and pulled the trigger, but the clip was spent.

Sam wheeled and fired. The last guerrilla tumbled down the stairs and collapsed.

Beno lunged for her pistol and she tackled him, screaming, 'Beno! It's over. They're all dead.'

He convulsed in her arms, weeping.

'I killed him. I killed him. I killed him.'

Sam started to sob, the nervous tension pouring out of her. A shot rang out and a bullet grazed her shoulder. Beno sprang to life, grabbed her pistol, spun around and blew off three quick shots. He saw a man on the ground below collapse with a final effort at revenge.

Paulo, the boy in the bar.

Beno dropped the pistol and stood, feet wide apart, a warrior in agony, heaving with sorrow.

The sirens drawing closer brought him to his senses. He bent over Sam, inspecting her wound, a graze that missed the bone.

'Does it hurt?'

'Not yet.'

'You'll live. Get out of here, now! Go out the back, circle the hotel and go down the beach. Find a car. You don't want to be here when the police arrive. Go!'

He shoved her toward the ladder which led down from the roof to the back garden. She hesitated, then swiftly climbed down the ladder.

'I'll find you in México City,' he shouted. 'I love you. Go.'

She ran across the garden, past the bodies of the fallen guerrillas, and disappeared over the wall.

A moment later he saw Elizalde's black Ford turn the corner and screech to a stop in front of the house. Three police cars followed, sirens screaming, lights flashing.

Beno descended the stairs to his bedroom and put on his pants. Elizalde and half a dozen policemen burst into the house, guns drawn.

That morning Máximo Levín had returned to El Partenón in order to contact Lucio Serdán. Suddenly, Inspector Velásquez burst into Máximo's temporary office and announced, 'A violent firefight has just taken place in Alvarado's house. Elizalde is on line two.'

Máximo was unprepared for Elizalde's first words.

'Director, Lucio Serdán and his guerrillas attacked Alvarado's house. Serdán is dead.'

Stunned, Máximo tried to maintain a cool demeanour. He said to Velásquez, 'Get a car.'

The inspector ran off to the garage.

To Elizalde he said, 'Is Alvarado alive?'

'He's unhurt.'

'Hold him there. Seal the area. Where's the woman?'

'Gone.'

'Alert the highway patrol. Find her and bring her back to the house.'

'Yes, sir.'

'Any prisoners?'

'No, sir. Five dead.'

'I'll be right there.'

'Yes, sir.'

Máximo did not hurry out to his car. He shut the door to his office and buried his head in his hands. Why had Serdán not called him first? What had possessed the man? He would never know. He did not blame Beno. Clearly, the man had defended himself.

Tlatelolco had claimed its final victim.

As alone and bereft as he had ever felt in his life, Máximo Levín wept.

After several minutes he composed himself and began calling the members of México 21. When he finished, he collected several documents into his briefcase and went out to the garage.

Sam had rented a car in the centre of town. Angry, confused and hurt, she pushed the Plymouth Acclaim to eighty miles per hour and was not surprised to see flashing lights in her rear view mirror for the second time that day.

No one had prepared the extremely polite Federal Highway Patrolman for the vehement fury of the woman he had been ordered to stop.

She refused to speak Spanish. Swearing in English, which the trooper did not understand, Sam flashed her diplomatic passport, quoted at the top of her lungs the pertinent diplomatic conventions, swore some more and peeled away, leaving the patrolman standing by the side of the road.

The Plymouth topped out at ninety-five. The five litre Mustang highway patrol cruiser easily caught up, came alongside, siren screaming, pulled in front and forced Sam off to the side of the road.

Still polite, the policeman approached the car with his gun drawn.

Waving her credentials in his face Sam snapped in Spanish, 'I have diplomatic immunity, you son of a bitch. Do you understand what that means? I'll have your job. I'll have your fucking head.'

Reaching inside the car, he took her keys and holstered his gun.

'I don't want to handcuff you, Miss,' he said. 'But I will if I have to. It is most unpleasant. Please step out of the car.'

Contrite but silent, she got into the Mustang. One of the troopers got into the Plymouth, and the two cars started back to Zihuatanejo.

23

Revelations

A grim-faced Alonzo Elizalde met Máximo in front of Beno's house.

'Director, the woman is being returned to Zihuatanejo.'

Máximo said to the local agent, 'Describe to me again the activities of this man Alvarado in the last twenty-four hours.'

Elizalde pulled a ragged notebook from his shirt pocket, flipped through a few pages, and recited, 'Yesterday afternoon he went to Plaza Mayor at 4:15 as is his custom. At 5:25 he returned to his house. In the evening he entertained a group of friends at home. He spent this morning in his house where I visited him at 8:30 according to your instructions. This afternoon he went to the *Playa Municipal* and met the woman. They returned to his house. Serdán attacked.'

'What is your general impression, Mr Elizalde?'

'Alvarado is well known in the town. He treats people with more respect than most of the gringos. No arrests, moderate public drunkenness, many women, no drugs. He travels the countryside frequently, goes to México City once or twice a month and, as you know, inquires persistently about Lucio Serdán.'

Máximo said, 'Yes, a model resident foreigner. Have you questioned him?'

'He refuses to talk.'

'Call everyone outside and remain here. I don't want to see or hear your men. Don't come in unless I call.'

'Yes, sir.'

'Your accounting of Alvarado's activities is excellent.'

'Thank you, sir.'

'Show me Serdán's body.'

The three dead guerrillas lay where they had fallen on the stone patio.

Silently, Máximo said, 'Good-bye, old friend.'

He asked Elizalde, 'Where are the other two?'

'In the rear.'

'Take the bodies to El Partenón. Call the morgue and tell them to send their people there. Keep the press and public away.'

'Yes, sir.'

'Have the woman brought here and hold her outside. Where is Alvarado?'

'In the house.'

Sitting in his kitchen, Beno saw a tall figure come through the door. With a shock, he recognized Máximo Levín, and a nervous grin stretched across Beno's face.

Máximo asked quietly, 'Mr Alvarado?'

'Yes.'

'I am Máximo Levín, Chief of the Directorate of Internal Security.'

'I know who you are, sir.'

'You don't seem surprised to see me.'

'After what happened today, nothing would surprise me.'

'Are you injured?'

'No.'

'May I sit down?'

Beno thought this polite question curious. He said, 'Of course.'

'Thank you.'

Máximo sat silently for a moment, calmly observing his prisoner, then asked, 'You know who these men were, I presume?'

Nervously lighting a cigarette, Beno answered, 'Yes.'

Máximo asked, 'In your estimation, why did Lucio Serdán attack your house?'

'The CIA is not exactly popular here in Guerrero. My cover was transparent to anyone who looked.'

Máximo said, 'Let me prompt your memory, Mr Alvarado. You frequent a tavern in Chilpancingo run by the Frenchman, Laluce. One might assume that among your other activities, you are a freelance mercenary.'

'A reasonable assumption, but not true. Sometimes I drink with Laluce. His place is full of useful contacts for someone in my line of work.'

'Your agency frowns on freelancers, I believe.'

'Indeed, it does.'

'Then,' said Máximo, 'perhaps you can explain why five nights ago, in Chilpancingo, you delivered to Lucio Serdán a sophisticated anti-aircraft weapon which you hoped he would use to destroy Alfredo Mendoza. That very weapon is now lying outside on your patio, next to the body of Lucio Serdán.'

Beno was shocked. Waves of fear and panic rolled through his body.

Máximo continued, 'Last night, Mendoza's plane was destroyed by an identical weapon. The newspapers reported that Lucio Serdán was responsible. I wonder where they got that information.'

'I don't know.'

'From you, perhaps?'

Beno said, 'If that were true, which it isn't, I certainly wouldn't admit it.'

Máximo said sternly, 'You should reconsider, Mr Alvarado. This is a trial. I am your judge and jury, and if necessary, your executioner. México has no death penalty, but attempting to assassinate the Minister of Government is a capital offence.'

'Naturally.'

With an earnest expression, Máximo explained, 'Conversely, killing a notorious revolutionary could be construed as a heroic act in defence of the republic.'

Beno said, 'I wasn't doing you a favour.'

Máximo stated, 'On three occasions, you met Serdán in Chilpancingo and sold him weapons. You did so either at the direction of Mr Lowry, your superior, or on your own.'

'I'm not suicidal, Director, but I have nothing more to say.'

'Lowry provided you with the Stingers. Is that not so?'

'Draw your own conclusions.'

Máximo said, 'In the press and within your own agency, Serdán was portrayed as a communist. You studied him. Do you think he was a communist?'

Beno asked, 'Studied?'

Máximo recited, 'You spent over a year investigating Lucio Serdán. You questioned every farmer in western Guerrero, his boyhood friends, his former colleagues at the *secundaria* in Chilpancingo and his family. I must say you've been thorough. I ask again, was he a communist?'

Beno groaned. 'Not in the traditional sense. He might have been a socialist, but he belonged to no party. He was an indigenous revolutionary.'

'Yes,' Máximo said. 'A revolutionary. If the CIA intended to kill Alfredo Mendoza, having it done by a revolutionary would exclude the CIA from the list of possible culprits. Very smart.'

'Why would CIA want to kill Mendoza? The idea is absurd.'

Máximo said, 'I don't find it so absurd, Mr Alvarado. Nothing CIA does surprises me. If your agency persuaded Serdán to kill Mendoza, then killing Serdán would remove the connection, no?'

'It would.'

'Do you regret having killed him?'

'Dr Levín, it gives me no pleasure to kill, even in my own defence. Strange as it may seem, I despise violence. These men attacked me.'

Máximo nodded slowly and said, 'I admire you, Mr Alvarado. You are unique. You're an incredibly brave man. Provocative.'

Máximo smiled with the corners of his eyes and said, 'There's no point in adding yourself to the list of the dead.'

Beno said, 'In my experience no one survives a DIS interrogation.'

'Were you alone in this house when you were attacked?'

'I was.'

'That's a lie. You were visited today by Miss Samantha Black from the US embassy.'

'That's true.'

'When did she leave?'

'About an hour before the guerrillas arrived.'

'Another lie. Miss Black was seen running from this house moments after the attack.'

'Your information is incorrect.'

Irritated, Máximo said with a sigh, 'If you lie, this will be a long afternoon.'

Beno lit a cigarette and stared at Máximo's long, curly hair and thick glasses.

The Director asked, 'Is Miss Black an employee of CIA?'

'Yes.'

'Did she show you a videotape?'

191

A simple search of the house would turn up the tape, so Beno answered, 'Yes.'

'What did you see?'

'Andrés Obregón boarding Alfredo Mendoza's plane. A little later Ramón Santiago and another man got on the plane. Then it took off.'

'Did she tell you where she got the tape?'

'Yes, from you. I told her I thought the tape was a fake.'

'Did she bring you instructions from Mr Lowry?'

'I quit the agency, Director. I told her I take no orders from Lowry or anyone else.'

'Please tell me what your instructions were.'

'I'm afraid that's classified.'

'I see,' Máximo said. 'Your instructions were to kill Obregón.'

Trying to conceal his surprise, Beno said, 'Whatever my instructions were, I refused.'

Máximo's heavily lidded eyes remained immobile while he listened to this statement.

Máximo said, 'I'm trying to assemble a puzzle from which several pieces are missing. Please bear with me. What you saw on the tape was genuine. Andrés Obregón was on Mendoza's plane last night. What I want to know is: who met the plane in Michoacan.'

Beno asked, 'Do you think it was me?'

'No,' Máximo said. 'You were here. Obregón is DEA. Perhaps his confederate was Antoine Bonmarche.'

Beno said, 'I can't help you. I was here.'

'Or Fred Lowry?' Máximo suggested.

'Only Obregón knows for sure,' Beno countered. 'Or Mendoza himself.'

Máximo smiled. 'That's an appealing scenario, but not correct. Do you know the source of Mendoza's wealth?'

Beno laughed, and listening to himself thought his laughter sounded like a death rattle. He said, 'A man like that has more sources than I could ever name.'

'Hazard a speculation.'

'Come on, Director. Have you already made up your mind to kill me? Are you looking for an excuse? Mendoza manufactures and sells heroin.'

'And Andrés Obregón?'

'He helps Mendoza smuggle the dope into the US. I'm not telling you anything you don't know.'

Beno had had enough. He was going to say his piece, kill Máximo Levín and take his chances. He said, 'Lucio was the only honest man in this country. He was trying to put scum like you and your patron out of business.'

Beno moved, but Máximo was quicker. Suddenly, a pistol appeared in the Director's hand and he backed away from the kitchen table.

'Please, Mr Alvarado, sit down. I don't want to call my men.'

Beno taunted, 'What's the matter, Dr Levín? Don't you have the nerve to shoot me yourself?'

'Please sit down.'

Defeated, Beno sat.

The Director paused, then asked, 'You admired Lucio Serdán?'

'I've already said so.'

'You say you wanted to help him to kill Mendoza.'

Resigned to his fate, Beno answered, 'Yes.'

'And you believe Serdán took orders from no one.'

'Correct.'

'That's not completely true. He took orders from me.'

'I don't follow you, Director.'

'Lucio Serdán was my friend.'

For a long moment Beno stared at Máximo, then he buried his head in his hands, rubbed his eyes, then said, 'That's crazy. Prove it.'

'You think I'm lying, trying to trick you.'

Beno retorted, 'It's the oldest interrogation trick in the book. Jesus Christ, you work for Mendoza. You're chief of DIS.'

Máximo said, 'Yes, and my position affords access to exceptional means of communication. Lucio Serdán kept me abreast of your meetings. I told him you were CIA a year ago. Furthermore, I know you were operating without CIA approval. You followed a dangerous course.'

Beno said, 'That doesn't explain why the man tried to kill me.'

'He believed you tried to frame him. Serdán reads the newspaper like anyone else. You gave him a Stinger. A man with a Stinger tried to kill Mendoza and failed. Serdán thought that man was you, but it wasn't. You were here last night.'

'You have my confession, Dr Levín. What more do you want?'

'I want Andrés Obregón. I want him to incriminate Fred Lowry. I'm certain Lowry was Obregón's accomplice, but I can't prove it without a confession from Obregón. Above all, I want the CIA to stop interfering with the internal affairs of this nation.'

'How noble.'

'Under the circumstances, I can understand your sarcasm. You know, Mr Alvarado, there are dozens of policemen outside prepared to lionize you. You are the man who killed Lucio Serdán, their enemy. I'm telling you, he was my friend for more than twenty years. Serdán was providing me with the critical information I needed to destroy Alfredo Mendoza. I must put the truth to you bluntly. In less than two weeks Mendoza will fall. Unfortunately, Obregón and Lowry are interfering with my programme.'

Beno shook his head in disbelief and confusion.

'Your programme? What programme?'

Máximo pleaded, 'Mr Alvarado, you must trust me. I'm telling you a profound secret. Alfredo Mendoza and the party which has supported him and his predecessors in power for three-quarters of a century will be demolished within a week. At the moment you need not concern yourself with the details.'

'A *coup d'état*?'

'Let's call it a palace revolution.'

'Why trust me with this information, Dr Levín?'

'I reiterate, Lucio Serdán was my friend. I think, in a way, he was your friend also. I believe you truly love México and her people. I'm prepared to trust you. I'm making a judgement based partly on expedience. You have a better chance of finding Obregón than any of my policemen, and you can search for him without alerting Mendoza, our common enemy.'

Beno asked, 'Why don't you simply arrest Lowry or make him disappear?'

'I have no wish to provoke a disastrous quarrel with the government of the United States. Lowry and Obregón are rogues. I wish to expose Mendoza, to destroy him. That is how we happened to film Obregón at the Zihuatanejo airport.

194

Obregón and Lowry are interfering like flies in the milk. I implore you to help me, in the name of Lucio Serdán.'

'Do you want me to kill them?'

'I want you to capture Obregón and hold him until I question him.'

The Director pocketed his pistol and placed several documents on the table.

He said, 'I fully intended to speak to you today before this unfortunate incident. I was as surprised as you when Serdán attacked. It was his custom to consult with me, but this morning's newspaper reports must have enraged him beyond reason. You must believe me. We both wish to achieve the same objective, the end of Alfredo Mendoza.

'I don't want Mendoza dead, and I assure you I can keep him alive. I want Obregón and Lowry silenced. Usually, I distrust instincts, including my own, but today I had a premonition that our conversation might turn out as it has. I am providing you with a DIS identity plate with the rank of Comandante, money, a Méxican passport, and several phone numbers you may call for assistance. Will you require anything else?'

'What if I refuse?'

'This is a delicate matter, Mr Alvarado. I could detain you. I could cause you to disappear. You know too much. You could agree to assist me and leave the country, or you can track down these two men and settle the debt to your own soul. This nation will be forever grateful for your assistance.'

Beno understood that if he didn't agree, he was dead. Perhaps he was anyway.

He placed the DIS identity plate he had carried for years on the table and said, 'I accept the promotion to Comandante.'

Máximo laughed quietly, appreciating the joke.

'I'll find him,' said Beno.

'Be quick. It won't be long before Mendoza discovers he's been betrayed.'

Beno stood up and said, 'I should go to Acapulco and start at Oakland Air Freight.'

Máximo contradicted, saying, 'We have the DEA under surveillance. If I were you, I'd start in México City. You can use my plane.'

195

Beno said, 'Okay. I need one thing. Stop Samantha Black before she gets to the embassy. I need her.'

Máximo asked, 'Will you take her into your confidence?'

'To a limited extent. She's a computer analyst. She can get the station computers to tell us where to find Obregón.'

Máximo smiled and said, 'She's right outside.'

The Director walked to the door and said to the guard, 'Bring in the woman.'

Sam rushed through the door to Beno's side.

He asked, 'Are you all right?'

'I'm scared,' she said. 'What's going on?'

'We're going after Lowry and Obregón. Let's get out of here.'

Elizalde drove them to the airport and put them on Máximo's plane. Máximo spent the afternoon in communion with the body of Lucio Serdán, then commandeered an AeroMéxico jet and returned to the glass pyramid.

24

Polanco

Sam slept on the short flight while Beno paced up and down the cabin of the empty plane. At the México City airport Beno bought a litre of orange juice, packed Sam into a rented VW Jetta and drove into the city, joining the thirty million citizens suffocating under a red bowl of industrial dust.

The cacophonous roar of the metropolis seemed to rise up and engulf the two Americans. They passed through the northern suburbs on the Periferico, a freeway that rings the outskirts of the city. Six lanes of nightmarish traffic crawled along in each direction.

Jammed with rural immigrants and daily commuters, thousands of buses spewed black smoke into the foul air. Horns blaring, airbrakes hissing madly, giant trucks bore down on rusted old Datsuns and pick-ups overloaded with peasants. Block after block of ragtag slums lined the shoulders of the bad-tempered road. Laundry hung on wires that stretched from the highway's chain link fence to back porches where black-eyed children watched the endless parade of shuddering steel boxes.

'Where are we?' she asked.

'Periferico.'

Sam stared out of her window at the grimy side of a bus plastered with a poster. 'Vota México. Vota PRI.'

From a giant billboard the immense face of Alfredo Mendoza loomed over the highway. Red and green neon spelled out 'Mendoza, Sí! México, Sí!'

Beno said, 'Maybe it'll rain and clear the air. How's your shoulder?'

'Still between my neck and my elbow.'

The pain had settled into a dull ache. She wrapped her good arm around herself and shuddered.

Beno asked, 'Where do you live?'

In a faraway voice she answered, 'Polanco. River Po Street.'

Sensing that Sam was retreating into post-combat shock, Beno reached into the back seat for the orange juice, handed her the container and commanded, 'Drink this.'

A long gulp revived her.

He asked, 'Do you want to talk about it?'

'Do you?'

'What can I say about the worst day of my life? There was one bright spot. You were beautiful, absolutely wonderful.'

Sam asked, 'What do I tell Lowry?'

'Considering what happened, you can tell him most of the truth. Lucio came after me for revenge, and you were there.'

'Five dead men,' said Sam.

'They didn't know,' Beno said. 'Lucio thought he had been betrayed. If I'd been him, I'd have done the same thing. They died as honourable warriors. Don't get eaten up by guilt. They were trying to kill us.'

'I never shot anybody before, Beno.'

'It doesn't get any easier, believe me.'

'Those were the good guys.'

Abruptly, Beno muscled the car across three lanes of traffic, cut off a bus, pulled off the road onto the shoulder, screeched to a stop, jumped out of the car and vomited in the bushes.

Afterwards, he stood by the side of the highway, watching the traffic, his mind flickering like a dying neon light. He lit a cigarette, forced himself to focus on the creeping traffic, then returned to the car. He started to slam the door but hesitated and shut it without a bang.

Concerned and confused, Sam asked, 'Are you all right?'

He turned over the engine, stared intently through the windscreen and said, 'There are no good guys. Not us, not them, not anybody.'

He switched on the radio, viciously ripped up and down the dial until he heard B. B. King slashing through a low-down, gut-searing emotional riff. Radio México. B. B. King. Lucio's cadres. Traffic on the Periferico. Sam Black. Above the car a billboard screamed Pepsi Cola. In the right lane a stalled bus full of what? *Damnificados*? Brown faces stared down at him with wide eyes. He could see their paper-bag luggage, their hopelessness, his own despair. Could he see anything? Could she?

Sam asked, 'Do you want me to drive?'

'No.'

He reconsidered and said, 'Yes.'

They changed places.

Sam pulled into the traffic, turned down the radio, and rubbed her shoulder.

Beno opened his window and let the dirty air wash over him.

Sam pointed the car straight ahead, silently reviewing the day in her mind. Standing naked in his bedroom, she had asked, 'Don't you feel anything?'

Now she knew that he felt things more intensely than anyone she had ever known. Life and death, sex and violence, blood and B. B. King. Anyone who thought the world was supposed to make sense was blind or nuts or both.

Sam's flat in Polanco contained all the plastic freshness of modern México City. Beno prowled through the air-conditioned, soundproofed rooms, reminding himself that after all, this was North America, interchangeable with Chicago, Saint Louis, Toronto or Los Angeles.

The phone-answering machine blinked incessantly, a Japanese cyclops. While Beno sponged the dressing on Sam's shoulder, she pushed the play button.

'Sam, this is Fred Lowry. Call me through the duty officer when you get home.'

'Hello, Sam, this is Lieutenant Alex Reynolds. We met in the embassy lounge last Tuesday night. Damn, I hate these machines, but I wondered if you would like to accompany me to dinner next Saturday night. You can reach me at the Marine detachment, nine seven six six. Thank you, good night.'

'Sam? This is your mother. Hi. You're not drinking the water, are you? I hope not. Oh, God, I sound just like a mother. Everything is fine here. Just fine. Call when you're not busy.'

'Miss Black, this is the duty officer. Please call Mr Lowry as soon as possible. Thank you.'

The machine beeped and turned itself off.

Beno said, 'Call your mother.'

Sam responded to his suggestion by putting on a Linda Ronstadt tape.

'Tomorrow,' she said. 'She phones me all the time. Should I call Lowry?'

'Fuck him. He'll call back. Let's have a look at your shoulder.'

Sam asked, 'What do I say when he calls back? Do I tell him you're here?'

Beno shook his head and answered, 'No, I'll be gone in an hour. Tomorrow morning you go to the embassy as usual and do your best to find Obregón's address.'

While Sam showered, Beno unpacked and cleaned his weapons. Then he took his turn in the shower, borrowed Sam's toothbrush, and found her waiting in bed.

As he slid between the covers, he said, 'Woman, haven't you heard of safe sex?'

Sam playfully backhanded his cheek and answered, 'It's a little late for that, isn't it?'

The second time around they took their time. The phone rang again, but Sam let the machine answer.

An hour later Sam called the embassy duty officer. Beno listened on the speaker phone.

Lowry answered and asked, 'Sam, are you okay?'

'Yes. I'm back in my apartment. Where are you?'

Ignoring her question, Lowry said, 'Máximo Levín called me

and told me what happened in Zihuatanejo. He said you were hurt.'

'It's just a scratch. Did he tell you who they were?'

'Yes. I hope that's the last of them.'

'I appreciate your concern, Fred. I'll be in in the morning.'

Lowry hesitated, then asked, 'Where's Beno?'

'He said he was going to Guadalajara to see the DEA people there. He's looking for Obregón.'

'Good. Excellent. See you in the morning.'

They hung up.

Beno left the Walther with Sam, packed the Uzi in his suitcase and left the apartment building through the ground-floor garage. He carefully checked under the VW, opened the bonnet and examined the ignition wiring, then drove a mile across town to Tomás Edison Street near the Revolution Monument.

He parked the car in a garage and bought a greasy taco and two bottles of Dos Equis from a stand on the corner. Carrying his supper, he checked into the seedy Paris Hotel and lugged his heavy suitcase to his second-floor room.

Over the years Beno had lived in the Paris for weeks at a stretch, making the acquaintance of its peculiar clientele. He found the hotel unchanged. Marijuana smoke oozed from cracks under the doors. Cocaine spiked the air like ozone in the subway. Floozy accordian music spilled down four flights of broken marble stairs, backing a raspy voice that chanted an improvised melody of love, betrayal, revenge and death.

Beno lay on his bed, drinking beer and humming the old Bob Dylan tune, 'Just like Tom Thumb's Blues'. He took one bite of the taco, threw the rest into the waste basket, and napped until three in the morning.

The young policeman on duty in front of Lowry's house remembered Beno.

'Good evening, *Capitán*.'

'Good evening, Noriega. You get your squad car yet?'

'Not yet, sir.'

'You will.'

'I hope so, sir.'

'Is the North American home?'

200

'No, sir.'

'Have you seen anyone go in or out of the house?'

'Not tonight. No, sir.'

Beno said, 'I'm going inside. If there's trouble, call DIS headquarters. Understand?'

'Yes, sir.'

Beno hoisted himself over the wall, went around the side of the house and disconnected the alarm system. He picked the lock on the back door, passed through the kitchen, and up the stairs to Lowry's study. A maid was asleep in a bedroom at the far end of the hall.

He picked up the phone and dialled the embassy.

'Four three nine one.'

'This is Alpha Seven calling on a secure line. Put me through to Flame.'

Beno and the duty officer went through the protocol and after several minutes Lowry came on the line.

'Hello, Beno. Where are you?'

'Guadalajara.'

Lowry asked, 'Find our boy yet?'

'I thought you could help me with that, Fred. I think you know where he is.'

'What are you talking about?'

'I bet you were real disappointed that there was no money on that plane. It must be painful, thinking about going home without all those millions.'

'Where are you, Beno?'

'Over here in Polanco looking at a nicely designed wall safe of German manufacture, wondering if I'll wake up the maid when I blow it. I guess I'll come back and check out the safe another time. Bye now.'

A minute later Beno returned to the street and the young policeman.

Beno said, 'Men will arrive here in a few minutes. Americans. You saw nothing, heard nothing. You were asleep on duty.'

'Yes, sir.'

Beno gave him ten thousand pesos and said, 'I'll put in a good word for you.'

'Thank you, sir. Thanks very much.'

Beno drove around the corner and parked. Ten minutes later

two carloads of embassy security heavies rushed toward Niagra Street and screeched to a halt in front of Lowry's house.

When Beno saw that Lowry was not among them, he drove back to the Hotel Paris, laughing without joy.

13 SEPTEMBER

25

Access Codes

Fred Lowry needed a better ruse to explain to his staff why he was encamped in his office. In normal fashion, México station was running several operations simultaneously, most of which involved spying on the Soviet Union.

Since the end of World War Two the Soviet embassy in México City had serviced the largest KGB station outside Moscow and Washington. For fifty years, the Mexican-American frontier had presented Soviet spies with an open door to the United States. With the cold war winding down, the KGB had ordered severe cutbacks in México.

From the moment he arrived in México, Lowry had declared frequently and loudly that glasnost and perestroika were nothing less than Soviet disinformation designed to lull the West to sleep. When Lowry assembled the staff in his office-cum-bunkhouse and made a long, blustery, anti-Soviet speech, no one was surprised.

At the end of this rhetorical exercise, Lowry ordered his operatives to increase surveillance on their KGB counterparts. Their mission was to determine which Russians were leaving México and the identities of their replacements. He wanted new agents inside the Soviet embassy on the other side of town on the Avenue of the Revolution. More than anything else, he said, he wanted the Russians to know, as far as México station was concerned, that the cold war wouldn't end until every KGB agent had quit North America.

Sam Black sat with the watchers, translators, cipher clerks, computer specialists, section chiefs, directors of personnel, operations, communications and security, defence, legal and DEA attachés, and the commander of the Marine guard, and rolled her eyes, trying to look earnest and dedicated. Alone among these stalwarts, she knew Lowry was blowing smoke to veil his terror of Beno Alvarado.

When, at length, Lowry dismissed his spies, charging them

with a final barrage of venom not to give the Russians a moment's rest, he asked Sam to remain behind.

Strained by his efforts, he had sweated through his off-white tropical suit. He patted his reddened forehead with a handkerchief of good Irish linen and said, 'Please, sit down, Sam. How's your shoulder?'

'Stiff.'

'Have you seen the medical staff?'

'Not yet. I was on my way there when I was called to your meeting.'

'Do you want to go down there now?'

'Thanks. It can wait. Nice speech, Mr Lowry.'

Lowry instantly detected her change in attitude from anxious novitiate to dangerous potential enemy.

He said, 'I'm going home in a few days. There will be a new station chief, and I want him to find everything in order.'

Sam smiled wryly and said, 'The new chief won't have to worry about Lucio Serdán and a nasty group of communist guerrillas running around threatening the security of the United States, will he?'

Fiddling with papers on his desk, Lowry watched her out of the corner of his eye and began to think that he had erred by sending her to see Beno a second time. Beno's notorious dissidence seemed to have infected her.

He commanded, 'Tell me what happened in Zee.'

In a turgid, factual manner, Sam recounted the attack by Lucio Serdán. When she finished, Lowry asked, 'You're certain it was Serdán?'

'Beno recognized him.'

'How many were there?'

'Five.'

'All killed?'

'Yeah. We both felt pretty bad. When we got back to México City, Beno barfed. Some tough guy.'

Lowry asked, 'Where is he now?'

'He told me he was driving to Guadalajara.'

'What for?'

'He didn't say.'

Lowry scribbled a note to himself, then said, 'The DIS called.

206

Máximo Levín and I agreed that they'll take the credit, and there'll be no mention of agency personnel being involved.'

Sam said, 'That's fine with me. There's probably more of them out there.'

With a patronizing smile, Lowry said, 'You're a blooded veteran now, Sam. You can be proud of yourself.'

Sam looked at Lowry as if he had made a wildly indecent proposition. She guffawed and said, 'Excuse my French, Mr Lowry, but that's bullshit. We had to defend ourselves or die. Only fools take pride in something like that. We lucked out. The guerrillas had rockets.'

Slightly ruffled by this exclamation, Lowry twisted his hand-kerchief and said, 'Nevertheless, you comported yourself bravely. I'm putting you in for a commendation.'

Sam told herself, 'Put up with this charade, girl. Remember what you want, Obregón's address.'

She asked, 'What about Beno? Does he get a commendation, too?'

Lowry prevaricated, saying, 'Well, I'm not sure about that. He's expected to deal with hostiles. He was only doing his duty. You went above and beyond.'

'Mr Lowry, I get the impression that you would be just as pleased if Beno had been killed.'

Lowry folded his fingers together into an arch, rested his chin on the support and said, 'I think your experience made you a little testy, Sam. It's understandable.'

She replied, 'It's bad enough being shot at, but being shot at by people you tried to help is less than fun. Somebody betrayed Lucio Serdán, but it wasn't Beno.'

'You don't really know that, Sam.'

Sam raised her eyebrows and stated, 'Oh, yes I do. Beno Alvarado is the only man working out of this station who sees México as more than a staging ground for the Russians. He noticed eighty million Méxicans living here. One Méxican was trying to make his country a better place, and Lucio Serdán is dead. Passing strange, that. Coincidence? According to you, Máximo Levín said that Andrés Obregón was trying to kill Alfredo Mendoza. If that's true, then maybe Obregón had some sense. Mendoza is the real bad guy, only now we're trying to save Mendoza's bacon by eliminating Obregón.'

207

'Is that what Beno said?'

'Yes, but you might be surprised to learn that I figured it out for myself.'

Lowry said, 'I take it you were able to persuade Beno to go after Obregón.'

Sam sidestepped the question and said, 'Look, I know you two guys are not exactly buddies, but I don't care.'

Lowry said, 'We have our disagreements, but we know how to put them aside in a common cause.'

Beno's voice echoed in Sam's head, 'No good guys, no bad guys.'

Lowry returned to the point by asking, 'Is Beno going to kill Obregón?'

Sam drummed her fingernails on Lowry's desk and replied, 'He isn't happy about it. I showed him the videotape, and he concluded the scene at the airport had been staged by Máximo Levín. Beno doesn't trust the DIS, especially Máximo.'

Lowry conceded, 'Beno doesn't trust anyone, but that doesn't make sense. Why would the DIS fake it?'

'Máximo Levín works for Mendoza. Maybe Obregón intended to expose the Minister as a heroin trafficker. After all, that's the DEA's business. It's too much of a coincidence that they caught him on videotape. If they staged the highjack and somehow persuaded Obregón to get on the plane, then Obregón is already dead. At least, that's Beno's guess.'

Lowry asked, 'How would they persuade Obregón to co-operate?'

Sam rubbed her thumb and fingers together and said, '*La mordida.*'

Lowry shook his head and said, 'Possible, possible, yes, no. No. Nonsense. That's a paranoid fantasy. We can't assume Obregón's dead and write him off. We have to keep looking for him.'

'Look where?'

'Beats me,' said Lowry.

Sam asked, 'In Acapulco?'

'That's a good place to start.'

Sam said, 'Beno was upset because you didn't give me an address for Obregón. He said you're sending him on a wild goose chase.'

Lowry frowned and claimed, 'I don't know where that little bastard is. I don't keep track of every DEA agent in México.'

Adamant, Sam said, 'Beno insisted that you know how to find him. He said to remind you that a simple phone call to the DEA would turn up a location for Obregón.'

Lowry replied, 'We don't need an inter-agency war around here.'

Sam said pointedly, 'We've got one anyway, Mr Lowry.' Then she added, 'Can't you access the DEA computer files yourself?'

'Yes, I can, but you know the computer audit procedures as well as anybody. The data processing system keeps a record of all inquiries into the system.'

Sam leaned back in her seat and said, 'Mr Lowry, every system has back doors and covert channels to gain access. There's no such thing as a completely secure computer base.'

'Be that as it may, Samantha, it's too risky. Remember, I'm honouring a personal request from Máximo Levín to find Obregón without a security leak. No publicity, no scandal. If the DEA were to find out, they'd hustle Obregón out of the country like that.' Lowry snapped his fingers. 'They protect their own, just like we do. I'm sorry.'

Sam asked, 'If the highjack was real and not staged, don't you think Obregón would have left México by now?'

'Good question, and I don't know the answer. Beno has to keep looking.'

Sam asked, 'Are you going to keep me as your go-between?'

Lowry waffled, answering, 'We'll see how the situation develops. Now, go downstairs and have your shoulder looked after. You'll find a lot of work stacked on your desk.'

As Sam rose to leave, she asked, 'Have you heard from Beno?'

The spymaster lied, 'No. All I know is what you told me last night, that he went to Guadalajara. He did go, didn't he?'

'That's what he said. Do you have reason to doubt it?'

'No. That's all.'

After a tetanus booster Sam had two sore shoulders. She felt that if the conversation with Lowry had continued much longer, she would have become lost in the maze of lies and counter-lies.

She was glad to return to her cubicle and computer in the secure documents room.

Overnight she had designed a simple program which would enable her to access the DEA personnel files. She turned on her terminal and quickly wrote thirty-two lines of code in the Department of Defense computer language, ADA. Cursory examination of her program would reveal nothing more than a security measure designed to monitor access to the DEA files. In fact the program would attach itself to any retrieval request by an authorized user, pull Obregón's file, route it to her, and then erase itself.

As a systems analyst, she had access to the mainframe's operating system. She retrieved the critical set of input/output programs, deftly inserted her new program, and waited.

On a normal day some two dozen authorized entries were made into the DEA personnel files. After fifteen minutes the first DEA request came through. Sam's program did what it was supposed to do and Obregón's file appeared on her terminal.

Obregón had two addresses in México City and one in Acapulco, which she memorized. She transferred the file to a floppy disc, then carefully retraced her steps to remove any evidence of her surreptitious entry into the DEA data bank.

For an hour she performed routine tasks, then shut down her terminal to go to lunch. As she reached for the door to her cubicle, it opened inward. A grim looking man with a tidy red moustache stood in the doorway.

He said, 'Samantha Black?'

'Yes.'

'Major Ross, data security. You're under arrest.'

26

Brig

With a firm grip on Sam's arm, Major Ross led her to the embassy's basement holding cells. As he locked her in, she said nothing. Knowing she was under observation, she sat stiff and rigid in a corner of the cell for an hour, arms folded across her chest, avoiding the stark toilet and sink.

Ross returned, locked himself in with her and said, 'You made an illegal entry into classified files. Do you care to make a statement?'

Sam replied, 'I want to see Fred Lowry.'

Ross repeated, 'Do you want to make a statement?'

'No.'

Ross said, 'We searched your office and found a disc with a copy of the file on it.'

Sam stared at the wall and remained silent.

Ross asked, 'Did you copy the file?'

Sam shook her head and said, 'Lowry.'

'He's unavailable.'

Slowly Sam revolved her head toward the security man and said, 'So am I.'

After two hours, Sam thought her bladder would burst. Squatting on the toilet, she heard the far doors clang and footsteps marching toward her.

She was pulling up her panties when Fred Lowry and a Marine guard appeared before her cell.

'Open it up,' Lowry commanded.

The Marine opened the door and Lowry said to Sam, 'Follow me.'

With the Marine trailing behind, Lowry led her to an interrogation cell, and the Marine locked them in.

Hot water, instant coffee and tea bags made it a party.

Sam tried to remember everything Beno had told her to do if she were caught. So far, she had made it through rule one: talk only to Lowry. Rule two: don't be intimidated. Remember that Fred is scared, too. Rule three: refuse everything and don't get comfortable.

Lowry asked, 'Coffee? Tea?'

'No, thanks.'

'Sit down, Sam.'

'I'll stand.'

'Sit down!'

'No!'

He moved toward her. Instead of shrinking away she said, 'If you touch me, I'll kick you in the balls and call the guards.'

Anger and confusion mingled in Lowry's eyes. Nervously, he smiled and made himself a cup of instant coffee, saying, 'I told you that going into those files was too risky. That's why I didn't do it.'

Sam demanded, 'Are you going to get me out of here?'

'I don't know. Should I?'

'For Christ's sake, Fred, I got Obregón's address. That's what you wanted, isn't it? Or maybe it isn't. What kind of dirty game are you playing?'

'I'm only doing my job.'

'So am I.'

Lowry sat down and stated, 'You broke the rules, Sam. There's no special reason why I should stick my neck out for you.'

'I'll ask you again, Fred. Are you going to get me out of here?'

'If I arrange for your release, you'll go directly to the airport and get on a plane to Washington.'

'Then what?'

'Langley will decide whether to prosecute you.'

Rule four: threaten him a little but not too much.

Sam leaned across the table and said slowly and clearly, 'I think I'd rather talk to Major Ross first. I think I'll tell him you ordered me to go into those files.'

'I wouldn't do that if I were you.'

'Why not?'

'He won't believe you.'

She leaned back against the wall and said, 'You're bluffing. I'll take my chance.'

212

Lowry knew that if she spoke to Ross, she would tell him everything, Lucio Serdán, the Stinger, the videotape, Máximo Levín, and the whole house of cards would collapse in his face. He said, 'Suppose I let you out. What would you do?'

Her voice rising, she almost shouted, 'Give Beno the information from Obregón's file. Jesus.'

'What else?'

'Nothing else. That's all there is to it.'

Lowry asked, 'Do you know where to find Beno?'

'As far as I know, he went to Guadalajara.'

Lowry shook his head, 'No. He's here in México City.'

Sam folded her arms across her chest and said, 'Then he lied to both of us. Somehow that doesn't surprise me.'

Lowry exclaimed, 'You've gone through quite an attitude adjustment, Sam. There's something going on here I don't quite follow, something between you and Beno.'

She leaned back toward him and said with relish, 'Right. I fucked him and I liked it and I like him and I don't like you.'

Not surprised, he said, 'I figured as much. Do you think Beno can get you out of here?'

'No, but you're locked in this building as tightly as I am, aren't you, Fred? You get me out of here or I'll make a statement to Major Ross.'

'And tell him what?'

'Maybe he'll let you read it.'

Lowry realized she wasn't going to crack. She had a new-found righteousness inspired by Beno Alvarado. The warped station chief suddenly perceived her as a dangerous enemy. He couldn't allow her to speak to Ross or anyone else in the embassy. Briefly, he considered offering her money, a large sum, but quickly rejected that scenario because he believed she wouldn't accept it. His only option was to let her go and set Obregón on her.

He said, 'Okay. I'll get you out. I'll tell Ross we were checking his security procedures, and he passed with flying colours. It's thin, but it'll have to do.'

'Do you still want me to pass on Obregón's addresses to Beno?'

'Yes. I'll have a Marine take you to your apartment. Beno

will get in touch with you there. If he doesn't, try his house in Zee.'

Lowry went to his office and called Obregón at his rooming-house on Avenue de los Insurgentes Sur in Coyoacán.

'Andrés?'

'Fred?'

'Yes.'

'Hey, man. You got my money yet?'

'It's in the safe in my house.'

'Give me the combination.'

'We have a new problem. One of our computer analysts is closing in on us. I want you to take her out. When that's done, I'll give you the combination.'

'You're a real shithead, you know that?' said Obregón.

'You want the money?'

'Tell me where and when.'

'Right now, in Polanco.'

Lowry gave Obregón Sam's address and a description of the car in which she would leave the embassy. He hung up and went down to Ross' office, explained the security ploy, and returned to the interrogation cell.

At the rear of the embassy, across the street from the garage, Beno sat in the black Jetta and watched cars enter and exit. When an unmarked Pontiac emerged with Sam in the back seat, he pulled away from the kerb and followed.

A block from Sam's house, he pulled up alongside the Pontiac and yelled at the Marine, 'DIS. Pull over.'

The Marine hesitated. Beno yanked the wheel to the right and crushed the Pontiac's front bumper, forcing it to the kerb.

Angry, the plain-clothed Marine protested in bad Spanish. Beno opened his jacket, let the Marine see his machine-pistol and put his finger to his lips.

He said, 'Are you going to be smart and alive or brave, stupid, and dead?'

The Marine stared straight ahead and kept quiet. Beno opened the rear door and ushered Sam out of the car.

To the Marine he said, 'If that thing still runs, go back to the embassy.'

The Pontiac roared off.

Sam walked around the Jetta, opened the door and got in.

Beno said, 'I don't think your apartment is safe any more.'

With a bright smile Sam said, 'I just got out of jail. How do you like that?'

'You what?' Beno exclaimed.

A motorcycle raced past. At the far end of the block the Pontiac stopped at a light in front of Sam's apartment building. The motorcycle stopped next to the Pontiac on the far side. Above the Pontiac's roofline Beno could see the motorcycle driver's helmet and smoked faceplate. At that distance the hiss of an assault rifle was audible but faint. People on the pavement suddenly ran and dove for cover. The cycle roared away and disappeared around a corner, but the Pontiac didn't move.

Beno said, 'Holy Christ.'

A crowd edged around the Pontiac. Several people lay on the pavement, some crying and holding their heads. Beno pushed Sam's head down across his lap and loosened his gun.

A uniformed cop, gun drawn, approached the Pontiac, opened the door, and the Marine sprawled onto the pavement.

Beno ordered Sam, 'Stay here.'

Uzi at the ready, Beno got out of the car and walked briskly toward the Pontiac, his DIS ID plate held high. The cop looked at the card and let him go first.

The Marine had taken three bullets in the chest but was still alive.

Beno bent over, put his hand on the man's forehead and asked, 'Did you see him?'

The dying man rasped, 'Motorcycle. Helmet . . .'

Beno leaned close to him and whispered, 'Semper fi, man, hold on, hold on. What's your name?'

The Marine's face froze in a grimace and he died.

Beno stood up and scanned the pavement in shambles. A woman lay moaning at the kerb bleeding from her leg. Sirens wailed, coming closer.

Beno shouted at the crowd, 'Anyone see the licence number?'

No one had seen anything. The crowd began to melt away. An ambulance arrived and hustled the injured woman toward the Social Security Hospital casualty centre.

Beno quietly ordered the arriving police to question all witnesses and to report directly to Máximo Levín.

215

In the car he found Sam pale and shaken, huddled on the front seat.

She said, 'Everywhere I go, somebody dies.'

Beno started to put his arm around her but sensed that that was not what she needed right then. Her eyes had grown cold and hard, field officer's eyes, and that made him sad.

Beno said, 'I think we'd better talk to Máximo.'

27

The Pyramid

Beno drove to DIS headquarters and parked the rented car on the street. He clipped his ID badge to his lapel and hurried Sam toward the spotless, sterile glass lobby.

Sam asked, 'When did you join the DIS?'

Beno answered, 'I was drafted. So far, so good.'

'Does Lowry know?'

'No. Máximo wants Lowry as much as we do.'

'What else haven't you told me?'

'Nothing that will get you killed, I hope.'

As they passed through the sliding glass doors, Beno's gun set off a loud, clanging alarm. Instantly, three female security guards in maroon blazers and grey flannel skirts surrounded them, pistols cocked.

Carefully, Beno loosened his jacket, unclipped his ID card and extended it for the nearest guard to read.

The guard said, 'You aren't supposed to come in this entrance armed, Comandante.'

'We're in a hurry,' said Beno.

'Don't move. I'm going to take your weapon.'

Beno allowed her to take the gun while another woman searched Sam. While being patted down, Sam glanced up at a huge mural which depicted the constant vigilance of the Méxican police against injustice. On the opposite wall giant photographs of Alfredo Mendoza and the President of the Republic added a dollop of irony to this cartoon.

With a wave of her hand the guard said, 'You may pass.'

At the reception desk, Beno asked to see Máximo Levín.

'Do you have an appointment?'

'Yes,' Beno lied. 'He's expecting me.'

The receptionist gave him a long, sour look. Normally, seeing Máximo entailed more difficulty than an audience with the Pope. Armed men did not barge into the Directorate to see The Genius. To her astonishment, the Director's secretary immediately cleared Beno and Sam to ascend to the seventh floor.

Máximo greeted them with formal cordiality. They shook hands.

'Good afternoon, Mr Alvarado, Miss Black. I've just been informed of a terrorist shooting on River Po Street. My operator is trying to contact the officer in charge at the scene.'

Beno said, 'Lowry tried to have Ms Black killed.'

Máximo said, 'Please, sit down. Ms Black, are you all right?'

'I'm okay. Thank you.'

Máximo asked, 'Why do you believe you were the target, Ms Black?'

'Fred Lowry sent me in that car, and there is no such thing as coincidence.'

'Where was the driver taking you?'

'To my apartment to call you from there.'

'Me? Why?'

'I have addresses for Andrés Obregón. I thought you would help me get in touch with Beno, but he found me himself.'

'Mr Alvarado, please tell me what you saw?'

Beno described the slaying of the Marine and his belief that the man on the motorcycle had been Andrés Obregón.

A speakerphone on Máximo's desk crackled, 'Twenty-third precinct, dispatch, Sergeant Digas.'

'Sergeant, this is Director, DIS.'

'Yes, Director, yes sir!'

'Patch me through to the officer in charge on River Po Street.'

A moment later a grizzled voice came through the speakerphone, 'Lieutenant Castillano.'

'Hello, Lieutenant. This is Director, DIS. I understand you have a dead American on the scene there.'

'Yes, sir. His identity papers say he's part of the embassy military detachment.'

217

'Any witnesses?'

'Several, but they can't tell us much. A motorcycle pulled alongside the American's car. The rider sprayed the car with what look like nine-millimetre bullets, then left at high speed. No plates. Japanese bike of uncertain make. Helmeted rider with a smoked glass faceplate. He's long gone. One woman injured, a bystander. She should be at the hospital by now. The Metro patrolman said one of your men was passing by in a cab. He stopped for a moment, then rushed off.'

'How do you read it, Lieutenant?'

'Professional, political, anti-American, or possibly personal. Hard to say until we know something about the victim. This is DIS business, international, embassy personnel and all that.'

Máximo said, 'Take the body to the morgue and try to keep the press away.'

'The paparazzi are already here, Director.'

'Yes, I see. Keep me informed.'

'Yes, sir.'

Máximo turned off the phone.

Beno interjected and said, 'I don't want to interrupt your train of thought, Director, but time is of the essence. I would like you to call Fred Lowry and tell him the Marine and Sam Black were both killed in the car. A woman was injured. That's enough of a fact to disguise the truth.'

Máximo asked, 'Won't Lowry want to identify the body?'

Beno answered, 'To do that, he has to leave the embassy, and that's exactly what I want him to do.'

'Supposing he sends someone else?'

'Then that person will report back that Sam is dead. I can see to that.'

Máximo folded his hands on his desk and said, 'Let me consider this for a moment, Mr Alvarado. There were many witnesses, none of whom saw a red-haired woman, alive or dead, in the car. The American legal attaché will make his own investigation. The press is already on the scene, and they probably have the injured woman's name. I'm afraid not.'

'It's worth a try.'

Máximo made a gesture of resignation and said, 'I wish it were. Truly, I do, but, as you say, time is of the essence, and it's too late.'

Beno repressed an urge to shout and throw a fit. Instead, his voice heavy with disappointment, he said, 'I guess you're right. But damn, those bastards tried to kill this woman.'

'I'm sorry.'

Beno suggested, 'What about an all points bulletin for Obregón as a common murderer?'

Máximo shook his head. 'That would alert Mendoza.'

Beno tried his last gambit, 'Why don't you have your people try the addresses for Obregón?'

Sam interrupted with, 'Lowry will have alerted Obregón to stay clear of all of them by now. You said that yourself, Beno.'

Máximo said, 'That's right. Mr Alvarado, I'm afraid you're still on your own in this matter. I can give you equipment, documents, anything material, but involving my agents means taking an unacceptable security risk. Police work is often tedious and frustrating. It's come to my attention that Mr Lowry has barricaded himself inside the embassy.'

Beno said, 'Yes, but obviously he's still dangerous.'

Máximo turned to Sam and said, 'Ms Black, if you feel you are in danger, I can protect you in this building.'

Sam said, 'I appreciate that, Dr Levín, but no thank you.'

Beno said, 'I need weapons and a car with communication gear, and Ms Black needs papers.'

Máximo responded, 'Of course.'

Máximo wrote out three chits and handed two to Beno. 'Take these to the motor pool and the armourer. They'll give you whatever they have. I'm sorry, but that's the best I can do.'

He gave the other to Sam and said, 'I'll call documents and your DIS papers will be ready in a few minutes.'

Máximo said, 'One more thing. We're watching the embassy and will alert you the instant Lowry leaves, if he does. You're in the Hotel Paris, no?'

Beno and Máximo exchanged stolid smiles. Beno said, 'Thank you, Director.'

28

Coyoacán

Sam and Beno went down to the documents division on the second floor. A clerk issued Sam an embossed red and gold brass DIS identity plate sealed in plastic. She was now Inspector Black.

From the armourer Beno chose a pair of Uzis, thirty-round clips, holsters and ten boxes of ammunition. Sam took a Ruger .38 Magnum revolver, holster and speed loader.

They took the elevator to the motor pool where Beno selected a dark blue Ford Taurus SHO, an inconspicuous factory hotrod. He checked the Motorola two-way radio, signed the chit, and drove out of the garage.

Sam expertly loaded the Ruger and pronounced the gun acceptable.

'How about a few rounds at a firing range?' she asked.

'We don't have time,' Beno answered, then asked, 'Where'd you learn to shoot?'

'Every Navy base has a firing range,' Sam replied. 'I made the Olympic trials in 1988.'

'It's a little different when people are shooting back, isn't it, Annie Oakley?'

'Hold and squeeze,' she said. 'And hit the target.'

'Don't forget,' Beno cautioned. 'We want Obregón alive.'

They crossed the city listening to police chatter on the DIS frequencies, a big city litany of rape, murder and pillage. After twenty minutes, Beno tuned the Motorola to the exclusive DIS channel, turned it down, and switched on the FM band. On an oldies station he found The Fabulous Thunderbirds and sang along with 'Tuff Enuff'.

When the song dissolved into a blast of screaming commercials, Sam plied Beno with a question.

'Where do you come from, Comandante Alvarado of the DIS?'

He chortled, 'What is this, kiss and tell?'

'Yes.'

'Well, like they say in México, I come from the other side.'

'That's no answer.'

'You're right. I don't talk about my past. I'm not trying to be mysterious or secretive, but I don't care where people come from. I was born and raised in San Francisco, but I've lived in México for twelve years. *La República* is home now.'

'Don't you ever go back?'

'To the other side?'

'Yeah. The U.S. of A.'

Beno slowly shook his head. 'Not often, and when I do, I don't like it. America is a broken promise. You don't want to get me started on this.'

Sam asked, 'What do you mean, a broken promise?'

Beno said, 'The Constitution, shredded. The Declaration of Independence, incinerated. Give us your tired and your poor. Forget it. We manufacture our own. That's what I mean.'

Sam felt Beno's words drill into her like a dentist's hard steel bit. Taken aback, she said, 'Those are surprising sentiments from a CIA officer.'

'Ex-officer, lady. I'm fed up with those racist assholes in the embassy.'

'Is that what you think they are?'

With great feeling Beno replied, 'You're white, Sam. Maybe you haven't noticed.'

'Then why did you stay in the agency so long?'

Beno lit a cigarette, let the smoke roll out of his nostrils, and replied, 'I stayed in because I know México. I filed my reports and did my job, but nothing I ever said or did made a damn bit of difference. Like everything else on the other side, the CIA is a big lie, a propaganda machine.'

'You sound bitter.'

'Ha! That's an understatement. With the world like it is, anyone who isn't cynical is an idiot with his head buried in the sand. How many wars started today? How many drug dealers bought how many prime ministers? How many millions did the Department of Defense spend on useless weapon systems? Want me to go on?'

Without waiting for an answer Beno continued, 'How many tons of radioactive material got dumped into the atmosphere,

221

the rivers, the oceans? How many children shot each other with assault rifles? How many drunks slaughtered families on the freeway? How many religious fanatics declared holy war on each other? What's for dinner, Mama? Frozen pizza with artificial cheese and real TV. The world is fucked, girl, and nobody takes the blame. It's always the other guy. When something goes wrong, lay the blame on the Russians, the Japanese, the poor people, the rich people, the Republicans, the Democrats, always the other guy. Our last three presidents have been a second-rate nuclear engineer, a third rate actor, and a fourth rate spy. And people thought Nixon was bad. The next one might be a TV preacher or a Nazi. Who cares? Half the people don't vote. The literacy rate is declining. Hospitals and schools and libraries are closing and every day a new hate group gets its own TV show. Tell me when you've heard enough and I'll stop.'

Laughing with delight, Sam said, 'I love a man with strong opinions, even if they are off the wall.'

'Off the wall? Are you kidding? It took me half a lifetime to think this shit up. Heard enough?'

'No, go on. This is incredible.'

'You think so? I'll tell you what's incredible. We're running around México City playing cops and robbers with two renegade Americans who tried to rip off one of the world's biggest dope dealers. Why do so many people take dope? Because life is fucking hopeless. Lower class, middle class, upper class, it doesn't make any difference. People are powerless. There's no democracy or equality or even a pretence of fairness. Instead you get the big lie. Congressmen are bought and sold like used cars by faceless corporations whose only concern is the bottom line. The bottom line, Jesus Christ, we're the bottom line, Sam. We're armed and dangerous and ready to do the dirty work.'

Outside their air-conditioned car, México City sank another millimetre into the ancient lake bed on which it was built. They rode in uneasy silence along Avenue de los Insurgentes, watching the endless crowds and limitless traffic. At a stop light a lane opened and Beno punched the powerful Yamaha V-6 that powered the Ford. The car lunged forward like a dragster, and he smiled with satisfied car lust.

Their first stop was an expensive hair salon in San Angel at the southern extremity of the city. Beno lost his moustache and added years of grey to his hair. Sam emerged a sandy blonde. With an agency American Express card they replenished their wardrobes in shops near the university.

Dressed as tourists outfitted by Banana Republic, they drove slowly down Fresnos Street in Coyoacán. The quiet residential block lined with hardy ash trees had a small grocery store at one end and a Pemex gas station at the other. Beno stopped beside the pumps, flashed his DIS card and showed the manager a photograph of Andrés Obregón.

'Oh yes,' said the manager. 'I know him. He has a funny accent, Puerto Rico or Dominica.'

Beno asked, 'Does he ride a motorcycle?'

'Yes.'

'When was the last time you saw him?'

The manager reflected, then answered, 'Yesterday, maybe the day before. He bought gas from me. Is he in trouble with the police?'

'We want to talk to him, that's all. If you see him again, don't tell him we were here. We'll be back.'

At the grocery store Beno and Sam repeated their inquiry. A fat woman surrounded by warm Coca-Cola and comic books recognized the photo of Obregón as 'that nice Mr Gutierrez from next door,' but he had not been in her store for a week.

She said, 'He told me he was planning to return to Venezuela where he was from, but first he wanted to visit Disneyland. Me, too, but it's so far to Texas where Mickey lives.'

Sam giggled as Beno asked, 'Does he live alone?'

'Oh, no. There's Donald and Goofy and those funny squirrels.'

Sam walked outside trying to suppress her laughter.

Patiently, Beno asked, 'Mr Gutierrez. Does he live alone?'

'Him? I think so. He's gone a lot.'

On the pavement Beno quipped to Sam, 'Do you think every goofball in the world lives in New York City? C'mon.'

Obregón's house hid behind a high wall topped with broken glass. Beno retrieved a tyre iron from the car, jemmied the locked gate and pushed it open.

A small brick house squatted at the rear of the lot, separated from the wall by a deep, unkempt patch of weeds. Beno sensed desertion and emptiness.

The house revealed signs of sudden departure. Drawers were left open, dirty dishes littered the sink, the bed unmade.

Beno shook his head and said, 'Next stop.'

They drove fifteen blocks to Obregón's roominghouse on Avenue de los Insurgentes. The desk clerk knew Obregón as José Pedregal and thought he came from Vera Cruz.

Beno asked, 'When did you see him last?'

'He got a phone call this morning and took off on his motorbike. He hasn't returned.'

'Show us his room.'

'No women allowed upstairs.'

'Listen, you . . .'

Sam interrupted, 'I'll wait, Beno. It's okay.'

Beno demanded, 'Give me a passkey.'

The clerk replied, 'I don't have one. He had the locks changed. It's on the first floor, number nineteen.'

Beno started up the stairs. Sam crossed the lobby to a red coke machine, dropped a five-hundred peso coin in the slot and withdrew a bottle. She popped the cap and was raising the bottle to her lips when the front door pushed open and Andrés Obregón took one step inside.

She screamed, 'Beno!'

Obregón saw the young blonde woman in the lobby, heard her shout, and hesitated, perplexed. Lowry had told him his target was a redhead. He had sprayed the car with automatic fire, but not until after the windows were shattered had he realized the back seat was empty.

Irrespective of hair colour, the blonde was the woman with the videotape. Obregón reached under his jacket for a pistol tucked into his belt.

Sam hurled the coke bottle at Obregón's head. He dodged and the bottle bounced off the steel door jamb. Sam dove for the floor and struggled to pull the Ruger from the stiff, new holster. She heard a loud gunshot and a bullet punctured the coke machine. A spray of icy freon squirted into the lobby. Beno bounded down the stairs in time to see the door swing shut. Keeping low to the ground, Uzi cocked, he crept out of the door and saw hundreds of legs and feet stepping off a city bus.

People saw his gun and scattered in all directions. Beno

looked left and right and rushed into the street, but Obregón had disappeared in the crowd.

Inside the hotel the clerk cowered behind the lobby desk.

'You can come out now,' Sam said. 'It's all over.'

Slowly the clerk raised his eyes above the counter, cautiously stood up, and frowned at his ruined coke machine.

Beno asked, 'Do you have a fire escape at the back?'

'Why?' asked the clerk.

Beno leaned close to him and said, 'Because our friend wired his door. If you had tried to go in there, the fire department would be scraping you off the ceiling.'

'Holy Mother of God.' The clerk rapidly crossed himself.

'Save it for Sunday. Fire escape?'

'Yes, yes. Come through here.'

Beno said to Sam, 'Clear everyone away from in front of the building. Don't let anyone in.'

'Sí, Comandante.'

Beno passed through the manager's apartment into a filthy courtyard and climbed the rickety steel ladder that served as a fire escape. Obregón had booby-trapped the door and window.

Beno returned to the lobby, picked up the clerk's phone and dialled Máximo Levín.

The Director's secretary answered.

Beno said, 'I need the bomb squad.'

'I'd better let you speak to the Director.'

Máximo came on the line. Beno rapidly explained the situation.

Máximo said, 'I'll get a bomb squad there in ten minutes.'

Beno said, 'When they defuse the bomb, I want to go in alone.'

'Certainly.'

'No questions. I don't know what I'll find in there.'

'Of course. I'll explain it to the Captain. Please hold for a moment.'

A few seconds later Máximo returned to the line and said, 'They're on their way.'

'Okay.'

Beno hung up and said to the clerk, 'Evacuate the building.'

The clerk cast a baleful look at his soda pop box and wailed, 'What about my machine?'

In a singsong voice Sam replied, '*Pepsi refresca mejor.*'

A three-man bomb squad arrived in an armoured truck. Beno led the Captain up the fire escape and they peered through the window.

The Captain said, 'The window is too dangerous. The detonator on the sill is a motion detector with a delay and a cut-off switch. That way, the guy who lives here can go in and shut it off. The best way always is to blow it.'

'Hell no,' said Beno. 'I want whatever is in that room.'

'So I'm told,' said the Captain. 'But it might be a small, shaped charge designed to kill an intruder but not destroy the valuables in the room.'

'I wouldn't count on it,' said Beno.

The Captain flicked on his two-way radio and asked the microphone, 'Is the building clear?'

'Yes,' came the answer.

'Cut off the power.'

The lights in the building went off.

'Smoke it,' ordered the Captain into his radio.

Grey smoke rolled under the door and filled the room.

The Captain said, 'There's no infrared. The sensors are ultrasonic. That's a bitch.'

Beno asked, 'What do you do now?'

'Go in there, Comandante.'

'Who?'

'Me.'

The two men climbed down the fire escape and re-entered the building.

A crowd had gathered across the street behind a police cordon. Andrés Obregón edged behind the onlookers and silently cursed the bomb squad carrying equipment into the roominghouse. He saw Beno step outside for a moment, speak to the blonde woman, then return to the lobby. He knew it was time to cut his losses and head for Acapulco, but he couldn't go until he learned if his boobytrap worked.

* * *

226

The Captain explained to Beno, 'We don't know how many sensors or how many charges. The sensors are point sources, probably high up on the walls and battery powered. They won't be pointed directly at the door. The cut-off switch can be anywhere.'

Beno said, 'Sounds like suicide.'

The Captain asked, 'How good is this guy?'

Beno answered, 'He's a pro.'

'Lovely.'

Upstairs two bomb squaders in heavy body armour gingerly removed the door from its hinges. The infrared detector smoke drifted into the corridor. When the door was out, the men directed a strong spotlight into the room. They saw a bed, an armoir, a table and chair, and an electronic device high up in a corner.

One of the men spoke into a radio, 'We see one detector, Captain.'

'I'm coming up.'

The Captain struggled into body armour, clamped on a heavy helmet and trudged up the stairs. He looked like a deep sea diver with a pair of wire clippers in his hand.

Beno ducked behind the lobby desk and watched the Captain enter the room.

Half a second later, his head wrapped in his arms, the Captain flew out of the doorway, knocking his men to the corridor floor. With a sharp blast, the bomb exploded and blew out a huge chunk of the corridor wall. In an instant the bomb squad rushed into the room with fire extinguishers. Black smoke filled the corridor, gushed down into the lobby and momentarily blinded Beno who had to feel his way to the front door.

The blast agitated the crowd across the street, but instead of running for cover the people pressed toward the building, causing the police to threaten them with batons.

Obregón smirked with satisfaction, then walked toward the entrance of the Insurgentes subway station and began his journey south.

When Sam heard the explosion, she clutched her belly and cried out, 'Beno!'

A moment later he stumbled out the door, coughing from the smoke and bleeding from a small cut on his forehead. Sam held him and dabbed at his wound with her sleeve.

Gently, he pushed her away and said, 'I'm all right. I have to go back in.'

Upstairs, the three members of the bomb squad stood in the corridor with their helmets off.

The Captain said to Beno, 'Three detectors. Very good, your pro. A shaped charge. The armoir is undamaged.'

Beno inquired, 'You all right?'

'Bruised, not bad considering. Go on in. It's safe.'

In the armoir Beno found eighty thousand dollars, an M-15, and a case of ammunition.

29

Mears

Beno locked the money and rifle in the boot of the Taurus and joined the riverine flow of traffic.

'Had enough excitement for one day?' Beno asked Sam as they drove along Avenue de los Insurgentes away from the roominghouse.

She asked in return, 'What do you have in mind?'

'We're burning Obregón's bridges. My guess is he stashed the rest of the money in Acapulco. This is getting sticky.'

'I could go for a little beach time,' Sam said. 'How about you?'

Beno grinned and said, 'Airport, driver. And make it snappy.'

As they neared the airport, the car phone rang.

Beno answered, 'Alvarado.'

'Dr Levín here, Comandante. I understand the bomb exploded, but there were no casualties.'

'That's right. Your Captain leads a charmed life.'

'What did you find?'

'Money and weapons.'

Máximo asked, 'But nothing that incriminates Mr Lowry?'

'No.'

'Mr Lowry just phoned me. Officially, he called to discuss his murdered Marine. Unofficially, he wanted to know where you were.'

'What did you tell him?'

'That I had no idea as to your whereabouts.'

'I appreciate that,' Beno said.

Máximo said, 'I have another piece of information for you. Mr Alexander Mears returned to México this afternoon. At the moment he's in the embassy.'

'Thank you, Director.'

The call ended.

Puzzled, Beno said to Sam, 'Lowry called DIS.'

Sam asked, 'Is he nuts? What for?'

'He's trying to find us. That's the good news. The bad news is that Al Mears showed up at the embassy.'

'The DDO? How often does he come to México?'

'A couple of times a year. He's one of Fred's old pals. The two of them can cook up a lot of mischief in a hurry. If you look back at America's unbroken chain of failure in Latin America for the last thirty years, Fred Lowry and Al Mears were responsible for most of it. They thought the Bay of Pigs was a good idea. Mears is a political animal who always has his finger to the wind. He's smart and squeaky clean.'

Sam speculated, 'They could be arranging the transfer of power to the new station chief.'

'I'm sure that's part of it,' said Beno. 'But not all of it.'

Sam asked, 'What could Lowry want from you?'

'There's only one way to find out.'

Beno pulled onto a side street and parked at the kerb. He picked up the car phone and dialled the embassy duty officer.

'Four three nine one.'

Beno spoke slowly and enunciated clearly into the phone, saying, 'Hello. My name is Andrés Obregón. I would like to speak to Mr Frederick Lowry, the station chief of the Central Intelligence Agency, please.'

Sam burst into laughter.

After a long pause, the duty officer replied, 'Is this some kind of joke?'

Beno answered, 'Hardly, my friend. You can hang up, try to trace my call, play all sorts of games, but I'll keep calling back until Lowry comes on the line. Or, I'll call his inside number. Let's see, that number is . . .'

'Hold on there, buddy. This is an open line.'

'No shit. I'm calling from a mobile phone. Why, anybody could be listening.'

Lowry's voice interrupted, 'Who is this?'

'Howdy, Fred. Heard you wanted to chat.'

The duty officer rang off.

Lowry asked, 'Alpha Seven?'

Imitating an officious monotone, Beno said sternly, 'Let's not mention names over the air, okay?'

Lowry demanded, 'Where are you?'

'What do you want, Fred?'

'I want you to come in.'

'I'm sure you do, just like your dead Marine. Why don't you give me his name. Maybe I'll write a letter to his family.'

'That's not very professional.'

'You want to hear something professional? He died in my arms.'

Lowry persisted doggedly, 'Some important people want to talk to you.'

'That's great. It makes me all warm inside to know important people are thinking of me. You, Obregón, nice people, dedicated public servants, champions of the free world.'

'I can give you guarantees.'

Beno guffawed, 'I can give you a guarantee, you son of a bitch. Care to guess what it is?'

Unfazed, Lowry continued, 'Things have changed. There's been a policy reversal. Call me back on a secure line.'

'No access, Fred. Now or never.'

'You're being insubordinate.'

'I'm retired. I can't be insubordinate. Who's in there with you, Freddie? Who're you trying to impress? Your important people?'

'Beno, I'm alone, but this is an open line.'

'You're an outlaw, Fred. You're fair game.'

A hint of uncertainty crept into Lowry's voice as he said, 'We have to meet.'

'I'll tell you what. I'll meet you at DIS headquarters.'

'No way.'

'There's no place else I can think of that would be safe.'

'DIS – that's impossible.'

'I don't trust you, Fred. If I were you, I wouldn't trust me, either. Speak now, or hang up.'

'Beno, this is of the utmost importance.'

'Not to me. I'm growing weary of this sparring. Bye, Fred.'

Lowry screeched, 'Wait. Don't hang up. Don't throw away your career.'

'I already have. My career isn't on the line. Yours is.'

'DDO doesn't see it that way.'

Beno laughed and said, 'I can imagine the line of shit you're feeding him. Old boy week, is it? Did you promise to split the take with him, Fred?'

'Let me name a place.'

'Think fast, faster than you did this afternoon when you tried to kill Sam Black.'

'Is she there with you?'

'No. Is DDO there with you?'

'No.'

'For a pro, you're a lousy liar.'

Lowry suggested, 'We can meet at drop eight.'

'No public places.'

'Drop twelve.'

'No private clubs. Don't you get it, Fred? I wouldn't meet you on top of a pyramid at midnight if you came naked bound hand and foot. I take that back. Under those conditions, I would gladly cut out your heart.'

'How can I persuade you?'

'You can't.'

'You name a place.'

'I did. DIS. You didn't like it.'

'It can't be there.'

'I wonder why. I thought you and Máximo Levín were kissing cousins.'

'Beno . . .'

'Adiós.'

Beno placed the phone in its cradle and drove away from the kerb. He said to Sam, 'Let's go to Acapulco.'

* * *

231

Al Mears sat in Lowry's office, listening to the speaker phone without expressing any sentiment, chainsmoking Salems, polishing his spectacles and wishing he were not in México City.

When Lowry hung up, he said, 'Sounds like he won't come in.'

Lowry said with disdain, 'I didn't think he would. I'm surprised he called at all.'

Mears asked, 'Where's your man Obregón?'

Lowry shook his head, 'I don't know.'

Frowning, the DDO said, 'You're botching this, Fred. The lid is about to be blown off Mendoza. Trying to use Serdán was a tactical error. The President is sick to death of people trying to embarrass the agency. If you can't bring in Alvarado, we'll have to go another route. None of this is making you look good.'

'What could I tell him over an open line, Al? He's in a DIS car outfitted with their electronics.'

Mears said, 'Tell me what happened with Mendoza's plane.'

Lowry folded his hands behind his head, leaned back in his chair and explained, 'There was a leak, and Mendoza wasn't on the plane. The only people who knew anything about the operation were me, Beno Alvarado, Obregón and the woman, Sam Black. We attempted to eliminate her and missed.'

'Why her? How did she know?'

'Obviously, Alvarado told her. He's gone beyond the pale, Al. He drummed up the idea of using Serdán. He thought Serdán was the second coming of Christ. I tried an end run. Obregón got onto Mendoza's plane, but the Minister wasn't on it.'

Mears folded his hands together, rested his chin on his locked fingers, and said, 'Too bad. Look at the record. You missed her. Obregón missed Mendoza. Our people are running around México City trying to kill each other, blowing up buildings. We have a dead Marine to explain. What the hell is going on here?'

'Beno Alvarado, that's what.'

'I thought you knew this man, Fred.'

Lowry said, 'He's never been one of us, you know. He's a foot soldier, a grunt. Clever, dangerous and highly skilled, but not really one of us, if you know what I mean.'

Mears' thin lips warped into the caricature of a smile as he said, 'You mean he's a Méxican, Tex-Mex.'

'California, actually.'

'I see.'

They sat quietly for half a minute, surrounded by Lowry's imperial maps, comfortable in the silence of their old-boyhood, confident of their supremacy.

Mears broke the silence by asking, 'Are you afraid of him?'

'I'd be a fool not to be.'

'Where do you think he'll go next?'

'Acapulco.'

'Get hold of Antoine Bonmarche. Have him arrest our loose cannon.'

Lowry dialled Oakland Air Freight. The phone rang ten times, but no one answered. He hung up.

Mears asked, 'How could you have let this affair go this far out of control?'

Angry, Lowry pursed his lips and said through his teeth, 'He's gone freelance. He's been in México too long. This place gets to everyone after a while.'

'Even you, it appears.'

Exasperated, Lowry sputtered, 'For God's sake, I didn't agree with the finding in the first place.'

'I think you're cracking, Fred. I'm bringing in the new station chief tomorrow. We need damage control, now, and your credibility is shot. I'm sorry, but that's the way it is.'

Mears puffed on his mentholated cigarette and said, 'The finding didn't say terminate Mendoza, did it?'

Shocked, Lowry stammered, 'You're going to lay this all on me?'

'Who else? You know the rule. Fail and fall.'

'You son of a bitch.'

'What would you do in my place, Fred? Be reasonable.'

'Sure, Al. I'll run right over to the Ministry of Government and tell Mendoza to be reasonable.'

Mears said, 'Calm down. It's only México. Nobody cares a damn about México. I'm putting you on administrative leave as of now. Relax, Fred. Go down to the commissary and have a drink.'

At the AeroMéxico ticket counter Beno and Sam bought tickets to Acapulco. At the gate their credentials allowed them to bypass the metal detectors. While they waited for the plane,

Beno circulated among the security personnel showing them a photograph of Obregón. No one had seen him.

Their plane was called and they took off for more fun in the sun.

Lowry spent an hour with his shredder, then descended a back stairway to the Marines' barracks.

The Captain of the Guard saluted and said, 'What can I do for you, sir?'

Lowry said, 'I need a detachment of four men to go over to Military Camp Number One. I've been asked by DIS to review a special regiment for the military parade on Thursday. Don't tell them where we're going. Security. And I need a uniform.'

'Yes, sir.'

'I'm going to join the Corps, Captain. I need a razor.'

'A little undercover work, sir? Always happy to help out the agency. Let's see. Forty-two regular?'

'I wish. Forty-six will do me.'

In the Marines' head Lowry spent thirty minutes shaving his scalp and clothing himself in Marine fatigues.

'Call for a van, Captain. Have the men meet me in the garage.'

A Lance Corporal and three privates were waiting with the van. The men in the DIS Ford parked behind the embassy scarcely noticed the van full of Marines pull away from the garage.

Lowry directed the Corporal to drive down Paseo de la Reforma and into the Zona Rosa. On Geneva Street Lowry waited in the van while one of the privates went into an Aca Joe and bought pants, a shirt, shoes, a belt and a hat.

The Marines loved it. Those CIA guys were so clever. Forty blocks south on University Avenue a bald civilian stepped out of an embassy van and disappeared into the subway tunnel.

Lowry found a phone booth and called the officers' club at Military Camp Number One.

He said to the receptionist, 'I would like to speak to General Vargas. I believe you'll find him in the bar.'

After a brief delay, the General came on the line.

'Vargas here.'

'General, Fred Lowry. I'd like to meet you in private as soon as possible.'

30

Red Line

Andrés Obregón stood absolutely still on the escalator that lowered him into the subterranean world of the Metro. At the bottom of the six-hundred-foot drop he bought a ticket and leaned against the white tile wall of Balderas station. Humanity swirled around, but Obregón preferred to watch the television monitors suspended overhead. Two dozen nineteen-inch monitors replicated the bleak fantasy of a well-dressed soap opera down the length of the platform. The flaccid dialogue echoed through the tunnel, 'Why are you having this affair?' 'I can't help myself.' 'I'll make you pay for this, you bastard.' Break for commercials. Tide. Buick. Kotex. Sony. The Party loves you. Mercedes-Benz, for the very few.

The Red Line train swept into the station. Decelerating, the lead car rocked back and forth like a swaying viper. Of French design, the subway rolled on rubber wheels over a wooden track, gliding silently through the tunnel like a slithering steel snake. Hydraulic pumps whooshed open the doors. Citizens crowded off and on the yellow cars, inhaling human odours, spying on shopping bags, assessing clothes and shoes. With a rubber pop the doors slid shut and the train slipped into forward motion.

Obregón shuffled to the rear of the last car, squeezed into a seat and hid his face behind a newspaper. No one followed him onto the train or paid him any attention. While the train remained motionless in the station, he dug into his pocket, brought out a small vial of cocaine, unscrewed the cap and tilted the bottle onto the tip of his little finger. With a quick, inconspicuous jerk he raised his finger to his nose.

Pow! The foetid air turned to ice. Rock music exploded in Obregón's ear. The vial tilted again.

The train began to move. Advertising posters on the platform wall whizzed past, blurred images of high fashion mingled with

235

the chunky shapes of excavated stone jaguars. Old blended with new in a subterranean mosaic.

Obregón twitched his nose and the train burst into the next station. Another bank of television monitors flashed past, heads talking beyond good and evil, talking silently, subliminally to the citizens on the platform, talking hard sell soft sell selling Tide Sony Mercedes Tampax lottery tickets, a jigsaw puzzle with infinite pieces. The train rolled on and the vial tilted again.

An old woman smelling of urine and cheap perfume pushed through the crowded car, plopped down next to Obregón and opened a romantic comic book. Obregón retreated behind his paper and sniffed more cocaine, anaesthetizing himself to her odour as the stations flashed past, Salto de Agua, Balderas, Cuauhtémoc, Insurgentes, Sevilla, Chapultepec, Juanacatlan, Tacubaya, until the names pushed him toward madness with their Méxican mix of Spanish and Nahuatl.

Pushing his face against the window glass, Obregón imagined his container full of money in the Oakland Air warehouse in Acapulco. With his mind's fingers he opened the heavy aluminium box and felt the solid bricks of bills, the sharp edges of the banknotes. The money was waiting, half a million dollars calling like deadly sirens over the Sierra, across the dry riverbeds and salt lakes until the sound reached deep beneath the floor of the Valley of México into the subway tunnel where Andrés Obregón rocked and sweated on a yellow train.

The coke intensified his anger and frustration. After waiting years for a chance to steal millions from Mendoza, the moment had slipped away. The money in the roominghouse was lost, and he faced the prospect of losing the half million stashed in Acapulco.

In retrospect, his first mistake had been not taking his money out of México before the fruitless highjack. His second mistake had been believing the money would be on the plane. With cocaine clarity Obregón understood that Lowry had intended to kill him. Assassinate the assassin. Lowry would never pay him a dime.

What a fucked up day. Balderas, Cuauhtémoc, he had come full circle on the Red Line. He had missed the woman twice, first in the car and then in the lobby of the roominghouse. The boobytrap had worked. Boom! Far out.

Every instinct for self-preservation told him the money in Acapulco was bait in a trap. Don't go. Split. Leave the country. Charter a plane, fly to Mexicali and cross the border in the high desert at night.

One two three four five hundred thousand American greenback dollars, in cash. If I'm going to die in this strange land, I'd just as soon die rich.

At Balderas station Obregón left the train, rode the escalator to the surface and flagged a cab.

'Airport. Charter annexe.'

'Yes, sir. Charter. Where you want to go, man?'

Obregón stared at the driver, considering his answer, then said, 'Acapulco.'

The cab driver turned around and said, 'I can get you there in eight hours, man. For a lot less than a charter plane which will probably crash and burn in the Sierra.'

Obregón asked, 'You got decent tyres?'

'Yeah.'

'You know how to keep your mouth shut? I don't want to hear the story of your life or answer questions.'

The driver smiled and said, 'I just drive, *amigo*. You want quiet, you got quiet.'

'How much?'

Obregón and the driver settled on a price and the cab headed south.

At five in the afternoon, about the time Obregón's cab was passing through Cuernavaca, Beno and Sam arrived in Acapulco and walked into the Oakland Air warehouse, just as the Raiders were closing up shop for the day.

Beno recognized Antoine Bonmarche sitting under a hard hat atop a forklift.

Beno inquired, 'Mr Bonmarche?'

'Yes?'

'I'd like a moment of your time.'

'We're packing it in for today, pal. Come back in the morning.'

Beno said, 'I'm looking for Andrés Obregón.'

'Haven't seen him today.'

Sam noticed the Raiders exchanging glances.

Beno asked, 'Do you expect him?'

'He comes and goes. You know how it is.'

Beno stepped closer to the forklift and said, 'Can we speak in private?'

Bonmarche peered down at the husky Méxican and knew something was not right. His first inclination was that the man and his lady friend were smugglers, perhaps the people Obregón had said he had met in México City.

He asked Beno, 'You want to ship some goods to the States?'

Beno answered, 'I want to talk.'

Bonmarche climbed down to the concrete floor, led Beno and Sam into his untidy office, and closed the door. He offered chairs, plopped down behind his desk, and asked, 'What do you want to ship?'

Beno said, 'I don't want to ship anything. I want to talk to Obregón.'

Bonmarche scowled and said, 'I didn't catch your name.'

'Alvarado. This is Ms Black.'

'Pleased to make your acquaintance. Do you know Obregón?'

Beno gestured with his head toward the door and said, 'I don't want any misunderstanding. Why don't you send your freakshow home.'

Eyes flicked back and forth between Beno and Sam, then Bonmarche said, 'Who are you, pal? What do you want?'

Beno replied calmly, 'I know you're DEA. I also know you're willing to co-operate.'

Bonmarche asked, 'You a DEA investigator?'

'No. Now, get those guys out of here.'

Bonmarche said, 'You're CIA. You're a spook.'

Beno shook his head and displayed his DIS credentials.

Bonmarche stood up, opened the door and hollered, 'Everybody go outside.'

A voice yelled back, 'You okay, boss?'

'Everything's under control.'

At that moment Sam reached under her seat and stuck a bug to the chair bottom.

Footsteps rattled over the concrete, the outer door slammed shut, and Bonmarche returned to his desk. Beno went into the warehouse and stood still for a moment, listening. Leaving the door open, he sat down again in his chair and laid twenty thousand dollars on Bonmarche's desk.

He said, 'Obregón has been fucking us around. Soon, today or tomorrow, he's going to be out of the picture. We want someone to replace him.'

Looking at the money, Bonmarche said, 'That's a very persuasive argument, but I'm not sure exactly what it's for.'

'Does it matter?'

Bonmarche folded his thick fingers together, leaned across the desk and snarled, 'Yes, because I won't take it. Fuck you. Get outta here.'

'Be reasonable, Mr Bonmarche.'

'I'll be reasonable. I won't kick your ass if you take your girlfriend and go bye-bye.'

Beno said, 'All you have to do is tell us where to find Obregón.'

'Find him yourself.'

'Why do you want to protect him?'

'My mother always told me not to tattle. Are you going to leave, or am I going to throw you out?'

Beno nodded to Sam and they stood. Beno said, 'You think about it.'

'Take your money.'

'Consider it a bonus, Mr Bonmarche. Give it to your favourite charity.'

Outside, Beno and Sam walked across the parking area toward their rented Ford Topaz. Beno stopped by the Oakland Air van, knocked on the windscreen, and yelled, 'You guys can go back inside now.'

As Beno drove away he watched in the rear view mirror as the van doors opened and the Raiders piled out. Sam turned on the portable receiver and they heard one of the Raiders ask Bonmarche, 'Who was that guy?'

Bonmarche said, 'I dunno. He said they were DIS, but I think they were spooks. They want that fuck, Andrés. They want him bad.'

'What'd you tell 'em?'

'I didn't tell them jack shit, but I sure am going to find out from Andrés why they want him. Go move his container. Stash it somewhere out of sight.'

'Okay.'

One of the Raiders said, 'Did you see that broad? What a piece of ass.'

Bonmarche's phone rang. He wasn't in the mood for the phone. He let it ring.

He said to his men, 'We're gonna stay here all night.'

Beno drove to the main parking area near the passenger terminal and pulled into an empty slot.

He said, 'Now we wait.'

Sam yawned. 'It's been a long day, a hell of a long day.'

'Get some sleep. It'll be a longer night.'

14 SEPTEMBER

31

Oakland Raiders

At three o'clock in the morning Andrés Obregón's México City cab arrived at the Oakland Air parking area.

The warehouse door was open and light filtered out into the night. Obregón told the driver to wait, got out of the cab, entered the building and waved at one of the Raiders.

The man shouted, 'Boss!'

Bonmarche came out of his office and signalled the Cuban to enter.

Standing in front of Bonmarche's desk Obregón placed his badge, American Express card and snub-nosed .38 revolver next to the telephone and a stack of files. With a wide grin he announced, 'I quit.'

Bonmarche blew out a lungful of smoke with a big sigh. Saying nothing, he yanked open a filing cabinet and fished around for a triple-sheafed resignation form. He found the form, tossed it onto the desk and said with a trace of irritation, 'Fill this out. Your cheque from the pension fund will show up next year if you're lucky.'

A mile away in the airport car park Sam had fallen asleep in the car. When Beno cranked the engine and jammed the transmission into gear, she woke up with a jolt.

'*Que pasó?*' she asked.

Beno answered, 'Obregón is in the warehouse.'

'What're you gonna do, Andrés?' asked Bonmarche. 'You got a job lined up?'

Obregón scribbled on the form and mumbled, 'Go back to Miami. Anyplace is better than México. This place sucks.'

Bonmarche said blithely, 'I could get you more money, an assignment stateside, Miami or Tampa. You can even join the Raiders if you like.'

'Nope. No way.'

Bonmarche chainlit a new cigarette, leaned across his desk on his elbows and said, 'Talk to me about Mendoza.'

Obregón reached the bottom of the form, signed it with a flourish, and replied, 'I can't tell you anything you don't know, Antoine. Red poppies, brown smack, and half the Méxican army to back him up. You'll never get him in a million years.'

'How many of our guys has he bought, do you think?'

'Hard to say.'

'Did he ever try to buy you?'

'Sure. He tries to buy everybody.'

'What happened? He give you a choice, take his money or die?'

'Something like that, yeah.'

Bonmarche leaned back in his chair and smiled. 'Why didn't you take the money?' he asked. 'Everybody else does.'

'Including you, Antoine? You wanna get personal?'

Bonmarche stroked his beard and cracked his jaw into a friendly smile as wide as the Mississippi.

He said, 'I can't blame you if you don't want to play Elliot Ness any more. We got prohibition all over again, and it doesn't work any better now than it did the first time. People are gonna drink, they're gonna fornicate, they're gonna take dope no matter how many fools preach, "Just say no."'

Obregón shuffled his feet and mumbled, 'I don't give a shit any more.'

Bonmarche drawled, 'Look, I can give you a phone number in Miami if you need work. A couple of ex-agents like you. When're you going?'

'Few days. Whenever I get my shit together. Who you got in Miami? Sonny Crockett? The Colombians? Fuck it, Antoine. I've had enough of this business.'

'I thought you were a player, Andrés.'

'Are you?'

'Like I said, everybody is.'

'Gimme the number. I'll think about it.'

Bonmarche jotted on a scrap of paper and said, 'It'll be worth your while.'

Obregón said, 'I'm just gonna collect my stuff and split.'

The Cuban was halfway through the door when Bonmarche

said, 'A guy was in here today asking for you. Said he was from DIS.'

Obregón felt an electric surge of adrenaline. He asked, 'Did he have a woman with him? A blonde?'

'That's the guy. You know him?'

'Yeah. You know where he is now?'

'Nope. Was he the dealer you mentioned from México City?'

Obregón didn't answer. He ran out into the warehouse and dashed into the corner where he had stashed his container. It was gone.

He turned to scream at Bonmarche and faced three Raiders with shotguns.

Bonmarche said, 'Who was the guy, Andrés?'

'Where's my container?'

'It's safe. Heavy sucker. Must be full of books. Who was the guy?'

'If he said he was DIS, I guess he was.'

'You know who he was, you son of a bitch. Did you rip off the Méxican feds?'

'What's it to you, Antoine?'

'This is my unit, you scumbag.'

Obregón snapped, 'Did you search your office? I bet he bugged it. You can give the container to me, or deal with him. He'll be back.'

Bonmarche said to one of the Raiders, 'Check the office. Check it good.' To another he said, 'Cover the door.' To Obregón he said, 'Let's wait for him.'

'I wouldn't do that if I were you, Antoine.'

Bonmarche drawled, 'I always co-operate with the local authorities.'

Growing desperate, Obregón said, 'He's CIA.'

Bonmarche smiled and said, 'Now we're getting someplace. What does he want with you?'

'He hired me to kill Mendoza. I missed. He wants to kill me to shut me up.'

'Kill Mendoza? Bullshit.'

'It's true. I swear it.'

'What's in the container?'

'My advance. He wants it back.'

'How much?'

245

'Half a million.'

The Raider at the door said, 'A car is pulling into the lot. There's a man and a woman in it.'

Bonmarche and the third Raider covering Obregón turned toward the door, giving Obregón long enough to take two steps and disappear behind a stack of pallets.

The Raider caught the movement out of the corner of his eye, turned and fired both barrels into the pallets. Obregón popped up and shot him in the throat. The man dropped like a sack of potatoes. Bonmarche dove behind a packing crate and heard Obregón scurrying away.

The big Louisianan dashed from his hiding place, picked up the shotgun and ran for the office. Obregón fired another shot on the run and missed.

Beno turned off the engine, coasted in neutral into the parking area and rolled to stop next to the Mexican taxicab. As he and Sam stepped out of the car, they heard the gunfire inside the warehouse.

Beno swore. 'God-damn. That guy is a moving combat zone. Stay behind the car and cover the door, Sam.'

Beno hustled toward the cab to question the driver, but the driver heard the shots and peeled out of the car park, leaving a trail of burned rubber. Beno had to dive out of his way as the taxi spun its wheels and roared toward the highway.

The warehouse door was open. Beno could see a human shadow extending into the doorway, a long, thin appendage attached to its torso. As he approached, he heard another pistol shot, then a shotgun blast, and a stumbling Raider collapsed across the doorway.

Obregón had taken out two Raiders. The third and Bonmarche were in the office, lying on the floor. From his prone position Bonmarche could see the bug attached to the seat bottom of a chair. He shouted, 'Break out the M-15s.'

Terrified, the Raider said, 'He killed Jacky and the Toad, man. I'm not goin' out there.'

Bonmarche crawled on his belly across the office, fumbled with his keys and unlocked the weapons case. He grabbed an M-15, shoved in a clip and scuttled back toward the office door.

Outside, Beno ran down the side of the building, counting

three windows and a rear loading bay. Cautiously, he tested the loading bay doors. Unlocked. He picked up a rock, hurled it toward the closest window and missed by a foot and a half.

Obregón heard the stone clang against the aluminium siding and knew it was a trick. He trained his gun on the loading bay doors. A second rock smashed through the window. A moment later the doors crashed open and Obregón fired three quick shots into the open space.

Bonmarche lifted himself to his knees, saw the muzzle flash of Obregón's pistol reflect off the far wall, and sprayed bullets in that direction.

Unhit, Obregón wheeled and shot Bonmarche in the belly. The big man screamed and fell back into the office, landing on the Raider, blood pumping from his wound. Obregón had two cartridges left. He crawled toward the front door and the shotgun lying next to the dead Raider.

Glancing over his shoulder toward the open bay doors, he reached the front door and was within two feet of the shotgun when he felt a steel ring press against the back of his neck.

'Don't move,' said Sam. 'Don't fucking breathe. Drop the gun.'

32

One Down, One to Go

Sam ordered, 'Put your hands behind your neck and lie on the floor.'

'You . . .'

'Shut up.'

'You cunt . . .'

Sam pulled the trigger, and Uzi bullets ripped through the packing crates like the teeth of a chainsaw. Bits of wood and styrofoam chips splintered around the flinching Andrés Obregón.

Snarling, Sam barked, 'I told you to shut up and lie on the floor.'

Silent and sullen, Obregón stretched himself prone on the concrete.

Beno came through the loading bay doors in a crouch. Sam called out, 'I got him. Here by the door.'

Beno shouted, 'You okay?'

'Yes,' Sam shouted. 'There's one dead here.'

'In a black shirt?'

'Yes.'

Beno stood up and walked quickly through the warehouse. As he neared the office, he heard moaning. He flattened himself against the wall next to the office door and called out, 'Mr Bonmarche?'

He heard an agonized groan and yelled, 'Anybody else in there?'

When the agonized moan trailed away, he peeked around the corner and saw a Raider cowering behind the desk, head buried in his arms, shirt soaked with blood, a shotgun at his feet.

Bonmarche lay on his back, eyes on the door. Beno went in, kicked away the shotgun by Bonmarche. The man's pupils were dilated and his pulse weak. He was going into shock.

Beno moved to the Raider, pulled his arms away from his face and asked, 'Are you hit?'

The man wailed without answering.

Beno slapped him and shouted, 'Snap out of it! Is there any morphine here?'

No response. Beno picked up the telephone and dialled zero.

'Operator.'

'This is Comandante Alvarado, DIS. I need an ambulance. Emergency.'

'Yes, sir.'

'I'm at Oakland Air Freight, at the airport.'

'Yes, sir. I'll connect you.'

A moment later a voice responded, 'Acapulco Police Emergency services.'

Beno repeated his request and hung up. He grabbed the sobbing Raider and tried to shake him into awareness.

'For God's sake, man. Do you have any morphine here?'

The man worked his jaw, forcing himself to speak. Slobbering, he finally pleaded, 'Don't kill me. Please, please.'

Beno dropped him. Behind him Bonmarche said weakly, 'Weapons case . . .'

Beno looked around frantically, spied the open case and found an ampoule labelled *Morfina*. He rolled up Bonmarche's sleeve and injected the drug.

Beno said, 'If you were going to bleed to death, you'd already be dead. You're gonna make it. The morphine will take effect in a few minutes. Ever have a root canal?'

Bonmarche's head moved slightly.

Beno said, 'That was worse. I gotta go outside. The ambulance is on its way.'

Beno started to move away, but Bonmarche grabbed his leg with surprising strength.

'Who are you?'

'DIS. Don't worry. We're on your side.'

'Did you get him?'

'Yes. Alive, the best way.'

'Were you telling me the truth, today?'

Beno broke away without answering, retrieved a pair of handcuffs from the weapons case and crossed the warehouse floor to Sam.

Sam held her Uzi in a two-handed grip a good six feet from where Obregón lay face down on the concrete, his hands behind his head.

Nodding his head in appreciation, Beno commented, 'Nice piece of work.'

He cuffed Obregón, dragged him to his feet and searched him. He found the vial of cocaine, an ankle holster with a small pistol and two knives.

Obregón asked sarcastically, 'Aren't you gonna read me my rights?'

Beno asked Sam, 'Does he have any rights?'

Sam grinned and said, 'This is México. He's guilty until proven guilty. Code Napoléon.'

Beno jammed Obregón's face into the concrete and said, 'You shithead. You have the right to talk now or later. The later it is, the more you'll hurt. If you're lucky, you might say something to save your life, if you call a Méxican jail life.'

The ambulance arrived, followed by a swarm of Acapulco police.

Mumbling encouraging words, Beno followed Bonmarche's stretcher to the ambulance. The morphine had worked its magic and the DEA man appeared tranquil. His pupils had returned to normal size. The distraught Raider was coaxed into a police car and driven to the hospital. The two dead Raiders were taken to the morgue.

The police lieutenant wanted to transfer Obregón to police headquarters. Beno insisted the Cuban remain in his custody in the warehouse.

'Orders from the Director,' Beno said. 'This is a DIS priority case.'

The Lieutenant protested, 'These are Americans. I'm supposed to notify the American consul.'

Beno commanded, 'You'll notify no one! The Director is coming here himself, and if you fuck up you'll answer to him.'

Cowed, the policeman responded meekly, 'Yes, sir.'

Beno ordered, 'Tell your men to stay off their radios. Understand?'

'Yes, sir.'

'Send a man to the hospital with orders to report to me when Bonmarche comes out of surgery. See that he talks to no one. Refer all inquiries to me. Leave two men here and get the rest away. No radios, no talk. *Silencio, absolutamente silencio.*'

Beno posted two policemen at the door with instructions to let no one enter without DIS credentials. Inside, Beno and Sam moved Obregón into the office.

Sam began searching the warehouse for Obregón's container. Beno retrieved the bug from under the office chair while Obregón lay on the floor and sulked.

Beno leaned over the handcuffed man and whispered, 'Before I call Máximo Levín to come interrogate you, is there anything you'd rather say to me?'

'Fuck you, you CIA prick.'

Beno ignored the insult and said, 'You've been a real screw up, Andrés. You got yourself videotaped getting onto Mendoza's plane. You let Lowry talk you into killing a US Marine. Your booby trap in México City only murdered a few cockroaches, and you lost eighty grand. You did all the dirty work, paid all the dues, and now you're taking the fall for Fred Lowry. I'll make a deal with you before Máximo Levín arrives. Tell me

250

Lowry's part in your operation and I'll let you walk. I'll take you to the passenger terminal and buy you a ticket to anywhere you want to go.'

'What about my money?'

Beno answered, 'That's mine now. You're bargaining for your life. Nothing more, nothing less.'

'You're conning me.'

Beno crouched down close to Obregón and said, 'I want Lowry. Give him up and you fly away. Once Máximo Levín is here, you're in deep shit, *amigo*. The Director is not a nice man. He'll question you, and when he has his answers, he'll turn you over to Mendoza. Imagine, you and Alfredo alone in the basement of El Partenón. Mendoza is a student of ancient Aztec torture. The Aztecs liked to skin a man alive, flay the skin right off him, then cut out his heart. You tried to rip off the heroin king of Guerrero. You highjacked Mendoza's plane and would have killed him if he'd been on it. I don't think he'll be real happy with you.'

Beno could see the effect of his threats. The arrogance in Obregón's eyes had been replaced by fear.

Obregón said, 'Suppose I talk to you. Suppose you put me on a plane. What happens when I get off? What's to stop you from having US marshals waiting for me?'

'Nothing. Only my word. You can fly to Jamaica for all I care.'

'All right. I'll talk. Take off the cuffs.'

'You don't need your hands to talk.'

'What do you want to know?'

'Start with Lucio Serdán.'

'It was Lowry's idea. You were supposed to set Serdán up with the Stinger, then we were going to blow the plane and blame the assassination on Serdán. Lowry wanted me to kill you, too.'

'Did you expect Mendoza to be on the plane?'

'Yes.'

'Were you supposed to kill him?'

'Yes, but what we were really after was the money.'

'Do you think Lowry was going to let you live?'

'No, but sometimes you take chances, right? What else do you want to know? I want to get out of here.'

'We've got time, Andrés. The Director won't be here for at least an hour.'

The phone rang and Beno picked it up.

'Comandante Alvarado?'

'Yes.'

'This is Officer Lopez calling from the hospital. Mr Bonmarche is in surgery. The doctors think he will live.'

'Thank you, Officer. Call me when he comes out.'

'Yes, sir. The other man is under sedation.'

'Okay.'

Beno hung up. Sam came into the office and whispered in Beno's ear, 'I found the container.'

Beno nodded and said, 'Wait outside. I'll be out in a minute.'

She exited and Beno said to Obregón, 'You tried to kill that woman this morning. Tell me why.'

'Lowry's orders. She knows too much.'

'You were trying to cover your own ass.'

'Yeah. Wouldn't you?'

'Sure I would, if I was a complete asshole like you, Andrés. You know what I think? I think you take too much coke. Gives you a big, fat head. That shit's no good for you.'

'Thanks for the advice. Are we done?'

'Get off the floor and sit in the chair.'

Obregón obliged. Beno went behind him, took another pair of cuffs from the weapons case and quickly locked one of the Cuban's thin ankles to a chair leg.

Beno said, 'Gee whiz, Andrés. You were right. It was just a con job. I ain't takin' you anywhere. Amazing what people will say if they're scared enough.'

Obregón screamed, '*Cabrón! Maricon! Cagado hijo de puta te faltan cojones! Chingate! Qué te jodas, follodero! Qué te la mame tu madre! Te voy a matar y tambien la raja. Chingate. Chingate. CIA cabrón.*'

'Save it, Andrés.'

The phone rang again.

Beno answered, 'Yes? Yes, this is Oakland Air. I'm afraid we're closed today. What? I'm sorry. There's nothing I can do about your package. No, you can't come pick it up. Sorry. Maybe tomorrow. Bye.'

Beno replaced the phone and said to Obregón, 'See what a

mess you've made of things? What am I gonna tell the guy? That his package has been all shot up?'

Sullen and deflated, Obregón stared at the floor. Beno walked around the desk, grabbed the back of Obregón's chair and dragged the chair and its manacled occupant into the warehouse. Obregón started to curse again, but Beno ignored him and after a minute he fell silent.

Sam was sitting on a packing crate, the Uzi in her lap, coming down off her adrenaline rush. Beno sat next to her, put his arm around her shoulders and asked quietly, 'You okay?'

'Yeah.'

'You did a brave thing. I told you to stay outside behind the car.'

She said, 'I wanted to shoot him. I still do.'

'I understand, but you did the right thing. I needed to talk to him.'

'What's going to happen to us, Beno?'

'I don't know. We got Obregón. We'll get Lowry, too.'

'What will they do to us?'

'The agency?'

'Yeah.'

'Anybody's guess, Sam. We're not the bad guys, but there's no way of knowing how they'll see it.'

'What did Obregón tell you?'

'What I already knew. I taped our conversation. You can listen to it later if you like.'

Sam yawned and said, 'Right now, I feel like going to bed for a week. I'm hungry.'

'Hang in there, girl.'

The phone rang again. Beno walked into the office and answered, 'Oakland Air.'

'Mr Bonmarche?'

Beno said, 'He's out.'

'This is Al Mears in México City. Would you ask him to return my call? He has my number.'

Beno said, 'Mr Mears, this is Beno Alvarado.'

'Alvarado? Alpha Seven?'

Instinctively, Beno answered, 'Alpha plus seven.'

Mears asked, 'Where's the DEA man?'

Beno told him, 'Bonmarche is in Acapulco Social Security

253

hospital. Obregón shot him and killed two more DEA agents. You can tell Lowry for me that he's responsible.'

'Where's Obregón? Does DIS have him?'

Beno answered, 'He's dead.'

'Did DIS question him?'

'No.'

Mears said, 'Flame took a bad fall. Blow to a head. Now he's a wildfire. Keep it quiet. I'll get you all the help you need to extinguish the blaze.'

'I'll call back,' Beno said and hung up. He called Sam into the office and said, 'Lowry has vanished from the embassy.'

'He got past the DIS watchers?'

'Looks that way. I'm going to call Máximo.'

Beno dialled the operator again and gave her Máximo's number in México City.

'Director's office.'

'This is Comandante Alvarado calling from Acapulco.'

'I'll put you through.'

Beno's call to the glass pyramid interrupted a meeting of México 21. Máximo put the call on a speakerphone.

Beno said, 'We captured Obregón alive.'

Máximo asked, 'Where are you?'

'The Oakland Air Freight warehouse in Acapulco.'

Máximo said, 'Hold him there. I want to interrogate him myself. I'll be there in two hours.'

'Yes, sir.'

Beno hung up and dialled Pizza Pie de Nueva York.

'Do you deliver to the airport?'

33

Interrogation

On the nineteenth floor of the glass pyramid, Máximo Levín and four members of México 21 were finalizing plans for Independence Day, now two days away.

Ricardo Solida, the Foreign Minister, hated meetings in

Máximo's library because the director forbade smoking. During the first part of the meeting, Solida had chewed an unlit Cuban cheroot while the conspirators discussed foreign relations after the sixteenth.

Solida had insisted, 'We can't afford to turn the United States into an enemy. If we blame our problems on the gringos, we'll never find solutions. And, gentlemen, after the sixteenth we'll have plenty of problems.'

'The gringos are the problem,' General Jalapa had argued. 'They've been the problem for two hundred years. Look at what they've done in Colombia. They used a phony drug war to start counter-insurgency operations. They sent advisors, just like they did in Vietnam. The drugs were just a smokescreen.'

Solida had asked the Minister of Defence, 'Do you think they would send troops into México?'

Jalapa had answered, 'That's my worst nightmare.'

Máximo had ended this dispute by saying, 'The Americans are guilty only of ignorance. We're not going to threaten their economic interests. No legal commercial transactions will be disrupted. As they say up north, it will be business as usual. Even Americans can distinguish between rhetorical bluster and reality. Please, let's move on with our agenda. Time is short. And Ricardo, light your cigar. Stop waving it like a banner.'

Máximo had turned to Guillermo Guzman and Manuel de la Roca, executive officers of the two television networks.

'Is the script ready?'

For an hour the five men had scrutinized the script for the broadcast of the Independence Day parade and ceremonies. When Máximo was satisfied the script was in order, General Jalapa had begun to describe the regimental order for the parade.

'The 42nd Armoured Battalion will lead the column through the city, followed by the 9th Special Forces Regiment. Thirty minutes before they leave Military Camp Number One, these units will be issued live ammunition.'

Guzman asked, 'What about the Presidential Guard unit in the National Palace?'

'Sabotage,' answered Jalapa. 'Superglue in the arsenal locks. The guard will be unable to deploy their ammunition stores.'

Máximo asked, 'Superglue?'

Jalapa grinned.

The phone rang.

'Comandante Alvarado is calling from Acapulco, Director.'

'Excuse me, General,' Máximo said, taking the call on a speakerphone. 'This may be important.'

The conspirators listened intently as Beno announced Obregón's capture.

'Thank you, Mr Alvarado,' Máximo said, and turned off the phone.

'Fantastic,' exclaimed Solida.

'Yes,' said General Jalapa. 'Máximo, you know what I'm thinking, I'm sure. What we're all thinking. This is bait for the trap.'

'Indeed,' Máximo said. 'This improves our chances immensely. Obregón will incriminate Lowry. With Obregón's confession, we can prove to Mendoza the CIA wants to kill him.'

Jalapa said, 'Then we take him with his own arrogance.'

Máximo stood up and declared, 'I'm going to Acapulco immediately to interrogate Obregón. Can you all make a meeting at the Ministry of Government this afternoon at eleven?'

Heads bobbed around the table.

Máximo ordered, 'Guzman, have a rough cut of the tape ready for viewing after our meeting with Mendoza.'

'Right.'

'Solida, inform the American ambassador that you wish to see him in the morning.'

'Done.'

Máximo stood up and assembled his papers.

'Gentlemen, I must leave. I shall see you at the Ministry of Government in approximately six hours.'

Máximo picked up a telephone, punched in a short series of numbers.

Máximo commanded, 'Send a four-man video crew from the green squad to the helicopter pad with interrogation gear.'

'Yes, Director. Please hold. Telephone Surveillance has a message for you.'

A moment later another voice said, 'Director? Telephone Surveillance here.'

'Go ahead.'

Máximo listened to a recording of Alexander Mears' call to

256

Beno at Oakland Air Freight. When the recording ended, he said, 'Lowry has vanished from the embassy.'

Smiling, Jalapa said, 'Mendoza will have to believe us now.'

Ninety minutes later in Acapulco a government van met Máximo and the video crew and drove them to the Oakland Air warehouse.

Police vehicles jammed the parking lot. Uniformed officers milled around the building, hoping to catch a rare glimpse of the DIS Director, but Máximo disappointed them by ordering his driver to pass through the loading bay doors.

Sitting in the office with Obregón, Beno and Sam heard the van roll in and stop. The door slammed and Máximo's footsteps clicked across the concrete floor.

Obregón sweated and cursed under his breath. Beno stepped outside and greeted Máximo by whispering, 'Lowry has escaped from the embassy.'

Máximo replied, 'I know.'

Astonished, Beno asked, 'Did you get him?'

'No. We learned by listening to your conversation with Alexander Mears.'

Sam blurted, 'That's supposed to be impossible.'

With a smile Máximo said, 'Don't worry, Miss Black. I don't divulge what I know to the Soviets.'

Beno asked, 'Is DIS searching for Lowry?'

Máximo said, 'Yes. This time we've issued an alert to DIS stations nationwide.'

Agitated, Beno said, 'Lowry is extremely dangerous. His career is ruined, his future shattered, he has nothing more to lose. He'll start a war of revenge, and he has substantial resources.'

Máximo said, 'We can deal with him.'

Beno insisted, 'You couldn't stop him from leaving the embassy. He'll try to kill you, Dr Levín, as well as Mendoza. I tell you, he'll start a second Méxican War by himself. Obregón was only a man with a gun. Lowry is an army. We'll find him.'

Máximo said, 'I'll have someone call the airport. In México City you can use the DIS suite at the Majestic.'

Beno started to protest, but Máximo interrupted, 'That's an order, Comandante.'

* * *

In a state of terror Obregón watched his enemies from across the room. Beno and Sam shook hands with Máximo and left the warehouse. Obregón sneered at their courtesy. Such ladies and gentlemen! He knew the DIS's reputation for interrogation. Everyone talked, but they hurt you anyway.

A technician carried a television set into Bonmarche's office, then two strong men picked up Obregón in his chair, carried him into the office and set him down facing the television. One of the men inserted a cassette into a VCR and a few seconds later Obregón was watching himself boarding Mendoza's plane.

The three-minute tape segment ran again, and again, and again. For an hour the tape repeated until it had run twenty times.

The technician returned, removed the cassette and replaced it with another. Obregón saw tape of the plane on the ground in Michoacan and shots of the bodies of Jesús Platón, Ramón, the pilot and co-pilot in the cabin. Next came a frozen still shot of the dead marine sprawled in his car in Polanco accompanied by an audio tape of Lowry's last phone call.

'Andrés?'

'Yeah.'

'Samantha Black will be leaving the embassy in thirty minutes in a blue Pontiac, licence DF 62B9755. She'll come down River Po Street in about forty-five minutes. She has the only copy of the tape of you at the airport. I want you to take her out. Can you make it?'

'No sweat.'

The conversation ended, the still dissolved and was replaced on the screen with a computer readout which Obregón recognized as a record of his telephone calls from his house in Coyoacán. The tape ended in white noise and did not repeat.

Máximo Levín entered the office, turned off the monitor and stood with his back to Obregón. He clasped his hands behind his back and remained motionless. He heard the small, sticky sounds of a man moving his dry lips, the noise of the chair legs scraping the floor as Obregón twisted and turned, the tiny rattle of the links between the cuffs, the swish of clothing moving over stiff muscles.

With a jarring din, the phone rang. Máximo let it ring and ring until it stopped.

Obregón vomited into his lap, gagged, and vomited again. Máximo didn't move. The acrid smell of fear permeated the office, but Máximo said nothing. He focused his eyes on an airline schedule pinned to the wall eight inches in front of him and memorized it. Lv ZNO Ar LAX Lv LAX Ar ZNO Lv MEX Ar ZNO Lv MEX Lv ACA Lv SFO Lv DAL.

Obregón said, 'I have some valuable information.'

Máximo didn't respond, didn't move.

Obregón said, 'I can be of great use to you.' He gagged again and stammered, 'I know things . . . this tape, it doesn't show you what happened on the plane, does it?'

Máximo slowly turned around and looked at his prisoner. Obregón's shirt and pants were soaked in vomit. His ankle had rubbed raw. His head and shoulders drooped, but his eyes were wide and bright.

Obregón asked, 'What do you want from me?'

Máximo wheeled Bonmarche's chair out from behind the desk, sat down and leaned close to Obregón.

He asked, 'Do you want to live?'

Obregón nodded enthusiastically and answered, 'Yes.'

'Are you going to co-operate with me?'

'Yes.'

'Answer my questions truthfully?'

'Yes.'

'Are you going to be brave and throw your life away in order to prove how macho you are?'

'No.'

'Are you afraid?'

'Yes.'

'Of what?'

'Torture. Pain. You.'

'Are you afraid of the CIA?'

Obregón looked confused. After a moment he answered, 'Yes.'

'Why? Do you think they will kill you if you answer my questions?'

'Yes.'

'I'll kill you if you don't.'

'I know. I know that.'

Máximo walked out of the room and returned a moment later

with a technician who set up a video camera and lights in front of Obregón. He turned on the camera and left.

Máximo said, 'Tell me your name, your full name.'

'Andrés Alonzo María Obregón Santiago.'

'Where were you born?'

'La Habana.'

'The date?'

'June 12, 1960.'

'Citizenship?'

'American.'

'How long have you been in México?'

'Five years.'

'Who is your employer?'

'DEA.'

'That's not true. I'll ask you once more. Who is your employer?'

'CIA.'

'How long have you worked for CIA?'

'Since 1979, in Cuba.'

'What was your responsibility in México?'

'Liaison with Alfredo Mendoza.'

'Did you illegally board the plane belonging to Alfredo Mendoza at Zihuatanejo on the night of September 11th?'

'Yes.'

'What happened on board the plane?'

'I shot and killed the pilot, the co-pilot, Ramón Santiago, and another man.'

'Did you force the plane to land?'

'Yes.'

'Where?'

'In Michoacan.'

'Was someone waiting there? Another man?'

'Yes.'

'Who?'

'Fred Lowry.'

'Who is that?'

'The CIA station chief in México City.'

'Why did you board the plane?'

'Lowry's orders. They'll kill me for this.'

'Why did Lowry want you on the plane?'

'The money. He wanted the money.'

'And Mendoza?'

'I was supposed to kill everyone on the plane, including Mendoza, but he wasn't there.'

'How did you expect to get away with this scheme?'

'Lucio Serdán was supposed to take the blame.'

'Why Lucio Serdán?'

'Lowry provided him with weapons. He was Mendoza's enemy.'

The interrogation continued for an hour. Obregón filled in details and Máximo forced him to repeat every statement, searching for contradictions. When Máximo concluded that Obregón had supplied enough evidence to crucify the CIA, he walked out into the warehouse.

He said to his men, 'Take Obregón to Acapulco city prison and keep him in isolation. We may need him later. And find me another plane.'

34

Hotel Majestic

When Beno and Sam walked into the lobby of the Hotel Majestic, the manager greeted them as if they were visiting heads of state. He introduced himself and escorted them to a suite overlooking the Zócalo.

'I received a discreet phone call from Dr Levín,' said the manager. 'He called you the most heroic officer in the directorate. I hope you're pleased.'

Flowers, baskets of fruit, trays of hors d'oeuvres and bottles of wine had been laid out in advance. Beno scrounged in his pocket for a tip, but the manager refused.

'Absolutely not,' said the man as he retired.

Exhausted, her shoulder aching, Sam lay down on the bed and asked, 'Are you going to search the room for bugs?'

'What's the point? I'll never find them. Just be careful what you say.' He paused, looked around the room and said, 'Fuck that. Say whatever you like.'

Ignoring the delicacies, Beno took a beer from the servi-bar and stepped onto the balcony to admire the panorama of the Zócalo.

The scrubbed paving stones glistened, free of chewing gum and dog exhaust. The newly constructed balcony jutted out from the façade of the National Palace. Six forty-foot DiamondVision screens faced the plaza. Flags, bunting and banners in the national colours adorned the buildings which surrounded the beautifully proportioned square, the National Palace, National Cathedral, Supreme Court, Department of the Federal District, arcade and hotel. In green, red, and white, the Zócalo was dressed for a night of patriotic frenzy.

Beno carried his beer inside and looked at Sam curled up on top of the bedspread. She opened her eyes and smiled.

She said, 'Somebody once said, "Be careful what you wish for. It may come true."'

Beno sat down beside her. Gently, he stroked her forehead and said, 'Sounds hippy dippy to me. Do you believe in the stars?'

Sam said, 'Two weeks ago I craved excitement. I think I got more than I bargained for.'

'Had enough?' he asked. 'You don't have to stay.'

'I'm in as long as you are, Beno.'

Beno said, 'I'm tempted to call the embassy and have them come and get you.'

'You wouldn't dare!'

'You've been lucky so far, Sam. Three firefights and only one scratch. Don't push your luck.'

'Don't patronize me, Comandante.'

Beno snapped, 'I'm not. I'll never find out who you are if you're dead.'

'I'm not planning on dying, you blockhead. I think I've handled myself all right so far.'

'That's true. You brought down Andrés Obregón.'

'Yeah! I did.'

'Proud of yourself?'

'You're damned right.'

He smiled, saying, 'Me, too. You saved my ass. Thanks.'

'You're welcome.'

Beno said, 'You could have blown him away, but you didn't. I think I would have.'

Sam said, 'You had the opportunity. There was nobody there but us.'

'I wanted Máximo to have him.'

Sam propped herself on one elbow and asked, 'What do you think of Máximo Levín?'

Beno answered, 'I think he's as crazy as they come.'

Sam said, 'He gives me the creeps.'

'I don't think he gives a shit about anyone's opinion.'

Sam laughed, 'That's something you and he have in common.'

A little embarrassed, Beno said, 'Some opinions count. Yours.'

'You're flattering me.'

'I hope so.'

Wrinkling her brow, Sam asked, 'How much time do we have, Beno? Before the agency comes after us?'

'I don't know. Not much, I'm afraid.'

'Do you think we can get away from them?'

Without hesitation he answered, 'I won't. After we find Lowry, I'm going to turn myself in to the embassy.'

'You mean that?'

'Yes, ma'am.'

'What will they do to you?'

'I don't know. It doesn't matter. I know I make a lot of noise. I bitch about the agency and the government, but I'm no traitor. In my own way, I'm a patriot. I'd rather face them and tell them straight up what I think than run away and hide for the rest of my life. They'll put the heat on me, not you. They'll cut you loose.'

'Do you think they might kill you?'

'Lowry would.'

Sam protested. 'When you gave the Stinger to Lucio Serdán, you were acting under Lowry's orders. Won't they believe that? Isn't Al Mears a reasonable man?'

'I wouldn't bet on it.'

'Do you think Mears still backs Lowry?'

'That's a fair assumption. If we don't kill Fred, he'll weasel out of it. Guys like him always do.'

'Do you think we'll get him?'

'Not lying around this hotel, we won't. And DIS doesn't have a chance in hell to neutralize good old Fred.'

'You sound tired, Beno.'

'I am. I'm beat, but there's no way I can sleep. Why don't you take a nap. If Mears is in México City, I want to talk to him.'

'Come on. Lie down beside me. Get some sleep.'

'Seems like every time we lie down together, people start shooting at us. Makes me a little leery.'

'I don't think that's going to happen here.'

Gently, she pulled him down and began unbuttoning his shirt. She could feel the tension rippling under his skin.

'We need each other, Beno. Make love to me.'

She unbuttoned his shirt to the waist and said, 'You taste like salt and lemons.'

'Want me to take a shower?'

'I want you to smell like a man, not a perfume factory.'

Beno sat up, pulled off his boots and peeled off his socks. Sam crossed her arms and slipped her light sweater over her head. Beno reached around her from behind and cupped her breasts. Her nostrils flared and she threw back her head onto his shoulder. He unhooked her bra in front and eased the straps over her bandaged shoulder.

'Does it still hurt?'

'Not now. Nothing hurts right now.'

They struggled out of their pants. He rolled over her as she reached for his erection, guided him into her, and slowly he began to pump his hips. She thrust her pelvis up to meet him, taking all of him, deeper and deeper until he burst inside her like a geyser. She moaned and clutched his buttocks and held him there, waiting for the tension to drain out of his body.

It never did. His back and legs remained as taut as spring steel.

Soaked in sweat, Sam asked, 'Aren't you going to relax?'

'I don't think so.'

'I can give you a back rub. I'm pretty good.'

Beno sat up and said, 'If fucking doesn't help, nothing will. It's just not our time yet, Sam. I need to be here in my mind, and I'm not. My head is out there in the city, scrambling after

Fred Lowry, trying to decipher Máximo, everywhere but here. It's just no good. I want to love you, have you, laugh with you, do silly, goofy things. I want to go to Paris and walk along the river, holding hands. No one has ever made me want to do that kind of thing, but none of that can happen until this is over. I have Lucio Serdán's blood on my hands. I feel unclean, and nothing will change that until this is put right. Does any of this make sense?'

'I love you, Beno. I don't care if you make sense or not.'

He took her face in his hands and kissed her softly.

'Let's talk about love when we get to Paris.'

Sam wrinkled her nose and said, 'It's hot and muggy in Paris in September.'

'I know. Good time to lie around in hotel rooms and screw all day. This is still México City. I'm going to call the embassy.'

'Four three nine one.'

'This is Alpha Seven. Skip the bullshit and put me through to Fire. Don't put me on hold. Put me through now or I'm gone.'

Al Mears came on the line.

'This is Fire.'

'Alpha Seven speaking. I want to deal with you alone.'

'Name it.'

'The lobby of the Hotel Majestic in twenty. Come alone.'

'And you?'

'My friends will be watching, but I can guarantee your safety.'

Provincial dignitaries crowded the ornate hotel lobby. Beno waited near the registration desk surrounded by men and women squabbling with the clerks and each other over reservations.

Al Mears passed through the revolving doors followed by two husky DIS inspectors.

Beno flashed his comandante ID at the DIS men and posted them by the door.

'Let's go into the bar,' Beno said to the DDO.

Beno led Mears to a booth where Sam waited.

'Al Mears, Sam Black.'

Beno ordered drinks.

265

Mears looked around the bar, picking out the young men in dark suits and skinny ties, and said, 'You have a lot of friends.'

Beno said, 'I'm a hero. I'm the man who got Lucio Serdán.'

'I see.'

'Do you? This has been the worst week of my life.'

Mears said, 'Does DIS blame the agency for Lowry?'

Beno answered, 'I don't know, but I wouldn't assume otherwise.'

The old spy said, 'I want you to convince them that Lowry is a loose cannon, a rogue.'

Beno said, 'You have to convince me first.'

'He misinterpreted the finding. No one was supposed to terminate the target, merely withdraw support.'

'Bullshit. I know how those things are worded and what they mean.'

'You are a very angry man, Beno. Try to see through your anger.'

'I don't need a shrink. Tell me how Lowry walked out.'

'He dressed up as a Marine, conned the Captain of the Guard, and adiós.'

'Brilliant. First-rate security.'

'Shit happens. We're in a damage control mode now.'

'And I'm the band-aid, right?'

'Do you have any idea where Lowry is, or what he's going to do?'

Beno shook his head.

Mears asked, 'What about DIS?'

'Call up Máximo Levín and ask him yourself.'

'Look, Beno, I'm appointing you acting station chief. You have full authority and full rights.'

'I don't accept. I've resigned.'

'Whether you resign or not, I know, you know, Miss Black knows, both of you are still on the job. You want Lowry and so do I. You can come into the embassy and use our facilities or not. It's your call. The important thing is to keep Lowry away from Mendoza. We can agree on that, I believe.'

Beno said, 'I'll take it under consideration. We can discuss it after we have Lowry, if we ever get him.'

'You will, Beno. I have complete confidence in you. Good afternoon, and good luck.'

Mears stood, saluted Sam, and walked out of the hotel.

Sam said, 'How do you like that, Comandante Station Chief?'

Beno said, 'I don't. He was trying to get me into the building, and that's not going to happen.'

'What do we do now?'

'Wait. Watch the Zócalo. If Lowry wants Mendoza, he'll try for him during the ceremony. That's what I would do.'

35

Mendoza

Máximo returned to México City and went directly to the Ministry of Government where the members of México 21 were waiting in an ante-chamber. Máximo led them into a meeting with Alfredo Mendoza whom they found seated in Porfirio's blue chair, which he had taken from El Partenón. The Minister greeted the seven men as members of the informal committee on national security.

'Gentlemen,' said Mendoza with a magnanimous wave. 'Please be seated.'

When Máximo and his entourage had arranged themselves around a conference table, the Director said, 'I appreciate your seeing us when I know you're busy preparing your campaign, Alfredo, but we have important news to convey. We captured the man who highjacked your plane.'

Mendoza chuckled, 'Serdán? You got Serdán alive? That's fantastic. What superior police work! That's the best news I've heard all day.'

Máximo interrupted, 'It wasn't Serdán. It was Andrés Obregón.'

Mendoza stood up, pounded his fist into his palm and grumbled, 'Obregón? Impossible! You're not making sense, Máximo.'

Máximo explained. 'The CIA tried to make the whole affair appear to be Serdán's doing, but it was disinformation.'

'Where's Serdán now?' demanded the Minister.

'He's dead, killed two days ago in Zihuatanejo by the CIA man who tried to set him up. Serdán is dead. Obregón is dead,' Máximo lied, 'but we have his confession. Alfredo, I hate to tell you this, but your friends in the CIA were trying to kill you.'

Mendoza reached for the phone and shouted into it, 'Get me the President!'

Máximo said, 'Wait a moment before you react. Let's discuss the implications of this.'

Mendoza thought for a few seconds, then nodded and said, 'All right.' He barked into the phone, 'Cancel that call,' and slammed down the receiver.

Máximo said, 'Let's keep this to ourselves for now.'

Mendoza said softly to his secret policeman, 'How long have you known, Máximo?'

'We knew within minutes of the highjacking.'

'Why didn't you tell me?'

'You're running for president. You have a campaign to organize. This information would have been a distraction. We took care of it. You've had more protection around you than you were aware of.'

'Who else was involved?'

'Lowry, the station chief, is the only one still alive.'

'Do you have him, too?'

'No. He's in the embassy.'

'I take it the President doesn't know?'

'Right, but I can't keep it from him forever.'

'Why did they do this to me, Máximo? I've given those bastards millions. They had complete access to DIS. We provided them with critical intelligence on the Cubans, the Nicaraguans, everything they ever asked for, and more, and more, and more . . .' His voice trailed off, his mind boggled.

Ricardo Solida, the Foreign Minister, answered this question, 'Because of the drugs, Minister. The CIA is under pressure from its own people. The American atmosphere is changing, becoming far less tolerant. You're far removed from them, and therefore an easy target. They tried to kill you and failed. I guarantee you that now, threatened with exposure of their involvement, they will attempt character assassination.'

'That works both ways.'

'Indeed it does,' said Solida.

Mendoza's rage boiled over. He screamed, 'I'll slaughter every fucking CIA agent in México. I swear, Máximo, get me a list. No, fuck the list, just bring me the bodies.'

'Calm down, Alfredo,' said Máximo. 'That won't put you in the National Palace, Alfredo. You have more viable options.'

'What options, Máximo?'

Máximo said, 'This committee has taken the question of options seriously, and this is why we have assembled here. We are all in agreement with what I am about to say.'

'Go on,' said Mendoza.

'We can throw Lowry out of the country, either publicly or quietly. We strongly advise that, no matter what.'

Solida said, 'I'm calling in the American ambassador in the morning.'

Máximo continued, 'We can sever relations with the CIA and make diplomatic war on the Americans, a dangerous choice. Or, Alfredo, you can take a bold step, the boldest step of all, what the CIA, the American government and our own people would never expect. You can seize the government at the ceremony on Thursday night.'

'A *coup d'état?*'

General Jalapa said, 'No less.'

Mendoza plopped back into his chair and stared at the man whom he trusted more than all his legions of sycophants. Then he looked each man in the face and saw that every one was deadly serious.

Mendoza repeated the words several times, '*Coup d'état. Coup d'état.*'

Máximo said, 'Otherwise, you're finished. No matter what you do, the CIA will ruin you. You might as well leave for Spain tonight.'

Breathing heavily, Mendoza said, 'Máximo, you make my heart stop.'

Máximo said, 'Do you have the nerve, Alfredo? If you want to be president, this is the only way.'

'Can a *coup* be arranged so quickly? My God, no one has attempted a *coup* in this country for more than seventy years.'

Máximo said, 'This committee on national security is prepared to make all the arrangements. We have a contingency plan. In fact, we prepared it years ago. The country will be taken by

269

surprise, Alfredo. I am convinced that the Americans will get to Salinas today or tomorrow, and he won't announce you as candidate at all. He's more afraid of them than he is of you.'

'Are you sure?'

'I am.'

'Tell me your plan.'

'The parade, after all, celebrates Méxican Independence. For once, México will declare true independence, freedom from the Americans. The first step will be to arm the troops before the parade.'

Mendoza interrupted and asked, 'General Jalapa, is that possible?'

'More than possible, Minister. Operational orders have been prepared. The stores are there. The army is behind you. We prepared for a *coup* when your nomination was in doubt. We have not lost our resolve.'

Máximo said, 'Salinas' speech is to be televised on both networks, but instead of his speech, a speech taped earlier by you will be broadcast in its place. During the day DIS will take control of all broadcasting facilities. It will be simple and virtually bloodless. By the time the telecast is over, you will be in control of the National Palace. The *coup* will be a *fait accompli.*'

Mendoza said, 'Astounding.'

Guzman, president of Televisa, said, 'You will be in control of the media, Minister. Salinas will be powerless.'

Máximo said, 'I've been with you twenty years, Alfredo, and what has happened in that time? México has lost its soul. The country is wracked by inflation and debt. And why? Because of men like Salinas, like de la Madrid, men with no guts, no balls. Unless you step forward, México will be lost forever.'

'What about the Americans, Máximo? How will they react?'

'As always, with pious statements and no action. After several weeks, relations will return to normal, only on our terms. Business will continue as usual. If it doesn't, we have nothing to lose. The future is south, only the past is north. We must gird ourselves for the twenty-first century, Alfredo. We will create a new body politic and call it México 21.'

'México 21?'

'As I said, we prepared this plan years ago. Nothing can stop you from returning Porfirio's chair to the palace.'

'What concessions must I make to the army in return for your assistance, General?'

Jalapa said, 'We want El Partenón. You won't need it any more.'

Mendoza exploded in maniacal laughter, 'This will wake up a few people, more than a few, won't it?'

De la Roca from Pemex said, 'All of Latin America will awaken behind you, Alfredo. They will call you the new Simón Bolívar.'

Mendoza stopped laughing, wiped his eyes with the back of his hand and asked, 'How long have you been planning this?'

Máximo said, 'We started making preparations two years ago, but I never thought it would be necessary until your plane was attacked. Then I knew. We chose the name México 21 several weeks ago. We've had posters printed, an entire propaganda programme prepared. Control of the media is critical. Control information and you control the people. Tonight, we can blanket the city with México 21 propaganda. No one will know what it means until Thursday night. Then, the world will know. The people of México will embrace you as their saviour.'

Mendoza asked, 'You are all in agreement on this?'

With one voice the seven men said, 'We are.'

Máximo asked, 'Are you?'

Mendoza said, 'México 21. It has the ring of strength.'

Máximo stood up and said, 'Call your managers back. Tell them nothing. We have much to do. Tomorrow we will tape your speech. Tonight we must lay the groundwork for México 21.'

Left alone, Mendoza dismissed his managers and ordered his aide to find General Vargas.

The aide tracked down Billy Vargas in the Officers' Club at Military Camp Number One, the huge army post on the eastern edge of the city where troops from all over the republic were assembling for the parade.

'This is Mendoza,' growled the Minister into the phone. 'Are you sober?'

'Almost, Chief.'

'Stop drinking and come to the Ministry.'

A few minutes later Vargas sat in Mendoza's office. The Minister appeared extremely agitated. For once he neither smoked nor drank but paced around the room, clenching and unclenching his fists.

Mendoza asked, 'Have you heard any talk among senior officers of a *coup*?'

Vargas said, 'Not since Salinas agreed to select you as candidate, Alfredo.'

'Do you think they were serious then?'

'Hard to say, Chief. Talk is cheap. Pulling off a *coup* is dangerous and risky.'

'What about Jalapa? Was he serious?'

'I don't know,' said Vargas. 'I was. I've been waiting for a *coup* all my life.'

Mendoza said, 'I just had the most amazing meeting with Máximo Levín, General Jalapa, and the other members of Máximo's national security committee. They claim that Salinas is going to back down and refuse to announce me. They proposed a *coup d'état*.'

Vargas felt instantly sober. He said, 'You're shitting me.'

'I shit you not, Billy. Máximo Levín sat right there in that chair and told me he has plans for a *coup* on Thursday night, during the ceremony.'

'Using Jalapa's troops?'

'Yes.'

'Do you believe it, Alfredo?'

'I want to, but there's something false. I can't put my finger on it, but something is not right.'

Vargas said, 'I've never trusted Máximo Levín.'

'He's made me a rich man,' said Mendoza. 'DIS provided the information I used to force Salinas to nominate me. I can't believe he would turn against me.'

'And the others?'

'Loyal to me for years, every one of them.'

'Then what's your problem?'

'I don't know, but I'm not taking any chances. How many troops did you bring here from Guerrero?'

'Only a token battalion. One hundred and fifty infantry with armoured personnel carriers.'

'How many more can you get here by Thursday?'

'Maybe a hundred, possibly two hundred.'

'Do it. I'll see that your troops lead the parade. We'll have a *coup*, by God. And Billy, keep your mouth shut.'

A laconic smile accompanied Vargas' salute. 'We'll have a *coup*,' he thought to himself. 'One hell of a *coup*.'

36

The Plaza of Three Cultures

The members of México 21 left the Ministry of Government and dispersed through the city to their offices. As Máximo was driven across town to the glass pyramid, he tried to focus his thoughts on Alfredo Mendoza, bewitched by Porfirio's chair, consumed by greed, dazzled by the idea of a *coup d'état*, but his memories of Lucio Serdán forced their way into his mind. He understood Lucio's death as a sacrificial suicide, but it had been so useless, so unnecessary.

In the next forty-eight hours, México either would free herself from her cursed history, or fall into a bottomless abyss of violence and revolution from which she would never escape. If México 21 succeeded, Lucio's death would be vindicated. If not, millions more would die.

When the car arrived at DIS headquarters, Máximo hesitated in front of the doors. Instead of entering the building he turned to his right, walked into the middle of the Plaza of Three Cultures and stood alone in the middle of the square.

The ancient district of Tlatelolco had been the site of the final battle between the Spaniards and the Aztecs, the heroic last stand of Cuauhatémoc, last First Speaker of the Mejica. Tlatelolco was the ultimate symbol of Méxican pride and Méxican shame. Since 1968 Máximo had never allowed himself to set foot on the square. He had built his glass pyramid adjacent to the Plaza of Three Cultures, but the square itself had been blotted out of his personal map of México City. For him, Tlatelolco was poisoned ground. He had avoided it, stayed away, shut it out.

Now, for the first time, he had returned.

He walked slowly over the tetzole flagstones looking for elliptical indentations in the rock. Within a few steps he found the first of many pockmarks in the stone of .50-calibre machine-gun bullets, worn smooth in a quarter of a century.

Máximo Levín sank to his knees and wept. His glasses smeared. Slowly, slowly he wiped them clean.

Rain fell that day, 2 October 1968. For months the students had marched, demonstrating solidarity with the students of Berkeley, Colombia, Prague and Paris. Hundreds were in jail. With México City's Olympic Games scheduled to start in ten days, the government was terrified of disruptions before a world-wide television audience.

An engraved stone in the Plaza of Three Cultures proclaimed the battle of Tlatelolco in 1521 as neither a victory nor a defeat, but the painful birth of the México people. Behind the ruins stood the colonial church of San Martín, built of stones looted from a demolished Aztec temple. On the far side of the plaza a forest of twenty-storey apartment buildings loomed over this vision of ancient and modern México. To one side rose the Foreign Ministry, surrounded by police motorcycles.

Five thousand shouting, chanting students and local citizens jammed the plaza, demanding freedom in the universities and an end to oppression. As Máximo and Lucio Serdán approached the plaza, they could see a battalion of police in riot gear lurking among the ruins of the Aztec temple. In command was none other than Alfredo Mendoza.

Suddenly a squad of police burst from the Foreign Ministry and charged the podium, pushing students out of their way. Gunfire erupted from an apartment building and two policemen fell to the pavement.

Máximo began to run toward the plaza but was dragged down from behind by Lucio.

'It's too late,' said the older man.

The police began to file up the steps of the ancient temple and quickly deployed to the north and west sides of the square. Mendoza gave the command, and .50-calibre machine-guns began a steady rattle, first ripping up the front of the apartment

274

building where the shots had come from, then moving slowly down into the crowd.

Máximo and Lucio retreated in horror as hundreds fell. The guns ejaculated death. As the stones of Tlatelolco turned red, Máximo Levín realized that everything he ever believed about his country was a lie.

After three minutes the machine-guns fell silent. Policemen and soldiers began moving through the crowd, firing rifles and pistols. Screams of the dying and wounded seared the mind of young Máximo Levín. He would never forget nor forgive.

Wounded and bleeding, Lucio said, 'We must get away. There is nothing we can do here.'

Máximo said, 'I have to get you to a hospital.'

Máximo carried and dragged his friend through the chaos of the square, pulled him into a car and drove him toward a private clinic in Las Lomas de Chapultepec, the wealthy neighbourhood where he lived. As they crossed the city they saw nothing but death, heard only the sickening thump of hard bullets in soft flesh. Finally, near the Monument of the Revolution, Máximo shouted through his tears, 'I want to kill them all.'

'No,' said Lucio Serdán. 'You are much too valuable. Peasants and workers will never bring this government down, Máximo. This is not Cuba. You must stay here. Study. Become rich and powerful. Find a *patrón*. Someday you will carry on the struggle from within.

'I am a poor man. I shall return to Chilpancingo and try to tell the young what has happened here. The world must know about this, but it will take a long time. You have time, my young friend. Never forget who is responsible.'

'I'll never forget,' said Máximo. 'I swear revenge.'

'No! Not revenge. Justice!'

'I swear.'

At the hospital they embraced and parted. Many years passed before Máximo saw Lucio Serdán again.

Máximo left the square, entered DIS headquarters. He said to the guards, 'Lock the doors. From this moment, no one enters or leaves the building without my authorization. That includes all of you. Let the morning shift in, but no one else. No exceptions. Prepare the third sub-basement as sleeping quarters.'

Surprised, the guards saluted and chorused, 'Yes, sir.'

Máximo went directly to the communications centre and switched on a microphone which allowed him to speak to everyone in the building.

'Ladies and gentlemen, this is the Director speaking,' he said, his voice resounding through all twenty floors of the pyramid. 'I have an extraordinary announcement.

'The Directorate of Internal Security has been given a sacred trust by the nation. This organization exists not to protect the government, nor one political party, nor one individual, but the people of México. In the next forty-eight hours the security of the nation will be threatened as it has never been threatened in this century.

'México is being threatened with a *coup d'état.*'

This pronouncement provoked cries of shock from the men and women in the building.

Máximo continued, 'We alone can prevent a national disaster. We have the responsibility of preserving the integrity of the nation. We will be forced to choose between two futures, between dark tyranny or peaceful democracy. If we are to have peace in México, a new political force must be born in this building tonight. In the name of peace, of democracy, of justice for the people of México, you, the agents and technicians of the Directorate, will be called upon to perform extraordinary service.

'Tonight, together, we shall take the first step toward a new México free of chaos and revolution. In this building we hold the keys to the future. In a few short years the twenty-first century will arrive. For us in the Directorate, the new millennium begins tonight. Much that will transpire will seem mysterious, perhaps dangerous, but if we persevere together, we will prevail.

'Ladies and gentlemen, the era of México 21 has begun. I must ask you all to remain in the building for the next forty-eight hours. For reasons of security, absolutely no personal calls will be allowed. I know this will be a hardship for many of you, but two days from now, you will understand. In order to accomplish the first step toward the preservation of peace in

276

the republic, I am going to cause a total blackout of power in the Federal District. That is all.'

No one dared challenge the authority of Máximo Levín. In the minds of many DIS employees, the disaster they faced came not from a *coup d'état*, but from being incommunicado, cut off from their families.

Nevertheless, after the first shock sank in, first one of the technicians stood up and faced the Director, then another, then groups of two and three until every individual in the communications centre was standing, a look of absolute devotion on his face.

For the first time DIS technicians saw their Director smile.

'Thank you,' he said with utter simplicity. 'México thanks you. Now, we must go to work.'

Máximo keyed his central monitor to a schematic of México City's electrical power grid. Another monitor showed the control room of the power company. Several more monitors replicated control panels which regulated the flow of power throughout the Valley of México.

He began punching buttons. In seconds he accessed the central computer which controlled the power system for the entire metropolitan area. A series of pre-programmed commands shut down the central processing unit. A second series of commands caused an overload in one sub-station near the airport. Key circuit breakers blew, shifting the overload to the next sub-station. A domino effect rippled across the city. Four minutes later, darkness enveloped thirty million.

Three million refrigerators stopped.

Two hundred thousand street lights blinked out.

Traffic lights stopped regulating traffic.

In most private hospitals, emergency generators kicked in. In the public hospitals, the generators failed.

Radio and television transmission ceased.

In Netzahualcóyotl two hundred trucks loaded with young boys and peel-back posters rolled out of a warehouse and fanned through the darkened city. Drivers dropped the boys in pairs, each pair carrying four hundred posters the size of large bumper-stickers. In the confusion of the blackout, no one paid attention to the bright posters suddenly appearing in every sector of the city. Sharply raked red block letters and numerals over a green stripe resembling a growling jaguar spelled out *MEXICO 21*.

By dawn four hundred thousand posters were plastered on buses, taxis, walls and subway tunnels.

Alfredo Mendoza first saw the poster as he returned to the Ministry of Government at seven o'clock. He sat back in his limousine and smiled, pleased with Máximo's efficiency and foresight.

15 SEPTEMBER

37

Persona non Grata

The Ambassador's receptionist took the call at nine a.m.

'Good mornin', Ambassador Christmas' office.'

A chillingly formal voice with a slight Méxican accent and upper-class inflection said, 'Good morning. I'm calling on behalf of the Minister of Foreign Affairs. The Minister has instructed me to tell you he expects the Ambassador to call on him in one hour at the Ministry.'

'I declare,' said the receptionist. 'That's rather sudden.'

'Is the Ambassador unavailable? If so, the Minister will see the First Secretary.'

'Well, honey, I'll tell the Ambassador. That's the best that I can do.'

'In one hour. Thank you. Good-bye.'

At ten Ambassador George Christmas, former United States Senator from Texas, anxiously paced the floor of an ante-room in the Ministry of Foreign Affairs. Portraits of President Salinas and his ministers lined the walls. Christmas stopped before a portrait of Alfredo Mendoza and contemplated the massive head and widely spaced eyes, imagining the future president as Aztec emperor, then as Spanish viceroy. The tragic history of México seemed to live in that cruel face.

Christmas moved to the window and gazed down at the ruins of the Aztec palace of Tlatelolco. At that moment lightning flashed over the city, casting an electric blue light over the historical shambles below.

A heavy oak door swung open and a tight-lipped aide informed him that his presence was requested within.

The interview was brief and to the point. Ricardo Solida, barely forty years old, immaculately tailored and coifed, stood behind a desk holding a large paper embellished with seals and ribbons.

'Good morning, Mr Ambassador.'

'Good morning, Mr Foreign Minister. I understand that you

wish to present me with an official notice from your government.'

'Yes, Mr Ambassador . . .'

Christmas smiled a wide diplomatic smile and said, 'Please call me George.'

'Certainly, George,' said Solida, 'but I must tell you in advance that this note is of an unpleasant nature. If you comply with the conditions stated herein, no public announcement will be made.'

'I understand. Please go ahead.'

The Minister cleared his throat and read from the paper.

'To the Honorable George Christmas, Ambassador of the United States of America: You are hereby informed that one Mr Frederick Lowry is declared *persona non grata* in the republic of México. Mr Lowry has engaged in activities detrimental to the republic of México, and is required to leave the national territory within seventy-two hours. By my hand, this 15th day of September, 1993, Ricardo Solida Rojas, Minister of State for Foreign Affairs.'

Solida held out the note with the tips of his fingers as if it were a squirming insect.

Trying to maintain diplomatic decorum, the shocked ambassador accepted the note with a nod of his head.

He started to ask, 'What is . . .?' but Solida held up his hand.

'Mr Ambassador,' said the Minister, 'We both know that yours is a political appointment, that you represent the President and the Department of State, and neither you nor any American ambassador is fully aware of the activities of the Central Intelligence Agency within your own embassy.

'I regret to inform you that four days ago, with an accomplice, Mr Lowry, your CIA station chief, made an attempt on the life of the Minister of Government, Alfredo Mendoza. Whether acting on his own or on orders of your government, I cannot say.'

Christmas blurted, 'That's preposterous! Fred Lowry thinks the world of Mendoza, and so do I. Mendoza is the most pro-American Mexican politician in fifty years. Kill him? I don't believe it.'

His hands shaking, the Ambassador stared at the paper

which made little crinkling noises as it shook. He repeated, 'I don't believe it.'

Solida said, 'Frankly, I didn't believe it myself when I first heard it. Unfortunately, it is true.'

Christmas stammered, 'Do you have proof?'

'We have the videotaped confession of his accomplice, a man named Andrés Obregón. Do you know him?'

'I've never heard of him.'

'Officially, he's an agent of the Drug Enforcement Administration. In fact, he's CIA, working directly for Lowry. I'm prepared to show you the tape and present you with other evidence now. Please sit down.'

Christmas took a chair. Although he had little diplomatic experience, he was a seasoned politician, and he understood an ultimatum when he heard one.

Solida said, 'I do not believe that this attack was prompted by your government. These two men engaged in a criminal act for their own personal gain. DIS agents captured Andrés Obregón yesterday, and his interrogation was conducted personally by Dr Máximo Levín.'

Solida pushed a button on his desk and a wall panel slid back, revealing a television monitor. Christmas watched the tape of Andrés Obregón boarding the Minister's plane, a brief insert from the Televisa Evening News report on the finding of the plane, then Obregón's confession.

When the screen went black, Solida said, 'My personal opinion is that Lowry and Obregón were motivated by greed. This was a robbery they wished to disguise as a political attack by Lucio Serdán. Now, please understand, Mr Ambassador, George, we do not want a diplomatic incident. We do not want to terminate the relationship between the DIS and the CIA. We do not want to embarrass your government.

'This is a serious charge, and under ordinary circumstances I would make this announcement in public. These are not ordinary circumstances. Neither the President nor the Minister is aware of the details. If they were, well, you could imagine the outcry on both sides of the border. Relations between our nations would be poisoned for years, well into the next century.'

The Foreign Minister came around from behind his desk and continued, 'Mr Lowry no longer has diplomatic immunity. By rights he should be shot. Executed. In the interests of continuing good relations between our countries, we are declaring him *persona non grata*, in private, in this office, nothing more.'

Christmas was stunned. Circuits began to pop inside the Ambassador's mind. Al Mears was still in the embassy, and the Ambassador was beginning to understand why.

The Foreign Minister added, 'There is always the possibility that Lowry was acting under orders, for reasons I cannot fathom. Obregón told us what he believed to be the truth, but only Lowry knows the real truth.

'I beg of you, George, because I know you are a friend of México, to talk sense to Washington. Let them know that this was a terrible mistake. If Mendoza is assassinated by the CIA, even if the assassins are acting on their own, you will unite all of Latin America against you. If Mendoza dies tonight in his sleep, these tapes will be made public. I will declare you *persona non grata* and recall my ambassador from Washington. You cannot interfere in our affairs!'

The Minister took a deep breath and continued. 'The United States has intervened in Latin America more than three hundred times since the declaration of the Monroe Doctrine in 1823. You have invaded México three times, but I guarantee you that the next time will be the last. The Monroe Doctrine is dead. President Salinas instructed me to make this perfectly clear: We are not afraid of you any more. If there is any further attempt on the life of any official of this government, we will ask for assistance from the Cubans, the Central Americans, the Argentinians and the rest of Latin America. If you think you can fight us all, you are sadly mistaken. Your arsenals of nuclear weapons, spy satellites and electronic countermeasures would be of no value in a war of the Americas. You could win all the battles but would lose the war, bankrupt your nation, and turn the entire world against you.'

The Ambassador held rock steady during this outburst. When Solida finished, Christmas said, 'It certainly won't come to that. My government does not promulgate a policy of assassination. Unofficially, as you are aware, the State Department supported you as your party's candidate, not Mendoza. You cannot pretend that Mendoza has popular support. You cannot believe that the other nations of Latin America will support him if he's elected. I don't believe your own people will support him.'

'This has nothing to do with the personality of one man! Don't be a fool, George. The people hate you, the *gringos*, more than they hate Mendoza. Presidents come and go, but the *gringos* will always be there. Perhaps in the next century we shall learn how to live with one another.

'Not every day must I declare a foreigner *persona non grata*. I find it distasteful. This interview is over.'

The Ambassador turned on his heel and opened the door.

The Minister said, 'One more thing, George, a private word. Check your inventory of Stinger anti-aircraft missiles. You may be several short.'

Speechless, the Ambassador left the Ministry.

Wind howled down the Paseo de la Reforma, driving raindrops like bullets. By the time the Ambassador's limousine turned onto the boulevard, the wild weather had swept away most of the traffic. The city was quiet, hunkered down in the storm.

Christmas rode through the deserted, ancient city. For days he had felt surrounded by an unspeakable, hovering violence. Instinctively, he turned and peered out of the rear window. A black Ford sedan followed the limo. The police? The Russians? Like everyone else in the embassy, the Ambassador lived in a fishbowl.

He wondered how soon he would be recalled. No ambassador, or president for that matter, could overcome centuries of indifference, neglect and racism. Under Democrats and Republicans, conservatives and liberals, the American posture toward México never changed. There was no policy. Instead there was only a desire for stability at any cost.

The limo passed in front of the embassy before circling to the garage. The stars and stripes fluttered wildly over the armoured front entrance. He was horrified to think that his name would be associated with an assassination. Despite his title and close ties to the President, he knew he was a figurehead, a minor character in a drama beyond his control. He felt helpless.

The limousine entered the garage and the Ambassador sent

285

word to Fred Lowry to meet him in the secure documents room.

Christmas found Al Mears sitting at a table inside the secure documents room, dressed in grey slacks, blue blazer and neatly knotted tie, calmly sipping coffee.

The Ambassador asked, 'Where's Lowry?'

Mears answered, 'We don't know.'

'What the hell do you mean, you don't know?'

'He left the embassy yesterday and no one's heard from him since.'

'Jesus Christ, that's the last thing I needed to hear. I've just come from a meeting with Solida at the Foreign Ministry. He accused Lowry of trying to kill Mendoza and declared him *persona non grata*. What the hell is going on here, Al?'

Mears set down his coffee cup, folded his hands in the middle of the table, smiled and said, 'Lowry went off his fucking nut, that's what.'

'Solida has a taped confession . . .'

'From Andrés Obregón?'

'Yes.'

'Under duress?'

'Obviously. He was bound.'

'Then it means nothing.'

'How can you say that? The Méxicans are throwing your station chief out of the country. This is a disaster.'

Across the room a uniformed Marine sat at his post behind a sheet of bulletproof glass. Mears spoke to him and the Marine unlocked a safe, withdrew a sealed document, copied down the number in his log, and asked Mears to sign for it. Then he keyed an electronic lock which sealed the room. No one could go in or out until the document was back in the safe.

Mears turned the document to face the Ambassador, who read the brief finding of the NSC.

'Why wasn't I shown this before?' demanded the Ambassador.

'Need-to-know rule, George.'

'This doesn't say kill the man.'

Mears smiled, 'They never do.'

'I'm going to have to call the Secretary of State about this before it backfires in our faces.'

286

'The Secretary knows, the President knows; don't be a fool, George. You're the only one who didn't know.'

Christmas protested, 'Mendoza is going to be presented tomorrow to the Méxican people as the party's candidate, and I'm going to be sitting in the front row of foreign dignitaries. It will be embarrassing, to say the least.'

'Shine it on, Mr Ambassador. There's a year before the election. A lot can happen in a year.'

'Sure. A civil war, a revolution, you name it. Hell, the Texas Rangers might win the World Series. One thing will happen for certain. I'll be gone. I'm not going to wait to be recalled. I quit. I didn't take this job to be a patsy for the CIA. I'll be there tomorrow, but tomorrow night I'll be in Washington, but not for long. That's the only town I can think of more corrupt than México City.'

The Ambassador stormed out of the secure documents room in the direction of the communications room. Like any good Texan, his first thought was to secede from the Union.

38

Camera, Camera

Military Camp Number One occupied a vast tract of land on the eastern edge of the Federal District. For days provincial regiments had been pouring onto the post, swelling the normal garrison of four thousand troops to twelve thousand.

Reunited with their dark blue DIS Taurus SHO, Beno and Sam were parked near the main gate, listening to tank engines revving inside the compound. A squadron of white F-14 jets streaked overhead, practising for the next day's flyovers.

The DIS radio dispatchers were directing cars away from DIS headquarters to sub-stations.

A nasty idea had been festering in Beno's head for the last twelve hours. During the blackout, while Sam slept, Beno had walked from the hotel onto the Zócalo. Just before the emergency generators restored power to the government buildings, a huge red neon light had burst into life atop the hotel.

287

He had seen the posters going up, and this morning they had been everywhere.

Blackout, México 21, Máximo Levín, *coup d'état*.

Finally, Beno no longer could keep his idea to himself. He said to Sam, 'I think I know why Máximo wanted Mendoza alive. The smart son of a bitch lied to me, lied like a champ. I'm such a sucker, I believed him. There's going to be a *coup d'état*. Tomorrow night, before the parade ends, Salinas will be dead and Mendoza will be President of México.'

Sam said, 'You're joking. Tell me you're joking.'

'I wish I were. These troops are preparing for something more than a parade. I can feel it. I can just feel it.'

'What can we do about it?'

'Not a damn thing.'

'You can tell Mears,' said Sam. 'He can have the Ambassador call on Salinas.'

'I could, but I won't. Whatever happens, it's a Méxican affair. Anyway, I can't make foreign policy on a hunch, and that's all it is, a hunch.'

Sam asked, 'Do you think Lowry knows?'

'Maybe. For all I know, he's in on it. He might be sitting in the Ministry of Government smoking cigars with Mendoza right now. We could go crazy trying to figure every possibility. This country is so strange, anything could happen.'

'Why not confront Máximo with your idea?'

'If I'm right, I'm dead. If I'm wrong, I'm a damned fool. Ah, well, we can't do any good here.'

Beno started the car and motored north toward Tlatelolco, up Avenue de los Insurgentes Norte past DIS headquarters. Instead of the usual activity around the building, no one was entering or leaving it.

The garage was locked. Armed guards, women in maroon blazers and grey flannel skirts, patrolled the pavements in front of the doors. México 21 posters blanketed the neighbourhood.

On the Paseo de la Reforma the American embassy appeared normal. A line of hopeful immigrants lined up on the side street outside the consular section.

On Avenue Bucareli DIS agents with machine-pistols surrounded the Ministry of Government. As Beno and Sam passed by, Máximo Levín's limousine entered the gates.

Mendoza's office had been transformed into an impromptu television studio. The Minister had made some changes in the speech Máximo had written for him and was reading it to the camera for the third time.

'Méxican independence is sacred. No longer can we tolerate a government which puts foreign interests before the needs of the Méxican people. Méxicans, we have been betrayed . . .'

He stopped, turned away from the teleprompter and said, 'Máximo, this must be more forceful in the beginning. I'm not satisfied with it the way it is.'

'Take your time, Alfredo. We have all day.'

'Have you been to Camp One?'

'I was there this morning. Jalapa is in perfect control.'

'The Americans?'

'They suspect nothing. No one does. Be tranquil, be calm, project strength.'

Mendoza puffed up his chest, straightened his tie, and looked straight at the teleprompter.

'Méxican independence is sacred . . .'

Beno drove to the city centre and used his DIS identity plate to gain access to the Zócalo. As he and Sam walked into the square, a cameraman testing equipment picked out Sam, and suddenly they saw her face thirty times life size repeated on the six giant screens placed around the plaza.

Her magnified lips trembled. Whistles and catcalls echoed around the square. Her giant blue eyes flickered like dragonflies on the screens. The camera moved on and came to rest on the neon México 21 sign above the hotel.

39

Hummingbird of the South

The military police van from Billy Vargas' 27th Infantry went round and round the Zócalo, round and round and round like a dizzying carousel with bobbing monsters, fierce jaguars, birds of prey, the awesome Huitzilopochtli. The driver wore a gleaming white helmet pulled over his ears, a colonel's eagles, a broad moustache, and eyes hidden behind reflector lenses.

Subminiature high explosive warheads exploded in Lowry's mind, one after another, pop pop pop, ripping across a deranged field of fire. Semtex! Whap! Twenty pounds of Semtex, whap! Enough plastic explosive to blow the face off the National Palace and take out half the square. Whap! Whap!

Choruses of hate. Kill 'em all. A symphony of destruction. Kill 'em all. An opera of death. Blow 'em all away. Why the fuck not? If I'm goin' down, I'll take 'em all with me, Mendoza, Máximo Levín, Salinas, the whole fucking government. Langley wants bodies, they'll get more bodies than they thought possible. Fuck with me and you fuck with the angel of death. You want history? I'll give you history. I'll write history in blood. I'll show you what it's about, you dumb fucks, you sanctimonious hypocrites. You like your violence nice and clean, far away, twice removed, veiled with euphemisms. Terminate, liquidate. We can't let the world see us kill Mendoza. Oh no. Must pretend Lucio Serdán did the job. Set him up, bring him down, terminate the loose ends. I'll stick it in your face, Al Mears, whap! Like an elbow that crushes your nose.

Scalp shaved smooth as a hummingbird's head, Fred Lowry ended his circular dance of death a block from the Zócalo at the edge of the excavated ruins of Huitzilopochtli's temple. A tiny green bird soared above the ancient blocks of black stone. Hundreds of tourists swirled around the deposed spy. To his right the National Palace. Behind him, the cathedral, in his mind, the diabolical flight of the hummingbird, the ancient legend come to life . . .

* * *

Huitzilopochtli smelled war everywhere now. From the north, from the south, the heady odour of fresh blood and flayed flesh wafted over the temple ruins, spattered by the rain. The old smell was accompanied by new sounds, mechanized sounds, the whistle of machine-gun bullets, the scream of rockets, the chatter of radios and the hum of computers, but the smell was the same, the men were the same. They bled and died and every day the sun rose over the great city, his city with his shattered temple at its centre.

Huitzilopochtli, Hummingbird of the South, God of War, darted among the ruins of the Great Temple raised so long ago in his honour. Here his people had nourished him with still-beating hearts sliced from the chests of prisoners of war. For this they went to war, to feed him so he might cause the sun to shine another day.

As Huitzilopochtli hovered high above the demolished sanctuary and darted through the gardens of the palace and among the stalls of flower sellers behind the cathedral, the night air carried the foetid scent which overpowered the jasmine and roses and clover. The palpable aroma of brutish violence and ritual murder was almost visible among the crevices and shadows of the excavation. The city reeked of fear, tears, sweat, and semen, the scent of Huitzilopochtli's victims in the instant before death.

He still counted time in the old way. Fifty-two cycles had passed. The sun was about to be extinguished and reborn again in fire and war. He could smell it in the air, read it in the stars.

The Spanish called him the devil and tore down his idols. They broke the stones and used them to build a church, a palace and a great square where Spanish priests sacrificed human beings with fire. Those stones now trembled as Huitzilopochtli, God of War, prepared to meet the ninth sun. He brandished his serpent of fire, and the high mountain air, long since choked with poisonous fumes, thickened with a terrible menace, then exploded as lightning and thunder. Blue light flashed over the monumental remnants of the Aztec capital, exposed and naked in the heart of México City, illuminating for an instant a tiny hummingbird's nest built into the crumbling mortar of the sacrificial stones.

Huitzilopochtli took shelter from the storm under the carved image of a jaguar. The nest was full. The Hummingbird of the South was hungry . . .

In the helter skelter chaos the night before the Independence Day parade no one challenged the Colonel of Military Police. His van was one of dozens of military vehicles mingling with the television crews, construction workers assembling stands and electricians mounting a huge red neon *MEXICO 21* atop the Hotel Majestic.

Slowly he drove away to spend the night criss-crossing the city, working the litany of death over and over in his mind.

16 SEPTEMBER

40

Military Camp Number One

A rosy smog-induced dawn broke over México City on the morning of 16 September. For a brief moment Popocatépetl and Ixtaccíhuatl, twin volcanoes to the south-east, were visible from Military Camp Number One, but their heavenly snow-capped peaks quickly disappeared in the onslaught of tank exhaust and jet condensation trails.

Twelve thousand soldiers ironed starched fatigues, polished boots and oiled rifles. Scarcely one in a hundred had ever seen combat. Of those, perhaps six hundred were blooded veterans of the guerrilla wars in the Sierra or the oil fields of the Yucatán.

General of Divisions Juan Jalapa, Minister of Defence, had mustered these six hundred into separate barracks and put them under the command of the 42nd Armoured Battalion, the honorary colour guard which would lead the parade through the city. The General had hand-picked fifty loyal officers to command these shock troops. These gentlemen were assembled in the general's command post where they were receiving the orders of the day from Jalapa and Máximo Levín.

The General and the Director stood on a podium with large schematic drawings of the Zócalo, the National Palace and a street map of the city.

'By ten o'clock,' said Máximo, 'the intelligence cadres should have accomplished their tasks and reported to me at DIS headquarters.

'At ten the President will rise to speak. The camera will be on him and both networks have scheduled his speech for broadcast nationwide. Mendoza believes his taped speech will be aired in its place, but I assure you, the broadcast will be of a radically different nature.

'At that moment on the balcony, in full view of the nation, General Jalapa will arrest Salinas, Mendoza and the officials of the party. General, please continue.'

General Jalapa cut a fine figure as he stood before his rebellious officers. Rapping hard on the map with a pointer, Jalapa said, 'There will be a certain amount of confusion in the square. It is of the utmost importance that the 42nd Armoured Battalion and the 9th Special Forces Regiment maintain discipline. The lead tanks of the 42nd will enter the Palace through the main gate. The Special Forces will enter the Palace here, here, and here.'

With the pointer the General indicated three entrances to the Palace.

'Control of the National Palace is symbolic. Once troops are inside the Palace, they will ring the Bell of Freedom, here, over the main gate. As the bell is being rung, Ricardo Solida will declare General Jalapa Head of State to serve until elections can be held in January. Leaders of all political parties, with one obvious exception, will be with him. I intend this to be a bloodless *coup*, gentlemen, but if you meet resistance, you must deal with opponents swiftly and without hesitation.'

Jalapa put down the pointer and said, 'If there are no questions, gentlemen, go with God.'

As the officers began to file out of the briefing room, they heard a commotion outside.

A muffled shout, 'You can't stop me from going in there. I'm a general officer!'

'Orders, sir! I will shoot you, sir!'

Jalapa snatched open the doors and saw two of his guards restraining General Billy Vargas. Another guard and two of Vargas' men faced each other, rifles at the ready.

Vargas said, 'General Jalapa, I must see you at once.'

Jalapa ordered, 'Let him go. At ease! Put your weapons down.'

The soldiers slowly slipped their fingers away from their triggers and stood at ease.

'Come inside,' said Jalapa, and the two officers retired to Jalapa's office.

Vargas said, 'I have orders from Minister Mendoza to place my troops at the head of the parade.'

'Mendoza has no such authority,' countered Jalapa. 'I command here.'

296

'The Minister is the Parade Marshal, and his wishes must be respected.'

'Why your troops, Vargas?'

'You know damned well why, Juanito,' hissed Vargas, insulting his senior officer by using the diminutive of his given name. 'I shall lead the *coup*! I shall arrest Salinas! I shall deliver México from the plague of socialism.'

'Are you saying Mendoza doesn't trust me? Are you trying to create discord and mistrust at this eleventh hour? I'll have you arrested.'

'Try it. My soldiers are armed and ready. We don't have to wait until tonight. We'll do it right now.'

Jalapa said, 'Let me talk to Dr Levín. Wait here.'

Máximo and his DIS inspectors were instructing army intelligence officers where to go and what to do on this night of nights. The Director excused himself, listened to Jalapa and said, 'We can't afford a petty squabble now. Let his troops go first. At ten o'clock sharp, have him shot. There's no other way.'

At four o'clock a drum and bugle corps struck up a march, and Billy Vargas' 27th Infantry led the long column out of Military Camp Number One, past the Hippodrome and onto the Avenue of the National Army. The 42nd Armoured Battalion, replete with twelve West German Leopard tanks, followed directly behind. The 9th Special Forces Regiment trailed the tanks. Ahead, motorcycle police cleared the streets and pushed back the crowds that lined the parade route.

The column turned right at Boulevard General Mariano Escobedu, left onto the Paseo de la Reforma, right onto Avenue Juárez and, three hours after leaving Military Camp Number One, entered the Zócalo.

A million people watched the parade from the city's pavements. Twenty-nine millions stayed home, trying to ignore the annual military display.

The air in México City was thick with smog. A camera on the roof of the National Palace panned ten thousand noisy party faithful crowded into the Zócalo and displayed the image on the six giant screens around the square. The party had been trucking in union members from the suburbs and farmers from the countryside for six hours.

A director in the Televisa studios picked a shot of a mariachi band strolling through the mass of humanity, and the image of sombreros and guitars appeared in giant magnification on the six DiamondVision screens.

A thousand México City police and five hundred military police maintained an ominous presence in the square as the troops began to file in. In front of the National Palace the Presidential Guard, resplendent in white helmets and white leggings, stood at rigid attention.

Military police vans roamed through the side streets and up and down beside the pavements surrounding the square. In one of them, Fred Lowry slowly worked his way toward the Palace.

The long, low, tetzole stone façade of the Palace faced the east side of the Zócalo. On the second floor, just to the left of the main gate and the Bell of Freedom, the new, wide balcony jutted over the pavement. At eight o'clock Lowry parked his van directly under the balcony. His detonator was primed.

Throughout México and the south-western United States, millions of eyes were trained on the Zócalo.

41

Drum Roll

At seven o'clock Beno and Sam watched from their hotel balcony as the first troops arrived in the Zócalo, then walked down through the lobby and into the square. Beno was dressed in the standard DIS uniform, a cheap grey suit, white shirt, and narrow tie. Sam wore the maroon blazer and grey skirt of a DIS security guard. Both carried Uzis tucked under their jackets and small portable radios with earplugs.

The 27th Infantry, 300 strong with 20 armoured personnel carriers, were stationed directly behind the ten thousand party members who had been sweltering in the square for hours. The six hundred seasoned troops of the 42nd, supported by potent

298

Leopard tanks, filed in behind the 27th. Next came a battalion of Marines, tough soldiers from Chiapas on the Guatemalan border. In all, regiments from the republic's thirty-two military districts and nine naval regions would be represented in the Zócalo.

Beno spotted General Vargas standing atop a French-built Panhard armoured personnel carrier in the front rank of troops, binoculars trained on the balcony. The armoured cars' guns were raised and aimed at the Palace, but no ammunition belts were in evidence.

On the balcony, the president of the government workers' union entertained the masses in the square with a two-hour speech extolling the virtues of the party and the unions. The party faithful cheered and waved their banners. The ordinary civilians who surrounded the Zócalo sat on their hands, cheered the colourful fireworks fired off every few minutes from an interior palace courtyard, and watched the giant TV screens.

Foreign dignitaries from the diplomatic corps began to arrive and take seats in the temporary stands erected along the side of the cathedral. Troops continuously poured into the square. At eight-thirty the sun dropped behind the spires of the cathedral, and the huge red neon México 21 sign on the Hotel Majestic suddenly sprang to life causing thousands of questioning fingers to point in wonder.

Beno saw the American ambassador arrive and pointed him out to Sam. George Christmas, accompanied by his wife, the Under Secretary of State for Latin America and her husband and an entourage of embassy officials, sat in the front row of the stands next to the Soviet ambassador and his party.

As the twilight deepened into purple a yellow moon rose over the Palace. A battery of Roman candles flared into the air from one of the inner courtyards to the delight of the crowd.

At nine o'clock the screens projected a half-hour film depicting Miguel Hidalgo's historic proclamation of freedom on 16 September 1810, which signalled the beginning of México's War of Independence from Spain. The film captured the genuine patriotic fervour of the occasion and enraptured the crowd, irrespective of political persuasion.

* * *

While the film rolled, Alfredo Mendoza, hitherto a man of no religion, entered the cathedral. The Minister wanted to take one small step into his past before making a desperate grab at the future.

The sanctuary was deserted, save for one cassocked priest.

The Minister said, 'Father, at this historic moment I wish to pray in silence and in peace. I wish the blessing of the church.'

The priest hastily lit candles. Amidst the marble and gold the General crawled on his knees and lay prostrate before the altar to ask the Virgin's blessing on his endeavour. Having utterly forgotten the catechism of his youth, Mendoza asked the Virgin to search his heart. After several minutes he stood, bade the priest pray for him and for México, then strode outside and walked toward the Palace.

At Military Camp Number One the final unit of the parade consisted of forty armoured personnel carriers. At the last moment, just before the APCs were scheduled to follow the penultimate regiment out of the gate, intelligence officers distributed city maps to the drivers while privates from the motorpool hastily plastered the APCs with México 21 bumperstickers.

A DIS inspector climbed into each car, and the APCs roared away from the post and fanned out through the city. Their destinations were the city's forty police precincts.

At 9:05 Máximo Levín activated a carefully written program from his terminal in DIS headquarters and the central police computer operating system crashed.

At 9:15 every police telephone exchange ceased to function.

At 9:30 police radio frequencies began to transmit only white noise.

At 9:45 the Director arranged a conference call on an open line with the chiefs of the federal judicial police, the federal district judicial police, the México City police, the bank police, and the police reserve brigade.

When all the chiefs were on the line, Máximo told them, 'As Director of Internal Security, I am declaring martial law. A *coup d'état* is in progress. Each of you is ordered to surrender your headquarters to army officers who will arrive within ten

300

minutes. Obey their orders. Failure to obey will mean imprisonment in your own jails. Resistance means death. There will be no questions. President Salinas and Minister of Government Alfredo Mendoza are hereby removed from office. The entire cabinet has recognized General of Divisions Juan Jalapa as interim Head of State. I repeat. No questions. That is all.'

Máximo closed down the phone lines, severing the chiefs' channels of communications.

At 9:50 a squadron of F-5 jet fighters roared out of the north and over the city at an altitude of four hundred feet. They climbed over the twin volcanoes in the south-east, turned, dived, and buzzed the city again.

Soldiers began to arrive at the police precincts. Local commanders had had no warning. Their swing shift patrols were on the street, isolated without communications.

At Precinct 32 in Coyoacán the Captain was still in his office puzzling over the failure of his communication systems when an army major in combat fatigues entered the station. The desk sergeant was sweating over paperwork while three brown-uniformed loafers drank coffee, smoked cigarettes and complained that the fancy new phone system built by that Jew Máximo Levín wasn't worth a shit.

The Major put his finger to his lips and waved his rifle in the direction of the sergeant.

'Where's your captain?'

The sergeant pointed upstairs.

The Major said, 'Martial law has been declared. You are to follow my orders and those of my men. Understand?'

The four policemen nodded vigorously.

'Do you have a television set?'

'Yes, Major, a poor one that shows all green.'

'Aren't you watching the Independence Day ceremonies?'

'No, señor. We only watch Mission Impossible and Miami Vice.'

'Turn it on and watch the parade. Keep quiet.'

The Major quickly deployed two troopers to guard the armoury, another pair to seize the motorpool, and spread the rest through the building. Then he went upstairs.

The Captain was playing draw poker with three friends when

the Major abruptly entered his sanctuary. Rifle at the ready and finger to his lips, the Major circled the table and looked at the men's hands. He smiled, pointed his rifle at the Captain and said, 'You lose.'

One of the men said, 'You like to sit down and play, señor?'

The Major swept the chips off the table and said, 'No more games, gentlemen. Martial law has been declared.'

The Captain wanted to argue.

'Who declared martial law? Mendoza?'

The Major answered, 'I take orders from General Jalapa. Mendoza is finished.'

The captain of police tugged at his moustache and nodded in comprehension.

'Gentlemen,' said the Major. 'Place your weapons on the table.'

At Precinct 17 in Iztapalapa the transition to martial law did not go so smoothly.

The Captain was convinced that communist guerrillas were responsible for the communications failure. He was standing in the station vestibule with his desk sergeant when two armed men in combat fatigues burst through the door. The Captain saw their military insignia, ignored them, pulled his pistol and shot one of the soldiers in the chest. The other soldier fired his rifle on automatic, tearing a line of holes in the ceiling of the room without hitting the policemen. The desk sergeant killed the second soldier. An army lieutenant entered the station and the policemen shot him in the leg. He crawled outside and told his major that two men were lying dead on the floor.

The Major shouted into a bullhorn that his soldiers were regular army troops and that martial law had been declared, but the policemen decided to hold their station until their headquarters ordered them to surrender. A siege developed with both sides determined to hold out.

By 10:00 the army was in control of the entire police apparatus of the federal district with the exception of Precinct 17. As the leader of each army team checked in that his precinct was secured, radio communication was restored. Army radio specialists sat with the police dispatchers and assigned the eight thousand México City policemen on duty to traffic control.

* * *

302

While regular army units seized control of the physical reins of the capital, crack military police squads moved on the political apparatus of the republic.

Máximo had provided army intelligence with addresses and daily schedules for hundreds of the most corrupt party officers, union officials and government bureaucrats. Armed with warrants, MPs swept in like piranhas and arrested officials in their homes, at their clubs in the Zona Rosa, and in the arms of their mistresses.

Not many went peacefully. Protected by bodyguards and private police, most of the officials put up violent resistance. The result was a slaughter of the republic's political élite, a Night of Sorrow for the survivors and their families.

Ten o'clock marked the end of México City's late rush hour. In subway stations throughout the federal district, half a million commuters had no choice but to watch the President's speech on hundreds of television monitors suspended over the platforms.

In millions of homes, tens of thousands of cantinas, and in front of hundreds of TV stores, people gathered to watch the speech.

In the Televisa studios, engineers in the control booth watched banks of monitors as the broadcast from the Zócalo was beamed via microwave to a satellite station in Tulancingo, one hundred miles north. Tulancingo bounced the signal off satellite Morelos F-1 to all México and the south-western United States.

The historical film on Miguel Hidalgo ended. Cameras spotted around the Zócalo focused on a battery of fireworks that shot up from the Palace. The colourful explosions high in the sky dissolved into shots of faces in the crowd, and then cut to a long shot of members of the government filing onto the presidential balcony for Salinas' speech.

In the glass pyramid thirty technicians in the communications centre felt like crusaders, armed with silicon shield and sword, prepared to sally forth and do electronic battle.

Máximo addressed his faithful, 'You all know what to expect,

303

but there can be no rehearsal. We are going to induce chaos, but it will be controlled chaos.

Máximo said, 'Send the units to the network studios.'

At 9:45 five armoured personnel carriers arrived at the Televisa studios, and another five at Imevision. Soldiers quickly filed into the buildings and established security perimeters.

An army captain in combat fatigues marched into the Televisa lobby and announced to the surprised security guards, 'This building is now under the control of the Ministry of Defence.'

Guillero Guzman, Televisa's executive director and a member of México 21, fidgeted nervously in the network control booth.

Beside him sat the broadcast director and his bank of monitors. The central monitor showed the scene in the Zócalo that was being simulcast on both networks and displayed on the square's six screens.

The director went to camera one, perched in a cathedral spire. The shot panned over the cabinet members filing onto the balcony. He selected a close-up of Mendoza, then Solida, then Jalapa, then pulled back to a wide-angle view of the entire balcony. For colour the cameraman panned the military police vans parked under the overhang.

On the six huge screens around the square the face of Fred Lowry stared through a pair of reflector lenses thirty times larger than life.

42

Zócalo

Ignoring the screens, Beno's eyes were locked on General Vargas.

Sam saw the huge images of Fred Lowry and screamed, 'Beno, look!'

Beno jerked his eyes toward the screen over the balcony and caught a fleeting glimpse of Lowry's face. The next instant the broadcast director cut to a shot of Salinas emerging from the antechamber onto the balcony.

The densely packed party members close to the balcony cheered the arrival of the President, a young, balding man with a tidy moustache.

Beno and Sam were two hundred feet from the balcony. Ten thousand wildly cheering people separated them from their quarry.

As Beno began to plough through the crowd toward the balcony, he tried to raise DIS headquarters on his radio.

'This is Comandante Alvarado. Put me through to the Director,' he shouted at the radio dispatcher. 'Emergency.'

'Impossible,' came the reply. 'The Director is taking no calls.'

'An assassin is loose in the Zócalo,' Beno told him, his voice strained with urgency.

'Listen, you fool,' said the anonymous dispatcher, 'a thousand assassins are in the Zócalo. Martial law has been declared. Clear this frequency.'

In the communications centre in the American embassy Al Mears recognized Lowry's face on his television monitor and experienced an eerie moment of helplessness. For the past hour embassy low priority communications had been intermittently jammed. Only Méxican military frequencies were working properly, and their signals were in a new code. Mears had sent couriers on foot to the British, French and Japanese embassies, and they had reported back that those foreign missions were encountering similar difficulties. The city telephone system had broken down, but off-duty embassy employees were pouring into the building with devastating rumours. Martial law had been declared. A *coup d'état* was about to occur.

In the glass pyramid Máximo Levín had a direct feed from Televisa. DIS monitors duplicated those in the television control booth allowing him to watch the Zócalo from twenty different angles. The large, central monitor showed the shot going over the air. As the camera panned members of the government sitting on the balcony, Máximo noticed to his amazement that his hands were trembling and his breath was coming in short gasps.

305

The fleeting image of Lowry's face penetrated Máximo's consciousness, but he had already dismissed from his mind the neutralized, impotent machinations of the CIA. For two weeks he had succeeded in his goal of keeping its staff members occupied with one another. At the last moment he had used their madness to deceive Mendoza.

President Salinas approached the microphone, saw his face reflected on the giant screens, and raised his arms to acknowledge the enthusiasm of the crowd.

On the roof of the Palace a Special Forces sniper moved into position and sighted General Vargas in his nightscope.

Máximo spoke into his headset to Guzman across town in the Televisa control room, 'Roll the tape.'

On the Zócalo screens and on fifty million televisions in every city and town in México the face of the President was replaced with the bright red logo of México 21.

On the balcony Mendoza smiled with grim self-satisfaction. Salinas stared speechless, confused.

The logo dissolved into a portrait of Alfredo Mendoza, taken from Máximo's studio tape.

A voice-over boomed through a thousand loudspeakers across the Zócalo with the words, 'This man is Alfredo Mendoza, Minister of Government, and this is his house.'

An aerial view of El Partenón appeared on the screens, followed by quick cuts of the casino, the swimming pools, the lavish furnishings and the accounting room. A close-up zoomed in on massive stacks of cash, pesos and dollars.

'And this is the source of his wealth.'

A sensual colour shot of white opium poppies rippling in a summer breeze. The film was a computer-enhanced version of Lucio Serdán's eight-millimetre videotape. A montage followed, a quick cut to the interior of the heroin factory, bags of powder and more cash, cut to the face of Lucio Serdán as seen on his posters, cut to rapid, flickering shots of Lucio lying dead on Beno's patio, cut to a tape of Máximo sitting in his library in the glass pyramid.

From a thousand microphones Máximo's voice intoned, 'I am Máximo Levín, Director of Internal Security. What you are about to see is more than an indictment of Alfredo Mendoza, the man called the heroin king of Guerrero. My duty tonight is

306

both sad and joyous. I feel great sadness that the ideals of our republic have been betrayed by this man and the corrupt political party which produced him, but I also feel great joy that I, with the co-operation of many others, have found the means to uphold the heritage of our nation and revere our spirit of independence.'

At that moment México stood transfixed. In subways in México City, hotels in Zihuatanejo, steel mills in Monterrey, auto plants in Hermosillo, cantinas in Guadalajara, and millions upon millions of homes in Cuernavaca, Puebla, León, Querétaro, Tijuana and Ciudad Juárez, citizens of the republic watched history in the making. The truth, the ultimate, damning, terrible truth was finally being told in incredibly spectacular fashion from an utterly unexpected source. After the first fifteen seconds of the broadcast no one needed to hear the words or see the images. As they had Miguel Hidalgo's cry of freedom in 1810, the people took the truth of México 21 directly into their hearts.

Beno neither saw nor heard the telecast. He saw only Fred Lowry in Méxican dress greens and white helmet standing in front of a military police van. Pumped up by adrenaline and days of relentless stress, Beno charged toward Lowry straight ahead through the stunned mass of humanity, brandishing his Uzi, forcing people out of his way, fighting through the crowd.

Sam kept her head and finessed the edges of the crowd. Citizens on the perimeter of the square remained motionless, awestruck, and Sam moved obliquely toward Lowry, approaching him from the side.

The Zócalo rattled with a violent din of shouts. Party faithful shook their fists, chanted slogans, and tore down loudspeakers. The citizens on the pavements exploded with laughter and cheers. The politicians on the balcony gaped in awe.

Fifty yards from the balcony, behind the mass of party banners and flags, General Vargas recognized Máximo's voice at the first words. Of all the men in the Zócalo who felt betrayed, Vargas was in a position to do something about the travesty on the screens. He quickly recovered from his first shock and ordered his infantry to storm the Palace. As the three hundred soldiers of the 27th Infantry surged forward, they pushed into the lake of humanity, the party faithful, antagonizing their only allies in the square.

Maintaining discipline, Jalapa's officers began to execute the orders they had been given that morning. The tanks began to move forward, pushing the crowd out of their path. Two companies of Special Forces flanked the square, sprinting around the crowd to seal the Palace doors and occupy the building. As they began to move, Jalapa ordered his sniper on the roof of the Palace to shoot Vargas.

In the sudden chaos the rifleman fired and missed.

During the first few seconds of the *coup*, the troops of the Presidential Guard froze, the officers failing to recognize the military nature of the calamity unravelling in the Zócalo. Within a minute the captain of the guard ordered his soldiers to open the armoury and issue live ammunition.

The armoury doors refused to budge, sealed shut with super-glue. Before the Guards could break through the doors, Vargas' troops reached the main gates, pushed the disorganized Guards aside and deployed in defensive positions with heavy machine-guns.

The first gunshots erupted in the square. As Jalapa's troops raced for the gates, Vargas' 27th opened up with their machine-guns.

The civilians panicked. Caught in a crossfire, party members fell by the dozen, slaughtered by the warring troops.

As the battle joined, Beno shouldered through the last of the crowd, shoving people out of his way until he stood ten feet from Fred Lowry. Bullets whizzed through the air around them. The rest of the military police fled.

'Fred!' Beno shouted. 'Fred Lowry! Don't move!'

Lowry smiled at Beno's Uzi pointed at his heart. He extended his arms toward Beno. One hand held a radio transmitter, the other a pistol.

'There's twenty pounds of Semtex in the van. Go ahead, Beno. Shoot. You can't stop it. It's going to blow.'

Beno said, 'Fred, Mendoza is finished. The Méxicans are bringing him down themselves. Listen. Can't you see what's happening? This is why Máximo wanted Mendoza alive, to have him sitting in the balcony for this. This is México 21, this broadcast.'

Lowry's left eye twitched. He sidestepped slowly to his right, moving away from the van and the battle.

He shouted to Beno, 'Máximo isn't in control, the generals are. Vargas and Japala are starting a war that could last all night, or continue for years. Do you think it matters who wins, Beno? This is a *coup d'état*. In the morning a general will be President of México. What could be better for us? A strong man in México will serve our interests, and that's what we wanted from the beginning. For stability, Beno. Anything for stability. In three minutes the Semtex in the van will destroy the balcony. For stability.'

A hundred yards away Vargas pulled the hatch of his APC over his head and shouted to the gunner, 'Load the gun. Shoot the screens!'

Grabbing an intercom, he yelled into the microphone to his Panhards, 'Gunners, shoot the screens!'

Vargas' gunner raised his gun until it aimed at the centre of the screen over the balcony and fired. The huge cathode ray tube exploded in a massive shower of sparks and glass.

The rest of Vargas' gunners began shooting wildly at the other screens. Four more ignited and fizzled into darkness, but one remained live. Hundreds of loudspeakers carried Máximo's voice, but by then fifty thousand people in the Zócalo had exploded into full-throttle panic.

From the balcony General Jalapa spoke into a radio and quietly ordered his tank commander to fire his gun at General Vargas' armoured car.

A turret on one of Jalapa's Leopard's revolved toward the centre of the square. The gun spat a jet of flame and the shell slammed into the rear of Vargas' car, pushed the vehicle twenty feet into the crowd, and exploded the fuel tank, killing Vargas and the crew.

Chaos overwhelmed the presidential balcony as civil war erupted below. Mendoza rushed from his seat and in the confusion sneaked past the soldiers into the Palace. Jalapa put his hand on the shoulder of the President and said, 'You're under arrest.'

Jalapa's shock troops fought past the outer defences of 27th Infantry, rushed through the courtyard, and onto the balcony.

Jalapa ordered his tanks into the Palace. Meeting resistance at the gate, the gunner of the lead tank fired high and the Bell of Freedom pulled loose from its ropes, crashed to the ground and shattered.

The tanks rattled through the open doors. Vargas' soldiers on the interior balconies turned their assault rifles on the tanks and infantry following behind. The defenders retreated into the courtyard, relentlessly pursued by the tanks. The night erupted with a cacophonous pandemonium of exploding grenades, cannon fire, and the screams of maimed and dying soldiers. Bullets defaced Rivera's murals. Artillery shells reduced ancient walls to rubble.

The hummingbird was in full flight.

Every television cameraman in México City was around the Palace. Three camera-equipped helicopters hovered over the maze-like structure, flooding the battle with light. One chopper caught an errant shell and crashed through the Palace roof.

The big red neon México 21 burned brightly over the Zócalo.

Deep in the interior of the Palace Alfredo Mendoza listened to the gunfire and knew his gambit had failed. He had prepared for this contingency. Calmly, he entered a workmen's locker room, shaved his moustache, combed a grey wash into his hair, and smeared brown television make-up over his face and hands. He strapped on a money belt which contained thirty thousand dollars in American hundreds and two million dollars worth of diamonds, dressed in a gardener's overalls and boots, stuffed a small pistol in his pocket, slipped into his secret tunnel and walked out of a back door of the Palace onto a deserted Tacuba Street.

Unrecognized, he walked half a block to the corner of Modena Street and unlocked the door to an unmarked garage. A moment later he backed onto the street in a rusted Toyota, and drove himself to a small airfield in Coyoacán. No one stopped him. Before the dust settled in the Zócalo, Alfredo Mendoza would be safely on his way to Spain.

Beno shouted to Lowry, 'Get out of my way.'

'This isn't your fight, Beno. Don't commit suicide for nothing.'

A zipper of stray machine-gun bullets stitched toward Beno's head and he ducked. Taking advantage of this momentary distraction, Lowry suddenly broke to his left, squeezing off rounds from his pistol. His first shot went into the crowd, but his second bullet caught Beno in the hip. A third shattered Beno's gun hand. The Uzi clattered to the pavement. Beno staggered and fell, clutching his leg.

Lowry took two more steps, looked back at Beno, turned and found himself face to face with Sam Black. Sam didn't hesitate. She pulled the trigger of her Uzi and fired six bullets into Fred Lowry.

A look of amazement on his face, Lowry toppled over backwards onto the pavement.

She ran to Beno.

'My God,' she sobbed. 'You're shot!'

She looked around frantically and said, 'I've got to get you out of here.'

'Never mind me,' he shouted. 'Run. Get away. Lowry's van is full of explosives, enough to take out half the Palace. Go.'

'I can't leave you here.'

He forced himself to stand on one leg and roughly pushed her away.

'I'll make it,' he said. 'Save yourself. I've got to get the van out of the square. Too many people.'

He started to hobble toward the van but his shattered hip crumpled under him and he fell.

Sam bent over him and kissed his forehead.

'I love you, Beno.'

She ran for the van, pulled open the door, saw the keys were in the ignition and turned over the engine. The Toyota roared to life. She gunned the accelerator, yanked the wheel to the left and tried to drive through the main gate of the Palace into the courtyard, away from the hysterical crowd in the Zócalo.

Jalapa's troops blocked her way. The front of the van was in the entrance but the rear was still under the balcony. She looked back into the interior of the van but couldn't see the detonator. Frenzied she pulled aside the tarpaulin which covered the explosives but still couldn't find any wires. She pushed open the rear door and saw Beno crawling after the van.

'Go back!' she shouted. 'You can't help.'

He saw her but couldn't hear above the noise of the battle.

Soldiers continued to run past Beno and the van into the

courtyard. The members of the government who had retreated from the balcony to a large room on the first floor cowered on the floors. The courtyard heaved with gunsmoke and the wild sounds of the mêlée between the 27th and 42nd battalions. Outside the door on the interior balcony that ringed the courtyard, Vargas' soldiers fired down on Jalapa's troops pouring in the gate.

Máximo's voice droned over the chaos. The one remaining screen displayed the face of Alfredo Mendoza while the voice-over ran a tape of Mendoza describing his heroin operation to Máximo in El Partenón.

Sam climbed back into the driver's seat, pushed the accelerator to the floor, and ran over six soldiers as she drove the van through the gate and into the courtyard.

She reached for the door handle, ready to leap. In the rear view mirror she saw Beno standing on one leg, supporting himself against the side of the building.

The door opened halfway. Beno saw one leg, then another, an arm . . .

. . . the Semtex exploded. The entire front of the Palace disintegrated in a cloud of pyrotechnic dust. Vapourized, Sam died instantly.

The walls of the Palace shielded the crowd in the Zócalo from the blast, but the courtyard and the rooms behind the balcony were blasted into dust. President Salinas, Ricardo Solida, Juan Jalapa and the rest of the government became part of the rubble. Two hundred soldiers were slaughtered by the explosion.

The shockwave of the blast hit Beno like a tidal wave, forced the air from his chest and rolled him backwards out of the gate and into the square.

The van and Sam had disappeared.

In the Zócalo Jalapa's remaining troops savagely suppressed Vargas' remaining soldiers and the vicious fighting came to an abrupt halt. A heavy cloud of smoke lay over the square. Thousands of civilians poured into the cathedral, seeking refuge.

Beno never saw them. Blood and tears poured from his body as he lay unconscious in the Zócalo. Behind him the one live screen glowed with a giant red México 21. The broadcast was over. México's uncertain future had begun.

* * *

Ambulances charged toward the Zócalo from every hospital in the city. Paramedics found Beno barely alive, discovered his DIS identity plate and rushed him to the Social Security hospital in Tlatelolco, close to the glass pyramid.

He awoke the next day clothed in plaster. Through a morphine haze he watched a television monitor suspended over his bed. The National Assembly had declared Máximo Levín Acting President of México. In his first decree he announced a general election to be held on the first day of February.

Outside the window Beno heard music and laughter. The people of México were dancing in the streets. A cheerful nurse came in to take his pulse and welcome him back among the living.

She wore a red and green pin over her heart.

México 21.